LIKE NO OTHER

Suddenly it was all too much for her – the tall thin body, the gaunt face, the mind that refused to be quiet and the temper that flared out of control sometimes and made enemies for her. Why had she been born like this?

Overwhelmed with shame and anguish, Rachel buried her face in a tussock of springy moorland grass and began to weep harshly. *Bill Withers!* If her father had to buy her a husband, he should look for a better bargain than that! *Buy her a husband!* Oh, dear Lord, the shame of it . . .

Like No Other

Anna Jacobs

CORONET BOOKS
Hodder & Stoughton

First published in Great Britain in 1999
by Hodder and Stoughton
First published in paperback in 2000
by Hodder and Stoughton
A division of Hodder Headline

A Coronet Paperback

10 9 8 7 6 5 4

A CIP catalogue record for this title is available
from the British Library.

ISBN 0 340 87449 X

Printed and bound in Great Britain by
Mackays of Chatham PLC, Chatham Kent

Hodder and Stoughton
A division of Hodder Headline
338 Euston Road
London NW1 3BH

To my grandfather, Fred Wild, who was also 'like no other'. He taught me to read and to make books well before I went to school, looked the other way when I stole pea-pods at his allotment, and was both creative and eccentric – two of my own traits! I wish very much that he'd lived long enough to read my novels.

AUTHOR'S NOTE

Anna Jacobs is always delighted to hear from readers and can be contacted at:

P O Box 628
Mandurah
Western Australia 6210

If you'd like a reply, please enclose a self-addressed envelope, stamped (from inside Australia) or with an international reply coupon (from outside Australia).

Anna Jacobs can also be contacted by e-mail on
jacobses@iinet.net.au

Part One

Part One

CHAPTER ONE

1753

Bored by the wench's halting attempts at conversation, Bill decided it was time to get some return for the tedious half-hour he had just spent listening to her talk as they walked up towards Whin Ridge. She had some right barmy ideas, this one did. But she also had a father with a bit of money in his pot, so Bill had been pretending an interest in what she was saying. Well, you had to court 'em a bit, didn't you?

'Let's stop an' catch us breath,' he growled, chucking his coat down on a grassy patch. 'It's a steep climb, yon.'

'Yes, but worth it for the view. Just look at that sky.'

He sighed and wished she'd shut up. He'd have to listen to her maundering on and stare at her plain face every day once they were wed, but not now! Now was for other things. At least there was some pleasure to be had in walking out, even if the lass was taller than you. There was little joy in marriage, as far as he could see, but now that his mam had died, he had to get someone to look after the house and spin the wool into thread for him to weave, and it might as well be this one, whose father was his good friend.

'That's enough o' talkin',' he growled, and reached out to pull her down with him on the grass, where her height wouldn't matter. With the ease of long practice, he thrust one hand down the front of her bodice and forced his knee between her legs – as well as he could, with the long skirt and petticoats she was wearing.

She didn't scream as any other wench would have done, she just yelled, 'Leave go of me!' and tried to shove him away.

'Ah, you'll like it,' he said, willing to woo her a little more.

She didn't give him the chance to prove this. A ringing slap on his ear was followed by a series of punches to any part of his body within reach, delivered by a hand as hard and muscular as most men's. Yelling, he rolled off her and scrambled to his feet.

She rolled in the opposite direction and jumped up facing him. 'If you try to touch me again, I'll make you sorry!' she panted, face flushed. When he made no further move, she began to set her clothing in order.

He tugged his breeches straight, keeping a wary eye on her. They all knew she had a hot temper. 'Damn you, woman! Why did you lead me on like this if you didn't want a bit of a fondle?'

She paused to gape at him. '*Lead you on?* How have I been doing that?'

'You agreed to come out walking with me, didn't you? What else did you think I meant by it?'

She glared at him, struggling to keep the tears back now.

He spat on the ground at her feet. 'Well, you can keep your precious body all to yourself from now on, Rachel Bloody Smedling. I'd as soon bed a viper as you. Sooner!' And so he'd tell her father next time they met, friend or no friend.

'Hah! Think I'd waste myself on a stunted weasel like you!' she flung back at him, trying to set her hair to rights by feel. 'I wasn't leadin' you on, an' well you know it, Bill Withers! When you asked me to come out for a walk, I told you straight there'd be no messin' around. I couldn't have said it plainer.'

'Aw, that's what all the lasses say when they're in the village, but they change their minds quick enough once you get 'em out o' sight o' their mothers.'

She bit back further words. What was the use in arguing? She'd been surprised when he asked her to go walking, for no other fellow ever had, but he'd been so nice about it she'd thought that once, just once, someone liked her well enough to find out if they got on comfortably together. But all he'd wanted was her body and – she scowled as she worked it out – someone to look after his house now that his mam had died. She should have realised that sooner, but she'd been so happy to have a fellow interested in her, like the other lasses. Well, she wouldn't fool herself again, indeed she wouldn't.

He snatched up his fustian jacket and began to drag it on, frustration making him want to hurt her. Stunted weasel, was he? He'd make her sorry she'd called him that, by hell he would! 'You should think yoursen lucky anyone's botherin' to take an interest. I haven't seen no one else askin' you to walk out with them.' He bent again to retrieve his hat and stick, winced at his sore cheek and added spitefully, 'Proper old broomstick, you are! Grateful to me, that's what you should be, grateful!'

She felt sick with anger, as much with herself as with him. 'Grateful!' she mimicked, with the biting sarcasm for which she was famous. '*Grateful!* To have an animal like you pawing at me.' She forced a laugh and tossed her head so that some of the soft, straight hair fell in front of her eyes and hid the tears still welling there. 'Well, I'm not grateful! I'm sickened by your slobberings. What's more, a hog'd not only have better manners than you, it'd smell nicer, too.'

Breath hissed into his mouth as he jammed the shapeless felt hat down on his greasy black hair. 'Well, there's other wenches as aren't sickened. Plenty of 'em.'

'Go an' slobber over them, then!'

He'd been a rough bullying sort of boy, she remembered suddenly, from the days when she'd been free to play out a bit with the other children. And he clearly hadn't changed much since.

'I will go an' find mesen a prettier bit of skirt, that's for sure,' he growled. 'Don't think I ever fancied you, you old horse-face! 'Twas the dowry I were after. An' someone to take Mam's place. A man can't see what's in bed with him in the dark, but a good dowry goes a long way in the daylight, an' so does a steady hand with the spinning wheel.'

He swished his stick at her, making her jerk backwards, then turned to leave.

'*What?*' The word was a gasp of air as his meaning sank in. She caught up with him in two leaps, barring his way with a ferocious look on her face. 'What d'you mean – dowry?'

He took a step backwards. He had no mind to provoke her further, not with that expression on her face. 'I meant nothin', nothin' at all. It were just words.'

''Tweren't just words, neither, Bill Withers. What did you mean by it?' Her voice was quieter now, but the fury flashing in her eyes and throbbing behind her words made him feel nervous. She was too strong for a woman, this one was. He preferred them soft and manageable.

'It were nothin', I tell you. Just a way o' speakin', like.' He kept a wary eye on her hands, which were curled into two very unfeminine fists, and tried to edge round her.

One of those hands shot out and before he could take a second step, Rachel had seized his stick. After a very brief tussle, she wrenched it away from him and used all the strength she could muster to send it whistling through the air, tumbling end over end as it bounced down the hillside.

He watched it open-mouthed, then edged back from her.

'I reckon I'm a match for you, Bill Withers,' she said, determination in every line of her body, 'so if you don't tell me what you mean by a dowry, you'll have to fight your way back to Upper Clough.'

'Well, then,' Bill's words came out in a rush, anger at being bested by a woman making him lash back at her in the only way he dared, 'it's your father as has talked about a dowry. He's offered five guineas to anyone as'll marry you an' take you off his hands. I could use the money, yes, an' a wife to spin for me, but I've changed my mind about havin' *you*! I'll find mysen a softer armful to warm my bed, by hell I will! You hardly even look like a woman! Proper old beanstick, you are! No, a maypole. They should tie ribbons round your neck an' save themselves the cost of that new pole they're talkin' about setting up.' He grinned at his own wit, then scowled again as she made no response, just continued to stare at him, grey eyes narrowed like a cat's. 'So you can keep that precious body of yours *untouched*, an' I'll look for a likelier lass.'

She moved out of his way then and flourished one hand in a gesture to him to leave, for she could not have spoken a single word. Sick humiliation sat in a cold lump behind her anger and she stood motionless, arms folded across her breast, as she watched him hurry down the path towards the village. A couple of times she saw him glance over his shoulder as if he was afraid of her following him, but she didn't move, couldn't, for very shame. It was all she could do to hold her head up and keep her back straight.

Only when he was out of sight did she allow her shoulders to sag. 'Oh, how could he?' she whispered, thinking of the shame her father had put upon her. Knowing him, she could guess he'd have made the offer in the Lower Clough alehouse for all to hear, because that's where he spent most of his time. Most of his money, too, lately. Oh, she could kill him!

And then, suddenly, it was all too much for her – the tall thin body, the gaunt face, the mind that refused to be quiet and the temper that flared out of control sometimes and made enemies for her. Why had she been born like this? Why couldn't she be soft and pretty like her cousin Nell? It would be a waste of time fussing over her appearance, whatever her mother and Nell said. When did she have time to primp, anyway?

And even if she did change how she looked, she would still be too tall and she wouldn't think like the other girls, would she? Or behave like them, either. When the lasses of her age had started to walk out with lads and sit with the older women of an afternoon, spinning and gossiping, Rachel Smedling had been at home learning to weave, as the brother who'd died would have done. For some reason it had amused her father to teach her – and when she'd shown an aptitude, he'd kept her at it, for her work brought him more money than she would ever have saved him by spinning wool for him. She was as good a weaver as any of the men in the village, but it didn't make her more popular – it only emphasised how different she was.

She moaned in her throat, misery trickling through her veins like slow, thick acid. What had she done to deserve this? She stood next to her father at her loom in the attic for as long as he did every day, longer since he'd taken to the drink. And when she wasn't weaving, she had to help her poor ailing mam to keep the house clean or else labour on the family's plot of land. It seemed sometimes that the work never ended. From early morning till she fell into bed, she was always behind with something.

Lately she had grown to hate him, whatever it said in the Bible about honouring your father and mother! And she knew he felt the same way about her. It had soured him when her poor little brother died and since then he spoke to her scornfully, mocking how she looked, not only at home, but publicly.

A grim smile sat briefly on her face. He didn't try to hit her any more, though. Last time he'd slapped her, she'd told him straight she'd thump him back if he laid a finger on her again. When he'd raised his fist, she'd grabbed a piece of wood and clouted him with it. Hard.

Her mother had got so upset he'd backed down, saying Rachel wasn't worth bothering about, and he hadn't touched her since, but it had never occurred to her that he would try to get rid of her by bribing the men from the Weaver's Arms to wed her.

She drew in a few deep breaths and tried to calm down, but the thoughts still twisted round and round in her skull. She could guess why he'd done it, of course. Last year she'd insisted on getting her share of the weaving money and had vowed she wouldn't work at her loom if she didn't get paid for it, though she had had to let the loom stand idle for five days to prove that. Then he'd given in, but with a sour grace. So now that he couldn't steal all she earned, she supposed he didn't see any use in her staying around.

And if it weren't for her mam, she'd leave home this very day, oh, she surely would – and take her savings with her. He knew she had money put by, but he didn't know where or how much, though he'd gone through her things once or twice looking for it, she could tell that. She was very careful nowadays when she added new coins to her store, making sure he was out at the alehouse before she dug up her little tin box.

Suddenly, it was all too much! Overwhelmed with shame and anguish, Rachel buried her face in a tussock of spring moorland grass and began to weep hoarsely. *Bill Withers!* If her father had to buy her a husband, he should look for a better bargain than that! *Buy her a husband!* Oh, dear Lord, the shame of it!

A few days before Rachel went for her walk, Maggie Kellett sat down in her sister-in-law's comfortable kitchen in Hepstone, in the big farmhouse where she had grown up and lived till she got married. 'Oh, Bella, if only Justin could have got somewhere closer to home. I'm going to miss you so.'

Bella sighed. Maggie's shoulders were drooping, her blonde hair was in tangles and her eyes were red-rimmed. The younger woman was a weak reed and it would be a relief not to have her living nearby, sending little Peg running to her aunt for help at every small crisis. 'You'll be fine once you get settled in,' she said bracingly. 'Mr Armstrong told your Justin the house in Upper Clough has three bedrooms and a proper parlour. Think how much better that'll be than the cottage you've got here, with only the open loft for the children to sleep in. And,' she looked suggestively at the other woman's swelling stomach, 'you're going to need more sleeping space once you've had the child.'

Maggie cradled her belly, but her face didn't brighten. 'I was later on than this when I lost the last one.'

'Well, you had two fine little girls before that, didn't you?'

'And lost two others. And I still haven't given Justin the son he wants.'

Bella ran out of patience. 'For heaven's sake, stop complaining, Maggie! Once the move is over, you'll be much happier in Upper Clough. You know you will.' She ignored the gulp and the trembling lips. 'Now, have you got everything ready for my Ned and Caleb Hesketh to load on the big cart tomorrow?'

'Everything except Justin's books and writing things. He wouldn't let me pack them till today because he was working on a sermon. You know what he's like, always reading in the evening. I can hardly get a word out of him sometimes.'

Bella wasn't getting into that argument again. 'Then you'd better go home and start packing the rest, hadn't you?'

Once she got home, Maggie began to tie the books into bundles. 'Justin thinks more of these than he does of me,' she muttered and brushed away another tear. She didn't want to leave Hepstone. The village might be small, but she had grown up there and her only remaining family lived just outside the village. Justin should have been offered the living here, for he'd been curate for eight years, but he wasn't the sort of man to talk softly to anyone, even his patron, especially when he saw an injustice or a better way of doing something. Eight years of living in a cramped cottage had made her feel very bitter. Well, who wouldn't be, in the circumstances? She'd come down in the world, she definitely had.

Her brother Ned was lucky. Men always had the best of everything. He'd inherited South Lea Farm from their father while Maggie had got nothing except some money, a few bits and pieces of furniture and her mother's silver locket. And of course her husband had immediately taken charge of the money, so she hadn't had the pleasure of spending it.

Why, even Caleb Hesketh, a distant cousin of Justin's, had a small farm of his own beyond the village, and *he* was bastard born. She sometimes thought she should have set her cap at him instead of Justin – except that Caleb was so big and stern he always made her feel a little nervous. And Black Top Farm, where he lived, lay right out on the edge of the moors, a bleak place where the wind whistled like a pack of demons in winter. She'd not fancy living there, nor enjoy living with his mother. Joanna Hesketh was a sharp-tongued woman and had nowhere else to go if her son married.

But her Justin was such a fine-looking young man that she'd been in a daze of love almost from the moment he came to the village as curate. He was still handsome; it was she who looked and felt worn out. She sat down on the edge of the bed and was tempted into lying down for a rest. Her back was aching again and she had craved sleep all the time she had been carrying this child.

Feeling guilty for her sharpness, Bella came round at dusk to help and found her still in bed, the books lying scattered on the floor, the little girls' needs forgotten. Eh, Maggie lass, Bella thought sadly, looking down on the sleeping woman, I don't know how you'll go on without me.

Justin returned home and frowned to see no evening meal ready and the packing still not finished.

'She's not carrying this baby easily,' Bella offered by way of an excuse.

'She never does. Thanks for your help, Bella, and for having the three of them to stay with you tomorrow.' He stifled his annoyance and went to shake Maggie awake. 'Time to get us all something to eat, love.'

As his wife yawned and took her time about getting up, he picked up the last few books and tied them together. He had finished his final round of farewells and duties as curate now, and was more than ready to leave Hepstone.

Only when little Peg came to try and help him did his expression lighten. But a shriek of dismay from the kitchen made the frown return to his face again, as he went to sort out his wife's latest domestic crisis. Perhaps she would cope better in a larger house. Or perhaps she wouldn't. Perhaps . . . he shook his head and banished such thoughts. She was his wife and whatever her faults, he owed her respect and love.

CHAPTER TWO

For a while longer Rachel sat there on the damp grass, her body hunched over and her arms crossed round her middle to contain the pain. But the beautiful vista gradually had its usual calming effect. The wide arch of the sky, the rolling moorland and the greenish-brown curves of Whin Ridge always made her feel better and she wished she could get up here more often.

Well, she decided eventually, being shamed doesn't kill you. I shan't heed 'em, whatever they say. I shall just go about my business as usual. But when Mam dies, she blinked away another tear at that thought, I'll leave him. I will that. I'll find mysen a little cottage and set up on my own as a weaver, take in a child from the foundling home to keep me company and help me with the spinning, maybe. It was a much cherished dream, for the last thing she wanted was to leave the valley and moors she loved.

With those thoughts she stood up and brushed the grass and seeds from her skirts. She didn't follow Bill Withers down into the village but turned on to the sheep trail that led up towards the tops. Whin Ridge was her favourite place in the summer, the only place where she could get some precious privacy during the few hours of leisure she stole when things got her down.

No wonder she was so thin, she thought, looking down at her bony right arm. She worked too hard. She knew it, but could change nothing. If she didn't plant and look after the oats, potatoes and vegetables, no one else would. Then she and her mother would go hungry, for if there was any doing without, it was never *him* that went short. It was all she could do lately to make him pay for the spun woollen thread they bought in for their weaving and give her enough money for his food.

She went swiftly up the hill with her long strides, skirts and petticoats hitched up. Once she paused to take a few gulps of clear, sweet water and wash her face in a tiny stream only a foot wide that trickled silently across the land. There were runlets everywhere, and they all built up into the River Whin, lifeblood of the valley named after it. As she walked, she breathed in deeply. Ah, but the air always smelled so fresh and tangy up here!

When she came to Whin Ridge itself, the going was harder and she paused for a rest. It was the highest point of land around and patches of bare rock jutted up here and there along its length, as if it had stood up and stretched during the night, shaking off some of the grass that clung to its flanks. She sometimes thought it looked like a gigantic hound when seen from below, crouching on the top of the hill, ready to pounce on the unwary traveller.

As she stood there, she saw a man come into sight striding across the tops from the east, and for a moment she hesitated, wondering whether to hide till he had passed. You had to be careful sometimes with tramping folk who could get desperate enough to steal the clothes off your back. But this fellow looked decent enough. In fact, when he drew closer, she decided he looked far too prosperous to be on the tramp. What was he doing, then, walking over the moors with a bundle on his back? Intrigued, she continued to watch him.

He was dark-haired, with a friendly expression on a face glowing with exertion and fresh air, and was wearing a plain suit of good black cloth, with sensible woollen stockings covering his legs below the knee breeches. His sturdy leather shoes were dirty, their buckles dull with dust, and one shoe was scraped across the toe, as if he'd stumbled on rocky ground. Since it was a warm day, he'd taken the jacket off and tied it to the pack on his back, and he was not wearing a hat. His waistcoat was full-skirted, as the gentry wore them, and showed a decent linen shirt below it, but somehow he didn't look like gentry, well not exactly. Who was he and what was he doing up here?

When he caught sight of the woman in the distance, Justin thought at first what a pretty colour of hair she had, honey-coloured with golden highlights from the sun. She had nice rosy cheeks, too. But as he drew closer, he realised it was only an illusion of prettiness, for she was gaunt and careworn, with unhappiness in the droop of her lips and anger in the fierceness of her eyes. She was tall for a woman, too, almost as tall as he was.

'Fine day,' he said, pausing a few paces away and taking out a handkerchief to wipe his forehead.

'Aye.'

He nodded towards the valley below them. 'Would that first village be Upper Clough?'

'It would.' She pointed. 'An' beyond it, Lower Clough, an' that's Setherby Bridge at the lower end of the valley, with the great house at Cleving Park on the lower slopes there. Were you seeking someone?'

He shook his head. 'No. I'm the new curate at Upper Clough and I'm looking for my church and house. Justin Kellett, at your service.' He sketched a bow.

She bobbed her head in acknowledgement. 'Rachel Smedling. I live just across the green from you. So what are you doing tramping over the moors, then, Mr Kellett? Folk like you usually come here on horseback.'

'I wanted to see what the countryside was like round here before I settled down.' He stared up at the sky. 'And the Lord always seems much closer up here on the tops.' Besides which, he had desperately needed a day away from Maggie, just one day – not too much to ask, surely.

She nodded. 'Yes, I know what you mean. Whin Ridge is the most peaceful place I know.'

'I set off early this morning on foot from Hepstone.' And Maggie had complained about that all over again when he woke her to say goodbye! 'My cousin Caleb is to bring my wife and children over to join me tomorrow in his big cart with our furniture, then I'll settle down to work.'

'You have children, then?'

He could not help smiling at the thought of them. 'Oh, yes. Two little lasses, and another baby on the way. Peg's five and Lizbet's three. My Maggie has her hands full with them, I can tell you. I intend to sleep here tonight and be there to greet them when they arrive.'

'How can you sleep there without furniture or blankets?'

He grinned. 'Oh, I'll manage, never fear. I can maybe lie in a pew inside the church, to be out of the draughts. I have a thick cloak here,' he indicated a roll of material lying under his coat on the top of the pack, 'and I dare say I can buy a bite to eat from someone in the village.'

'My mother can lend you some blankets, if you like. We've plenty to spare.'

'I couldn't trouble you.'

She shrugged. 'Where's the trouble? 'Tis no effort to bring some bedding across to the church when I get back, and a pillow, too, if you like. Finest goose feathers. I cleaned them and made the pillows myself.'

'That's very kind. Thank you.' Then he turned again to stare into the valley. 'The three villages look pretty from here, almost as if they're tied together by those grey stone walls running down the hills.'

'Not always as pretty when you're down below, though.'

Her voice was full of bitterness. He glanced sideways at her. Poor lass. She looked hard done to, somehow, and had obviously been weeping. Well, he would no doubt find out more about her once he'd settled in.

'I must be going now.' He was suddenly eager to see his new home and church. 'I'm happy to have met you, Rachel. Thank you again for your offer of blankets.'

'I'll bring them round later. And something to eat as well.'

As he walked away, he glanced back over his shoulder. The lass had a nice smile and a direct way of looking at you, and from her clothing she came of decent folk. His Maggie could do with a friend in the village.

It'd seem funny living here. It wasn't all that many miles away from Hepstone if you had a horse – which he didn't – but it seemed a lot further on foot and the folk from the two valleys rarely came into contact. Why, he didn't know a soul over here, while in Hepstone, the Kelletts, Heskeths and Garstons had known one another for several generations, and married one another sometimes, too. Then there were the Armstrongs nearby in Todmorden. He came from one of the poorer branches of that family and when Nathaniel Armstrong had inherited Cleving Park from his uncle, he had almost immediately offered the vacant curate's position to his distant relative.

One day, of course, Justin hoped to get a living of his own, then he and Maggie would settle somewhere for good. It had been a hard path for him, a mere farmer's son, to get where he was, but now that he was to assist the old parson here in Whin Vale, surely things would improve.

Rachel watched him walk away, then climbed a little further before sitting down on her favourite rock near the summit, her arms loosely clasped round her knees. She gazed down at the long, narrow Pennine valley where she had lived all her life. From here, the hamlets seemed as small as the wooden toys her cousin Nell's children played with. From here, her troubles always seemed smaller, too.

'How could my father do it?' she repeated, but sadly now, the anger used up by the stiff climb to the ridge.

Later, when she realised the sun was starting to dip towards the horizon and the air had a damp feel to it, she got up with a sigh to begin the hour's walk down into Upper Clough.

Life went on, she thought grimly, as she approached the village. It just went on regardless and you had to go with it wherever it led, putting up with whatever it brought you. Only when you died did the pain stop, and perhaps not even then.

★   ★   ★

17

Further down the valley at Cleving Park, Nathaniel Armstrong sat in the library and looked round in satisfaction. He could not have been happier at how things had turned out. He had expected the estate to go to his elder brother, who was Reuben Armstrong's godson. But the will had said plainly that John would have more than enough with the family's Todmorden properties, so Cleving was to pass to the next living nephew. Which meant him, Nathaniel. For his father had four surviving sons and Uncle Reuben had none.

'You'll *have* to get wed now, son,' his mother had said immediately she heard the news. Not, 'I'm happy for you!' or even, 'How kind of your uncle to think of you.' No, just, 'You'll have to get wed now.'

She'd been on at him to do that for years, urging him to find a wife with a decent dowry, but at thirty he still had no desire to marry, though he supposed he'd have to give the matter some consideration later. A gentle wife who kept a quiet house and could bear him a son or two might not be too bad, but he didn't want a nagging wife like his mother, who was never satisfied with anything and whose voice rang out shrilly from dawn till dusk. But before he did anything, he wanted to savour his inheritance and get used to his new status as a landowner.

There was no need to rush into anything because his widowed aunt had agreed to stay on with him and manage the big house for the time being, been glad to, in fact. It was a condition of the will that he provide for her in comfort, and if he wished to house her away from Cleving, it was to be in a genteel residence suited to her station and well supplied with servants. Funny that Reuben had not left anything to her, but then his uncle had had little faith in women's ability to manage money and property – and Nathaniel rather agreed with him on that.

He got up and went to look out of the window at the splendid view. Justin Kellett had said he'd tramp across the tops from Hepstone today. A stout fellow, Kellett, or he'd not have got the curacy, relative or not. Nathaniel had no time for clerics who spent their days buried in books and neglected their parish duties, as St John had been doing in this parish for the past decade or two. It was too late to change the old parson, who was seventy if he was a day, but Nathaniel would take care about choosing a new one. Justin Kellett would have to prove himself worthy if he wanted to win the living when St John died.

In fact, Nathaniel decided, leaning back and stretching luxuriously, he meant to take an interest in all that happened in the three villages in Whin Vale, much of which belonged to the estate. He intended to be master here in more than just name. His uncle had let things slide in recent years, but Nathaniel did not crave parties and soirées, and he intended to set his hand firmly on the reins – as the land agent, Tam Barker, would find out, for a start. The fellow had not impressed Nathaniel at all, but it was only fair that he be given a chance to prove himself. After all, an idle master made for an idle man. And the villagers would find out too, especially the less thrifty among them. A landowner had many obligations and Nathaniel didn't intend to neglect any of them.

That same afternoon, Caleb Hesketh went across to South Lea Farm to finish loading the big dray and check that Maggie and the girls would be ready on time in the morning. He peered through the kitchen window and saw her weeping on her sister-in-law's shoulder, with Bella looking frazzled.

The two little girls were sitting together in a corner, with five-year-old Peg cuddling three-year-old Lizbet. Peg was a little mother to her sister already and knew to keep out of her mother's way when she was in one of her moods. He heard a sound from the barn and went to investigate. Ned Garston was in there, tying some stained canvas over the loaded cart. Caleb went to help him.

'How are things going, then?' he asked.

'My dear sister hasn't stopped weeping all day. I don't envy you the journey over to Upper Clough with her tomorrow, lad.'

Caleb sighed, forbore to comment and when the canvas was firmly tied in place, he and Ned went into the house.

'Hello, Bella, Maggie,' said Caleb. 'I came over to check that everything's all right for tomorrow.'

'Don't worry. I'll make sure it is,' Bella replied, with a definite grimness of tone.

'I'll be over before dawn, then. I want to make an early start.'

'It'd have been better for you to sleep here, as I offered.' Bella patted Maggie's back absent-mindedly, as she would have done to a child.

'I don't like to leave my mother alone in the house at night, and I'll be gone tomorrow night as well.'

'You're a good son to her,' Ned said.

'Well, she's been a good mother to me.'

As he walked home, Caleb reflected that Joanna had indeed been a good mother to him, whatever some folk said about her sharp ways. Well, she'd had to be forceful to make a living. Her own family had disowned her completely. Justin Kellett was the only relative who had acknowledged him at all, and that had come much later when they were both lads. He was only a distant cousin of the Kelletts and often thought how wonderful it must be to have a close family – brothers, sisters, aunts, uncles. When he grew older, his mother had told him something of her struggle to make the Singleton family do something for the bastard son, who was the only child Isaac Singleton had left behind him when he died suddenly of a fever. They hadn't provided generously, just gifted a small piece of land and a tumbledown cottage to the child, and nothing to her.

He remembered his grandparents, the dour Beth, whom he greatly resembled physically and to whom he had never spoken. His grandfather, John, had been more kindly and on their occasional encounters at the Rochdale markets had always stopped to chat and advise the growing lad about improving the small piece of land. Good advice the old man had given, too. And once he had slipped Caleb some money to pay for drainage and buy a nearby field that was for sale.

His mother had been huffy and said he should have given it back, out of sheer pride, because they could manage without charity, thank you. But he'd sensed somehow that this money was his legacy from John, the final recognition of him as a grandson. And sure enough, the old man had died soon after.

Caleb and his mother had not been invited to the funeral, though he had gone anyway, to stand on his own at the back of the church, ignoring the whispers, then to hover behind the other mourners at the graveside, determined to pay his respects. That had won him some black looks from the younger Singletons but a grudging nod from his grandmother.

If it hadn't been for Joanna's spinning and the vegetables she grew, he did not know how she would have managed. But he had never gone hungry. Not once. Many of his childhood memories were of her spinning – the big wheel turning on and on, every minute she could spare devoted to it, though she would chat to him as she worked. Soft hands she had from the grease in the sheep's wool, and she was a noted spinster. Nowadays, there was not only a steady demand from a clothier in Rochdale for the fine, even woollen thread she produced, but that thread came from their own fleeces. They had enough sheep now to put spinning out to some of the other women in Hepstone and then Caleb took the finished yarn to the clothier, who was paying the more skilful weavers to produce the new lightweight cloth with a napped surface that they were starting to call 'Rochdale flannel'. Good warm cloth it was, too, and you could be proud of your part in producing it.

He had grown up expecting to work hard and had developed a man's frame by the age of fourteen. Over the past ten years he had used his size and strength to develop the smallholding and build some more rooms on to the tiny two-room cottage, with stone he picked up on the moors and dressed himself, though he'd had to buy in the roof slates. He had worked for other men to earn extra pence, living mainly off his mother's earnings and the food they grew themselves, and saving his money to buy more land. Well, now he had enough fields to feed a small flock of sheep, for he had laboured doggedly over the years to dig the ditches and do whatever drainage work was necessary to make the poor marshy fields more productive.

He smiled, remembering how he had been scorned at first by other farmers for wasting his time and money learning such stuff from books. 'That land's allus been poor and allus will be,' they'd told him over and over, as if it was set in stone like one of the Ten Commandments. 'No book's going to change that.'

But once drained, his land had begun to increase its yield. The sheep dung from his flock had improved it still further, and he'd paid village lads a penny a time for buckets of horse dung, not caring whether they'd stolen it or acquired it legally, so long as it enriched his land.

Young as he was, still only twenty-two, he had won grudging respect for his efforts. When he heard older farmers comment, 'He's a hard worker, that 'un,' his heart swelled with pride. And because he and his mother shared a passion for reading, he had read also of men who were improving their breeds of sheep, so he was trying to do the same himself. At tupping time he had separated those sheep which produced better fleeces from the others and not let them mate indiscriminately. Last year he had found the money to buy in a couple of new rams from a like-minded farmer over Rochdale way to improve the flock still further. That had started the tongues wagging again. 'He's gone mad ovver them sheep, young Caleb has.' 'Eh, was there ever a chap like yon?'

But he had not gone mad. The new lambs seemed bigger to him, as well as having longer threads of wool, much better for spinning. And he was not done yet, oh, no. No one knew he had an agreement with James Trotter to buy their small farm when old Jed Trotter passed away, for James had no desire to stay in Hepstone and spoke longingly of going to work in a town where there was more to see and do. Once he had that land, Caleb would be able to increase his flocks still further and hire men to work for him all the year round – though he'd have to build a cottage or two for them in order to do that.

So, for all his mother's hints, he had not married, not even considered it yet. He was not going to let anything stop him making a respected place for himself in the community. And he had only to see foolish Maggie Kellett to know he was doing the right thing. If he couldn't find a sensible woman to work hard by his side, he simply wouldn't get wed at all.

When Rachel got home from her walk, she found her mother sleeping and the kitchen in a mess where *he* had sawed at the hunk of cheese she'd bought for tea. He'd taken a full half of it and left the rest uncovered to get dry and stale. The door of the bread cupboard was swinging open again so that flies could get into it. She clicked her tongue in exasperation, took out two pieces of oat bread, then closed it firmly. Inside were stored several weeks' supply of flat clap bread, which she'd made herself from oats bought from a neighbouring farmer. Sometimes, for a treat, they ate wheaten bread, which she bought from the baker in Setherby, but like everyone else round here, they ate oat bread most of the time.

'Just like him!' she muttered as she set the kitchen to rights and went to draw a jug of small ale from the barrel for herself and her mother. 'He's a greedy, slummocky pig, he is.' She knew where her father would be now – drinking strong ale in the Weaver's Arms in Lower Clough. He went there most evenings as soon as the light failed, sometimes even before that, and usually came home fuddled.

She swung the kettle over the fire to give them some warm water to wash in, then tiptoed upstairs. 'Ah, you're awake, Mam. Shall I bring you up something to eat and drink? Father's gone out, so you've no need to come down.'

'Nay, I'll get up now and sit with you.'

But it worried Rachel that her mother's face was white and pinched, and that she sat down at the table like a woman who'd done a hard day's work, not one who'd just had a long sleep. The lump in her mother's breast was large now, and smaller lumps were appearing on her body here and there, while the rest of her seemed to be wasting away. They'd even gone to see the doctor down in Setherby, with Rachel paying, of course, for *he* wouldn't. The doctor had made a cursory examination, then talked about 'the Lord's will', before admitting there was nothing anyone could do to help Mrs Smedling. It seemed very unfair that God should inflict such suffering on a good woman like her mother, and so Rachel had told him.

After they had eaten, Rachel went to sort out some blankets for the curate and tied a piece of bread and the last of the cheese in a cloth as well. He'd be used to eating wheaten bread all the time, no doubt, but he didn't look the sort of man to scorn her offering. As she worked, she told her mother about the meeting on the tops, speculating about what the new curate's wife would be like. Youngish, if she had small children, but would Mrs Kellett think herself above the other village women? Well, she was above them, of course she was, but with some people that didn't matter, while others made a big thing of their superiority.

Old Mr Armstrong had been friendly with everyone, rich or poor, but as he grew older, he got out and about less. His agent, Tam Barker, now acted as if he was king of the valley. Rachel didn't like Tam, but he was a friend of her father's as well as being the man who collected their rent, so she could not take open exception to the scornful way he spoke to her.

It remained to be seen what the new Mr Armstrong would be like. She'd seen him once in Setherby on market day and he looked to be full of his own importance. He was youngish, a stout sort of man, with brown hair and a square, pale face. Not married, the servants said, and fussy. Wanted things doing just so.

Her mother's voice jerked her out of her idle musing. 'I thought you'd gone out walking with Bill Withers today, love. You should have brought him home for a sup of ale. It's thirsty work climbing up those hills.'

Rachel hated to wipe away that hopeful expression but couldn't lie to her mother. 'I soon parted company with him. He – he wasn't really interested in me. Father had offered to pay him five guineas to wed me, an' he wanted to sample the goods first.'

'Oh, no! Oh, surely not!'

Her mother looked so distressed Rachel wished she'd kept some of the information to herself. But it still hurt, festering inside her like a dirty cut, and she hadn't been able to hold the hot words back. 'Eh, don't bother about that,' she said gruffly. 'I wouldn't have taken up with Bill Withers anyway. He's a nasty, spiteful sort of fellow an' always has been.' She gestured to the bundle on the table and changed the subject. 'I'll just walk over to Church Cottage and take these things to Mr Kellett, shall I? Then I'll pop in to see Nell for half an hour, if you don't need me.'

'Aye, you do that. Eh, it'll be good to have a curate here again and church services every week.' Alice brightened up at the thought. She knew she hadn't long for this world and it'd be a comfort to go to the tiny church each Sunday and listen to the Lord's word again, a great comfort, for she had not been able to manage the walk down to the big church in Setherby for a while now.

She went slowly over to the door and stood there as dusk settled around her, watching her daughter stride across the village green and disappear into the church. Eh, the poor lass! It wasn't fair of Walter to shame her like that. And yet you couldn't blame him for being bitter, with his only son dead. But he had no need to take that out on Rachel. What had happened wasn't her fault. The lad had died of a fever that had killed several children in the valley, and Alice had only ever borne two children, Rachel and poor Paul.

On that thought, she went back into the house. She'd been meaning to write the letter for a while now. She couldn't go to her Maker with so much on her conscience. She'd talk to the new curate, then ask him to pass the letter on to Rachel after she was dead. It'd be safe with him. She didn't want Walter finding it and destroying it out of sheer spite. Her daughter deserved to know the truth, should have been told before, really, but Walter had insisted not.

She was glad Rachel was strong-willed. The lass would need to have all her wits about her if she was to make something of her life with a father like that. It had been a bad mistake marrying Walter Smedling, though he'd not been nearly as selfish and bitter when they first wed. But what choice had she had? He had been the only one willing to take her, money or not.

CHAPTER THREE

Late the following afternoon, Rachel was walking back through the village from Nell's when she saw a farm cart pulling slowly up the hill. It was piled high with furniture and the six horses drawing it looked weary.

Something about the man driving it caught her attention and she couldn't help staring at him. He was very tall, you could see that even when he was sitting on the cart, with a hawk-like profile and eyes that burned darkly, as if he was angry at the world. Everyone else in the village was staring too, with folk standing openly at windows and doorways, because strangers were not common in this upper end of the valley where the road came to a dead end.

She suddenly realised who the driver must be – the cousin who was bringing the new curate's furniture, of course! And that'd be Mrs Kellett sitting up beside him, a fair, fluffy woman, looking blurred somehow, as if there was nothing definite about her. Where were the children? Ah yes, one was sprawled behind the driving seat on top of the canvas cover staring around her, and the other was curled up asleep with her head in her mother's lap. Rachel smiled. There was something very appealing about a sleeping child. She loved children and often played with Nell's four, enjoying their honesty and their curious views of the world.

It was at that moment Caleb Hesketh first noticed her, a strong woman, from her looks, unlike this bleating fool beside

ANNA JACOBS

him. The sunlight was gilding her hair and she was smiling
tenderly, the smile lighting up her whole face. He ignored
the other villagers, pulling to a halt nearby and hailing her
simply because he wanted to speak to her. 'Can you direct
me to Church Cottage, please, mistress?'

She stepped forward, nodding. ''Tis the house beyond the
church – you can just see the end of the garden wall there.'

Even as she spoke, Justin came striding towards them, calling, 'Caleb! I had given up hope of you getting here today.'

Rachel did not miss the scowling glance Caleb shot at the
woman beside him.

'We had a later start than I'd have liked.'

Mrs Kellett pushed the child aside and held her arms out
to her husband to be lifted down. 'You didn't say how hard
a road it was, Justin. We've been near jolted to pieces and it's
taken all day to get here.'

Rachel was amazed at the whining tone of the greeting,
but felt she should not be lingering here like an eavesdropper,
so turned to leave.

'Mistress Smedling!'

She turned back at Justin's call.

'Come and meet my Maggie.' He bent over the short,
fair-haired woman and said coaxingly, 'Dearest, this is Rachel
Smedling. She and her mother have been very kind to me,
lending me some bedding for last night, and today they've
brought us some griddle cakes to welcome us to our new
home. 'Tis nice to have friendly neighbours, is it not?'

The smaller child woke up and began to call to her father to
lift her down. The other lass didn't wait to be helped, but started
climbing down by herself, though it was a steep drop for a child
of her size. Rachel saw trouble looming and rushed forward to
catch her, bumping into the stranger, arms outstretched on the
same mission.

She already had hold of the child, so Caleb simply held
Rachel steady while she set the little girl on her feet.

'I'm sorry!' she said, confusion spreading through her at
his touch. It felt so strange to look up at a man instead of

28

down. How very tall he was! The tallest man she'd ever met.

'That's all right.' Caleb let go of her and stepped backwards.

Rachel didn't want to meet his piercing gaze, which seemed to see right into her soul, so she bent to straighten the little girl's pinafore. 'There you are, love.' She could still feel his eyes boring into her, though, and still feel the impression of his hands holding her steady, too. Why was he staring like that? She could not stop the warmth rising in her cheeks. Then there was a tug on her skirt and she looked down, grateful for any diversion.

'Is this Upper Clough? My mother said we'd never get here.' The little girl was staring round her, bright-eyed. She was blonde like her mother, but she had her father's intelligent eyes and open interest in the world.

'You mustn't speak so rudely to the lady, Peg!' Maggie scolded from nearby.

Rachel turned with a smile. 'Eh, she means no harm. She's a bonny little lass.'

Beside her, Caleb nodded agreement, his eyes thoughtful now, but still fixed on her.

Rachel's confusion grew. Did she have a dirty mark on her face? Was her hair slipping out of its pins already?

The two of them looked at one another, glanced away, then both turned back for another look at the same time.

Rachel was greatly relieved when Maggie Kellett broke the spell.

'Yes, folk do tell me my daughters are pretty.' She smiled down at the child, for she was very proud of her girls' looks and loved to hear them praised.

Justin turned to Rachel. 'I wonder, would you have time to take my wife and the children over to the cottage while I help Caleb with the cart?'

Rachel forgot the stranger, wishing now she had walked on, because interesting as it was to meet the newcomers first, she was already behind with the day's work she had set herself.

'Do you live in Upper Clough, Mistress Smedling?' Maggie

paused delicately to choose a path round a muddy patch, then paused again to assess the next stretch of ground.

Rachel, who never bothered about a bit of mud for she had good solid shoes on her feet, sighed for her companion's slow progress and looked enviously at the dainty feet in their soft leather shoes with the silver buckles. 'Aye. And have lived here all my life.' She stole a glance down at her own feet and was suddenly unhappy with how large they looked.

'And your husband? What does he do?'

'I'm not wed. I live with my mother and father.' She pointed across the green. 'That's our house.'

'I see.' Maggie stopped to take a good look, pleased that it was one of the larger houses in the village. She would not want to make friends with just anybody.

Caleb, who had been unashamedly eavesdropping, also turned to look at the house, then Justin asked him something and he forced himself to pay attention to his cousin.

Rachel pointed towards the left. 'That's Goody Bentley's place. She's a widow and sells bits and pieces of food and such to make herself a few pence. We don't have a market or any proper shops here in Upper Clough, though there's all you could need down in Setherby Bridge.'

'That's a long way down the hill,' Maggie looked resentfully at her belly, 'and I'm not in a state to do much walking at the moment.'

She didn't seem of a mind to do much of anything, thought Rachel, and had to bite her tongue not to speak brusquely. Perhaps Mrs Kellett was just overtired today. Women at her advanced stage of pregnancy didn't always feel well.

Then they were at the cottage and an astonished Rachel found Maggie waiting for her to lead the way inside, waiting for her to show off the rooms, waiting to be invited to go upstairs in her own house, instead of rushing round to explore as Rachel would have done.

'It's very nice,' Maggie said at last, rubbing her back. 'I do hope they bring my settle in soon, though. I'm too tired to stay on my feet.'

Rachel felt like shaking her, so drooping and spiritless did she seem, but there were the children to think of, poor little mites, looking lost and clinging to one another, so she found them each a scone to eat, then scolded herself for her impatience with the mother, who did indeed look white and exhausted.

When the men appeared at the kitchen door, it was Rachel who took the basket of provisions from Caleb Hesketh and found the tinderbox to light the fire. Then she sent a neighbour's lad down the hill to buy a household barrel of small ale from the Weaver's Arms, since the Kelletts had nothing but well water to drink. She found the kettle for herself among the bits and pieces, and set it ready near the fire, then strode across the green to fill the bucket from the village well, which was noted for its sweet, clear water. No need to filter this water through muslin, or leave it to settle for a day like the water in Setherby.

'There,' she said bracingly as she swung the kettle crane over the fire, 'that'll soon get hot.'

Her only answer was a sigh.

While they were waiting for the lad to trundle the barrel back on the alehouse's handcart, Rachel went home and got a jug of small ale for them all, giving her mother details of what had happened so far, ending, 'As if I haven't enough to do!'

'We must all help one another,' Alice said, with one of her sweet smiles. 'It doesn't matter if you have to leave a few of your tasks here, love. It'll be nice for you to have a friend.'

'I've *got* a friend. My cousin Nell.' Rachel picked up the jug of ale and made her way back across the green to Church Cottage, calling, 'Would you like a drink?' to the two men who were still carrying pieces of furniture into the house.

As they stood in the kitchen drinking, Caleb Hesketh moved over to stand beside Rachel. 'You're from Upper Clough, then?' he asked as he gave her back the empty beaker.

'Yes.' What a serious expression he had. Nice dark hair, tied back in a queue and, from his clothes, not a poor man. He had a kind way with the little girls, too. Rachel liked that in him.

'And your family? Are they from round here?' he went on.

'My father was born in Rochdale and my mother came from over Todmorden way. But they settled here when they married.' Then she realised how time was passing, put her beaker down and turned to the curate. 'I really must go now, Mr Kellett. My mother is not well and needs me to help her.'

'Yes, of course. We thank you for your help, don't we, Maggie?'

'Oh, yes. I'm very grateful indeed.' Maggie sighed and pressed one white hand against her brow. 'I don't know how I'm ever going to manage everything on my own, though.'

'I dare say it'll all get done in the end.' Rachel moved purposefully towards the door.

Caleb smiled to see that she was not taken in by Maggie's ploy of helplessness. How Justin bore with the woman and her foolishness so patiently, he could not understand! One day alone with her on the cart had nearly driven him mad.

One or two men from the village turned up then to offer their help in unloading the cart and Maggie pulled herself together to direct them where the furniture was to go; some of it was the old stuff that her parents had left, which had been stored by her brother until she got a larger house. She wept for joy to see it used again then started unpacking her cooking utensils and dishes.

Caleb Hesketh stood by the cart and watched Rachel cross the village square, admiring her strong body and firm tread. He would like to get to know her better. He *would* get to know her better! He had never met a woman who had attracted him like this one did.

'Where's my food?' Rachel's father grumbled as soon as she opened the front door. 'I'd expected it to be ready by now.'

'It'll be ready in a minute.'

'Couldn't resist all the fuss over the new curate, could you? That's a woman for you, always ready to abandon her duties.' He jerked a thumb towards his wife. 'And *she* never lifts a finger nowadays.'

Rachel felt anger flare in her at the look of dumb suffering on her mother's face. 'You know very well she's too ill to do much,' she said in a low, angry voice.

'Then *you* should be here helping her, shouldn't you, not going out gawping at the new curate's doings.'

She turned and set her hands on her hips. 'If you talk to me like that, you'll get no food prepared by me at all.'

Her mother's voice was hesitant. 'Rachel, love . . .'

Why did her mother always try to placate him? Why did she never stand up to him? But her mother's face was so white that Rachel bit back an angry response and started slamming things down on the table. He only wanted to get off to the alehouse, so the sooner he went, the sooner they'd have a bit of peace. Rachel stood on a chair to unhook the ham hanging from the ceiling, unwrapped its muslin cover carefully and shaved off a few slices, before starting to wrap it up again.

Her father thumped the table. 'I want more than that!'

'If I give you more, it'll not last, then you'll have no ham at all till Rob's next litter has grown big enough to be slaughtered.'

'If you didn't take all the weaving money for your fripperies, I'd have enough to buy another ham in Setherby any time I liked.'

She didn't answer, for this was an old argument, just wrapped the meat and hung it up again. She watched in disgust as he wolfed down his portion like a hog at a trough, then slammed out of the house without a word of thanks.

'He's likely tired,' her mother offered.

'He's likely less tired than I am, for he lay abed half the morning with an aching head from the gin. Strong ale's bad enough, but now he's on the gin as well.'

Alice's eyes filled with tears. 'I'm sorry, love. I got you a poor father, I know, but he's better than none.'

Which seemed to Rachel a funny sort of remark to make, but then her mother's mind had been wandering a lot lately, and she talked about the past more often than the future. She realised her mother had spoken again and looked up. 'Sorry. What was that?'

'Will you ask the new curate to come and see me when he has a minute?'

'Yes, of course I will.' And she would tell him that her mother had not long for this world and beg him to set her mind at rest over whatever had been worrying her lately. The thought of what life would be like without her mother upset Rachel so much she lost her appetite and had to force the rest of her food down. Afterwards, she went to get some wool to spin as they sat together for an hour. They didn't say much, but then, they didn't need to. She might not have a good father, but she had a wonderful and loving mother.

One day the following week, a panic-stricken Maggie came hurrying across the green to beg her new friend to come and help out that afternoon.

'I have my weaving to do,' Rachel insisted, determined to stand firm today, whatever the reason for this fuss, for she had already learnt how ready Maggie Kellett was to lean on someone else.

'But *he* is coming to tea! He's just invited himself, sent up a groom with a note not an hour since. And us not settled in properly yet. Why couldn't he have waited till next week? It's so important to make a good impression on him.'

'Sit down, Mrs Kellett, and tell us who is coming,' Alice urged, smiling at the two children hovering near the door and beckoning them inside as well.

'Mr Armstrong himself!'

'Do you mean Mr Armstrong from Cleving Park is coming to tea at your house?' Alice asked, impressed.

'Yes. He's a distant relative of my husband's, you know. Only I'm still having trouble with that fireplace, and how I'm to get the place ready for him in time, I don't know. But Justin will be so angry if I let him down.'

Rachel had never seen Justin Kellett even remotely angry. In fact, she thought him too soft with his wife altogether and could not help wondering how two people so unlike had come to marry.

He had been to her own house twice now and she knew how comforted her mother was by his visits. Whatever had been preying on Alice's mind must have been confided and dealt with, and last Sunday she had even attended church, which meant Rachel going too, to help her across the square and back.

Behind the visitor's back, Alice frowned and jerked her head to indicate that her daughter should go and help out, so Rachel bit back a refusal and said, 'All right, Maggie, I'll come over in a minute.' Then she stared the other woman in the eyes. 'But not if you treat me as a servant while he's there.' This had happened once or twice already and had annoyed her intensely. She was no one's servant and never wanted to be.

'No, no! Of course I won't do that. I didn't mean to before, I'm sure.' Maggie's hand fluttered to her belly. 'I'm just – not myself at the moment. The baby's been very quiet lately. It must be getting ready to be born.'

'They often lie quietly towards the end,' Alice said comfortingly.

Rachel's tone was much brisker than those of the other two. 'You go back and make a start, then, Maggie. I'll follow shortly when I've settled my mother for a rest.' She watched the other woman trail across the village green, followed by the two little girls, who were skipping together and holding hands. 'Are you sure you'll be all right, Mother?'

Alice smiled and patted her hand. 'Of course I will, love. You go and help poor Maggie. But first put on your Sunday gown. If you don't want to be treated like a servant, then you shouldn't look like one.'

When Rachel had changed her clothes, Alice sighed and shook her head. 'You really will have to make time to sew yourself a new gown. That one's growing so shabby it's only fit for everyday use. A nice round gown, I think, in blue, and with some lace at the neck. I'll help you as much as I can. Wait! Come here so I can fix your hair.'

'Oh, Mother!'

'Sit on the stool. I can't reach you else.'

35

The result of Alice's efforts was that Rachel went across to Church Cottage with her soft hair pinned back neatly and her mother's best cap on her head, not to mention her mother's finest lace-trimmed fichu tucked into the bosom of her Sunday bodice.

When she opened the door, Maggie stared. 'I had not thought you could look so fine!'

Rachel flushed. 'My mother thought to do you honour in your dealings with Mr Armstrong.'

'Yes. Yes, of course. Well, come in.'

Thereafter, it was necessary to work quickly to set the parlour to rights and prepare some refreshments to offer the landowner. And it was Rachel who did most of the work.

Justin returned a short time before Mr Armstrong was due and hurried upstairs to get ready.

When he came down again, Rachel thought how much a gentleman he looked, and how well his wife looked too, for once, and wondered what she was doing in such company. These two were far above someone like her. Maggie called her a 'friend' but the two of them had nothing at all in common, and their conversations consisted mostly of Maggie's complaints or reminiscences and Rachel's bracing responses.

'Thank you for helping us,' Justin murmured when his wife had bustled upstairs for a final check of her appearance.

Rachel shrugged, feeling embarrassed by his praise.

'Maggie will go on better once the child is born, I'm sure,' he added in his quiet way. 'She doesn't carry them easily.'

''Tis hard on women.' But in spite of her words, Rachel was coming to the conclusion that Maggie Kellett simply used people to remedy her own weaknesses and would always find some excuse for not doing things herself.

There was the sound of a horse's hooves clopping to a halt on the harder ground outside the low garden wall, and both of them turned towards the window to see Nathaniel Armstrong swing off his horse and tie the reins to one of the rings in the churchyard wall. He stood for a moment studying the cottage thoughtfully as he took off his riding gloves, then strode towards the door.

Rachel tried not to stare as Justin went to greet the visitor, but she was very interested to see the landowner. There were no real gentry apart from this man in the valley, just the lawyer, the doctor and a few shopkeepers and farmers who had more money and possessions than their fellows. Nathaniel Armstrong was healthy and strong-looking and was wearing his own faded brown hair tied back in a queue with a small black bow. Rachel had expected him to be taller, somehow, but he was not even her own height, though he carried himself with great confidence.

She had expected him to dress more grandly, too, but although his linen was very fine and white, and his clothes were made of good broadcloth, they were neat and little different to those of the doctor and the lawyer. He wore a dark green frock coat over a lighter green waistcoat ornamented with braid and fastened down the front with silver buttons. His knee breeches were the same colour as a mouse she had killed only the day before, and were worn over grey stockings, very finely knitted, just visible over his boot tops.

By this time Maggie had come downstairs and was standing near her husband looking flustered and nervous. Justin drew her forward to introduce her to his patron, and she managed a graceful curtsy, in spite of her large belly, then beckoned Rachel to join them. 'Mr Armstrong, this is my friend, Rachel Smedling, who has been helping me settle in at Upper Clough. She and her family live just across the green.'

Rachel followed her hostess's example and dropped a curtsy, feeling stiff and awkward, wishing now that she had stayed in the kitchen.

Mr Armstrong stared at her, eyes narrowed. 'Smedling? Walter Smedling's daughter?'

Her heart sank. He could have heard little good of her father lately. 'Yes, sir.'

He studied her again, not attempting to hide his surprise and curiosity.

'I'll go and brew a dish of tea,' she said. No small ale for this visitor, but the best china tea, though the cost of a pound of this precious substance would have kept a poor family in bread for a week. Her father scoffed at tea as a drink, but her mother loved it, so Rachel occasionally bought an ounce or two for a treat, and they re-used the leaves several times.

Voices followed her down the corridor and into the kitchen. Nathaniel was saying in his fussy yet penetrating voice, 'She appears more respectable than her father, at least. They tell me he's become a heavy drinker.'

Justin replied quietly, 'She's a hard-working young woman, and has been very kind to Maggie and the children.'

'I've heard she weaves like a man. Not sure I approve of women doing such things. Still, if she ain't married, I suppose there's no harm in it. Tall, though, ain't she?'

Rachel flushed. She hated to be spoken about like this, as if she hadn't any feelings, as if she couldn't hear every word they were saying. She banged down the china pot that was to hold the tea and piled the little dishes beside it, annoyed that Maggie had not come out to help her.

In the parlour, Nathaniel had also noted with disapproval the way his hostess leaned back in the chair with a fade-way air, fingertips massaging one temple as though her head was aching.

Rachel brought in the tray and would have retreated to the kitchen again, but Justin insisted on her sitting down and frowned at his wife to remind her of her duties.

The tea was black and strong and Rachel enjoyed the rare treat of drinking it without feeling guilty about the cost as she listened to the men talk and Maggie add the odd comment, usually foolishly off the point. Rachel tried not to push herself forward. However, when Justin asked her opinion of the way old folk could be helped when times were hard, she dared to respond. 'What they really want is independence. They hate taking charity. I've seen them starve before they'd ask for help. And I would, too.'

Nathaniel nodded his approval. 'So you think we should find ways for them to earn a little extra?'

'If you can. Sometimes they're not strong enough to do anything. Though you could perhaps pay someone else in need to look after them. That way, they'd know at least that the charity was helping one of their neighbours.'

He nodded again and said, 'Yes, you make a good point there.'

He was a very solemn man, Rachel decided as the conversation continued. If he hadn't been the landowner, she wasn't sure whether people would have liked him as a neighbour, because although he was clearly trying to do his duty and be gracious, he seemed very fixed in his views, if not downright arrogant.

'They tell me you weave like a man,' he remarked later.

'Yes, sir. I do. If I didn't, my mother and I would go short.'

'Can you find no other way to earn your bread? Something more suited to a woman?'

She held back her resentment. People like her didn't speak sharply to people like him, however much they deserved it, but she did allow herself to say, 'I'm a good weaver. Better than most men. And I earn good money by it.'

His expression said he didn't believe that she was as good a weaver as a man, so she breathed in slowly and deeply and allowed Justin to turn the conversation to another subject.

When she got home, she told her mother everything she could remember, and even her father was interested to hear about the great man's visit – as was almost every other inhabitant of Upper Clough over the next day or two, but Rachel was quite curt with them. Being a friend of the curate's wife was rather wearing and she would have preferred the honour to fall upon someone else, someone who had the time and energy to spare.

When Nathaniel got back to Cleving Park, he went to look for his aunt. He found her in the stillroom where she was supervising the making of cordial for winter coughs. 'Do you care to take a turn round the gardens, Aunt?'

She looked at the cordial, then nodded to the maid. 'Be sure to cover it before you leave it to cool. We'll bottle it together later.'

Outside, Nathaniel offered her his arm and they walked along slowly.

Although moving was painful because of her twisted joints, Hannah Armstrong was very determined not to give in to her infirmity so she struggled to keep up and asked brightly, to distract his attention from her, 'So, how did your visit go, Nathaniel?'

He pursed his lips. 'I continue to like and approve of Kellett, but I didn't take to his wife at all. When she is delivered of the child, we must invite them to dine here, then you can give me your opinion.'

She nodded. Not a detail was too small for her nephew's attention. She had learned by now how firm a control he intended to keep of his valley and its inhabitants. He was very different to her husband who had, she admitted, been a rather lax landlord, relying too much on Tam Barker.

'The wife had a friend visiting her, one Mistress Smedling.'

'A young woman or the mother?'

'Young.'

Hannah nodded. 'Rachel. She's three and twenty, but seems older. She's a hard worker.' Hannah might not be able to get out and about these days but the gossip and news still came to her through her maids.

'I've heard little good of the father, but the daughter seems decent enough. Very capable, in fact. 'Twas she who prepared the refreshments for Mrs Kellett. And looked neat and cleanly in her person, too.'

Hannah smiled at him wryly. 'So weaving like a man has not coarsened her?'

He shrugged. 'I still say 'tis not a suitable occupation for a woman, but she seems modest in her ways. Had I been here while she was being taught, however, I would have had a word with the father and dissuaded him.'

Hannah shook her head fondly. She could see no wrong

in a woman weaving, but then she often thought men under-estimated their womenfolk. Nathaniel would never change, though. He was already settled in his ways. A kindly, responsible man – as long as you allowed him to be master. He would look after her when she grew too twisted to manage the household, she was sure, and she had no desire to leave Cleving Park, which she considered her home. She only hoped he would choose his wife carefully and that it would be someone she could get along with.

In September, Maggie Kellett went into labour and insisted she needed Rachel. For once, she was not putting on an act. She had a thin, narrow sort of body and the contractions were not strong. After a couple of hours, Rachel went downstairs to find Justin and ask him to call in the doctor from Setherby Bridge and to send for Grandma Lowther as well.

His face turned bone white. 'Is she – in difficulty?'

Rachel hesitated, then said carefully, 'I've had some amount of experience with birthing and this is – it's not going well, so I would prefer that we get help.' She didn't want sole responsibility, definitely not. Her cousin Nell's births had been so easy compared to this one.

'I'll go for these people myself.'

Rachel grabbed his sleeve. 'No! We'll send someone else. I just wanted your permission. Your wife is calling for you.'

He swallowed. 'I – surely I'd be out of place in a birth chamber?' He had not attended any of the other accouchements, for Bella had been there.

Rachel felt that any man would be out of place in such circumstances, but Maggie was insisting she needed her husband and it seemed best to humour her. 'Go to your wife, Mr Kellett. I'll ask Thomas Thorpe to take a message down to Setherby.' Nell's husband was a kindly man who would do anything for anyone.

She watched Justin go upstairs, then took the two children round to Nell's to be looked after, for Maggie was starting to scream now and was clearly in great distress.

Grandma Lowther arrived within the hour, and the doctor an hour after that. The three of them worked on Maggie Kellett all night but got the baby out only as dawn was streaking the sky with first light. It was a boy, but it never breathed and it looked to Rachel as if it had been dead for a while.

By that time, Maggie was only half conscious and had screamed herself hoarse.

'I'll go and inform the father,' the doctor said, rinsing his hands briefly in the only fresh water left then rubbing them dry on a waistcoat that seemed filthy to Rachel. 'You two clean her up and see to the infant's body.'

'That's a man for you,' Grandma said sourly when he had left. 'Takes all t'clean watter, then goes off and leaves the real work to the women. He'll be collecting his money now. He allus asks for it straight off.' She looked down at Maggie, lying whimpering in an uneasy doze. 'Eh, she's had a hard time of it, poor lass. I didn't think we'd save her. Another baby will kill her for sure.'

It was the child Rachel was looking at, the shrivelled baby, with its blue-white skin. She felt tears rise in her eyes. 'Poor little thing. It never even drew breath.'

The doctor found Justin pacing up and down in the parlour below. 'I'm afraid your baby was born dead – and had been dead for a day or two *in utero*.'

Justin looked at him in misery, his throat thick with tears. 'Maggie?' he managed.

'Is exhausted and sleeping now, but if she lives the week, she should recover. Another babe would certainly kill her, though. She's not made to bear children easily. Narrow hips and not a strong woman.'

'Oh. I see.'

'You should refrain from congress, to be certain.'

'Yes.'

'You have your daughters, at least.'

But like most men, Justin wanted a son to follow in his

footsteps. And now, it seemed, this was to be denied him. As was the comfort of his wife's body.

The doctor coughed to regain his attention. 'That will be five shillings, if you please, sir.'

Numbly, Justin paid him, then remained in the parlour, one hand on the mantelpiece, staring down into the fire. No son. No chance of a son, either. And a weakling for a wife. There were times when it was very hard to bear.

After a while, he knelt to pray for the soul of his dead child and to pray also for the strength to be tender with poor Maggie and to manage from now on without a wife's attentions in bed.

Upstairs, Grandma Lowther agreed to stay on and keep an eye on Maggie at a shilling a day, on top of her two shillings for attending the birth, then Rachel came wearily down the stairs to tell Justin of the bargain she'd made on his behalf.

She found him sitting in the parlour, head in his hands.

When he looked up, his eyes were bright with tears. 'Do *you* think Maggie will recover?'

'Yes. But she'll be weak for a while and will need tending. And there are your daughters to be looked after. So Grandma Lowther has agreed to stay for a while and help out.'

'*You* couldn't?'

Rachel had had more than enough. 'No. I'm happy to come in an emergency, Mr Kellett, but I have weaving waiting for me at home, a sick mother to care for and a house of my own to run.'

'Oh. Yes. I suppose we've been very selfish lately, asking for your help.'

'Yes, you have a little.' She looked him in the eyes. 'I cannot *afford* to keep coming across here, Mr Kellett. I already have more than I can manage on my own account.'

'I'm – sorry.'

She shrugged and turned to leave, so blind with tiredness she knew she would have to sleep for a while, not get on with her weaving until later.

★   ★   ★

When Caleb came over to see them a few weeks later, Maggie insisted on telling him her tale of woe in graphic detail, ending, 'And Rachel has not been across to help since. I do not think much of a friendship like that.'

'But didn't you tell me her mother was ailing?'

She sniffed. 'And so am I ailing. She calls herself my friend but has been of little use to me in my time of need.'

'I think you are being unjust to her.' The words were out before Caleb could prevent himself. On his way through the village he had caught a glimpse of Rachel's mother sitting by her front door and had thought how ill she looked, as if she had not long for this world.

'Well! What a thing to say!' Maggie's eyes narrowed and she stared at him. 'I hope this partiality does not mean you are *interested* in her? It will not do, you know, Caleb. They are only common weavers and the father is a drunkard.'

'Well, and I am bastard born,' Caleb tossed back at her.

'*Maggie!* Mind your tongue,' Justin thundered.

She made a little bleat of protest but fell silent, staring down sulkily at the embroidery on her apron and smoothing it with one finger as she listened to the two men speak of other matters.

When Justin was showing his cousin out, he said awkwardly, 'I ask your pardon for what Maggie said – about you and Mistress Smedling, I mean. 'Tis none of her business.'

Caleb shrugged. 'I was only sorry to hear her criticising one who has stood her friend.'

'She means naught by it.'

'Then she should not say it.'

They both stared across the village green and saw Rachel walking to the well with her usual brisk stride.

'She is a fine woman, though.' Caleb flushed as he realised he had betrayed himself.

'*Do* you have an interest there, then?' Justin asked in surprise.

Caleb scowled. 'You know full well I can't afford to have an interest in anyone yet.'

But Justin saw the hungry way his cousin stared at Rachel and drew his own conclusions – which he did not share with his wife, who seemed to have an ambivalent attitude towards their helpful young neighbour nowadays. Besides, no other man was courting Rachel, nor was likely to, so what did it matter? If Caleb were to show an interest in her later, that was his business. There was plenty of time for them to get to know one another.

CHAPTER FOUR

1754

Towards the end of winter an outbreak of fever more viru-
lent than any ever seen before hit Whin Vale. Upper and
Lower Clough were particularly badly affected, though strangely
enough Setherby Bridge escaped the worst.

When Nell and her sons fell ill, Thomas Thorpe was beside
himself with worry and knew not where to turn for help.
Without hesitation Rachel abandoned her weaving, ignoring
her father's indignation at this, and went to nurse her only real
friend and the little boys who were only two and four years
old. The two girls, Ruth and Kitty, seemed untouched by the
fever and Rachel found them sitting in a corner of the kitchen,
weeping softly, cuddling one another.

She liked Thomas Thorpe best of all the men she knew
because of his sensible nature and temperate ways, even though
she sometimes thought him a slow-speaking man, lacking in
ambition. As the first night passed, she sat and shared his anguish
as they watched the two little boys die, their lives snuffed out
with little more ceremony than candle flames. Young children
were always at risk and you couldn't expect to rear all you
bore, but it was dreadful to see the children she had played
with from the time they were tiny babies die and then lie
like wax dolls in the small coffins Thomas made for them
himself.

She tried to keep the sad news from Nell, but the next day
her friend heard the sound of hammering and guessed what

it signified. At that she lost heart. She closed her eyes and it seemed to Rachel that she willed herself to die too.

Even as a stunned Thomas was struggling to cope with this new grief and Rachel was trying to comfort his little daughters, there was a hammering on the door. She opened it to find her father standing there, his face red with ale and anger.

'You're wanted at home, madam – *if* you can spare us the time, that is. Your mother's took the fever now, and badly. But of course you might be too busy here to help *her*!' His eyes flickered to Thomas suggestively, but the latter was too upset to notice.

Rachel closed her eyes for a moment, too weary to summon up the anger she usually used to defend herself against her father. When she opened them again, she was calm enough to turn to Thomas and say quietly, 'I'll have to go, lad. I'll be back later to lay Nell out.'

'Stay with your mother. I'll tend to my lass myself.' He came across to take her hand briefly. 'And I do thank you with all my heart for your help, Rachel.'

A tear slid down her cheek. 'It did little good.'

'No one could have done more and it's a comfort to me that you tried, that we both did everything we could.'

She looked past him at the girls. 'How will you manage now?'

'I'll find a way. Ruth is a good child and will help me look after Kitty, won't you, my pet?' As the child nodded solemnly, he gave Rachel a gentle push. 'Go now. Your duty's at home.'

'Well, I'm glad one of you admits that!' Walter cut in, his voice too harsh and strident for a house of mourning. Without waiting for an answer, he turned and strode away into the darkness and his daughter followed, trying to summon up the strength to face this new situation.

Within two days, Alice Smedling was also dead, too weakened by the canker in her breast to fight for her life. She managed to whisper her love and gratitude to her daughter for all the tender care of her in the past few months, then asked to take leave of her husband privately, commending Rachel to his care and wishing him well in the rest of his life.

Then, as her daughter came back into the bedroom, she closed her eyes and seemed to give herself up willingly to death.

After his wife had breathed her last, Walter indulged in a bout of stormy weeping that astonished his daughter, who had not thought he still cared for her mother. When he recovered, he made it plain that he blamed Alice's death on her, then went off to seek consolation in the Weaver's Arms.

'But the funeral. We have to—'

'*You* arrange it! You've nothing better to do, have you? No other friends to go and nurse?'

'What about money to pay for it?'

'You pay for it! You've plenty of money and I'm a bit short this week.' He was gone before she could argue.

When Walter came home late that night, he was in the foulest of moods and began at once to taunt Rachel with any nasty insult that came into his mind. 'Sitting here all alone, are you? Well, you'll die alone and unloved, you will – unlike *her*. You've never been wanted by a man and you never will be.'

Rachel refused to respond to his insults but that didn't stop him from finding other hurtful words to throw at her. She let them pass over her head, her usual anger seeming to have vanished, swallowed by the black hole of grief she felt for the double loss of her mother and her best friend. She couldn't help wincing at the crude things he said, though, and eventually she walked out of the room and locked herself in her bedroom, leaving him downstairs roaring with triumphant laughter.

As the days passed after Alice's simple funeral, only Rachel's promise to her mother that she would look after her father made her stay on in the house that did not seem a home any longer without her mother's quiet smile to greet her. It was hard indeed to have a father who seemed to hate the sight of her. What was wrong with her that he should feel like this? She had pondered on that many a time since her brother's death and never been able to work it out.

But her mother had made such a point of her promising to stay, saying it was only right that she should look after her father, that she tried to ignore his ill humour and lack of gratitude for all she did, telling herself that things would get better as he recovered from his loss. But it was hard to bear, very hard.

Old Jed Trotter of Hepstone also died of the fever, though that village had not been as badly affected as those in Upper and Lower Clough.

The day after the funeral, his son James came round to see Caleb Hesketh. 'Dost still want to buy the farm?'

Caleb nodded, excitement surging through him. This land would make all the difference to his plans. 'Aye, I do that.'

'Price we agreed on, then?'

Caleb nodded again. 'Done. It'll take me a while to get the rest of the money, but I'll give you five guineas now in earnest of my good will.'

'That'll suit me, lad.'

'I have a bit of paper ready for you to sign.'

When James had laboriously spelled his way through their simple agreement, he signed it, shook hands with Caleb and left.

Joanna, who had been sitting quietly by the fire, looked at her son. 'How will you get the money?'

He shrugged. 'I have some saved, but I thought I'd ask Mrs Bretherton to lend me the rest.'

'Eh, you'll never!'

'Why not?'

'But she – well, maybe she won't want to deal with such as us.'

'She doesn't mind stopping to chat to me when she's out riding. And she talks to me about sheep-breeding, asks my views. I think there's a good chance she'll help me.'

The next day, he dressed in his best, saddled the pony and set off through the village of Hepstone along the road that led towards Rochdale. High Fell House was a stark square edifice of stone built on the edge of the moors, 'looking down over Lancashire and turning its back on Yorkshire', as local folk jested.

Leaving the pony in charge of a stable lad, Caleb allowed himself to be taken into the house itself. He had never been inside it before and looked round curiously as he sat on a hard upright chair in the hallway, which was as large as his whole home, he reckoned, and had six doors leading off it. He could not help wondering what a woman on her own needed with six rooms, and there must be more upstairs.

The hall floor was of polished wooden blocks set in a pattern and the walls were also panelled in wood, so the place was rather dark. But he liked the brightly coloured carpet on the floor in the middle of the hall, and the red upholstery on the various chairs. He fingered the one he was sitting on surreptitiously, enjoying the feel of the rich material. Pictures graced the walls and there was a mirror at one end, with a heavy gold frame. He'd have examined the pictures more closely and looked at himself in the mirror, for he had only a tiny square of mirror, but he did not want to seem inquisitive.

The elderly maid reappeared and beckoned to him, tutted and took his round felt hat from his hand, setting it down on the hall table. Then she gave him an odd look and showed him into a large, square room, whose fire was crackling pleasantly and whose occupant was seated in a large armchair near the hearth watching him. He wasn't quite sure what to do, so bowed his head and said, 'Good day to you, Mistress Bretherton'.

Georgiana nodded and studied him for a moment, this serious young fellow who might have been handsome if he had bothered about his appearance or smiled a little more often. What had brought him to see her? Never mind what. She was feeling moped today and was pleased to have some company. Her husband had died a few years previously, she had no children and her other relatives had moved away from the district, and although she kept herself busy, she had to admit she grew lonely at times. But she'd been born in this district, loved the moors and this house, and had a fancy to live out her days here, whatever her nieces and nephews said. She still had one relative here, Hannah Armstrong at Cleving Park. Hannah was the last friend of her youth still alive. They enjoyed each other's company greatly.

Georgiana spoke to her young visitor gently, because he looked nervous. 'Come and sit down over here, Caleb Hesketh, and tell me what business brings you to see me.' For it had to be business. He was a small farmer, even though, unusually, he owned his own land, and he would never have presumed to call on her socially. She knew all the people round here, by sight at least, and was well aware who considered her their equal and who did not.

Caleb sat down, enjoying the warmth of the fire and the sight of the lady clad for indoors in green figured silk, her hair neatly arranged under a pretty lace-trimmed cap. 'I need to borrow some money to buy more land and thought of asking you first.'

She hid a smile at his bluntness. 'Oh? And why should I wish to lend it to you?'

'You may not wish to. But you've stopped to talk to me a time or two when you were out riding, and – and you seem interested in the breeding of sheep, so I thought why not try?'

'What is the money for?'

'To buy more land. And if you did lend it me, I'd pay you back as soon as I could, with a fair rate of interest, for I can't abide to be in debt. I'd allow my rams to tup your ewes, too, which would help improve your flocks. I have some good rams, which breed healthy young. I – I think such an arrangement would benefit us both.' For him it was a long speech. He could think of nothing else to say, so closed his mouth and waited.

She questioned him gently. 'How do you know so much about the breeding of sheep?'

He shrugged. 'I correspond with one or two gentlemen farmers who are interested, and who have kindly instructed me.' He grew animated suddenly. 'I even went down to Derby to meet one of them. I enjoyed that greatly and Mr Lowerby treated me most kindly.' A pause, then, 'And I read what I can – about that and about the world.'

'You read a great deal?'

Another shrug. 'What else is there to do in the long winter evenings? There's just Mother and me at the farm. Besides, I do not like to be ignorant.'

'You've never thought of marrying, getting yourself an heir?'

He gave her a long, level look. 'Who from round here would want to marry a bastard like me?'

'Many young women, I'm sure. You're a good-looking young man.' She chuckled as he flushed. 'Has no one told you that before?'

He shook his head, then added thoughtfully, 'Besides, I don't intend to marry until I'm well set up in the world.'

She nodded. 'I approve of ambition in a young man. As long as it's allied to hard work.' Which in his case it was, for everyone in the district knew how hard he had toiled to get so far. She had liked him the few times she had talked to him when out riding. She liked him even more as she understood what he was trying to do with his life. From such a beginning, that was a great credit to him – and to his mother, as well. The Singletons were stupid to have disowned him. She would have to see if she could meet the mother properly, talk to her. Joanna Hesketh must be an exceptional woman to have bred a son like this. 'Very well,' she said suddenly. 'I shall do it.'

'You – you mean you will lend me the money?'

'Did I not say so?' She smiled encouragingly. 'We shall, of course, have my lawyer draw up an agreement, but I can see no problem to this. I have one condition: you must bring your repayments here in person each quarter day and take tea with me, telling me how your venture is progressing.'

He looked at her uncertainly, for it seemed a strange condition.

She decided on frankness to match his own. 'My only close relatives are my sister's children who live too far away to visit, and my cousin Hannah at Cleving Park. My nieces and nephews would come rushing to visit me if they thought I could be induced to leave them my house, but I do not intend to encourage them. They would sell the place, not live here. I shall leave it to someone who will love it, as I do. I shall enjoy your company on quarter days, Caleb Hesketh, and I shall take an interest in our mutual breeding of fine sheep. The services of your rams will be welcome. I shall also ask your advice about buying more rams for myself, which you may in turn use to – er – assist in breeding your flocks.' She paused to study him again. 'And you may expect to see me riding over to Black Top Farm from time to time. I like to keep an eye on my investments.'

He watched in surprise as she grinned – lady or not, it was definitely a mischievous grin – and could not prevent an answering smile. 'I have only a small farmhouse in which to entertain you, Mrs Bretherton. And there are those who would not sit down with me or my mother, for she never wed my father.' He wanted to make sure that was understood from the start.

'I knew that already and am not one to scorn folk for human weaknesses, nor am I too proud to sit at your table, Caleb.' She held out one hand. 'So, is it a bargain?'

He grasped her hand and shook it warmly. 'Aye, it is indeed, Mrs Bretherton, and I thank you from the bottom of my heart.' He was amazed at how soft the hand was, how sweet the fragrance she seemed to exude. His mother always smelled of wool or damp or cooking. This lady smelled of summer flowers in a meadow.

'I shall send my head shepherd over to talk to you about breeding better sheep,' Georgiana said. 'And now, let me offer you a dish of the tea that everyone delights in nowadays.'

He accepted, because to try something new was always interesting.

The dark liquid was nice and hot on such a chilly day but it tasted so bitter he pulled a face.

She chuckled. 'I felt like that the first time I tried it, but now I've grown to like it. You shall have a dish or two with me every quarter day.' She carefully refilled the small dish he was clasping in his hands, adding, 'And you should hold it like this to drink from it.'

He tried to do as she showed him and sipped again. 'Is that my punishment for daring to borrow money from you?' he asked, forgetting to stay respectful.

'Nay, 'tis an introduction to the strange ways of the gentry. It never hurts a young man to polish his manners.'

And from then on something very close to friendship began to grow between them, for all their differences in age and station. He had often wished he had an aunt or grandmother, and gradually he began to feel that Mrs Bretherton was behaving more as an aunt to him. She was not at all like the disdainful Singletons, but treated him as an equal, riding out to see him quite often when the weather was fine.

She also lent him books, for she shared his love of reading about the world. In that they seemed almost equals, discussing what they had read with great vigour, though of course he could not read as much in the summer as in the winter. He wondered about their friendship sometimes, but it was impossible to feel uncomfortable with such a kind lady, who did not stand on her dignity with anyone, not even her servants.

He did not forget, however, that it was hard work which would make his dreams come true.

Walter Smedling was spending even more time down at the alehouse. The only peace Rachel knew was when he was out trying, he said, to drown his sorrows – though the ale always seemed to put him in a pugnacious mood. The family's small jar of savings soon vanished and Rachel had to dip into her own 'pot', as she called it, to buy food until the next piece of cloth could be carried to the clothier. And when Walter did carry the pieces of cloth they had both woven into Rochdale, he at first refused to give her any of the money he'd been paid for it.

She felt the old anger start to simmer inside her again. 'If you don't give me my share, if you try to cheat me like this again, then I shall leave. There's nothing to keep me here anyway now that Mam's dead. *You* don't want me, that's for sure.'

They stood staring at each other. His breathing was harsh, laboured, and he looked as if he was about to burst forth with more complaints. After a minute or two, however, he threw some coins down on the table. 'There y'are, y'unnatural *daughter*! Just like you to rob your poor father of his last few pence!'

She picked them up, counting them quickly. 'It's not enough.'

'It's all yer gettin'! All I can spare.' He slammed out of the house.

'Then you'll find no food ready for you tonight,' she shouted after him.

During the days that followed, they lived in a state of open warfare. Walter did some weaving intermittently but was down at the alehouse by mid-afternoon most days. And how he was getting the money to pay for that, Rachel couldn't understand. She tried to get on with her own piece, but her progress was slower than usual, for she kept staring into space and worrying about her future. She had no intention of letting her father pocket the money she earned to throw away on ale, no intention of even staying with him if he didn't pull himself together.

She wept into her pillow most nights at the things he'd said to her lately. He'd never spoken so harshly when her mother was still alive. Evenings became a great trial, for now he often brought the sots whom he called friends back home to drink with him until the small hours – a thing he had never done while his wife was alive. For the first time, Rachel began to lock her bedroom door, even placing a chair under the handle for extra security. More than once someone stayed the night, too drunk to stagger home – but not too drunk to try her door handle after Walter had gone stumbling up to his bed.

The first thing she missed was her mother's favourite vase, and when she asked where it had gone, her father slapped her face, sending her spinning across the room. 'None of your bloody business.'

She grabbed the cleaver and brandished it at him. 'If you ever touch me again, I'll hit you with the nearest thing to hand – and lay you out senseless, too.'

For a moment, she thought he would make her prove it, but after glaring at her he spat in the fireplace to show his disgust and turned away.

Other bits and pieces began to disappear from the house to finance his drinking. He was buying food at the alehouse, too, which was a costly way to eat. One day she went round the house checking and found many of her mother's little treasures missing, so she took a few pieces she valued particularly and hid them in her room, locked in the sailor's tin trunk where she stored her few possessions. She kept the key to it hanging round her neck.

When he noticed that things were missing, more harsh words passed between them, but he would not agree to mend his ways.

The next day, the best cooking pot vanished.

He didn't try to hit her when she accused him of taking it, just sneered, 'I can do as I like with my own things.'

'And how will I cook with no pots?'

'There are other pots left.'

'None as good as that. Father—'

'Don't you "father" me! I'm shamed to call you daughter, downright shamed, so ugly you are! I shouldn't have agreed to—' Then he gasped and clamped his lips together, rocking to and fro on his heels and muttering to himself.

'Go on! Go on, why don't you? Finish what you were saying. You shouldn't have what?' He'd said similar things to her lately and Rachel couldn't help puzzling over what he was concealing.

'Ah, you'd like me to do that, wouldn't you? Break my promise to *her*. Well, I won't an' you shan't drive me to it, you ugly old maypole, you. No wonder no man ever wanted you. Nor ever will. An' when you could make it up to me – which is only right, considering – when you could help a poor, grieving widower to make hisself a decent living, you

57

won't do it. Well, you're nothing but a greedy grasping old spinster, trying to chouse me out of the money.'

That night she lay awake for a long time, not even hearing the voices downstairs as she agonised over the decision she had to make. 'I can't keep my promise, Mam,' she whispered at last. 'I just can't stay with him.'

But if she left this house, she would need somewhere to go, and to get a house of her own she'd have to approach Tam Barker, Mr Armstrong's agent – only he was a crony of her father's, one with whom she'd had sharp words more than once, and she suspected he'd take great pleasure in refusing. She could go to Mr Armstrong himself, but it was hardly likely that the landowner would look on her request more kindly, even though several cottages were vacant after the outbreak of fever. Women on their own usually went to live with relatives, but she had none.

Should she try to get a place in service, then? No, that went against all sense, for she could earn far more money as a weaver. And anyway, she didn't fancy being at someone else's beck and call all day. From what she had heard, although the servants at Cleving Park were treated kindly, every move was watched, their free time strictly limited, and she didn't think other large houses would be much different. As for farm servants, they were either drudges or women with skills in the dairy. And she had none of the latter.

Should she move into Manchester, then? There would surely be many chances to make a living in a great city like that, for she had heard Justin Kellett say that over ten thousand people lived there now, an amazing number, frightening, too. But somehow she shrank from cutting herself off from the only life she had ever known. Why, she had never even visited Manchester, wouldn't know where to go, who to talk to. Even Rochdale and Todmorden seemed busy places to her, with more folk about than you could ever hope to know, so that you were glad to get safely home again. And anyway, she loved the moors round Whin Vale and simply didn't want to live anywhere else.

That night was wet and windy, and when someone knocked at the door, her father made no attempt to answer. Lips tight with disgust that anyone should call and find men like these gambling with dice in her house, Rachel peered out of her bedroom window, seeing only an indistinct figure with a piece of sacking over its head. The knocking sounded again. Clicking her tongue in exasperation, she ran down to open the door.

She found Thomas Thorpe standing there with rainwater running down his face. He clutched her arm. 'It's little Ruth. She's took ill of the fever, just when everyone thought it'd passed. Your father said you'd done enough for us when I spoke to him yesterday, but I'm desperate, Rachel lass. I've sent Kitty to my cousin's, but I don't know what to do for Ruth. I've tried everything they said. *Everything*. And she just gets worse.'

She could see in his eyes the fear of losing another of his family and her heart went out to him. 'I'll come over at once. I'd have come before if my father had told me.'

She hadn't noticed Walter get up from the fire and stagger over to join them.

'You'll not go round there again!' he roared. 'You brought the fever back here once. It was you as killed your mother, but you'll not bring it back here again!' He made a threatening gesture with one clenched fist.

Rachel grabbed the broom to defend herself, but Thomas placed himself in front of her. He was not as tall as her father, but he was younger and stronger, and he had not been drinking. 'Shame on you, Walter Smedling, for threatening your daughter like that!'

Walter took a step backwards, more in surprise at this reaction from a man noted for his quiet manner than in fear of the threat being carried out.

'Rachel, I'll understand if you decide not to—'

'Of course I'm coming, Thomas. As if I'd not do my best for Nell's daughter.'

Walter glared at them out of bloodshot eyes. 'If you go with him, y'unnatural doxy, you'll not come back to live under my roof again!'

There was a moment's silence, with even the dice players pausing to watch and listen, then Rachel tossed her head. 'I was leaving here anyway. I'm not earning good money for you to spend on boozing and gaming.' She turned back to Thomas. 'I'll have to get my things together first. I'm not leaving them here for him to sell. Can I bring them to your house and will you wait on a minute or two till I've packed my trunk?' She was afraid of violence from Walter and his cronies.

Thomas laid one hand on her arm, concern on his face. 'Nay, I can't ask you to give up your home, lass.'

'You don't need to ask. I'm coming for Ruth's sake – and for Nell's, too.' Her voice dropped and she whispered, 'I really was leaving anyway.'

'I meant what I said!' roared Walter, furious at being ignored.

'I'll not want to come back.' When Rachel looked at her father, he seemed like a stranger, a drunken, violent stranger. And yet she had memories of him dandling her on his knee, of him swinging her and her brother round in circles till they were dizzy. But all the kindness had stopped abruptly when Paul died. Overnight she'd seen her father start scowling at the mere sight of her, begun to feel the weight of his hand, too. And had never understood why. Yes, he'd lost his son, but he still had a daughter. Only he didn't seem to want her. She sighed and turned back to Thomas. 'Can you help me carry my things?'

'Of course.'

'And – is there someone who'll help you carry my loom?'

He blinked at her in surprise. 'Your loom?'

'Aye. It's mine by right, that is. 'Twas my earnings paid for it, and *he* never gave me more than half of what I earned for my weaving. Beside, I'll need the loom afterwards – to earn my bread.'

'You'll not take it!' yelled Walter, swaying on his feet. 'You'll not take anything save your clothes.'

'You'll not stop us,' answered Thomas quietly but with steel under his words. 'If Rachel feels she's earned it, then that's all right with me. An' I've friends aplenty who'll be glad to help me if you try to make trouble.'

'I'll smash the loom to pieces first.'

Walter's cronies drew in their breaths audibly.

'Then we shall have to take yours in its place, shan't we?' Thomas Thorpe was slow to rouse, but tenacious once he grew angry. And he was disgusted at the way Smedling was behaving. Nell had always felt sorry for her friend, but he was beginning to think that even his wife hadn't known the half of it, if this was how that sot spoke to his daughter in front of folk.

Walter stared at Thomas for a long moment, hands bunched into two fists, then shrugged and spat on the floor. 'Ah, take it, damn you! If it'll help me get rid of that foul-mouthed witch, you're welcome to it.' He flung himself back down on the settle next to his friends and seized the flask from the man next to him. 'Down with all women!' he roared and poured a good measure of gin down his throat.

They echoed his toast one by one, and Bill Withers eyed Rachel with such malevolence as he lifted the flask to his mouth that it made her feel sick. Ever since that day on the moors, he had glared at her when they met and once or twice had paused to whisper that he'd not forgotten and would make her sorry one day for treating him badly. She leaned against the doorpost for a moment, suddenly terrified of what she was doing, shaken by the hostility and anger which seemed to be aimed at her.

Thomas's voice was quiet in her ear. 'Come on, lass. Let's get it over with. I don't like to leave Ruth too long with only the neighbour's daughter to watch her.'

Rachel went quickly round the room, her eyes so blurred with tears she could hardly see what she was doing. She selected what she believed to be a fair share of the remaining household goods and piled them on the table, watched resentfully by Walter and with open interest by his friends who were already anticipating the pleasure of telling everyone how she'd robbed her own father.

When she was ready, Thomas went to borrow a handcart.

'Shall you be all right while I'm gone, lass?' he asked in a low voice.

She nodded. 'Aye. I'll keep the broom handy.'

When he had left, the three men just sat and stared at her. The expression on her father's face was beginning to worry her. Surely he wouldn't try to harm his own daughter.

To her relief, Thomas soon returned. When the cart would hold no more, the two of them left the house, pushing it together through the darkness and rain. It seemed to Rachel to take a very long time to cross those few hundred paces to the small but comfortable house that stood slightly downhill from the village, a house which already showed the lack of a mistress and seemed echoingly empty without Nell to smile a greeting and give her a quick hug.

But when Rachel found the neighbour's daughter fretting to leave and little Ruth hot with fever, she instantly forgot her own troubles. Within minutes she had warmed some water and was sponging down the thin body and murmuring soft encouragements to the child, who kept calling her 'Mam'.

Thomas unloaded the things they'd brought, dumping them in the little front parlour. Then he returned reluctantly to Smedling's cottage to get Rachel's loom, taking the neighbour with him. He ignored the muttered remarks tossed at him by the group near the fire, but then Walter started to say, 'That bloody Rachel—'

'Yes?' said Thomas sharply, wheeling round. 'What about your daughter?'

Walter breathed deeply, but did not say any more.

'Eh, it's a bad business, this,' Thomas's neighbour muttered as they worked together.

'He's a nasty sod, that one is,' Thomas whispered back. 'The things he said about that poor lass tonight don't bear repeating.'

'He never does have a good word for her.'

'She's a decent, hard-working lass, Rachel is. My Nell was that fond of her!'

'She's got a tongue like a gutting knife, though.'

Well, Thomas thought as he took the handcart back, if that poor lass ever needed a friend, it was now. Yet even in the midst of all her troubles, she had come to help him with Ruth. He would never forget that and would make sure she was all right afterwards. She had no one else to turn to, that was sure, and Nell would want it.

CHAPTER FIVE

Nathaniel Armstrong frowned at his groom. 'What did you say, Timothy?'

'Rachel Smedling has left her father's house and has moved in to live with Thomas Thorpe.'

'Where did you hear this?'

'From the lass's father. Upset, he was. Said she was living in sin and her mother would be turning in her grave.'

'Is this true? You know I don't like malicious gossip.' And he didn't like immoral behaviour in his valley either.

'I wouldn't pass it on if it was just spite, sir. I was right shocked to hear this. She's never behaved loosely before.' He gave a snort of laughter. 'Well, with her face I doubt she's had many chances to misbehave. Everyone thought she was set to stay a spinster.' He thought over what he'd said, then in fairness added, 'Mind you, I'm not much taken with that Walter Smedling either, sir. He's turned into a right old toss pot since his wife died. But in this case, him being the father, everyone is on his side. She not only walked out, she took half the furniture with her too.'

Nathaniel was shocked. 'Then she must give it back. As magistrate, I shall go and see her myself about that.'

Timothy shrugged. 'If she gives it back, he'll just sell it and spend the money on drink, sir.'

'Mmm.' Nathaniel didn't like the idea of a daughter plundering her father's house, but he didn't like drunkards. 'What has she done with the furniture?'

'Taken it over to Thomas Thorpe's house.'

'And she's still there?'

Timothy nodded.

'Send for Mr Kellett. He will be the best person to look into this.'

For three days, Rachel's bed and other bundles lay in a corner of Thomas's parlour, and the pieces of the loom lay in a heap beside Thomas's own loom in the top-floor attic room with the big windows which gave the extra light needed for weaving.

In the daytime, she persuaded him to get on with his work, as much to distract him as for the money he would earn. Ruth had been brought downstairs to the kitchen for convenience, and never for a moment, not even to herself, did Rachel admit the possibility that the child might die.

Justin Kellett called every day to see how Ruth was, not seeming at all worried about catching the fever himself. He prayed with them next to the bed, setting one gentle hand on the burning forehead as he spoke a blessing.

To Rachel, these were just empty words spoken out of kindness. Talking to the curate might have consoled her mother, but prayers hadn't stopped Alice Smedling from suffering griev-ously for the last few months of her life, had they? And what good would prayers do for a child burning up with fever? Then she saw Thomas's face, realised the visit and prayers were helping him and berated herself for her insensitivity. *She* might not be able to take any comfort from religion, but others did.

'Yon's a decent fellow,' Thomas said one day after the curate had left. 'Better nor most parsons. Mester Armstrong chose a good 'un for us this time. Mester Kellett understands what life is like, an' t'other parson understands nowt but what's in them books of his.'

On the third night Thomas, who had gone to snatch a few hours' rest, woke to the sound of the child raving in delirium and Rachel's low voice forming a soothing counterpoint to its gasping, childish treble. Realising guiltily that he must have been asleep for longer than he had intended, he flung himself out of bed and rushed downstairs.

'Is she . . . ?' His voice faltered at the sight of the thin, flushed face of his daughter. He couldn't speak for a moment because his throat was so choked with the fear that he would lose her, lose everyone he loved, as he had lost his Nell.

Rachel's calm tones brought him quickly back to his senses. 'She's still fighting, Thomas. Don't you lose heart. She's at the crisis, an' a good thing, too, for she couldn't stand much more of this. We mun keep her cool now. I'm glad you've got up, though, because I need some more water fetching from the well. Then you could warm it up a bit to take the chill off, if you would?'

'I'll go and get it.' He grabbed the wooden pail and was out of the house in a flash. When he came back, his eyes were suspiciously bright, and she guessed he'd been weeping as he wound up the heavy well bucket.

When he'd swung the kettle over the fire to heat the water, she said, 'Come and sit by me now, Thomas. 'Tis weary work, keepin' watch at this hour of the night.'

He brought a stool and did as she asked. 'Is she — any worse?'

'She's a bit better, I think.'

He clutched her hand. 'Do you really think so, Rachel lass? She looks right poorly to me. You're not — not just sayin' it to comfort me?'

She looked down at his hand, enjoying its warmth on hers and making no attempt to pull away. 'Nay, I do truly think so, Thomas, else I wouldn't say it. 'Tis cruel to give someone false hope.'

Suddenly he could not hold back the tears and he didn't care if it was weak and unmanly. 'I can't *bear* it if she goes too. She's the most like Nell of 'em all. I've lost the two lads. I *can't* lose the lasses as well.'

Rachel put her arm round his shoulders. 'You won't lose her. I shan't let her go.' And, indeed, her touch seemed to calm the child, who still thought it was her mammy looking after her.

He buried his face in Rachel's shoulder and fought to control the sobs.

'Nay, lad. Nay, then.' She rocked him against her, feeling fiercely protective of this gentle fellow who had faced so much sorrow of late. But she kept an eye on Ruth and after a moment she pushed him aside to wipe the child's hot face, sponge down her body and lay another cool, damp cloth on her forehead.

When she turned back to Thomas, he gave her a shame-faced smile. 'Eh, Rachel. You're a right comfort to me!'

'I'm glad of that, then.' She didn't take much heed of his words. Folk always said such things when they were sick or needing her, for she was a good nurse, but they soon forgot it when they were better. Afterwards, they stood silent and let others mock her in the street, the others usually being her father's cronies.

The two of them sat up with the child all night and by morning it was clear the fever had indeed abated and Ruth was sleeping more peacefully. As it grew light, Rachel stood up and stretched, feeling quite stupid with tiredness. 'I mun get some rest or I shall be falling asleep on top of her today.' She yawned. 'Can you watch her for an hour or two, Thomas?'

Her father would have refused and told her watching the sick was woman's work, as would many of the men in the valley, but Thomas merely nodded and said, 'Aye. Of course. But you mun tell me what to do.'

When Rachel woke up a few hours later, it was full daylight and Thomas was still sitting by the truckle-bed, but she thought he looked better, more at peace with the world. And Ruth was better too – sleeping, her face pale still, but with a forehead cool to the touch.

'Did she wake?' Rachel asked.

'Once or twice, and wanted a drink.'

'Good. She's on the mend, that's for sure.' Rachel felt a rush of joy run through her that she had saved Nell's daughter. She went to get herself a piece of Nell's oat bread from the cupboard, suddenly ravenous, but as she ate it, she glanced sideways and saw Thomas looking at her strangely.

When she had eaten her fill, he said gently, 'Come an' sit down a minute, Rachel lass. We need to talk, you an' I do.'

She was puzzled, but did as he asked.

'I've been trying to work out what to do while I've been sitting here, an' I think I have it figured right now.' He didn't tell her he'd been the target of snide remarks about 'off with the old, on with the new' as he fetched water. He didn't tell her that thanks to her father, gossip was rife about what she was doing in his house. He wouldn't insult her by repeating such lies.

When she came over to sit with him, he took her hand and looked at her very solemnly. 'What shall you do now, Rachel? You can't go back to your father. Have you made any plans yet?'

'Nay, there's been no time for that. I were bound to leave him, sooner or later. I only stayed with him so long for Mam's sake.' She smiled sadly. 'I shall try to find myself a cottage, set up my loom an' start earning my bread, same as anyone else.'

'I don't reckon they'll let you have a cottage, not a woman on your own. Mester Armstrong refused to rent one to Pamela Grey only a few weeks gone, and she's a widow and older than you. And besides, Tam Barker's no friend of yourn.'

She shrugged. 'Well, then, I shall have to go into Manchester an' look for a place in service, shan't I? I'm strong, Thomas, an' I have a bit of money saved, so I shan't starve. I reckon Mr Kellett will give me a bit of paper to tell folk I'm respectable and hard-working, don't you?' She was more worried about her future than she let on, but her companion had enough troubles of his own and she wasn't going to burden him with hers.

Thomas seemed to find it difficult to choose his next words, so she waited patiently. Nell had always said you could never rush Thomas Thorpe into anything, but he still got things done, and well done too.

His words came slowly, with pauses and frowns. 'I've been puzzlin' it out as I sat here, and what I think is, well, you could wed me instead of going off among strangers. That might be a better thing for you to do, lass.'

She froze, not certain she had heard him aright.

He looked down at his hands, flushing a little as he added, 'I know I'm a fair bit older nor you, and – and I won't bother you in bed, not if you don't want it – but I think it'd be the best thing for all of us if we got wed, best for me *and* for the children.'

'I – you can't be serious, Thomas.'

He gave her one of his steady, direct looks. 'Of course I'm serious! Do you think I'd torment you like your father does? Look how you nursed my Ruth. No mother could have done more for her. You love childer. I've allus knowed that from watching you play with mine. An' – an' I'm comfortable with you, Rachel.' He saw the doubt in her eyes, the way she was shaking her head, and took hold of her hand. 'Nay, listen to me, lass! I shall have to wed again, for the children's sake, you know I will. What other choice is there for me? But I'm not – I don't get on easily with new folk. So I'd rather it were you I wed.'

'But you *loved* Nell! And she's not long dead.'

'Aye. She were a good wife, my lass was. But I shall not love her less if I wed again. She'd understand – why, I think she'd even approve.' He went through it all again, to make sure Rachel understood, for she looked stunned. 'There's the childer to see to – I cannot weave and look after them like I should. An' there's the house to see to as well. I'm no hand at cookin', let alone sewing and such. So I *must* wed again, and before too long.' That was how things were done. It was the only way for a widowed man to manage.

She felt as if the room was spinning round her, as if Thomas was one minute far away, the next close to hand. She felt dizzy and happy and sad all at the same time.

'So do you think you could give it some thought, lass? If you could see your way to . . . Nay, Rachel, what's wrong? Rachel, don't!'

For she was weeping, sobbing silently, her whole body shaken with emotion. And now it was he who put his arms round her and held her close, patting her shoulders awkwardly and saying, 'Hush, now! Hush, now!' as he would to one of his children.

At length she drew away from him, her eyes searching his face. 'Did you really mean it?' She whispered the words, as if she daren't even say them aloud.

'Why should I not mean it?'

'Because,' she forced herself to say it, 'I'm so ugly.'

He was patently astonished. '*Ugly?* You're not ugly, Rachel!' He could see she didn't believe him and struggled to find the right words to set her fears at rest. 'Oh, I'll not pretend you're pretty. I know you're not pretty. But you're not ugly, never that, lass! Ugliness comes from inside a person. You're too wholesome to be ugly.'

She had to be sure how he felt. 'What am I, then, Thomas, if I'm not ugly?'

He shook his head. He was not one for fancy words, but she was waiting for an answer, and it obviously meant a lot to her. 'You're – you're like that loom up there,' he managed at last. 'A serviceable piece, it is, with all the parts fitting in the right places. It isn't pretty, neither, but it does what it's meant to do – an' does it well. You're – well, you're just Rachel and – and I'm comfortable with you.'

The tears had stopped now and she was smiling at him. 'Like an old clog, eh?'

'Not like an old clog,' he teased back, relieved, 'more like a shoe, one made of good leather that's been worn in nicely, with years of wear left in it yet.'

She stood up and went across to the window. 'I never thought to marry.'

'Didn't want to?'

'Of course I did! Only–' she bowed her head, '–no one's ever tried to court me. I'm too tall and too – too forceful. I'm not easy to live with, Thomas.'

He chuckled. 'Eh, lass, no one's easy to live with. Why should you think you're that different? We all have us own ways of goin' on.'

ANNA JACOBS

She turned round. 'I should think you'd be easier to live with than most.' Suddenly, her face was radiant and she stretched out a hand to him. 'So I thank you for asking me, Thomas Thorpe, and I shall be proud to become your wife.'

His face creased into a wide, gentle smile. 'Eh, I'm right pleased, I am that.' Clumsily, he placed a kiss on her cheek.

She put up one hand to touch the spot he'd kissed, wondering at how soft and warm a man's lips could feel.

He patted her arm, his eyes looking into the distance for a moment. 'Nell would approve of this, I know she would.' He still felt riven with grief for his wife, and wished he might wait a little before taking this step. But Rachel had no home to go to, so he could not do that, and anyway, his house and children needed tending. 'We'll wed as soon as Ruth is well an' Kitty comes back from my cousin's, eh?'

Rachel bent over the sleeping child, needlessly fussing with the covers, terrified all over again as she said gruffly, 'Yes, all right. An' Thomas – I'll be happy to be a proper wife to you in bed if – if that's what you really want.'

He nodded in his usual placid way. 'Aye, well, it'd be better like that. If you're sure you don't mind. A man has his needs.'

'I'm certain.'

He gave her a knowing look. 'A woman has her needs, too.'

She found it hard to believe a woman could enjoy it. She knew her mother hadn't for she had overheard protests and whimpers, and sometimes her mother had made bitter comments about what women had to endure in bed from some men. She had heard other women complaining about their husbands' demands, too. But it was the price you paid to be wed, and – her breath caught in her throat at the thought that her dearest dream might now come true – to have children. Oh, how she ached for a child of her own!

When she turned to beam at Thomas, he blinked in surprise, because she was suddenly glowing with happiness. He had not realised Rachel could look like that. She was not even plain at this moment. Handsome would be the right word for her now.

72

Maybe – he pursed his lips as he considered it – maybe it was the unhappiness which made her look so gaunt and worn, and the work. Everyone in the valley knew Walter Smedling was an idle fellow. And everyone knew how hard Rachel toiled. Well, she wouldn't have to work so hard with him, by hell she wouldn't.

The next day, Rachel and Thomas went to see Justin Kellett about getting married and he frowned to see them as he opened the door, for he'd received a message from Mr Armstrong asking him to look into the situation. He led the way into the small front room which he used as his study.

As he indicated chairs, Rachel wondered why he was looking at her so disapprovingly, then realised why and snapped, 'If folk have been gossiping, Mr Kellett, I'll tell you to your face that Thomas and I have *not* been sharing a bed.'

Both men looked startled by her bluntness.

'Shh, love!' Thomas took her hand and looked at Justin. 'Rachel came round to help me look after Ruth – and her father grudged me that help, so he turned her out. She had nowhere else to stay but with me.'

Justin turned to Rachel, noting how tired she looked. 'I hear the little girl is better now.'

It was Thomas who answered. 'Yes. The fever turned the night before last. I do truly b'lieve Rachel saved her life.'

'Good, good.'

'We came to ask if you'd marry us.' He stared Justin in the eyes. '*Not* because of the rumours, but because I can't manage on my own. I need a wife and Rachel's been a good friend to me and mine, so I think we shall do well together.'

A look of sheer relief on Justin's face made Rachel stiffen again.

'We haven't done anything wrong,' she repeated. 'We're marrying because it suits us.'

Thomas made a soft tutting sound and patted her shoulder. 'Nay, then, lass. Nay, then.'

She clamped her lips together and stared down at her tightly clasped hands.

Justin nodded, but with his patron's words in mind, said thoughtfully, 'Until you are wed, however, it's best you move out of Thomas's house, Rachel.'

She gave a bitter laugh. 'Where to? I can't go back to my father's house.'

Justin ran over the alternatives in his mind and made a quick decision. 'You can come and stay here, if you like. We can put a mattress in the kitchen for you at night.' He wasn't at all sure how this would work, because Maggie had been the one who had related the gossip to him and had seemed to believe it, talking very scornfully about how she had been deceived in her so-called friend.

Thomas looked sideways and saw Rachel's face cloud over. 'Or I could move out of my house, perhaps, and stay with someone else.'

Justin shook his head. 'That would not stop the gossip, I'm afraid.' Nor would it please Nathaniel Armstrong, he was certain.

Rachel made a sound of muffled exasperation.

Once again, Thomas patted her hand and made soothing noises and once again Justin saw her calm down, though she gave her companion an unhappy look.

'They always gossip about me, Thomas,' she told him sadly. 'I'm not like the others, never have been. So they talk about me. You'd do better marrying someone who fitted in.'

'You're a fine woman,' he said stoutly, 'and I don't want to marry anyone but you.'

Rachel felt the anger leave her. 'Eh, Thomas, you're a lovely man.' She looked back at Justin. 'Very well. I'll come and stay here.' She stared round, noting the small signs of neglect. 'Your wife will no doubt appreciate my help around the house in return for the favour.'

'You will be coming here as a friend, not a servant.'

She smiled at him then, a very knowing smile. 'But a friend

74

can still help out, can't she? Besides, I can't stand to be idle. Never could.'

He got up. 'I'll go and tell Maggie the good news in a minute, but first I have something for you, a letter from your mother. I'm sorry, but with so many people dying, it slipped my mind.

Rachel stared at him in surprise. 'A letter from my mother? But why would she need to write to me? We saw one another every day.'

'There was something she confided in me, and we thought you should know about it.' He unlocked his desk and got out a folded piece of paper, hesitated, then looked at Thomas. 'You may wish to read this alone, Rachel.'

She was puzzled now, for she could see nothing to fear in a letter from her mother. 'I shan't be keeping any secrets from Thomas.'

'You can always tell me about it later, love.' He stood up. 'I'll come with you to the door, Mr Thorpe.'

In the passageway, Justin put a hand on Thomas's arm. 'She may need your support and comfort after she's read the letter. It contains a surprising piece of news. Though I'll let her tell you about it herself. Let's take a turn around the green together, eh?' Thus he would lend them his public support. Besides, he still had to inquire about the goods Rachel had taken from Walter Smedling's house, see whether they were fair. His patron had charged him with that duty as well. And afterwards, he would write to Mr Armstrong, whose note had worried about blatant immorality in the village, and say he believed there to be no foundation for the rumours, but that for propriety's sake, now the child was better, Rachel Smedling would be staying with him and his wife until the wedding.

When he went back to his own house, after inspecting the goods Rachel had taken with her and finding nothing like so many as on the list Smedling had made, there was no sound from the front room and the door was still closed. He tiptoed over and set his ear to it, hearing the sound of muffled weeping, so nudged Thomas and went into the kitchen where his wife was sitting.

'Maggie, my dear, I've invited Rachel Smedling to stay with us.'

'*What?* But why?'

'She has nowhere else to go until her marriage.' He saw her frown. 'And please understand that I would have you make her welcome here.'

'But . . .'

He looked at her very sternly. 'Mr Armstrong himself has asked me to deal with this matter.'

To his relief, his patron's name worked its usual magic, but Maggie still didn't look happy.

'I do not believe there has been any immorality between the two of them,' he added for good measure, then became practical and discussed setting up a bed in either kitchen or parlour.

Maggie let out a scornful snort but made no further protest.

When the two men had left her alone, Rachel sat and stared at the folded letter with its red wax seal, reluctant to open it. She could not think what her mother would be writing about. Surely anything important had been said before she died, for they'd always been very close. She borrowed a paperknife from the desk and lifted up the wax seal, unfolding the square of paper and reading it quickly.

She had not gone very far when she gasped and went to start at the beginning again:

My dearest daughter,

I know not whether I should tell you this, but if I do not, I shall be going to my Maker with it on my conscience.

I have spoken to our kind curate and he has assured me the Lord will forgive me for what I have done if I truly repent. I dare to hope you will forgive me too, my dear girl. And afterwards, if you are troubled, Mr Kellett has promised to be of comfort to you.

When I was young, I lived over Todmorden way, as you know, and to my shame I fell in love with a gentleman. I do truly believe he was fond of me too, in his own way. He was married to a good lady who was both sickly and barren, and since he did not wish to hurt her, when I found myself with child, he gave me money to find myself a husband and asked me to leave the district.

Dearest Rachel, you are that child and Walter Smedling the husband I found. He is no kin to you, though he promised to treat you like a daughter all the days of his life, and so he did while our son was still alive. But when Paul died, Walter grew bitter, for I never quickened again. That is the cause of his anger against you — that his child should die and mine live.

Sadly your real father is dead now as well, so I feel it best to keep his name secret. He was such a handsome, kindly man, Rachel dear. I wish you could have known him and he you. You can be very proud of the man who bred you.

Oh, my dearest girl, do not be angry with me. I was so young then. I was tempted and fell, but have lived to regret my sin and have paid for it, too. I can't bear to think of you growing bitter, thinking your own father does not love you, which is another reason to tell you the truth that Walter is not your father.

You have been the best of daughters and should think no shame to your birth. The shame has been all mine. Hold your head up among any company and live an honest and fruitful life, my own dear child.

Your loving mother,
Alice

Tears were rolling down Rachel's cheeks and she could no longer see the paper. With a low cry of pain, she dropped the letter and buried her face in her hands, sobbing. And yet, for all her pain, a weight seemed to have fallen from her shoulders, because Walter Smedling was not her father — she was not so unlovable that her own father hated her.

As she sobbed, the door opened, but she did not turn round. Then an arm went round her shoulders and Thomas was there, pulling her to him. 'Lean on me, lass. Lean on me.' He held her very close, stroking her hair back from her flushed and damp face. 'Tell me what troubles you. Let me help.'

It was at that moment she began to love him.

That same night, a man breathed his last down in Setherby Bridge. He lay in a large bedroom full of elegant furnishings, but none of the comforts were of any use to him. Justin Kellett had been sent for and sat there with Peter St John all through the long hours of darkness. Just before dawn, he felt the parson's hand slacken in his as the old man gave up the struggle for breath.

The housekeeper, who had been popping in and out, entered the room at that moment and would have spoken, but Justin held up one hand and gestured for silence. He stood up and closed the staring eyes, then bent his head to say a prayer for the departed soul.

'He's gone, then?' she whispered when he had finished and moved away from the bed.

'Yes, I'm afraid so, Mrs Charnley.'

'The fever took him quickly. He hasn't been well for some time.'

Justin nodded. He flexed his shoulders slightly and moved his head from side to side, feeling tiredness sweeping over him now.

'If you'd like to lie down for an hour or two, sir, I've prepared a bedroom. I'll send Lal over to the big house with the news as soon as it's light. Mr Armstrong asked particularly to be told what happened – and he may even want to see you before you go back to Upper Clough.'

'Yes. I suppose so. I'll accept your kind offer of a bed, then.' He took a couple of steps and halted. 'You'll see that all is done to prepare the body?'

'Bless you, yes, sir. I've laid people out before and know what to do.'

Justin let her show him to the bedroom, refused an offer of refreshment and bent with a sigh of relief to take off his shoes. But even though it was still dark, he could not sleep, could only lie there in the dimness and pray again that Mr Armstrong would now offer him this living. Not only for himself, but for his poor foolish wife and his two little daughters, who deserved more than a lifetime of struggling along on a curate's meagre stipend.

And also for the chance to live his life here in Whin Vale, which he had grown to love and whose sturdy, independent inhabitants he cared about too.

CHAPTER SIX

Georgiana Bretherton was bored. She sighed and stared out of the window. I'll go for a ride, she decided at last, and set her bell pealing. She would ride over towards Caleb's farm, for she took great pleasure from their friendship. He was careful never to presume on their acquaintance or overstep the social boundaries that separated them, but *she* could and *did* cross them. Lately, he was beginning to relax, confide in her a little. She smiled. What did social boundaries mean when she had found a friend? She could do so much to help him, this solemn young man.

For perhaps five minutes, she trotted sedately along the narrow track that led up towards the moors, her groom a little way behind her. She breathed deeply, enjoying her freedom. Suddenly, she heard an exclamation behind her and reined in her mare.

'I'm sorry, but I'm afraid we shall have to return, Mrs Bretherton,' Hawkins said. 'Brandy here has just cast a shoe.'

She turned round, scowling, not wanting to be penned up when a fresh breeze was blowing and the sun was shining after days of rain. 'You go back, then, Hawkins. I'll continue on my own. I'm perfectly all right with my dear old Honey. She's very sure footed.'

'But madam, it's not safe.'

'Oh, pooh!' She waved one hand in dismissal and encouraged her mare to go faster, calling over her shoulder, 'Don't expect me back in less than an hour. Honey and I know our way home well enough by now.'

She didn't look behind her again, but once she was away from him, she allowed the horse to slow down and trot quietly along. They were both showing their age, after all.

Later, as she paused on a hilltop to enjoy the view, she noticed two figures lying behind a drystone wall some distance below her. They were watching another man walking towards them. She was puzzled. Why were they hiding like that? What were they up to?

The other man continued to approach the wall, clearly unaware of their presence, and as they picked up cudgels, she suddenly realised they were lying in wait to attack him. Without hesitating, she began to spur down the hillside, waving and yelling, 'Watch out! Robbers!' She turned in the saddle, shouting 'To me, Hawkins!' and making wide gestures with one arm as if to her groom.

Her mere presence was enough to send the two rascals running away across some rocky terrain over which a horse could not follow safely, so she contented herself with reining in near the wall and watching them go. The man was now close enough for her to make out his identity. Caleb Hesketh! Now why would anyone want to attack him?

He had also stopped to watch the two men. When they had disappeared from view over the brow of the hill, he strode over to where she sat waiting and swept her a quick bow. 'I owe you my thanks, Mrs Bretherton.' Then he looked behind her, his forehead creased in puzzlement. 'You called to someone – did he not come to your aid?'

She grinned then and sat back more comfortably. 'I was only pretending I had my groom with me.'

His mouth eased into an answering grin, then he grew serious again. 'That was very brave of you, ma'am, and I thank you for your assistance. You saved me from attack today – though why anyone should want to attack me, I don't know.'

'I enjoyed myself, actually.' She looked wistfully in the direction taken by the would-be attackers. 'I wonder who they were. If the ground wasn't so rough round here, I'd have given chase.'

'I'm glad you didn't do that, not on your own. And you really shouldn't ride alone, you know. Not out here, anyway.'

She pulled a face. 'I started out with my groom but his horse cast a shoe so he had to go back. I *am* a bit tired now, though.' She looked ruefully down at herself. 'I'm getting old, and that is not always pleasant, Caleb. Sometimes, just for a few minutes, one likes to pretend one is still young.'

He could see she was feeling a reaction and was worried about her pallor. 'My farm isn't far away. Would you care to come and rest for a while? I'm sure my mother would be glad to offer you some refreshment.'

She brightened up. 'I thank you. I am rather hungry.' She considered this statement, head on one side. 'And that's something new, for I have been sadly lacking in appetite lately.'

'Have you been ill?'

She shrugged. 'A little moped, that's all. A woman without a husband to escort her leads a rather restricted life. Besides, he was a personable man, my Ralph. Good company. I miss him.' Who would have thought that he would die so suddenly? Barely five-and-forty and had seemed in excellent health until the day of his death. She shook away the sad memories. 'Lead on, then, my young friend.'

As soon as it was light, Mrs Charnley sent the maid, Lal, with news of the parson's death to Cleving Park and Justin received a message asking him to delay his return to Upper Clough and wait upon Mr Armstrong at ten of the clock. Realising how important this interview could be, he went to ask the housekeeper if there was some way of perhaps running a smoothing iron over his crumpled shirt so that he would not look too dishevelled.

She stared at him, eyes narrowed, for she, too, understood exactly what this coming meeting might mean for him. 'You could wear one of Parson's clean shirts, sir. He'll have no more need of them, poor man.'

'I don't like to . . .'

Since Jane Charnley had her mind set on staying on as housekeeper under the new parson, she coaxed him into taking the clean shirt, then swept him downstairs to consume a hearty breakfast. She said nothing openly of her own ambitions but did manage to let drop a hint that she had no relatives who could take her in and was now worried about finding herself a new position. No need to labour the point. Mr Kellett was not a stupid man.

When Justin was shown into the spacious, marble-tiled entrance hall at Cleving Park, he was struck yet again by how large the house was and how comfortably appointed, the sort of place only a rich man could own. He felt nervous, as he always did when he came here, but told himself that all men were equal before the Lord and followed the footman into the library.

Nathaniel set his quill down carefully on the inkstand and got up from his desk to extend a hand in greeting. 'Ah, Justin, come and sit down.' He waited until his guest was seated before taking a chair opposite. 'So, St John is dead?'

'Yes, sir.'

'Did he die easily?'

'He did.' Justin furnished particulars of the previous night and how he had sat with the old man, who had seemed while conscious to find comfort in his presence and prayers.

'Good, good. We'll set the funeral for two days hence, I think.'

'Yes, sir. I presume you'll want me to officiate.'

'Naturally. And your wife should be present too.' He leaned back. 'I am considering offering you the living.'

Justin felt relief rush through him, then realised his patron and relative had said 'considering' not 'I wish to offer you' and his heart sank.

Nathaniel steepled his fingers and looked thoughtfully into the distance. 'Should you be happy to spend the rest of your life here in Whin Vale?'

'Yes, sir. Very happy. I've come to love this valley, and the moors around it.'

He could not have said anything which pleased his patron more, for Nathaniel, too, had grown fond of the place he now thought of as 'his' valley. 'And your wife? Would she be happy to continue living here? I've heard she pines for her family and old home. Especially since she lost the child.'

Justin tried to put the best light on things. 'It took her a while to settle down, sir, I will admit. It was a sad blow to us both to lose the child. She's much happier now, though.' He stole a worried glance sideways as this information was greeted by silence and a frown, only too well aware that poor Maggie was not the best of wives for the parson of a far-flung and busy parish like this.

'Hmm.' Nathaniel looked down at the desk, then across at his curate, trying to make up his mind. Then he thought how much he liked the fellow; indeed he respected him greatly, as did the parishioners, so he decided to take a risk with the wife and stretched out his hand on the thought. 'Will you accept the living?'

'Gladly, sir.' Justin shook the hand, feeling quite giddy with relief for a moment and hoping this didn't show in his face.

'Then you may consider yourself appointed parson as from today. We'll have to gain the approval of the Bishop, of course, but that is a mere formality. I'll write him a letter at once. And of course, before you can move down the hill, we must clear the parsonage out.' Then he saw a way to help his somewhat impoverished new parson. 'Unless you'd be willing to do that for me.'

'Clear it out? What do you mean, sir?'

'St John had no family and was a very distant connection of my mother, so has bequeathed his worldly possessions to me.' He tapped a document on this desk. 'I have his will here. However, although I shall be delighted to accept his library, I have neither the desire nor the need for anything else of his. In fact, you may keep anything you wish for yourself – the furniture is quite good.'

Justin looked across at him. He was not going to pretend about this, or about anything else. 'I think you know, sir, that

85

I am not well provided with worldly possessions, so I wish to say how much I appreciate your kindness. I'm not too proud to accept the gift.' Indeed, Maggie would be thrilled and happy.

Nathaniel was pleased by this honest response. 'Very well, then. Get the funeral over, then you can move in. Say Friday next, so you're in time to hold a service here on Sunday. I'll have to appoint a curate for Upper Clough now. I do not like to leave my churches unattended, however small the congregation.' He made a mental note that it should be someone with a very practical and energetic wife. 'One last thing. It might be a good idea for you to keep on St John's housekeeper and maid, if they're satisfactory to your wife. I don't like to see good servants left without a way to earn their bread.' He glanced sideways as he added, 'After all, Cleving endows the living for two hundred and fifty guineas per annum, so you should be able to afford their services now.'

Justin gasped. 'I had not realised it was so much, sir. But Maggie will indeed need some help to run a larger house and I find Mrs Charnley efficient and helpful.' Which should make things easier for Peg and Lizbet, too.

It was with a heart overflowing with joy that Justin strode back up the hill and greeted his wife by sweeping her off her feet and swinging her round and round, laughing aloud.

The day before the Kelletts moved down to the new parsonage, Caleb rode over to see his cousins, having heard their good news from Mrs Bretherton. He was also hoping to see Rachel Smedling while he was there, for he had not been able to get her out of his mind. She might not be pretty, but there was something about her which appealed to him, a directness and strength unusual in a woman. He would not rush into anything, that was not his way, but he still wanted to get to know her better.

As he rode, he mulled over his recent conversation with Mrs Bretherton who seemed to be a woman of a similarly direct nature. She had invited him to dine with her after their meeting on the moors – to his mother's great delight – and had asked him openly why he was not married. He didn't know how she had managed to worm out of him that he had met a woman who had caught his interest, but she had urged him to do something about it before it was too late.

''Tis sad to grow old without children,' she had added quietly, her eyes blind with memories. 'This woman, if she is sensible, will not care that you are still building your fortune.'

When he found Rachel actually living with Maggie and Justin, he thought fate had smiled on him for once – until he found out that she was to wed Thomas Thorpe the following week.

His good humour evaporated abruptly and he could not prevent his responses becoming curt, his scowls frequent, so that everyone stared at him. When Justin offered to walk down the hill to Setherby with him to set him on his way home and to show him the new parsonage, he accepted at once.

As they strolled down the hill, with Caleb leading his horse, they chatted sporadically. He could not help feeling low, though he refused to tell Justin why. He did not want anyone to pity him. He was not sure he'd visit Mrs Bretherton again either, because she'd be sure to worm the story out of him and he did not want her trying to find him another wife. No, he would stick by his original decision and not marry anyone until he was firmly established with a thriving farm – if he could find someone, that was.

On the way back across the moors, he let his horse slow to an amble, frowning into the grey-green distance, heedless of the state of the road or the possibility of another attack. For the first time he had found a woman who attracted him and look what came of it! It was all of a parcel with the rest of his life. He was the bastard son whom the family had provided for but who was never invited to spend any time with them. He was the lad whom other children had taunted, especially when he grew so much taller than they did. He looked down at his long limbs. He was several inches past six feet now and he'd seen the expressions on lasses' faces, their fear of his size. He knew what they thought of him – too tall, too serious, too blunt in his speech.

Well, it seemed very clear now he was not meant to marry, or at least not meant to marry the woman who had caught his fancy. Bitterness flooded through him. He would go home and mind his own business from this day onwards, and forget about wives and families. He'd keep himself busy and to hell with all women.

Rachel and Thomas were married by Justin down in Setherby church, since Maggie said Justin was too busy to come to Upper Clough simply for a wedding. They strolled down the hill in a party, taking Thomas's two daughters with them, as well as his old friend Rob and Rob's wife Jane, to act as witnesses. The sun shone brightly, for once, and the air seemed filled with the fresh tang of wind from across the moors. Rachel thought she had never been so happy in her whole life and her only regret was that her mother was not here to see her married.

When they crossed the River Whin at the old footbridge just below Lower Clough, the water was bubbling merrily down the hill, clear and sparkling. 'I used to plodge in that as a lad,' Thomas said, pausing to smile at the rushing water. 'Eh, I got my backside tanned many a time for coming home wet and muddy.'

The church was quiet and peaceful that day, with sunlight streaming through the two tall stained-glass windows behind the altar. It seemed strange to see the place so empty, though just before the ceremony started a couple of old women slipped inside to sit at the back and watch the ceremony. Had they nothing better to do with their time? Rachel wondered, wishing there need be no one here except herself and Thomas.

Justin Kellett's voice was firm and resonant, filling the echoing space with the well-known phrases of the marriage ceremony. I really am getting wed, Rachel thought. Whatever anyone else said about her, this man did want her. She glanced sideways and saw a smile on Thomas's face, gentle and encouraging. She looked down to her other side and saw the two little girls beaming up at her and their father. Joy coursed through her. She wanted to weep. She wanted to laugh out loud. Instead, she listened carefully and made her responses in a clear, firm voice.

'You are now man and wife,' Justin finished.

For a moment, the whole world seemed to Rachel to be filled with wonder and the echo of his words in her mind, 'man and wife, man and wife', then Thomas bent forward and kissed her lips, a brief kiss, but its warmth lingered. She didn't hesitate, but took hold of his shoulder and pulled him gently towards her to place her own salute on his cheek. 'I'll make you as good a wife as I'm able, Thomas,' she promised in a low voice.

'Nay, I have no doubts about that, lass.'

Then she bent down to kiss each of the girls. 'I can't take the place of your mother, my dears. We shall all miss her, shan't we? But I'll look after you as well as I can.'

Behind them, Jane nudged her husband. 'She's a good lass under that sharp manner.'

'Did you doubt it?'

Yes, Jane had doubted it. And still had some concern about Rachel's famous temper – about her family background, too. Alice had been a nice enough soul, but Walter Smedling was not only a drunkard but nasty with it, and had gathered together a group of cronies of the same ilk. They were a disgrace to the valley, those men.

They left the church and set off walking together. When Thomas stopped outside the Ram's Head in Setherby, Rachel looked at him in surprise, for he wasn't a drinking man.

'I've arranged for us to have our dinner here,' he said, smiling at her. ''Tis a surprise for you, lass. A celebration of this special day.'

'Oh.' She was touched by that, and a little nervous, too, for this was a proper coaching inn, and it was a cut above the alehouse in Lower Clough.

The landlady came to greet them at the door, beaming. 'Congratulations, Mrs Thorpe! I hope you'll have a happy and fruitful married life!' She led the way to a back room where a table was set ready and within minutes had produced a fine meal of mutton pie and roast fowl.

'You shouldn't have done this,' Rachel whispered to Thomas. 'What is it all costing?'

'It's costing no more than it should. This is our wedding day, lass. A time to celebrate. Something to remember.' He touched her sleeve. 'If not, why did you make yourself a new gown?'

She could only blush and smile.

'You look well in it,' he said, for her ears alone. 'We must get you another good gown or two.' For he had noticed how worn and shabby her other clothes were.

When she would have protested, he stopped her words with a fingertip on her lips and she smiled at him, mouthing the words, 'Thank you.' Then she noticed how solemn the two little girls were and included them in the conversation. 'Well, I'll have to get my new daughters to help me choose the materials for some new gowns, then, shan't I?'

The children both brightened up at that and began to tell her their favourite colours.

Thomas bought them all a drink of mulled ale, in celebration and to warm them up on such a cold day. When they had finished, they walked up the hill to Lower Clough, where Thomas and Rachel said goodbye to their two guests, then turned to complete the walk to Upper Clough arm in arm, with a child on either side.

As they were passing the Weaver's Arms, Walter Smedling staggered out and planted himself squarely in their path.

Rachel's heart sank, for his expression was malevolent, his face twisted with spite.

'So you've getten yoursen a man at last, have you, *daughter*?' he sneered. Then he raised his voice. 'Come out an' see a miracle, lads! A gawky old beanpole wed to a—' He didn't complete his sentence, because with a growl of anger Thomas stepped forward and punched him squarely in the mouth.

The men who had poured out of the alehouse to mock stopped dead as Walter staggered backwards and fell to the ground.

Thomas glared at them all. 'I should think shame to treat a child o' mine like that. And now that Rachel's my wife, I shall know how to deal with anyone as tries to speak ill of her, whether in my presence or out of it.'

Walter scrambled to his feet, furious at being shown up like that. 'She's no daughter of mine, that one,' he yelled, keeping out of Thomas's range. 'Her mother's belly were already full when I wed her. She's a bastard, she is, a whore's bastard.'

Thomas took another hasty step forward but Rachel grabbed his arm and pulled him back. 'I was glad when I found you were no father of mine!' she spat at Walter, furious that he had spoiled her lovely day and blackened her mother's name into the bargain. 'Who'd ever want to be related to a drunken old ale swiller like you? Just look at you – dirty linen, greasy hair an' drunk afore the afternoon's half over. Better to have no father than one like you, I say.'

There was total silence from all the bystanders, for this tale was news to everyone. Thomas was still standing with his clenched fists raised, ready to fight. Rachel held her head high but could feel how shame had sent hot colour flooding her cheeks. Then she realised that the girls were clinging to her skirt, weeping, so she put her arms round the children's shoulders and waited, half expecting someone from the crowd to call her names.

Instead, an older man called Jim Belton stepped forward and offered her his arm. 'Mrs Thorpe, let me escort you home. You and the children look tired.'

But she couldn't move, not until she'd seen that Thomas was all right. 'My husband . . .' she said faintly. 'I don't want him to fight. Walter Smedling isn't worth it.'

'Take her home, Jim lad. I intend to stay and deal with anyone who wants to blacken my wife's name,' Thomas said loudly, without turning his head. 'I'm ready to do that today and any other day, too. Starting with you, Smedling.' He took a step forward again, bunched fists raised, and Walter, seeing the iron determination on his face, took a stumbling step backwards.

The onlookers gasped, for no one had seen Thomas Thorpe in fighting mood since he'd been a young fellow.

'You're quite right, Thomas lad,' Jim said loudly. 'An' I

for one will tell you if I hear anyone speak ill of your wife when you're not there.' He took hold of Rachel, tugged her into motion and began walking up the hill.

But she dragged on his arm, looking over her shoulder, afraid for her husband if Walter's drinking cronies joined in.

'There's others to help him, lass,' Jim whispered. 'Don't let them fellows see you looking so worried.'

Beside her, little Kitty began to sob again and that sound made Rachel pull herself together. She let go of Jim's arm and picked the child up, cuddling the small body against her. When she risked another glance backwards, she saw Thomas still standing there, arms folded, eyes steady on the little group of men.

'I can't leave him,' she whispered to Jim, so they stayed where they were.

As the silence dragged on, Rafe Whiteside, another of the older men, stepped forward. 'Thee get on thy way, Thomas Thorpe. A wedding day's no time to be fighting an' I think shame of them as have spoiled it for thee. No one'll speak ill of thy wife in my presence. Tha's allus dealt fairly wi' me an' I'll do the same wi' thee and thine.'

There were murmurs of agreement from some of the other men. 'I thank you, Rafe,' Thomas said. He looked at the crowd, saw several men nod at him encouragingly and turned to walk away.

'Look out!' A voice yelled.

Thomas spun on his heels and the rock that had been hurled from behind a corner whizzed past his head harmlessly.

There was a growl of anger from the crowd and calls of 'Coward!' and 'Shame!'

Bill Withers, who had thrown the rock, scowled, but let a second one drop to the ground and edged forward to join his mates. 'Ah, he's not worth the bother, Walter lad,' he said, his voice slurred. 'Come on, there's good ale waiting for us inside.'

Walter fixed Thomas with a baleful gaze that said this quarrel was not settled yet, then followed Bill.

Only when he'd gone inside did Thomas let out his pent-up breath and nod his thanks to his friends.

When he caught up with his family, he wrung his friend's hand. 'Thank you, lad.'

'We'll keep an eye on them sods for you,' Jim said quietly.

Kitty pushed to get down from Rachel's arms and went to hug her father's leg, so he swung her up on to his shoulders. Ruth went to walk on his other side.

For a minute, Rachel felt alone, then Thomas said mildly, 'Come on, love. That's a cold wind.' He put his free arm round her shoulders and led her away, feeling how she was shaking, though whether with the rage for which she was famous or for some other reason, he did not inquire.

And only then, as they walked slowly towards the cottage which stood on its own just below the village of Upper Clough, did Rachel realise how wonderful it was that she was no longer on her own in the world.

Behind them, Rafe looked at one of his friends, an old fellow like himself, as the crowd slipped away. 'It's a bad business, that. She'll not live such a scandal down easily, that poor lass won't.'

'Was Smedling speaking the truth about not being her father?'

'I reckon so.'

'Didst thou know about it, then? I mean, the child had already been born when Walter and Alice came to live here. Thou'st never said owt about it.'

Rafe shrugged. ''Tweren't my business. But I used to see poor Alice at the market in Todmorden afore she were wed.' And he'd seen her with a gentleman, too, several times, her face lit up with love and happiness, so he had a fair idea who had fathered the child. But that wasn't anyone else's business either, so he was not going to mention it. 'The baby were born six months after they wed, and I didn't see how Walter Smedling could have got it on her, seeing as he'd hardly spoken to her afore – well, not that I'd seen.' He chewed thoughtfully on the stem of his empty clay pipe and added, 'And not only did

Smedling get wed in a hurry, but afterwards, when he moved to Upper Clough, he had enough money to buy a new loom and some decent furniture. An' he were a man who'd never saved a farthing in his life. Though he settled down for a time with poor Alice, seemed fond of her, too. She were a bonny woman until she took ill.'

'Well, Walter's getting slack again since she died, he is that.'

'Aye. An' spiteful with it. Nor I never did like that Bill Withers.'

'Rachel will be safe with Thomas Thorpe, though, an' I reckon she'll look after him and the little lasses all right.'

'Aye. She may have a temper, but she's a hard worker an' she was right good to her mother. You can't fault her there. She's loyal to her own.' Rafe nodded as if that settled matters and went back to his weaving.

At home, Rachel was still looking anxious.

'Eh, it's all right, lass,' said Thomas, and gave her a quick hug.

'You're that good to me,' she said gruffly, then set about tidying her new home and making them all comfortable.

The rest of the day passed quietly, and when it came time for them to go to bed, Thomas could see that Rachel was nervous. He didn't say anything, but let her go upstairs first, then followed a few minutes later.

As he got into bed with her, he said quietly, 'If you'd rather wait . . .'

'No. No, let's – do what's necessary.'

He could not help chuckling at that. 'Rachel, lass, it's not only necessary, it's a great pleasure.' Very gently, he set about proving that.

Afterwards, she lay awake staring into the darkness with tears of joy on her cheeks. He was a lovely man and she had never thought to be so happy.

'I'll make him happy, too, Nell,' she whispered into the night, then let herself sink into sleep.

* * *

As the days passed and the gossip died down, Thomas Thorpe would have agreed with Rafe absolutely about Rachel being a hard worker. He had never seen anyone get so much done in a day. He thought about it one night in bed, with his new wife sleeping soundly beside him, not wanting to curl up in his arms as Nell had done, but preferring to stretch out on her own next to him. He was now living in great comfort with a woman who stood weaving beside him like a man – no, better than most men – yet who never neglected the children and still kept the house in excellent order.

The Lord had taken away from him with one hand, then given back generously with the other. He was a fortunate man, he was indeed. He must make sure Rachel did not regret her decision, that she had a good life with him. And the little lasses seemed happy with her too. Yes, it was all working out well – as well as could be expected, given the circumstances, though he sometimes missed Nell's gentleness. You couldn't call Rachel gentle, not even when she was in a good mood, for then she simply radiated more energy than ever.

He had told her several times that she had no need to drive herself so hard, that she could now take things more easily, but she just laughed at him.

'It's the way I'm made, my lad,' she always replied. 'I doubt I'll ever be able to sit down and just do nowt. I'd go mad in a day if I tried.'

But she would smile as she said this. She often smiled nowadays, and that pleased Thomas. She had even put on a little weight and she looked better for it, though she would never be a soft, rounded sort of woman, like Nell had been.

And in bed – well, she was a woman with hidden passion, that was sure. He had trouble keeping up with her. He smiled as he thought about that, then turned over and sighed into sleep. But it was Nell, he dreamed of, Nell whose name he murmured as dawn crept into the corners of the room and chased away the darkness. He knew he did that sometimes and wished he could prevent it, but he could not. Fortunately, Rachel didn't seem to have heard him.

Of course she had heard him, today and other days too, but she said nothing. What good would it have done to complain? You couldn't expect miracles. How could any man love her as much as he had loved Nell? Thomas was certainly fond of her and that was far more than Rachel had ever expected from life. She didn't mind him saying his first wife's name – well, not much – and she certainly didn't *blame* him. After all, he and Nell had been married for near ten years and had been happy together.

But she was determined to make him happy with her as well and she loved caring for their comfortable home. She had everything she wanted in life, had never expected to be so happy. She shivered at this. You should never think things like that. It was tempting providence.

CHAPTER SEVEN

From the very first day, Maggie Kellett loved living in Setherby parsonage. With a cook–housekeeper to organise things and a maid to do the rough work, she felt she was at last living the genteel life she deserved. And when her brother and his family drove over to visit (which was much easier now they did not have to go right up the hill to Upper Clough) or when Caleb popped in on market day for a chat with Justin, she did not now feel ashamed of her house or hospitality.

They hadn't seen much of Caleb for a few months after their move. Justin said he was busy, but people like him were always busy and it hadn't stopped him coming to see them before. Maggie didn't believe that excuse. Justin clearly knew the reason, but she could not worm it out of him, and then Caleb started calling more regularly, so she stopped worrying.

Another thing she enjoyed was visiting Cleving Park, for they were invited to dine there every month. She took great care to dress nicely, and always to flatter and agree with Cousin Nathaniel, as he told her to call him. However, she did not get on as good terms with their patron as she had hoped, and maybe that was Hannah Armstrong's fault. Nathaniel's aunt was horridly shrunken by her years and moved about with the aid of a stick, but her brain was as sharp as it had ever been, and so was her tongue. She might be a lady by birth, but she was as blunt in speech as any villager from Upper Clough. Maggie did not really like her and resented the fact that she was never invited to take tea with her at Cleving.

'You'd think that woman would set a better table,' she grumbled to Justin on the way home the first time.

He looked at her in surprise. 'I thought the food good and plentiful.'

'Plentiful, yes, but not – not *stylish*. Anyone might have served a meal like that. Why, I could do so myself. A great man like your cousin Nathaniel owes it to his position to keep a better table.'

'I don't think Nathaniel is interested in pomp and show, Maggie, and I hope you'll not grumble to anyone else about such things.'

She tossed her head. 'Of course not. But it'd be a fine thing if I couldn't discuss it with my own husband. And look how Mrs Hannah dresses. So plain and ordinary. If I were in her position, I'd be wearing silk and fine brocades, not plain blue wool.'

'Wool is warmer in winter.'

She made a scornful sound. '*Warmer!* As if people like them couldn't afford to have a fire burning day and night in each room.'

He stifled a sigh. What had got into Maggie lately? He had thought she'd be happy here in Setherby, would become her old self again, but she seemed to have settled into this permanently aggrieved frame of mind and he didn't know what to do about it.

She grumbled about the parish duties that were expected of her, and she particularly disliked visiting the sick. Justin begged her several times to make more effort, though in vain, and only when Nathaniel asked her pointedly one day when she was going to attend to her parish duties did she begin to make a token effort. She visited the sick, carrying a basket of food prepared by Mrs Charnley, though she rarely penetrated beyond the doorway of their cottages.

Maggie watched resentfully as Justin bustled around each day from dawn, then tumbled into bed – a separate bed! – exhausted at night. He seemed to have less time for his wife than ever before, and she missed having him in her bed, even if only to cuddle up to. But when she told him, he said sleeping apart was easier for a man who was not allowed to make love to his wife.

If it were not for her new acquaintance, Mrs Payne, the wife of the linen draper, Maggie would have been very lonely. But dearest Lydia shared her love of clothes and finery, not to mention her love of gossip, and the two soon became firm friends.

There was only one thing that upset Maggie about Lydia, and that was her family. The Paynes had two buxom daughters and no less than three stout sons, while she had not been able to give Justin even one son. She knew he regretted that. So did she. Not that she missed being pregnant. Oh, dear me, no! But she did wish she and Justin had a son to carry on the family name and to look after them in their old age. Daughters weren't the same thing at all. They got married and went off to live with their husbands, forgetting their own families. She had noticed that time and time again.

Most of all she hated to see how proud Mr Payne was of his boys – and how wistfully Justin watched them sometimes after church when folk lingered to chat in the churchyard. She absolutely hated that! Life could be so unfair. She should have had a son, not two daughters.

One day a few months after Rachel and Thomas's wedding, Rob came running across the green and banged on the Thorpes' door, shouting, 'Thomas, come quickly, lad!'

Thomas and Rachel exchanged startled glances and both left their weaving to hurry down the stairs.

'It's your Uncle Fred. He's had a seizure. Your Auntie Susan needs you.'

'I'll come with you,' Rachel said quietly. 'Let me get my shawl.'

They went out to the tiny hamlet near Upper Clough where the last member of Thomas's family lived, all the others having died or scattered to other towns. There they found that neighbours had lifted Fred Thorpe's body on to his bed and some of them were still in the house, keeping watch with Fred's wife.

Rachel went to stand by Auntie Susan but could see at a glance there was nothing anyone could do for Uncle Fred. It made her shiver suddenly to see how much the man on the bed resembled her husband, though he looked much older, of course.

'Eh!' muttered Thomas by her side. 'That's the last of my dad's brothers gone. Uncle Fred lived longest of 'em all. The others all died afore they were forty.'

Rachel shivered again, then told herself not to be silly. Her Thomas had had an easier life than his father, so he'd be bound to live longer. And he'd always eaten well, too, for Nell had kept a good table. That made such a difference.

Auntie Susan looked up at them blindly from beside the bed. 'What am I going to do?' she whispered. 'They'll put me in the poorhouse now, without my Fred to weave for me.'

'Nay, we'll not let them do that, Auntie,' Thomas said. He began to shepherd the neighbours out of the house, then sent a message down to Mordrew Bates in Setherby, who was the only undertaker in the valley. He would make sure his uncle had a proper send-off, with a good coffin.

Rachel helped Auntie Susan lay out the body and tried to console the still weeping woman, whose anguish seemed to be divided equally between losing her husband and fears for her own future. 'Do you want to come and sleep at our house?' Rachel asked as dusk began to fall.

'Nay, I'll stay and keep watch over my Fred.'

'Shall I stay with you?'

Auntie Susan shook her head, then patted the capable hand resting on her shoulder. 'You're a good lass. Thank you for your help, love. But I'll see this night out with just him and me, the way we've allus been.'

Back at the house, Rachel was very pensive as she prepared something to eat. When she and Thomas were in bed, she suggested, 'Why don't we ask Auntie Susan to come and live with us?'

'I'd be happy to do that, but – well, are you sure?'

'Of course I am. Your aunt's one of the best spinsters there is round here. She'd be a big help to us.'

'Yes, but,' Thomas struggled to put it tactfully, 'how shall you get on with her, two women in a house, like?' Nell had always said she would not like to share her house with any other woman.

Rachel just laughed. 'Nay, my lad, I'm not quarrelsome. Susan and I will manage well enough together. She needs a home and we need more thread spinning, so we shall all benefit. And anyway,' her face grew sombre, 'she's terrified they'll put her into the poorhouse. I don't like to see her so fearful.'

He gave up the attempt to talk it over. With Rachel, he sometimes felt he was being rushed along like the River Whin which poured itself rapidly down the lower end of the valley without knowing where it was going, gathering to itself any stream which happened to come within reach and growing wider with each mile it travelled.

As long as he could feed his family, Thomas didn't really care about making extra money and building up savings, beyond a sensible amount in case he fell ill and was unable to weave for a week or two, of course, but Rachel seemed to crave money. This was not for greed or for show, he had realised as the months passed, but simply for the security that money represented. Still, he wished she did not feel so driven to making money above all else.

When Auntie Susan came to live with them, things turned out better than Thomas had expected. Rachel was quite happy to leave many of the household tasks to the older woman and concentrate on her weaving, so he breathed a sigh of relief that his peace and quiet were not to be disturbed by quarrels. Under Auntie Susan's expert tuition, little Kitty started learning to spin, and Ruth's spinning also improved tremendously, though the two girls were now going to learn her letters from the new curate's wife three mornings a week. It was Rachel who'd insisted on that, who said that girls needed educating just as much as boys.

So gentle Thomas Thorpe found himself at the head of a thriving household and with more money than anyone else he knew, for his new wife was a better manager than poor, generous Nell who had always liked to share what she had with her friends. It worried him sometimes to think of those coins lying there in the tin box doing nothing when there were folk in the valley who hadn't enough to eat.

Still, the increased production didn't seem to give him a heavier burden of work; less in fact. Rachel was far quicker than he at calculating how much wool and thread they would need. But it was he who went with the other men to fetch the raw wool for spinning and he enjoyed these outings. Every week or two, weavers from the village would walk into Rochdale, carrying their pieces of finished work. It was something of a social occasion for the men. In the longer days of summer, if the weather was fine, they might walk back the same day, but more often they came partway and spent the night in the barn of a friendly farmer who'd been lodging the weavers from Whin Vale for as long as anyone remembered for a penny a head. But with twice the amount of finished cloth to sell, thanks to Rachel, Thomas found his load rather heavy to carry, and there was, of course, no question of a woman coming along on the trip to help him. Some of the older men were also beginning to grumble about the long walk. It upset Thomas to see his friends ageing suddenly, to hear of one dying, then another.

'I s'all have to make me a handcart, I reckon,' Thomas told his wife one Sunday as they were sitting at ease after their evening meal. 'There's too much stuff to carry to Rochdale comfortably now. Yon pieces of cloth are heavy.'

She frowned. 'It'll still take a full day and a half for you to get there and back, even with a handcart.'

He realised she had some idea for improving matters and waited to see what it was.

'Will you see the children to bed, Auntie Susan?' she asked. 'Me an' Thomas have summat to talk over.'

Once they were alone, she said thoughtfully, 'It's a long walk into Rochdale, my lad. Tiring for you, too.'

'Aye.' He pulled contentedly on his clay pipe, his one indulgence. 'But we have to take in the cloth to get our money, and we have to bring back the wool and thread, so there's no help for it.' Some men had enough womenfolk to spin their own thread, others bought thread ready-spun, increasingly from Caleb Hesketh, who had, with his mother's help, organised the spinsters of Hepstone into spinning the very finest of thread. Farmers' wives and daughters, widows, all sorts of women were eager to earn a little extra money and Caleb's wool was beautiful to work with, longer in staple than that of most other farmers.

'I reckon that walk's a waste of your time, a waste of everyone's time,' Rachel went on. 'Two whole days away from your weaving sometimes! You should have accepted that clothier's offer to send his cart for the stuff.'

'If we had, he'd have paid us less. And he'd be telling us what to do. The lads wouldn't like that. We're an independent bunch here in Whin Vale.'

'Well, I still think there has to be a better way to do it.'

He took the pipe out of his mouth and looked at her indulgently. 'What have you got in mind now, my lass? Come on. Out with it!'

Rachel smiled and patted his hand. 'How well you know me, Thomas. I'm so happy with you. If only . . .' She left the sentence unfinished. She had hoped to bear him a child or two, but they'd been married for well over a year and there was no sign of a baby starting.

Thomas squeezed her hand sympathetically. He, too, would have liked another son. Sometimes he went to the graves of the two little lads who'd died and just sat there, remembering them. He remembered Nell every day and set flowers on her grave from time to time.

'There's no way but to go to Rochdale oursen, for we haven't got a putter-out to fetch it for us,' he said.

'Not yet we haven't,' Rachel said quietly. 'But there could be one.' She paused to eye him expectantly.

Pipe forgotten, he waited for her to explain, thinking idly how well she looked in that dark green Sunday dress. He'd chosen the material for her himself, against all her protests about it being an extravagance, and Auntie Susan had helped her make it up into one of the simple closed robes that suited her so well. The neck was cut low and – he smiled at the memory – how Rachel had protested about the frivolity of that! But Auntie Susan had got hold of a dressmaker's moppet from Mrs Payne in Setherby, to show her the more fashionable styling. She and the girls had had their say about trimmings, too, so that there was lace on the edge of the kerchief tucked round Rachel's neck and modestly filling the low-cut bodice. Why, even Rachel's two everyday dresses were fuller in the skirt and more flattering than the things she'd had when they first married.

Not exactly pretty, his Rachel, but a healthy-looking woman, and when her eyes were sparkling with excitement as they were now, he thought her very fetching. She had completely lost that gaunt, angry look that had made him and Nell feel sorry for her.

'If we had a cart, with a donkey to pull it,' she said, the words tumbling out in a rush, 'we could maybe come to some agreement with Harrison's, as well as with the men here. You could become a sort of putter-out, collecting the packs of wool or spun thread and taking in the pieces of cloth for the whole of Whin Vale. You wouldn't need to charge much for doing it, but the pennies would mount up. It'd save everyone a lot of time and trouble and you could do it easily, my lad. Everyone trusts you and you know your cloth. Harrison wouldn't be able to say any pieces were of lower quality without your agreement.'

He started to play with his cooling pipe, twisting it round and round in his blunt fingers, saying nothing, just frowning down at it.

She bit her tongue, waiting for him to speak, for he did not like to be hurried in a decision. But it was hard for her to sit quietly, with the ideas bubbling up in her brain.

'Where should we keep a donkey and cart, though?' he asked at last.

She nodded approval of this sensible question. No fool, her Thomas. 'We should have to move to a bigger house, of course, one with more rooms and a bit more land, for we'd need to grow hay for the donkey as well. Should you mind moving?'

He shrugged. 'Nay, you live where you need to. Me an' Nell didn't allus live here.' And maybe if they did move, he'd not think of his first wife so often. Even now, it was sometimes a shock not to find her waiting for him when he got back from an outing.

He removed some more tobacco from his leather pouch, an unusual extravagance, filled the pipe slowly, paying meticulous attention to how the tobacco was packed in, then took a wooden splinter from the jar by the fire and lit it, another lengthy process, involving much puffing and re-application of the burning splinter.

Rachel could have screamed at him to hurry up, but she knew his ways by now, so clasped her hands together tightly and forced herself to stare into the fire, leaving him to sift through the ideas in his mind.

A few more puffs, then, 'Nancy Clegg an' her family are movin' out of North Beck Cottage up the hill, now that Paul's died. I could ask Tam Barker for it. It's a fine big house, that. Six rooms, a big attic *and* a shed. We'd need bigger windows in the attic, though, with the two of us weaving.'

She let out her breath in a whoosh. Could she have persuaded him to do it so easily?

He gave his slow, lopsided smile. 'I shouldn't bother to do it on my own, we both know that, but with you beside me, lass, I don't mind having a try.' He didn't add that the extra work involved would also keep her mind off her failure to give him a child.

As they got into bed, he murmured, 'I think we'd better get oursen a dog, too, if we move. A good watchdog. It's a bit lonely, that cottage is. Jim's bitch has just had pups. A rare clever dog, she is. I believe I'll ask him for one. I like dogs.'

She would have let him keep six dogs if he'd wanted them. Her love for him was deep now, but more easily shown in deeds than in words. 'Then we'd better speak for one of the pups tomorrow.'

'Right.' Thomas smiled and drew her into his arms, saying softly and happily, 'I allus wanted a dog of my own, but Nell couldn't abide them under her feet. Eh, but you're a grand lass to me!'

She burrowed her head against his chest. A simple man, her Thomas, simple and good. Why couldn't she be more like him? Why did she always want so much more out of life? Questions like that tormented her on wakeful nights and she could never find any satisfactory answers. Why, even now, when she had everything a woman could ask for – except children – her happiness was not unalloyed and she was always wanting to try new things. And that did not always please Thomas.

The next day the two of them walked up to look at North Beck Cottage in the late afternoon. It was the best property in Upper Clough, being only ten years old, with two acres of good arable land attached.

'I'll speak to Tam Barker,' Thomas decided.

'Do it tomorrow.'

So the next day he walked down the hill and went to knock on the back door of Cleving Park.

Tam let him speak his piece, then looked across his desk and frowned. 'I had thought to let that cottage to someone more substantial than a weaver. A retired sea captain, perhaps, or someone of that ilk.'

Even gentle Thomas took exception to this tone and, as the interview progressed, grew angry enough to raise his voice and thump the desk, demanding to be given a chance since he could pay the rent as well as any sea captain. Tam was, he realised suddenly as the objections continued, just being spiteful – no doubt for his friend Walter's sake.

The noise of the quarrel brought Mr Armstrong himself to see what the matter was.

Barker, with occasional scornful looks at the visitor, explained.

Thomas folded his arms and waited his turn to speak, but had no need to plead.

'Let Mr Thorpe have North Beck Cottage,' Nathaniel said as soon as he understood the problem. 'He and his wife will make good tenants.' He was well aware of the worth of all who lived in the valley and was pleased with the match Rachel had made, delighted to see such an industrious household. It had also pleased him that the Thorpes had taken in the old widowed aunt. People should look after their old folk. It was their bounden duty. There were those who tried to put old folk on to the poor rates instead.

'But sir, we shall have to put extra windows in the attic and—'

'Barker, I am happy to let Mr Thorpe and his family have the cottage.'

Tam knew better than to argue with Mr Armstrong when he spoke in that tone. 'Yes, sir.' But the look he threw at Thomas was full of resentment. 'I'll see to it at once.'

Two nights later, Rachel was awakened by faint sounds outside. When she got out of bed and opened the window to stare outside, the sounds stopped and she decided it must have been a fox.

In the morning, she and Thomas woke to a foul smell, and when they went downstairs found piles of stinking debris dumped in their back garden.

'Nay, who's done this? What a nasty thing to do!' Thomas said sorrowfully.

'It'll be him, of course,' Rachel raged.

'Who?'

'Walter Smedling, who d'you think?'

'Surely not?'

'Who else holds a grudge against us?'

Tam Barker turned up unexpectedly in Upper Clough

that morning while they were still clearing up the mess. He came round to the back of the house without invitation and stood staring round in disgust. 'Clear this place up at once!' he ordered.

'What do you think we're doing?' Rachel demanded.

'How can you have let things get so foul? Did you not know better than to leave your rubbish lying around?'

'*Us* leave it!'

'Shh!' Thomas pulled Rachel back towards him and said mildly, 'This is not our doing, Mr Barker. Someone came and dumped this mess here during the night.'

The land agent made a scornful noise in his throat. 'It'd take more than one person to dump all this. It must have been building up for weeks. Shame on you for your slovenly ways! You've kept your show of industry for the front of your house, where folk can see it, but you've let things get into a proper mess here. Well, I can't possibly let Mr Armstrong rent North Beck Cottage to people who create a stinking midden like this. You can consider our agreement terminated.' He turned and strode away, hiding a smile.

Thomas put his hand across Rachel's mouth as she would have yelled after the land agent. 'It's not worth causing trouble and bad feeling, lass. That fellow has been dead set against us having North Beck Cottage from the start, and it's him we'd be dealing with, not his master. It's just not worth it. We can manage here as we have been doing.' Besides, he wasn't totally convinced he wanted to become a putter-out. It would be a lot of responsibility to take on. He would just get himself a handcart.

Rachel spent the morning fulminating, but two attempts to convince Thomas to complain were useless. In the end, she put on her warm cloak and said curtly, 'I'm going out to walk off my anger.'

'Eh, lass . . .'

She was gone before he could say more.

Down in Setherby, she hesitated, wondering how best to approach the matter, but when she saw Justin in the distance, she said, 'Ah!' and hurried over to him.

After she had explained what had happened, he took her back to the parsonage and insisted she take tea with his wife and wait for him to return. 'I'll go and see Mr Armstrong about this matter myself.'

Rachel half rose from her seat. 'Surely I should come with you.'

He shook his head. 'Mr Armstrong does not think it suitable for women to discuss business matters. It's not the best way to approach him, Rachel, believe me.'

So she sat and tried to take an interest in Maggie's gossip about her household doings, but failed lamentably.

Maggie grew angry at the signs of inattention. Her friend, Lydia Payne, had been hinting that this woman was not a suitable acquaintance for a parson's wife, had been hinting, too, that Mrs Thorpe did not get on with the womenfolk because she was more interested in the men. Maggie had protested about this, but today, seeing how finely dressed Rachel was, how much better she looked these days – who would ever have believed that she could look so handsome? – she began to wonder if Lydia were not right. And Justin had hurried to help her. Was Rachel interested in him? Mr Thorpe was an older man. Perhaps his second wife found him lacking in certain ways?

The conversation faltered to a halt as jealousy crept in and Maggie's mouth took on a hard line. Was Justin – could he be finding consolation elsewhere?

Nathaniel frowned at his parson. 'Explain that to me again, if you please.'

So Justin passed on the tale Rachel had poured out to him, then added his own opinion that if Thomas Thorpe said someone else had piled the rotten rubbish in their back garden, then he was telling the truth, since the man was known to be honest to a fault.

'I shall come and see for myself. Pray ride up the hill with me.'

Justin nodded. 'I'll meet you near the church, shall I?' He

took great pleasure in having a horse of his own and being able to get around the valley so conveniently.

After telling the groom at the livery stables to saddle his horse, he hurried to tell the two women what was happening, whereupon Rachel took her leave. She made a few purchases in Setherby and walked home alone, hoping Mr Armstrong's visit had gone well. She still felt angry that she had not seen the landowner herself. How foolish to say that women were not suited to discussing business matters! Why, she was far more suited than Thomas. And as for Maggie Kellett, the woman got sillier every time she saw her, always fussing about unimportant things like ornaments and ribbons instead of schooling her daughters or managing her household herself. Fancy leaving so much to a housekeeper.

She had hoped to pass Mr Armstrong and the parson on their way back and perhaps get some idea of what had happened, but she only saw them in the distance, riding out towards the moors. With an exasperated click of her tongue, she quickened her pace.

'What happened?' she asked, bursting into the house.

'Thomas is weaving,' Auntie Susan said placidly. 'But all is well, I think.'

Rachel clattered up the stairs. 'What did Mr Armstrong say?'

Thomas set down his shuttle and looked at her with a rather stern expression on his face.

'Well, what happened?' she repeated impatiently.

'Mr Armstrong came and inspected the back of our cottage. He found where someone had broken through the fence, then discovered tracks where a handcart had been wheeled up the hill. But we didn't find where the handcart had come from because the ground was too hard further down.' He paused, then said quietly, 'I gather you went to see Mr Kellett.'

She nodded.

'Why did you not tell me what you were doing, Rachel?'

She flushed. 'I thought you might try to stop me.'

He looked sad. 'I don't like you lying to me, lass.'

'I didn't lie exactly, I just – didn't tell you. I was so *angry*.'

'Well, it's all turned out all right, I suppose. But don't deceive me again, Rachel. It doesn't please me.'

It was as near as he'd ever got to reprimanding her and she felt it very keenly, more because he was hurt by her actions than because he was angry. She'd do anything rather than hurt him. 'We are to get North Beck Cottage, though?'

'Aye.' He went back to his weaving.

'Aren't you happy about that?'

'I suppose so. It'll mean a lot more work, though.'

She looked at him in exasperation. Sometimes it would be nice to see him get excited, nice if he wasn't quite so placid. But that was his nature and who was she to try to change it? 'I'll go and put on my working clothes and join you. I've lost a lot of time today.'

'There's no need. Why don't you take a rest? We're well ahead with our pieces—' But he was talking to himself, for she had already gone downstairs to their bedroom to change into her working clothes, with their shorter skirts.

'Eh!' He shook his head and paused to stare blindly out of the window. 'I don't know where all this will lead to, I really don't.' But at least him becoming the putter-out would help the older men as well as earn extra money for himself and his family, so it was worth doing, really. He didn't know why he'd been dragging his feet about it. Maybe he wouldn't get so tired when he had a donkey cart to ride on. A smile crossed his face. And a dog to run beside the cart.

On moving day, Rachel was in her element, organising everything and feeding the helpers. It was only as they all stood around in the new house afterwards that she realised there were no women among the helpers, and that most were older men, friends of Thomas, for he did not get on nearly as well with the younger men who thought him too settled in his ways.

They all enjoyed their new home, which had a small room for Auntie Susan downstairs as well as a very large attic for the two looms, with a fine new window in it.

Later that first day, Rachel and Thomas went up to the weaving room together.

'Look at that view!' he said, standing by the new window. 'I shall enjoy working here.'

'Look at all this space!' said Rachel, beginning to sort out her bits and pieces. 'We could fit another loom in. Take on a third weaver, a young fellow who can't afford to buy his own loom yet, perhaps.'

He sighed. 'Let's leave it with you and me, lass, eh? I enjoy being just the two of us together when we're weaving.'

She stifled a sigh and got on with her work.

Caleb went to take tea with Georgiana Bretherton that same day. His resolve to have less to do with her had not lasted long after his disappointment with Rachel. Georgiana was able to discuss all sorts of things about the wider world that he sometimes longed to go and experience, and he listened to her in fascination. Today he ventured to hint that the man who managed her home farm was perhaps not doing his task as enthusiastically as he ought to have been.

'I've been wondering about that myself,' she said thoughtfully. 'And yet he's brother to Tam Barker who is land agent for Cleving Park. He ought to know his job.'

Caleb shrugged. He hadn't told her the half of it and was beginning to wonder whether Tam Barker was cheating his master as well. Both the brothers seemed to be involved with one of the market stalls, though neither was associated with it openly. But he'd seen them talking to the man who ran it, selling farm produce and whatever fruit and vegetables were in season. Maybe some of that produce came from the gardens of the big houses.

He rode slowly back to his own farm, pleased that his new ventures were going well. He was paying back the money he owed to Mrs Bretherton more rapidly than he had expected, so the land he had bought from James Trotter would soon be clear of debt. In fact, life was going very well for him financially. This was better than the old days with the big communal fields.

Then he looked up at the glorious sunset sky and sadness filled him. Sometimes he felt as if he was empty inside, however busy he was outside – especially when he had seen Rachel Thorpe in the distance. He gave a snort of bitter laughter as her image rose before him. Although his mother had introduced him to one or two eligible young women, the thought of spending his whole life with any of them set a chill in his blood that made him stiffen and draw back, even from the most amiable lass. None of them had Rachel's intelligence, her sturdy body, her brisk way of walking and talking. And yet she looked happy with Thomas Thorpe.

Why did she still affect him like this? Was he never to be free of this longing for her?

CHAPTER EIGHT

The pup was brought to join the family at North Beck Cottage as soon as it could leave its mother, and promised to grow into a large dog. They chose a male, because whelping would cause too much trouble with a bitch. The dog was very much Thomas's own and he called it Dusty because of the indeterminate greyish colour of its coat. He would hold long conversations with it when he was out walking and it acted as though it understood every word he said. Best of all, as far as Rachel was concerned, the little creature yelped at the approach of visitors before it could even bark properly.

'That,' said Thomas, 'is the sign of a good watchdog. He'll be well worth keeping, our Dusty will.'

Rachel exchanged smiles with Auntie Susan. They all knew he had grown fond of the little animal and would have kept it whether it was a good guard dog or not.

Although the older men of Upper and Lower Clough were loud in praise of the new system of putting-out, and expressed relief not to have to make the long trek into Rochdale, some of the younger ones refused to join in the venture, insisting they enjoyed their walks, the only time they got out of the valley and away from their wives.

'They'll change their minds come the winter,' Rachel said. 'They don't know when they're well off, that lot don't.'

'It matters not,' Thomas chided her. 'There's room for doing it both ways.'

But objections to the new system continued. One day Walter Smedling blocked the path through Lower Clough, arms akimbo. 'You want to watch what you're doing, Thomas Thorpe.'

'What do you mean?'

'I mean you're trying to take over in Whin Vale and it won't do. We won't allow it! Mind,' he blew ale-smelling breath in Thomas's direction, 'we all know it's *her* doing. You wouldn't have done this on your own.'

Anger made Thomas ask sharply, 'Are you trying to cause trouble for my Rachel again?'

Walter rolled his eyes. 'Me? When have I ever done that? It's *her* as causes the trouble round here, all sorts of trouble. And don't tell me *you* thought up this stupid scheme, for I'll not believe you. You're not a grasping sort of fellow – or you weren't till you wed *her* and I've no doubt you're regretting that now.'

'I don't regret my marriage in the least. Rachel is a good wife to me, a wife any man could be proud of. You go back to swilling your ale and mind what you say about her in future.'

Walter spat on the ground, narrowly missing Thomas's foot. 'Ah, you're governed by the petticoats, you are.'

'And you're governed by the ale and gin.' Thomas turned away. It was no use arguing with a man in that condition.

Walter stood and glared after him until he was out of sight. 'It's all *her* doing,' he muttered. 'She's stopped us enjoyin' oursen an' set us at one another's throats.'

It surprised no one when Walter and his cronies refused to let Thomas take their pieces into Rochdale. But after a while, as an unusually severe winter took away much of the pleasure of the long traipse, even the group who drank in the Weaver's Arms succumbed to temptation. One by one, they asked Thomas to take in their finished pieces to sell to Harrison's.

Last to do it was Walter, stiff and aggressive as he made his request. He went back to the alehouse afterwards and jeered at how soft Thorpe was. 'He just told me his terms an' took my piece. I'd never have worked for my enemies like that.' He raised his pot of ale in a mocking toast.

'Nay, he's no one's enemy, Thomas isn't,' one of the older men protested.

Walter fixed him with such a malevolent look that the man blinked in shock and from then on began to drink in the front room of the inn. Gradually the back room became the recognised territory of Smedling and his cronies, none of whom would deal with Rachel when they brought their pieces up to North Beck Cottage

Walter had found himself another wife, a woman called Hetty from a hamlet near Todmorden. Since the marriage, he had settled down a bit, doing enough weaving to earn a decent living and he now blamed his period of heavy drinking on Rachel's troublesome ways.

Bill Withers had also married, but his wife had brought him nothing except a full belly every year and that made him feel angry whenever he saw Rachel, looking not only prosperous but surprisingly handsome. She should have married him when he asked her, then he would be the one to benefit from her hard work. Now he was weighed down with a child (a girl, too) and another on the way, not to mention a wife who kept telling him complacently that all her family were good breeders – as if he wanted a house full of bloody brats. Resentment festered within him, though like Walter Smedling he was careful to hide his feelings when Thomas or his friends were around.

'Thorpe won't allus have so many folk on his side,' Bill said to Walter when another of the older men died. 'There's one more of his precious friends gone. We s'll have our day. Just you wait an' see.'

'What do you mean, "have our day"?'

'The day when we'll get our own back on that shrew. She's turned uppity since she got wed. Won't give anyone the time of day now.'

Walter nodded agreement. 'I raised an ungrateful one there, I did that.' And had lost his own son while he was doing it. 'If I had my rights, she'd have stayed home and paid me back by working for me, then I wouldn't have had to marry Hetty Parks. She's nowt in bed, that one, nowt!' And had shown no signs of bearing him a child, either. Well, not a daughter, but a son, like the one who had died. He often thought of what Paul might have been like now. It had always seemed unjust that Paul had died and Rachel had lived. A man had a need for a son somehow. Well, *he* did.

Soon after their move, Rachel began to suspect that she was with child. There had been other false alarms, so she did not dare put her trust in her body's irregularities until there could be no doubt about her condition.

When she had to rush across the room to be sick into the wash bowl as she got up one morning, Thomas grinned at her from the bed. 'That's settled it, my lass.'

She stared at him, then burst into tears and came back to the bed, snuggling against him and burying her face in his chest.

He put his arms round her and patted her gently on the back. 'Nay, then, nay! I thought you'd be glad of it.'

'I am g-glad. I've n-never been so h-happy in my life.' And she wept even harder.

So he just held her till she'd recovered and when she ordered him not to tell anyone about the child or her foolish bout of weeping, he nodded.

Although they didn't say a word, even to their own family, Auntie Susan announced a few days later that Rachel had better rest a bit more. 'Havin' a first one at six and twenty isn't easy.'

'What? How did you know?' For once, Rachel was blushing and stammering like a young girl.

'You haven't had your courses for two months now. And anyway, it shows. Put on a bit of flesh around the chest, haven't you? Your face looks fuller, as well.' She paused, then added complacently, 'I'm right, aren't I?'

'Well, it – it seems so,' admitted Rachel, trying to speak calmly and failing. 'But it's early days yet and I'm not one to coddle myself, Auntie.'

'It's not you as we're out to coddle. This is for the child's sake.' Auntie Susan wagged a determined finger in her face. 'Mind what I say now! If you want to keep that child, you'll take an hour's rest of an afternoon. Can't beat it. Saved many a one, resting has. An' you can afford to do it. Don't tell me you and our Thomas need every penny you can earn to put bread on the table.'

So for the first and only time in her life Rachel allowed herself to be 'spoiled silly', as she put it, and the household conspired to keep her calm and happy. Thomas would not let her overtire herself with too much weaving, Auntie Susan took care of the cooking and, with the girls' help, the washing, and Rachel was encouraged to rest regularly – which was a good thing, because she had never been so sleepy in her life.

On the first of June, Rachel's child was born. It was not an easy birth. Rachel was two days in labour and Auntie Susan refused point-blank to let the doctor come near her.

'But I want the best for my lass,' Thomas protested, almost beside himself with worry, for Nell had borne children easily and he knew how much it must be hurting for Rachel to cry out like that. 'Let me go and fetch him.'

'This is women's business, Thomas Thorpe.' Susan frowned. 'Mind, it wouldn't hurt to have a bit of help, like. Rachel's a bit old for a first child, that's what the trouble is. At her age, her body's too strong for its own good an' it won't give way easily to let the child out. Sithee, why don't we send for Grandma Lowther to come up from Setherby? She knows more nor yon fool of a doctor about bringing babbies into the world.'

Thomas rushed off down the hill to do as she suggested.

The reason for the difficult birth became apparent when the child at last made its way into the world.

'Will tha just look at this one, Susan lass! Largest babby I ever did see!' exclaimed Grandma Lowther. 'Eh, I never thought we'd get it out safe, but we did an' just look at the way it's kicking now.'

'My baby . . .' came a thread of a voice from the bed.

'You've a fine, lusty son, my lass,' said Susan briskly, bringing a flannel-wrapped bundle to her.

'A son!' Rachel managed a tearful smile, but was too tired even to take the babe in her arms. Her eyelids flickered closed.

Auntie Susan set the baby in its cradle and went down to the kitchen, where she scolded the girls for neglecting their spinning, and sent one of them running to fetch Thomas who had been banished from the house because he would insist on standing outside the bedroom door and peering in whenever anyone opened it to get something – which had upset his wife.

When Rachel's eyes next fluttered open, she found her husband sitting by the bed, his eyes on his new son, and realised from the lightness of her body that her ordeal really was finished.

'Thomas.' Her voice was a mere rasp of sound.

He turned and beamed at her. 'Who's my clever lass?' Leaning forward, he kissed her cheek and smoothed her hair back.

'The baby's all right, isn't he?' She could not help worrying that there would be something wrong with her son, that he might be different from other children.

'He's a fine little lad. Perfect in every way.' Thomas beamed at his wife, tears of joy welling in his eyes.

'You great soft lump!' Auntie Susan scoffed, nudging him gently. 'You'd think no one had ever produced a son afore!' Then her glance softened as she stared down at the cradle. 'Still, he *is* a fine little lad. *Little!* Grandma Lowther's right. He's the biggest newborn babby I ever did see! I doubt whether some o' those clothes we made will even fit him.'

'Then we'll make some more.' Rachel smiled at her husband and reached for his hand.

As if aware that he was the centre of attention, the baby woke up and began to quest around for food, his little mouth sucking busily at the air, and his face gradually growing red as he wailed out his frustration.

'Eh, look at him! Only three hours old and wants his dinner!'

cackled Auntie Susan. She picked the infant up and rocked him in her arms for a moment, then passed him over to Rachel.

Mutely Rachel took the baby and put him to her engorged breast. As he began to suck, tears started to roll down her face. My son, she thought in wonderment, my son! And was seized with such a deep love she thought her heart might burst.

'Nay, lass!' exclaimed Thomas. 'What's wrong now?'

Rachel shook her head, almost incapable of speech; then, as she saw how worried Thomas was, she managed to choke out, 'I'm just – so very happy!'

Tactfully, Auntie Susan left them alone together.

Thomas stroked his wife's cheek with one callused fingertip. 'Nay, then, you've a funny way of showing your happiness! You've done naught but weep all the time you've been carrying him.'

She managed a tremulous smile but could not keep her eyes for long from her son's face, for he seemed a miracle to her. 'What shall we call him?' she asked, after a while.

'Do you still fancy the name Adam?'

'Yes, love. If it's all right with you.'

'Then Adam it is.'

'Adam Thorpe.' She gave a deep sigh of satisfaction and, as soon as the child had had his fill, she allowed Thomas to take him from her. Within seconds she was asleep again, a smile still lingering on her face.

Thomas stayed to stare down at his son, so different from the smaller babes his Nell had produced. A strong child, this one, like his mother. 'You'll do me,' he told the sleeping baby in a voice thick with emotion.

Going up to the attic, he settled down to his weaving. But every now and then a smile would cross his face and once or twice he said aloud, 'Adam. Adam Thorpe. Eh, it's a right good name for a man, that is. A strong name. I reckon he'll make summat of hissen, our Adam will.'

When he heard that *she* had had a fine, lusty son, Walter Smedling grew even angrier, for his own wife still showed no signs of getting with child, though it was not for lack of trying on his part.

'She'll not make a good mother, Rachel Thorpe won't,' he told anyone who would listen. 'And I pity the child, I do indeed. She'll chivvy it round from morn till night, poor thing.'

Bill Withers gave a sour smile. 'Eh, having a babby's nothin' to be proud of. My Mary can have 'em as easy as shellin' peas. I'm just surprised yon Rachel is woman enough to get a man to the point.' He guffawed and poked his friend in the ribs, but could get no smile from him.

Walter remained sour and angry for days. Even his new wife was beginning to tell him he was being unreasonable about this, but he'd given Hetty a good clout and she'd not spoken out of turn since. He should have clouted Alice more, stopped her from spoiling her daughter. Made her take better care of his son. Stopped her from favouring Rachel.

For a moment, he wondered, as he often had, who Rachel's father was, but Alice had always refused to tell him – and what did it matter now anyway? The only thing that did matter was paying back that ungrateful doxy! And one day he'd do it, by hell he would!

At the parsonage, Maggie Kellett felt jealousy sear through her like sharp vinegar when she heard that Rachel Thorpe had given birth to a son, a child so large and lusty that Grandma Lowther was still talking about it.

'Have you seen the miraculous Thorpe baby, then?' Maggie asked Justin scornfully when he came back from a visit to the new curate who was settling down well in the valley and whose wife did much to remedy Maggie's lack of interest in caring for the poor of the parish.

'I have indeed. A fine little boy. They are to have him christened next week and, um,' he shot a sideways glance at her, 'have asked me to stand as godfather.'

'Well! They're looking a bit above their station there! I hope you refused. You can't be standing godfather to every mewling babe born in this valley.'

'I was going to say no,' he admitted, 'but somehow, he's such a fine baby that I found myself saying yes.' It had been a strange moment, that, with sunlight slanting through the window of the kitchen in North Beck Cottage and Rachel seeming almost Madonna-like as she sat cradling her baby in a rocking chair. Marriage and motherhood had softened her and she was so different nowadays from the gaunt woman he'd met on the moors when he walked across to Upper Clough that sometimes he blinked in surprise when he saw her in the street, glowing with health and vitality.

Maggie threw up her hands in despair and tried to persuade him to send word that he'd changed his mind, but he would not.

'Wait till you see the baby,' he told her. 'You'll be enchanted by him too.'

She let out a scornful puff of air. 'When am I ever likely to see him?'

'You're surely going to visit Rachel? You openly called yourself her friend in the past and she has done nothing to deserve the insult from you of ignoring the child's birth. Besides, Thomas Thorpe is a leading citizen of Whin Vale and Mr Armstrong will expect us both to call. He's very pleased at how the putting-out is going, says it's a more modern way to do things.'

'*Go and see her!* But it's a long walk up the hill and the weather has been wet and rainy all week.'

'Then you must be sure to wear stout shoes and your cloak of oiled wool.'

When she opened her mouth to protest, he held up one hand and said, 'Tomorrow!' in such stern tones that she flounced one shoulder and said oh, very well, she would go.

And to her great surprise, Justin was right. The babe was quite delightful, so well grown for his age and so lively, kicking and panting and throwing his little hands around, that Maggie quite lost her heart to him. As for her daughters, whom she'd taken with her, they passed him from one to the other, and cooed over him as if he was their little brother.

When it came her turn to hold him, something seemed to grasp her heart. The baby's eyes were still unfocused, but they were large and beautiful, and the way he held on to her finger made emotion thrill through her. 'He's going to have dark eyes, I think,' she said to the proud mother, her voice softer than when she had arrived. 'You have a fine son.'

Rachel nodded. 'So we think. And he's going to be very like his father.'

Maggie looked disapprovingly at the kicking limbs. 'You didn't think to swaddle him?'

'Oh, no! He enjoys moving about so much it'd be a shame to bind his limbs.'

'But you'll want to be sure his legs grow straight.'

Rachel laughed. 'I'll feed him so well they'll have no chance to grow otherwise. Good food is the best medicine of all, to my mind.' Her breasts were overflowing with milk, and anyway, she wouldn't like someone to bind her limbs tightly so she wasn't going to do it to Adam.

Maggie bent her head over the baby again, wishing desperately that he was hers, then she drew in a long, quivering breath, told herself not to be silly and handed him back with as good a smile as she could manage. 'You must bring him to visit when you come down to market. You'll want somewhere to sit and nurse him.' She was surprised to hear herself offering this, for she had not attempted to pursue the acquaintance with Rachel since she moved down to the parsonage. 'We haven't seen much of you in the last year or two.'

Rachel gave her that glowing, luminous smile which surprised everyone who saw her with her son. 'Why, that's a kind offer. I *will* need somewhere to nurse him.' Thomas had said he'd be happy to drive her down into Setherby and back in the pony cart, but she had laughed at that idea. It'd be a poor look-out if she couldn't manage to get up and down the hill on her own two feet.

On the way back to the parsonage, Maggie tried to puzzle out why she had invited Rachel to come and see her, and could find no answer except the child. As Justin had said, he was delightful, the sort of baby you couldn't help loving, the sort who seemed destined to survive infancy, unlike so many others. Mind you, Rachel had improved greatly since her marriage, and dressed better, too, Maggie thought. She would not be ashamed to be seen in Rachel's company nowadays, she decided.

And that's how she explained it to her friend Lydia, who expressed astonishment at her changed attitude to the Thorpes. But Maggie couldn't explain, even to herself, her growing obsession with young Master Adam Thorpe. She wept several times after she had seen him, longing for a son of her own, a son exactly like that. She even tried to persuade Justin to try again for a baby, just once more, but he refused, saying he did not want her death on his conscience. She didn't agree with him, sure she'd have no trouble bearing a healthy child living as they did now, with servants to help and care for her. Why could he not understand that?

Caleb now managed a stall at Setherby Market which sold farm produce from Mrs Bretherton's estate, as well as eggs and other bits and pieces from the women of Hepstone. The stall was doing well in a small way, and gave employment and cheap food to a needy widow who stood behind it for him, and who took no nonsense from anyone. Mary Shaw also helped Caleb's mother out at Black Top Farm. This employment of a poor woman had seemed to please Mrs Bretherton more than the money the stall brought in, but Caleb welcomed the extra income.

As he had expected, once Mrs Bretherton began to take an interest in her business affairs, she had discovered that Peter Barker was more than negligent; he was downright dishonest, in fact, and she had sent him packing, hiring a man recommended by Caleb instead.

Since then, Tam Barker had openly accused Caleb of cheating his brother out of a job and its tied house, and now refused to speak to him. This did not make the slightest difference to Caleb, who disliked the whole Barker family. Tam's parents had lost most of what they'd once owned through mismanagement and now had only a tiny, run-down farmlet on the edge of the moors a couple of miles away from Caleb's own Black Top Farm. Old Mrs Barker had recently died and since then Mr Barker did more ale-swilling than caring for his sheep, and looked likely to follow her before too long. The place was a disgrace to the neighbourhood.

Caleb came face to face with Rachel near the market cross one day. He gasped to see how radiant she looked, her skin glowing with health and her face lit up with happiness. He saw her glance down at the babe in her arms, then say something to the little girl skipping along beside her, and a pang shot through him. 'Good day to you, Mrs Thorpe.'

She stopped. 'And to you, Mr Hesketh.'

His eyes were drawn downwards. 'So this is your son.' The baby looked up at him with large eyes and waved one chubby fist. 'He's a fine child.'

She beamed at him, which made his heart twist in his chest. He wished the child was his, wished he had been the one to make her so happy. He wished – oh, what was the use in wishing? You took what life brought to you and that was that.

The less he had to do with this woman now, the better. In fact, the longer he stood talking to her, the more he felt out of his depth. He looked away, and caught sight of a man on the other side of the square looking across at them so malevolently that he blinked in shock. Before he could say anything, Bill Withers turned and walked away.

'I must be going,' Caleb said abruptly.

Rachel opened her mouth as if to say something, but with a bow he walked away, angry with himself for reacting to her still. He was a fool. More than a fool. He should find himself a wife and breed some sons of his own, not drool over someone else's wife and child.

But when he reached the other side of the square, he couldn't resist looking back over his shoulder. And found her staring across at him, her brow wrinkled in puzzlement. He knew he had been rude to her, but that was better than betraying how he felt.

★　　　★　　　★

Nathaniel Armstrong, too, heard of the Thorpes' lusty son and deigned to stop his horse and dismount for a word with Rachel one day. Motherhood clearly suited her, but he had heard that she was still doing her weaving, something of which he definitely did not approve. Weaving, in his opinion and in that of most other folk, was men's work, and although he had understood Rachel Thorpe's desperate need to earn money when she was living in her parents' house, she had no lack of money in her new position. Thomas Thorpe was a good breadwinner. His wife should cultivate more of the household skills instead of leaving that to the old aunt. Rachel Thorpe was a strange woman, but not too strange to make a good mother, from all accounts, and was a loving wife, too.

'The babe seems to be thriving, Mistress Thorpe.'

'Yes, he is, sir.'

'How old is he now?'

'Four months.'

'And you carry him with you to market every week? He must be heavy.'

'He's getting a bit heavy, but Ruth helps me with the baskets and, small as he is,' she smiled down at the little face, 'Adam loves to get out and about.'

'My congratulations on your fine son.' Nathaniel nodded farewell and remounted, surprised by a sudden desire for a son of his own. Justin had said the Thorpe baby was 'a grand little lad' and he was right. Nathaniel inclined his head. 'And pray give my regards to Mr Thorpe. I hear his business venture is doing well.'

'Yes, very well.' Only it was her business venture, really, and it annoyed her sometimes that no one ever gave her credit for the idea. Or for the fact that she did all the accounts and calculations. Even Thomas sometimes spoke as though it had all been his own idea.

Eh, why was she taking on like this? What did it matter whose idea it was, as long as there was good money in it for her and her family? And what did anything else really matter when you had a son like this? She planted a quick kiss on Adam's rosy cheek, then caught someone watching her and blushed. But the other woman just smiled and nodded. So Rachel smiled too, and continued on her way. It was such a lovely day.

CHAPTER NINE

In spite of Walter Smedling's sour and oft-repeated prognosti-cations about Rachel Thorpe making a bad mother, Adam Thorpe continued to thrive. He was larger than other babies of his age, cried more lustily and ate twice as much, and folk said he'd be a big man when he grew up. Rachel, lost in wonderment at the miracle of her son, was convinced he was the most handsome child ever seen.

She did not quicken again, and it was no wonder, for Thomas seemed to have lost interest in that side of marriage. She missed the loving greatly, but did not chide him. He looked so tired sometimes, his complexion sallow and greyish, and she didn't want him feeling guilty about anything. She concentrated instead on her son, this splendid male child she had created, and tried not to long for more children.

Even Thomas, who had bred and lost other sons, felt this child was somehow special. He called him 'my lad' in such a tone of pride that it brought tears to Rachel's eyes, tears she quickly blinked away, for fear of seeming soft.

She enjoyed living at North Beck Cottage, and couldn't imagine being as happy anywhere else. From her front doorstep she had sweeping views of Whin Vale and would often snatch a moment just to stand there and enjoy the land spread out around her in a patchwork of fields and walls and rocks. She loved to see the rain sweeping across the hills, to breathe deeply of the fresh moorland air, and she even enjoyed the sight of snow carpeting the tops, so that blue shadows were cast everywhere and the whole world seemed a quieter place, more at peace with itself.

Thomas got more pleasure from his trips to deliver the finished pieces and from his sleek grey donkey and lively dog than he did from the extra money they made, and he continued to leave the accounts to his wife. Every month she told him proudly how much they had earned and how much they had saved, and he would say, 'There, now!' in a tone of wonderment, but he rarely wished to spend any of it.

The man and dog were so inseparable that even Auntie Susan, who hadn't much time for animals, would say, 'That dog's a rare thinkin' creature. Bless him, how did he know our Thomas was going out? You'd swear someone had told him, the way he was standing waiting at the door.'

As the patient Sukey hauled the cart slowly along the badly-rutted valley tracks and more rapidly along the broader road that led into Rochdale, Thomas would talk to the animal in his slow, soft voice, to encourage it along. Dusty sometimes sat on the cart beside him and at other times gambolled along beside the vehicle, but he never strayed far from it and at a word from his master would sit or lie or simply stand and wait.

On the bad stretches of road, or on muddy days going uphill, Thomas would get out and walk beside the cart to ease the burden on Sukey. Sometimes he would stop to rest the patient creature and indulge in a pipeful of tobacco. He took pleasure from the ever-changing landscape and the little sights nature offered to his gaze, a nest of fledglings, the hawthorn blossom in the hedgerows in spring, the first snowdrops of the season, or just a pattern of clouds that caught the eye.

'Come on, my lass! There's a girl!' he would say when he was ready to set off again. 'It'll be downhill soon. An' you just see if I don't give you a fine nosebag of oats when we get there!' The donkey would toss her neat head at him and pull the cart with a will, encouraged by the mere sound of his voice.

Occasionally Walter Smedling and his cronies, who still bore Thomas and his wife a grudge, would appear by the road, shouting insults or even throwing stones. Thomas didn't tell Rachel about these encounters and he hoped no one else would. He worried, however, that they were getting more frequent and that ignoring them didn't seem to be doing much good. Only he didn't want to lay a complaint before Mr Armstrong, who was the local magistrate, and thus get drawn into a worse feud.

After one particularly rowdy confrontation, which Justin had witnessed and put a stop to, the parson had a word with Nathaniel.

Nathaniel summoned his land agent and asked why he had not mentioned the incidents before.

'Oh, they're nothing, sir, a bit of harmless fun.'

'It is lawless behaviour, of which I disapprove strongly. I am displeased with you, Barker, very displeased. If you cannot prevent these minor troubles, I shall find myself a land agent who can. You are to speak to this group of troublemakers and stop the harassment of a decent, hard-working man. Do you understand?'

'Yes, sir. I'll see to it, sir. I, er, hadn't realised how bad it'd got.'

But Nathaniel was not to be appeased. 'Well, you should have done.'

So Barker went to the Weaver's Arms that night and had a word with his drinking cronies. 'Come on, lads. What good does it do attacking Thorpe? Mr Armstrong says it's got to stop.'

'Thorpe has no right to run things,' Walter muttered, scowling down into his pot of ale.

'And no doubt *she* put him up to complaining to Mester Armstrong,' Bill added.

'It were Parson as complained, not Thorpe.'

'Well, *she* is a friend of the bloody parson's wife, isn't she?'

Tam sighed. 'Just stop it, lads. It's doing no good.'

'We s'll find a way to deal with her one day,' Walter muttered to Bill when their friend had gone.

'Aye, I'm with you on that.' Bill was against the whole world at the moment because Mary was having another baby and had decided she didn't want him in her bed till after it was born. She was also complaining about the amount of money he gave her, which was not nearly enough to keep them all fed properly. In fact, she did nothing but complain lately and he was sick to death of it. He had hardly enough money to buy himself a pot of ale. He'd have to find a way to get more, or what sort of a life would he be leading?

One of Rachel's treats was to walk the first mile alongside her husband when he set off for Rochdale. She strode out happily beside him in all but the worst weather, setting off early in the morning when most folk were still abed, even in the dark in winter, as long as there was enough moonlight to show her the path. At first she carried the baby with her, wrapped in a shawl, but as he grew bigger she had to leave him at home. When he started to walk, both parents would hold his chubby hands and he would totter along between them on his sturdy little legs, or sometimes they would sit him on the cart. The little donkey ambled along at a steady gait and Dusty darted here and there, chasing rabbits and other wild creatures.

These were some of the happiest times of Rachel's life.

Just beyond Lower Clough, where the lane turned off to the main Rochdale-Todmorden road, they would stop. Thomas would kiss his wife and son goodbye, and Rachel would stand waving till he was out of sight. On the way back she would talk to her son and point out things of interest to him, even when he was only a baby, as if he understood every word she said. Perhaps for that reason Adam spoke sooner than other children of his age, and developed an interest in anything and everything he could see and touch.

When they got home, Rachel would return to her weaving, while Ruth and Kitty took turns at keeping an eye on their little half-brother, on whom they both doted, being gentle, maternal girls. On days when she was too busy to take her son out for an afternoon walk, she would let the girls have turns at leaving their spinning or their other chores to take him for an outing, for Adam must get plenty of fresh air and exercise so that he would grow up strong and healthy. Rachel was no believer in coddling children. Let him develop good muscles to carry him through life, as she had.

It was a good thing her two stepdaughters had their mother's happy nature, or they might have grown jealous of their little half-brother, for although Rachel did not neglect them, she certainly did not give them half the attention she gave her son.

Rachel took Adam everywhere with her. One day, when he was just over two and walking strongly already, she was down in Setherby Bridge at the markets when she ran into Maggie Kellett, whom she had not seen for a while.

For a minute, the other woman hesitated, so Rachel would have passed by with a simple nod. Then Maggie looked at Adam, her face softened and she came forward to chat. 'I haven't seen you to talk to for a while, Rachel. How are you? Not that I need ask. You always look well nowadays.' But her eyes were on Adam, standing staring up at her with his big brown eyes, his cheeks rosy and his legs firmly braced.

Rachel thought the parson's wife looked very finely dressed for a work day in a gown with pleats flowing at the back from the shoulders, and a flounced petticoat revealed by the split in the overskirt at the front. No one could get much work done in such garments, that was sure.

'I mun get going,' Rachel said, not having the patience to stand and gossip about nothing. 'I've got work waiting for me at home.'

'Surely you can spare half an hour to take tea with me,' Maggie begged. 'Your son will enjoy a drink of milk and a piece of cake, won't he?'

'I like cake,' Adam announced and when Maggie held out one hand to him, he hesitated, gave her a thorough inspection, then put his own hand into hers. As they walked along, he reached out to finger the material of Maggie's overskirt, fascinated by its bright colours and silky gleam.

So Rachel found herself being led towards the parsonage and installed in the parlour, to sit there like a fine lady with nothing better to do. A young maid brought in the tea tray and

Maggie talked to Rachel a little but seemed more interested in playing with Adam.

'He's a fine lad,' she said, offering him a second piece of cake. 'You're a lucky woman, Rachel Thorpe.'

'You have two pretty daughters yourself.'

'But no son.'

Which made Rachel stare at her and wonder why Maggie was making such a fuss of someone else's son. It seemed strange. As soon as she decently could, she left, but remained disturbed by the incident. Maggie's attention had been all for young Adam. Why?

Over the next year, Maggie often caught Rachel at the markets and insisted on taking her home for a dish of tea. This happened so frequently it could not be chance and Rachel began to suspect that the other woman kept a watch for her from one of the upper windows of the parsonage, which looked out over the village square. Sometimes Justin would come into the parlour and sit with them, saying he must see how his godson was doing. Once Caleb Hesketh was visiting at the parsonage and Justin brought him in to take tea with the ladies as well. He stopped short at the door when he realised who the other visitors were, and it seemed to Rachel that he was not happy to see her. But after a moment, the surprise vanished from his face and it fell into its usual severe expression. He continued to stare at her quite openly, however.

She soon felt very uncomfortable and whispered to Maggie, 'Why does he stare so?'

Maggie shrugged. 'Ignore him. I'm sure he means nothing by it.' She returned to playing with Adam.

When Rachel and her son left to walk back up the hill, she saw Caleb across the market square, and clicked her tongue in exasperation, for he was staring at her again. She could still feel his eyes on her as she walked away and was so puzzled she went to stare in the mirror when she got back, worried that something was wrong with her appearance. But nothing was. It was all very strange.

★   ★   ★

When Adam was five, there came the first of his real tussles with his mother. He started wandering off on his own, returning home muddy and sometimes so late that Rachel was worried sick that he had come to harm.

'Nay, let the lad be!' Thomas would say. 'It's natural for youngsters to go off explorin'. Just you be thankful we can afford to let him enjoy hisself. Other childer mun earn what they can by that age.'

'Well, I don't want him running off an' gettin' into trouble.' And she was also somewhat worried that Walter Smedling or Bill Withers might do him harm. She wouldn't put anything past them, for they still shot her glances full of hatred when she passed them in the street, still refused to deal with her when they brought their pieces of finished cloth for Thomas to take into Rochdale.

For a time Adam continued to wander the valley, and no amount of scolding would make him stay near his home. He continued to be tall for his age, with solemn brown eyes, a nose that was losing its childish softness and promised to jut out further than average when he grew beyond childhood, and a wide mouth that rarely smiled, a proper Thorpe mouth, folk said indulgently. His mother kept his dark wavy hair cut short, for she couldn't abide to see children squinting through a tangle of hair. And even by the age of five he had developed a habit that he was never to lose, of planting his feet wide apart, putting his hands on his hips, looking people straight in the eyes and firing off a series of questions about what they were doing. The folk in the village found it amusing and would wink at each other as they answered the lad's questions, but they would tire before he did and tell him to run off and mither someone else.

The only way to stop his wanderings, Rachel decided in the end, was to keep him busy at something else. 'I shall go an' talk to the curate, Auntie,' she said abruptly one day. 'Mr Lasson takes a few lads for lessons in the mornings. Me and Thomas have taught him to count and cipher, and he's learned his letters, but I reckon he'll need to be able to read an' write better than we can. Me an' Thomas are too slow at it, though he does like to read his newssheet, my Thomas does.'

More thinking and she added, 'Nor we can't write fancy, like Parson and the land agent do. Their writing's all joined up with fancy curls to it.' She nodded her head firmly. 'I shall speak to Thomas tonight, an' then I'll go an' see Mr Lasson tomorrow.'

All Thomas said was, 'Nay, we mun think about that, my lass.'

She resigned herself to waiting several days for him to chew things over, as usual, but the next day he surprised her over breakfast. 'You're right about speaking to the curate,' he said. 'I'd like the lad to get hisself some learnin'.'

Across the table from him Adam listened, all agog. 'What do you mean?'

'I mean we're looking to send you to the curate to learn more than we can teach you, son.'

Adam frowned. 'Why?'

'Because you'll need to know a lot more than we do by the time you grow up, the way the world is changing.'

So Adam found himself excused all chores and sent off across the village each day to learn more than just his letters with the curate of Upper Clough in the house where Justin and Maggie had once lived. Nicholas Lasson, being chronically short of money to feed his growing family, was happy to teach anyone who could pay, whatever their station in life, and made no objection to young Adam joining the small group of farmers' sons studying with him in the mornings.

Fortunately for the peace of the Thorpe household, Nicholas was a born teacher, a gentle soul, who spent all the money he could spare on books and newspapers which he shared with the people around him. He believed that universal literacy would provide a solution to wars and strife, though this belief did not greatly please his patron, for Nathaniel Armstrong was against educating men above their station in life.

At first highly reluctant to sit all morning indoors, Adam was soon won over by Nicholas Lasson's love of knowledge and also by the fascination of what lay inside the books. He gradually made friends with one or two of the younger lads, but as he refused to be bullied by the older ones, he got into fights regularly. Even when the older boys won the fights, Adam would not back down or do as he was told, and in the end they stopped trying to bend him to their ways and left him more or less alone.

Rachel could not help worrying about this, for she didn't want her son to grow up like her, different from other people around him. But Mr Lasson said Adam was different, and she should just be grateful that the Lord had given her a son with such ready intelligence and interest in the world.

During that same year, Justin and Maggie began to quarrel, and the arguments always covered the same old ground.

'You could at least *ask*!' she would complain. 'You've never even tried.'

'Why should I? No one would want to give up their son. It's a foolish idea, Maggie.'

'You don't care how I feel, do you? You never have done. All you care about is your stupid parish, all those poor folk who call for your help. But when I call for your help, what do you do? You refuse me. I don't know how you can live with your conscience, indeed I don't.'

He closed his eyes and prayed again for patience. It was her age, likely. Women got strange ideas as they grew older, but none as strange as this. 'Maggie, the Thorpes love their son. Why on earth should they give him up to us?'

'Because we can offer him so much more than they can. If they loved him at all, they'd let us adopt him, bring him up as our son, educate him properly, give him all the advantages they can't. You can talk to them, show them that there are a lot of good reasons.'

'But they love him dearly and he's Rachel's only child. I wouldn't even insult her by asking.'

Maggie burst into loud sobs.

'Maybe we can find another child to adopt,' he said one

day. 'If you want a son so much, there must surely be other children in need of homes.'

She pushed him away from her. 'I don't want other children. I want Adam. And I'm sure he wants me!'

'No, Maggie.'

'But—'

'I refuse even to speak of it again.'

But she could not stop thinking about the possibility and liked to sit in her little parlour and imagine that Adam was her son.

In the year Adam turned six, Gracie Berris, a relative of Thomas's, sent word that she wished to come and visit the Thorpes. She was an older woman, a widow whose only son had left the district to go to sea, then been reported lost when his ship sank.

'What does she want?' Rachel wondered. 'She's never visited us afore.'

'Well, I suppose the lasses are her only relatives now,' Thomas said easily. 'I see her sometimes in Rochdale. We were good friends when we were childer, Gracie and me. It's only natural she'd want to see Ruth and Kitty now she has no child of her own to think about. She were very fond of Nell, too.'

Gracie turned up on the Wednesday as arranged and walked up the hill with Thomas who had gone to meet the carrier's cart. She spent a couple of hours with the family, mostly ignoring Rachel and Adam but paying a lot of attention to the two girls.

As Thomas accompanied Gracie back down to Setherby to catch the carrier's cart back, she turned to him and held his arm to stop him walking. 'I'd like to take your Ruth to live with me, lad.'

He could only blink in surprise.

'I've thought it all out. Those two lasses and you are my only relatives now and it's only fair that I leave my things to one of them when I die. My shop does well, too, selling sewing stuff and other women's things – well enough for me, any road. But it's lonely, living on my own. And what's to happen to the place when I'm gone? So I thought if I took Ruth – she's the elder, so that's the right thing to do – and trained her up, I could leave her to run the shop after I die.'

Thomas stopped to think about this for a moment. 'Eh, Gracie, I'm not sure about that. I'd miss the lass sorely.'

'Well, there'd be nothing to stop you seeing her every time you come into Rochdale, would there? And it'd be a fine chance for her.'

'I s'll have to think about it.'

Thomas wanted to say no to this offer straightaway, but Rachel disagreed and thought it a fine opportunity. She persuaded him to ask the child what she thought.

Ruth sat there for a moment, then said, 'I think I'd like it. Auntie Gracie seems nice.' She looked sideways at her father, sorry to see him frowning. 'Maybe I could go there for a visit and see how me and Auntie Gracie get on together?'

Thomas sighed. 'Well, all right, we could try it for a bit. Eh, I shall miss you, though, love.'

Ruth smiled back at them both with an expression that grew more like Nell's by the day. 'I shall miss you all, too. But I'm twelve now, an' it's time I found something to do with myself, don't you think? Besides, it's always so interesting in Rochdale.' Her father had taken her with him a few times for a treat. 'I think I might enjoy living there.'

So it was all settled.

As Rachel had feared, however, tongues wagged about her 'getting rid of' her poor stepdaughter, or alternatively about the child 'wanting to escape'. She knew to whom she owed these rumours, but she could do nothing about them save hold her head up and ignore them. And at least Ruth seemed happy with Gracie.

Nathaniel Armstrong studied his Aunt Hannah, who was looking tired and in pain. 'I think you need help managing the house, Aunt,' he said in his decided way. He had expected her to protest, but she didn't.

She stared down at her twisted hands. 'I fear you're right, Nathaniel. I can't get about the place like I ought to, to keep an eye on things.'

'I'll look for someone to help you, then.'

She nodded, resigned by now to an increasing dependence on others. 'And a wheeled chair might be useful, as well. One of the maids could push me around, I dare say.'

'All right. I'll get one made.'

Finding a suitable woman to help out was much harder than they had expected. They tried first one, then another, but did not find one who did the work to Hannah's satisfaction, for although her body might be failing, her mind was as acute as ever and she noticed more of what was going on than most people realised. And Nathaniel was horrified when one woman he had hired as companion to his aunt set her cap at him. He dismissed her out of hand.

He had begun to think seriously about marriage, but he wanted a woman with both breeding and sense, a quiet person who would not nag him as his mother nagged his father. He did not intend to rush into anything. Finding a suitable wife was too important.

Part Two

CHAPTER TEN

With a weary sigh, Thomas sank into his chair by the fire. 'By, it's clemming out there!' he exclaimed. 'Put Sukey away for me, Kitty and Adam, will you? I'm gettin' too old to enjoy drivin' out in all weathers.' He reached down to pat his dog who was already stretched out in front of the fire, then leaned back and closed his eyes.

Stunned by this outright admission of weakness from one who had always been noted for his strength and stamina, Rachel hurried to heat the poker and mull him some ale. She stood over him while he drained the pot, surreptitiously studying his face and noting the strain and the greyish hue to his skin. How long had he been looking so – so old? And why had she not done something about it sooner? She'd get him a herbal tonic from the apothecary the very next time she was in Setherby, yes, and see that he drank it, too.

Guiltily she admitted to herself that she had been too engrossed in her son and in making money. She said nothing, but vowed to keep an eye on her husband in future. It had been a hard winter, with more snow than anyone ever remembered seeing, and there had been a damp biting cold, even when the snow melted. She would get Thomas a warmer cloak for his trips into Rochdale and send him off with two hot bricks from now on.

And she had other worries. Auntie Susan was failing visibly, and Kitty was missing her sister, complaining that she hadn't been asked to go and live in Rochdale as well. Lately the girl had been making disparaging remarks about Upper Clough where, she said, nothing interesting ever happened.

Why was it that troubles never came singly? Rachel wondered. Well, sufficient unto the day is the evil thereof. She concentrated on Thomas, who was her chief worry at the moment.

For the rest of the winter he found himself wrapped in a brand-new muffler and ordered to wear a thick sheepskin shepherd's waistcoat under his cloak and over his other clothes. He was also supplied with two heated bricks for his journeys into Rochdale, as well as being given strict instructions to get them changed for hot ones for the return journey. Mulled ale would be ready the instant he returned home and Adam would go out to feed and stable the donkey without being asked. Young as he was, he could be trusted to do such things.

'You're right good to me, lass,' Thomas said quietly one day before he left, patting his wife's shoulder and kissing her cheek. 'Eh, it were a good thing we wed, weren't it? I've never regretted it for a minute and I hope you haven't neither.'

Rachel returned his compliment, heedless of the people around them. 'Neither have I, Thomas lad.'

She stood and watched him leave, not able to walk along with him as usual, for Auntie Susan seemed worse this morning, coughing and wheezing. They would all be glad when spring arrived, she told herself. A bit of sun always made you feel better. Behind her Dusty was whining because he was shut up in the house. The dog had come in lame and bleeding the previous evening and they had decided to keep him at home. He must have got into a fight with another dog, though that wasn't like him. The sore foot would make it difficult for him to travel such a long distance.

At three o'clock that afternoon, the dog suddenly started howling, long, doleful cries that made Rachel leave her weaving and come rushing down to the kitchen where Dusty stood by the door, still howling and scratching to go out.

'Nay, what's wrong with him?' exclaimed Auntie Susan

from her rocking chair near the fire. 'He were outside only half an hour ago.'

Rachel called, 'Come here, boy!' and tried to catch the dog's attention, but he would heed no one. In between his long ululations, he pawed and scrabbled at the door, pleading in every way but words to be let out.

'Shall I open the door?' asked Kitty.

'They say dogs howl like that when someone dies,' contributed Auntie Susan.

'Don't be silly!' snapped Rachel. 'An' just you get back to your spinning, Kitty! You're well behind today.'

Still the dog went on howling and Rachel could only stare at it in frozen apprehension. Something was wrong. She knew it.

'Nay, we cannot let him go on like that,' said Auntie Susan at last. She banged her walking stick on the ground. 'Quiet, boy, quiet!'

The dog redoubled his frantic scrabbling at the door, looking back over his shoulder at Rachel and whining pleadingly.

At last she moved. 'I reckon I shall have to let him out.' She looked at the new clock that took pride of place on her mantelshelf. 'I'll take him to meet our Adam from his lessons. He was going to stay late today, but he'll be done by now. Maybe a walk will settle Dusty down a bit. His foot seems a lot better now.'

She did not dare put into words her fear that the howling was indeed a portent of disaster. She did not, *would not* believe in such superstitions. Only – Thomas was late back. Her hands trembling, she took her new winter cloak from the peg behind the door and put the dog on a leash, something they rarely did.

'Keep a good fire going, Kitty!' she called as she left. 'Your dad will be chilled through in this weather. I reckon it's going to rain again.' She opened the door and let the dog, still whining and occasionally howling, pull her down the deeply-rutted track. A few people came to their doorways as she passed and asked what was wrong with Dusty, but she could only call out that she didn't know, for he would not stop.

Adam rushed out of Church Cottage. 'I saw you coming from the window. What's wrong with our Dusty, Mam?'

'I don't know, lad. He just started to howl, all of a sudden, like.' Suddenly she had to share her worries with someone. 'I – I've been wondering if your father's had an accident. They say dogs can tell.' Her voice shook.

He stared at her. 'Is that where you're going, to meet Dad?'

Taking the rope from his mother's hands, he spoke sternly to the dog, but to no avail. Dusty continued to drag them along and to howl as if he had run moon-mad. They stumbled down the rough track together, slithering over the half-frozen mud in the wheel ruts. After the first brief exchange of words, they said nothing, saving their breath to stumble along as fast as they dared in the icy conditions.

After Lower Clough, they reached the lane that led to the Todmorden-Rochdale road. Without hesitation Dusty turned right, in the direction of Rochdale, not howling now, just whining in his throat, his limp worse, though he hadn't let that slow him down.

From time to time Rachel exchanged glances with her son but neither spoke. A solid band of terror had clamped itself round her heart. *Thomas*, she kept thinking, over and over, *please, God, let my Thomas be safe*.

A mile or so along the road, Dusty suddenly tore loose from Adam's grasp and flung himself forward towards what proved to be Thomas's cart. It was canted over in the ditch by the side of the road, and the only sign of movement was the threshing legs of the donkey trapped beneath it.

With a cry, Rachel ran over to the cart. She saw a hand protruding from underneath it and called, 'Thomas! Thomas! Are you all right?' When he didn't answer, she began shoving frantically at the cart to try to move it. Together she and Adam managed to lift the vehicle and prop it up on some of the scattered packs of spun yarn.

Thomas was lying very still and quiet on the ground beneath the damaged vehicle. He had not moved, had not acknowledged their arrival in any way.

'Dad!' Adam cried out hoarsely.

Rachel could not make a sound and just fell to her knees beside her husband, reaching out to feel his temples and throat for signs of life.

It took only a minute for her to confirm the obvious and gently close the staring eyes. Thomas must have been thrown from the cart and cracked his head on a stone. His face, under the mask of dark dried blood on one side, bore a look of mild surprise, as if at the suddenness of his end. The stone lay beside him in mute testimony. One wheel of the cart was smashed beyond repair.

Sukey was miraculously unhurt except for a few grazes and cuts, but she was lying on her side tangled up in the harness and reins.

'Cut Sukey free, will you?' said Rachel in a voice thickened by tears she could not shed. She remained where she was, holding Thomas's hand.

Adam fumbled through the leather bag of small tools his father kept on the cart to find a knife and cut the harness. He jumped back as Sukey rolled round and managed to scramble to her feet, snorting and tossing her head. He stood by her for a moment, stroking her quivering neck until he judged her to have recovered enough to stand quietly on her own. When his mother didn't move, he said, 'You'll have to help me now, Mam.'

It took them a while to wedge the cart to hold it off the rest of the body, using more wool packs to prop it up. Then they pulled Thomas gently out from underneath it.

Dusty sat and whined beside the cart, a soft sad sound now.

'He's dead,' Rachel said, needing to say it aloud to believe it. 'Your father's dead. *He's dead!*'

For the first time in his life, Adam saw his mother give way to her feelings. She fell on her knees by her husband's body and burst into loud, ugly sobs as she cradled him in her arms and begged him to come back to her, not to leave her.

Instinctively the lad stood aside and left her to her grief. Tears were trickling down his own face, for he loved his father deeply. But Rachel was unaware of him, unaware of anything except that she had lost the man she loved, the man who had given her so much.

Adam kept praying for a vehicle to come past, but none did, so after a few minutes he went over and put his arms round his mother. 'Shh, Mam. Stop cryin' now. Shh.'

Gradually the dreadful racking sobs quietened, and seeing the fear in her son's eyes, Rachel tried to pull herself together.

'Shall I go for help, Mam? We'll need to get Dad home.'

When she replied, it was in a harsh, choking voice. 'Yes, lad. You go for help. I'll stay with your father.'

'It'll be dark soon, Mam. And it's freezin' over again. You can't just sit here.'

She raised her head and glared at him, saying with something of her usual spirit, 'I can and I will stay here. You get off towards Setherby and find someone to help us. I'll not leave Thomas lying here on his own!'

When she had that expression on her face, it was useless to argue with her. 'All right, Mam. I'll be as quick as I can.' And so he set off running along the road, stumbling and slipping on the icy ground. Twice he fell but hardly noticed it, up and running again almost immediately.

Left to herself, Rachel sat holding Thomas cradled in her lap. Gradually she calmed enough to look around her, wondering how the accident had happened. It was then that she saw the footprints in the soft earth by the side of the lane. And beside them, lighter, curling impressions – like – like the coils of a rope! She stared at the marks for a while, wondering who had been standing there, for not many people came down here on foot, it being the main route to the highway and little else. She turned and stared down the lane as she realised that the footprints approached from the direction of Lower Clough. She looked the other way. The mud was smooth, its half-frozen surface unbroken. No one had walked on down the lane. They had stopped just here, and even in the fading light, she could see that the same footsteps led back again towards the village.

Then her eyes fell on the piece of rock that had been lying near her husband. It was bloodstained, and she shuddered to think how hard he must have hit his head when he fell. But what had made him fall in the first place? Sukey was usually so sure-footed and placid. Nothing ever seemed to upset her. The poor creature was still standing beside the ruined cart, shivering and snorting gently from time to time, but not attempting to run away.

As Rachel turned her head this way and that, she saw on the opposite side of the lane the footprints of someone else, and some more of those faint, curling marks nearby. That meant two people had been standing here, one on either side. And they'd both had pieces of rope. She looked from one side to another, then back at the piece of rock. How she wished it had been lying somewhere else, then her Thomas might still be alive!

It was at that moment the pieces of the puzzle fell into place, for it was the only piece of rock to be seen just there, a pale lump of limestone, darkened in one corner by Thomas's blood. There was a drystone wall along each side of the lane, of course, but it was old, the stones greyed and weathered. And – her eyes traced slowly along the uneven lines of rock – it was in good repair, with no gaps. The single rock on the ground was lighter in colour, much lighter; it could not have fallen out of the wall.

She drew in one long, shuddering breath after another as the realisation spread through her. 'Someone set upon him!' Her words hung in the air in front of her mouth on a cloud of frosty breath as she wailed, '*No-o-o! Oh, no!*' But when she looked again from one sign to another, she could not deny the evidence. The curling marks were clearly made by ropes. Someone must have used them to stop the cart. Maybe they'd pulled it tight to make Sukey stumble and fall. And the rock – someone must have thrown it at Thomas and hit him on the side of the head. She looked down at his dear face and sobbed aloud. They must have thrown it very hard. Why? Who had he ever harmed?

She was weeping again, but she knew – knew with utter certainty – that it could only have happened that way.

She didn't need to think about it for long to realise there was only one set of people who might wish Thomas ill – no, who wished *her* ill and who might have attacked him to get at her.

It was dark by the time Adam returned with a group of men. Rachel hadn't moved, but neither had she resumed her wild sobbing. Her face seemed to have taken on new and deep lines of sorrow.

'Eh,' one man told his wife later, 'she looked years older, Rachel Thorpe did, all gaunt and hollow-cheeked like when she were younger. You couldn't help feeling for her. She thought the world of Thomas, an' so did I. He were a grand fellow.'

The men Adam had brought from the village gathered round to assess the damage, speaking in hushed voices. Rachel took not the slightest notice of them until two came to lift Thomas's body on to the gate they'd brought with them.

'Careful!' she said harshly as they took the weight off her. 'Don't bang him about!'

'Fair gave me the creeps, she did,' one of them whispered to another as they walked back to the village behind the gate and its still burden. 'She spoke just as if he could still feel it.'

Some of the men worked together on the Thorpes' cart – they had borrowed a spare wheel from the blacksmith. By the light of two lanterns, they fitted it in place, then went to pick up the scattered packets of wool and yarn that had been thrown all over the ground by the impact of the crash. They were sorry about Thomas Thorpe, but their livelihood depended upon these packets.

When they set off back to the village, Adam walked by his mother's side, touching her when she stumbled, for her eyes were fixed more often on her husband's body than on the ground underfoot. After a while she sighed and put one hand on her son's shoulder. 'I cannot seem to walk straight,' she muttered once, and later, inconsequentially, 'I mun see he rests easy.'

It took them over an hour to get Thomas home again. The men stopped in Lower Clough to get more lanterns and spread news of what had happened, and a couple of lads trailed along behind the little procession, anxious to miss nothing. The men were kind in their rough way, but Rachel had withdrawn into herself and wanted none of their sympathy.

'I thank you all for your help,' she said in a tight, harsh voice as they carried the body into the house and laid it in the small, little-used parlour as she directed. 'We can manage now.' Her voice was calm, her face expressionless. Only her hand betrayed any feeling, gripping Adam's shoulder so tightly he found a bruise there the following day.

'Looked like a corpse herself, she did,' one man told his wife.

'I asked her if she wanted help layin' him out,' said another to a friend. '"My wife'd be glad to help," I said. "None better. Does a lovely job of laying out." But she just looked through me an' said no, thank you, she would do it herself, but I could send word to Mordrew Bates in the morning, if I would, to bring up a coffin. Looked like a wild woman, she did, her eyes were that strange.'

'She's got her son to comfort her, at least. He's a sensible lad, that Adam,' said a third, draining a welcome pot of mulled ale in the Weaver's Arms. 'Wise beyond his years.'

'Aye,' agreed the first man, holding chilled hands out to the blazing fire. 'I never did see a lad of his age so well-growed. He'll be the tallest man in these parts one day, I reckon.'

'Favours his mother. Eh, I mind when Rachel were a gawky young lass herself. Taller nor most of us lads, she were. Still is.'

'The lad takes after his father's side as well, though. They're built sturdy, the Thorpes. You can see already that he'll be a well-set chap one day.' He stared into his empty pot. 'Well, I don't know about you, but I could do with another sup of ale. It's thirsty work bringing a body back.'

They spent an hour or so in comfortable reminiscences about Thomas Thorpe, for they had all grown up together and knew each other's strengths and weaknesses, not to mention all the skeletons in each family's closet. That, of course, led them into consideration of their own futures.

'Well,' one said thoughtfully a little later, 'he were a good man, a good putter-out, too. Dealt fair with us all. They aren't all so honest, I can tell you. What'll us do now with our woven pieces? Shall us have to start traipsing into Rochdale again?'

This aspect of the accident had not struck any of the others yet, and it furnished a subject for discussion and heated argument. Some thought Parson should be consulted about what to do. Others reminded everyone that Mr Armstrong's agent would also have to be consulted, because if they found themselves a new putter-out, he would need to move into North Beck Cottage, which was the only place with an out-house to store the packs of yarn and the bundles of finished cloth, not to mention having stabling for a donkey.

Life had to go on, after all, and they'd no mind to start those long walks again, like in the old days. And anyway, what would Rachel Thorpe need with such a big house now that she'd lost her man? She'd want to move out, no doubt about that, and find somewhere cheaper to rent.

In the back room of the inn, Walter Smedling was very quiet.

'Aw, pluck up, lad!' Bill said quietly at one stage, after glancing round to make sure no one was close enough to overhear. 'It were an accident.'

Walter shook his head. 'No, it weren't. You did it a-purpose. You didn't need to have brought along that stone, Bill Withers. We had the rope to stop him and were just going to tell him to leave the putting-out to someone else from now on. We could all see he were getting old. Only fair for someone younger an' fitter to take over. Better for him, too. We were only meant to *talk* to him, not kill him.' His voice had risen and people were looking at him.

'Shut up, you fool!' Bill hissed, grasping his arm and giving it a little shake. 'Shut *up*, will you!'

Walter gave a long, shuddering sigh, took a slurp of ale,

then continued in a lower voice, 'But oh no, you had to take a bloody great piece of rock along with you an' chuck it at him hard, didn't you?'

'I've telled you an' telled you, it were an accident, that. It were just to frighten him, like. I didn't mean to hit him.' Well, not hard enough to kill him, anyway, Bill acknowledged silently.

But once he got hold of an idea, Walter was slow to let it drop. 'Well, if they hang us, it'll be your fault an' so I'll tell 'em. It were all your doing, that rock were.'

Bill grunted in annoyance, then growled in a low, angry voice, 'They won't hang us, because no one will know about it if you will just keep your soddin' – mouth – shut.'

'They'll find the rock an' see the blood on it. Someone might figure out it were chucked at him.'

They stared at one another, then Bill said slowly, 'They won't figure any such thing, 'cos they won't find nothing. Eh, I should have picked up that rock again, got rid of it.' But he'd been terrified by what he'd done and had only been able to think of coiling up the rope and running away. Besides, the rock had been underneath Thomas's battered face and he hadn't wanted to touch the man, hadn't been able to.

Walter nodded and stood up. 'Reckon we'd both better see to that.' He saw that people were still looking sideways at him and said loudly, for effect, 'Poor old Thorpe. He were no friend of mine, but I'm sorry for him nevertheless. Yes, sorry for him.'

A man at the next table nodded. 'It's a sad way to end, isn't it? All alone like that. What'll become of his wife now, eh?'

Bill muttered something, but as they walked out, he nudged Walter and said, 'With a bit of luck, we shall get rid of *her* now.'

Walter stopped in surprise at the expression on Bill's face. 'I'm not doin' owt else like that, think on.'

'We won't have to *do* anything. She'll have to earn her own bread now, won't she, an' if we speak to Tam, we might be able to make it a bit hard for her to do that in Whin Vale. Then she'll go somewhere else an' we'll be shut of her.' In the darkness, he smiled. He'd waited a long time to pay her back, and now his time had come. Really, it was a good thing Thorpe had died, a very good thing. He'd make sure he profited from it.

That night, after everyone else had gone to bed, Rachel sat by the fire, thinking about what had happened. Her husband lay on the table in the small parlour, and although she'd been to sit with him, she'd been unable to settle.

'It were murder,' she muttered and looked at the clock. 'An' something ought to be done about it.' Another silence, then she decided that since the gentry didn't go to bed till later, she would go and tell Mr Armstrong about her suspicions. He was the magistrate. He would do something. She went upstairs to get her cloak, then quietly let herself out of the house.

Alone in the darkness of a moonless night, she strode down the hill, knowing the path well enough to find her way without a lantern. The cold clamped itself round her like a vice. She tucked her hands under her cloak, shivering from time to time, but didn't slow her pace or even think of going back.

Within the hour she was approaching Cleving Park. The gates were shut fast, so she rattled them and then went to bang on the front windows of the gatekeeper's cottage. When Jimmy Buckley came to the little side gate in his nightshirt, gaping to see a woman out alone at this hour, she said, 'I have to see Mr Armstrong.'

He raised his flickering candle, about to give her the sharp end of his tongue, then realised who she was. 'It's Mrs Thorpe, isn't it?'

She nodded, impatient to get to the big house.

His voice became gentler in respect for her loss, for the news had spread rapidly among the servants at Cleving Park. 'Eh, love, Mester Armstrong will be in bed now. You'll have to come back in the morning.'

'No. No, I have to see him tonight. It's too important to leave.'

'I can't let you in at this hour, lass.'

For a moment she stood there, then she simply pushed him out of the way and set off down the driveway.

He called after her, then cursed and ran back into the house. 'Rachel Thorpe says she's going to see Mr Armstrong right now,' he told his startled wife. He snatched up his breeches and dragged them on, fumbling around for his shoes.

'At this hour? Has she run mad?' His wife sat bolt upright in bed. 'Eh, poor woman. It's turned her brain.'

But she was talking to empty air, for Jimmy had grabbed his cloak and run out of the house, trying vainly to catch up with Rachel.

He found her hammering on the front door of a darkened house. She continued to bang insistently, waiting only a few seconds, then banging again. A light rain had started to fall and Jimmy's teeth were chattering, but she seemed heedless of that, for the hood of her cloak was hanging down and the cloak itself was flung back over her shoulders.

A faint light appeared and wavered its way along the first floor of the house, but only when she saw the hall illuminated from within did Rachel stop thumping on the door.

Bolts were crashed back and the door flung open. 'What is going on here?' demanded Nathaniel Armstrong, peering out. 'Who is knocking at this hour?' He was wearing a banyan and nightcap over his shirt and breeches, and had been about to go to bed.

'I need to see you, sir,' Rachel said. 'Now. It's very important.'

He goggled at her wild appearance.

''Tis Mrs Thorpe,' the gatekeeper said. 'She just pushed past me at the gate, sir.'

'Ah.' Nathaniel knew the woman's husband had died that day, but he could not imagine why she was here at this hour. 'I'm sorry to hear about your husband's accident, madam.'

'It was no accident, sir. It was murder. That's why I've come to see you.'

There was silence, then Nathaniel held the door open.

'Come inside and tell me why you say this.' She must be crazed by grief.

Inside, he indicated a chair in the hallway and took a seat next to her, whispering to the gatekeeper, 'Go and rouse the coachman. Tell him to harness a trap to take Mrs Thorpe home afterwards.' Then he turned his attention to his visitor. 'Tell me why you think your husband was murdered.'

She explained all she had seen while she was waiting with Thomas's body, words falling over one another in her rush to make him understand. From time to time she brushed the tears impatiently from her eyes, but although her voice faltered sometimes, she did not stop until she'd told her tale. Then she sat with a burning gaze fixed upon him.

'What do you expect me to do about this, Mrs Thorpe?'

'Send men to check that what I said is true.'

'At this hour?'

''Tis coming on to rain. The marks will all be washed away by morning.'

He looked towards the window and shivered. 'We'll go at first light. We'd not see enough at this hour to prove anything.'

'If you took lanterns—'

'Mrs Thorpe, I realise you're upset, and your husband will be a sad loss to this community, but you mustn't let your distress make you see trouble where there is none.'

'You – won't go?'

'I will. I'll go in person, but not until first light.'

She sagged back in her chair. 'It'll be too late by then. The marks will be washed away.'

'The stone will still be there. We shall be able to tell if it's been carried there from somewhere else, as you seem to think.'

The room seemed to turn black for a moment, then she took a deep, sobbing breath. 'They murdered him,' she said brokenly. 'They murdered my Thomas.'

By the time the gig drew up in front of the house, she had realised it was useless to press for more action. And Mr

Armstrong was right. The stone would still be there. She would go to the place herself first thing, even before it was light, to make sure no one tried to remove it.

He tried to persuade her to ride home in the gig, but she shook her head. 'Nay, I cannot sleep tonight, sir. I may as well walk.'

As the three men stood and watched her figure disappear into the darkness, cloak flapping behind her, the gatekeeper said, 'She's allus been a strange one, sir.'

And those words stayed with Nathaniel as he made his way upstairs, took off his clothes and put on his nightshirt, before huddling down beneath thick woollen blankets on a soft feather mattress. She was indeed a strange woman. And what her future would be now that she was widowed, he couldn't think. She would be unlikely to marry again, for folk did not speak kindly of her. Indeed, his own land agent was always very scornful when he mentioned her name, though the parson spoke well of her.

Nathaniel frowned. Obviously she could not stay on at North Beck Cottage, not a woman on her own. She would not be able to afford the rent, and anyway she would not need such a large house.

He said a short prayer for Thomas Thorpe's soul, then turned over in bed and tried to get comfortable. But his thoughts still lingered on the man's sudden death. Life was very hard at times. You knew not your hour.

CHAPTER ELEVEN

The following morning Adam woke before it was light and decided to get the fire burning to warm the house up. His Auntie Susan had been coughing in the night and she sounded worse.

To his surprise, he found his mother downstairs, fully dressed and asleep in the rocking chair in front of the fire. The embers were still glowing, so he put some wood on quietly and went out to draw water from the well. But the sound of the door opening and the chill air on her cheek woke Rachel. She started and stared around the dark room, muttering, 'Is it morning, then?'

Adam came back. 'It's just getting light, Mam. I was—'

'I mun go, then.'

'Where to?'

She grabbed her cloak and pushed past him without answering, and went rushing down the hill as if pursued by a mad bull.

When Auntie Susan made her slow and painful way downstairs, wheezing and coughing, she found a blazing fire and a worried child sitting next to it. She sank on to a chair and held her hands out to the blaze. 'Eh, it's sad not to see Thomas here, it is that. What shall we do without him?'

Adam's eyes were blind with tears for his father, so that the bright colours of the flames all ran together. 'I don't know.'

As his voice broke on the last word, she took him into her arms and held him close, trying to explain gently that people died every day, and the ones left behind just had to get on with living. She wondered where his mother had gone. Some women went strange for a time with the grief, but surely not their Rachel.

The world seemed unreal as Rachel strode down the hill. It was still dark, though there was a greyness growing in the sky to the east. An iron chill sat on the land, binding the valley into a hushed silence. It had rained heavily during the night, but now it had stopped and her progress was marked by the faint chinking sound of ice-rimmed pools under her feet and a sodden thumping noise as she walked on more solid ground. She didn't see another soul moving out of doors until just past Lower Clough. There she came upon Mr Armstrong and his groom, both trotting along on horseback heading towards the lane where the accident had occurred. The groom was yawning widely, but Mr Armstrong seemed his usual alert self.

Nathaniel caught sight of her and slowed down. 'Good morning, Mrs Thorpe. As you see, I am going to inspect the place where your husband was killed.' After a restless night, he had decided he must do this as early as possible, to set her mind at rest. He doubted anyone really had set upon Thomas Thorpe, not in Whin Vale. It wasn't a lawless place, his valley.

'Thank you, sir.' She hurried along behind the horses, not wanting to hold him back. In the increasing light, she saw how the night's rain had washed away any traces of footprints from the sides of the lane, and her heart sank. By the time they got to the place where Thomas had been killed, she was already sure there would be little left to see there except for the chunk of stone.

'Stop, sir!' she called. 'It was here it happened. A few paces ahead. See, there are some pieces of the wheel lying in the ditch.'

Nathaniel got down from his horse, handed the reins to his groom and surveyed the ground. 'I'm afraid the rain has been rather heavy. As we feared, there are no foot-prints left.'

'There was a rock, though, a big chunk of light-coloured

rock.' She turned from side to side, but could not see it. 'It was over there.' She pointed with one finger.

Nathaniel exchanged glances with the groom. 'I see nothing.'

She moved forward, searching desperately everywhere. 'It's gone! They must have come and took it away! See there's a little hollow where it lay.' She stood frozen as she realised this meant the culprits might get away with their dreadful crime.

Nathaniel came to stand beside her. He patted her on the shoulder and said gently, 'I think you refine too much upon the circumstances, Mrs Thorpe. It was an accident – a dreadful accident for you – but no one *murdered* your husband, believe me.'

As she looked at him, the wildness left her face, leaving both bitterness and determination. 'It happened exactly as I told you, sir, and I shall not say otherwise. But I can see I have no way of proving it, so I'm sorry to have got you from your bed so early.'

'Wait! I wish to—' But she had gone again, striding off into the misty chill of that grey morning.

'She'll be upset, like,' the groom said. 'She was very fond of her husband, sir. Though she was always, well, a bit headstrong.'

'Yes.' For a moment longer Nathaniel stood there, staring down, and there was a small hollow – as well as the faintest of imprints around it which might or might not have been the last traces of footprints. And he remembered that a few years previously he had had to send Tam Barker to stop people from throwing rocks at Thomas Thorpe. Had it happened again? There was no way of finding out. But he would bear it in mind. He mounted his horse. 'We'll say nothing of this to anyone, I think, Timothy. Kindly see the gatekeeper and tell him to keep quiet too.'

It was sad to see the woman so overset and haggard, for only a week ago he had noticed her at market and thought how handsome and vigorous she looked. It was sad about Thomas Thorpe, too; he had clearly been well loved by his family. Well, since she would have no husband to protect her now, he would make it his business to arrange something for her, some way of earning a living. It was his Christian duty.

What would be best, though? She claimed to be a weaver but had always worked under the supervision of a father or husband. Now that she was on her own, she would no doubt find the whole process of turning the woollen thread into finely woven cloth too much to organise. He would have to think about that, consult his aunt, perhaps. Between them, they would work something out.

At the parsonage that day, Maggie also woke early, smiling in the darkness as she remembered that Thomas Thorpe had been killed the day before. Oh, she was sorry for the poor man, of course she was. And for his family. Naturally. But this meant – she took in a breath of deep satisfaction on the thought – it meant she would get the boy. Rachel would be glad to have him provided for now, and Justin would not be able to say it was an unreasonable request to adopt him, either. She was simply being charitable, helping her neighbour, taking in an orphan.

And Adam – she would let him keep that name, because it suited him, though he would of course change his family name to Kellett now – Adam would come and live here. She pictured him in her mind, so rosy-faced and sturdy – and intelligent, too. She would start getting a bedchamber ready for him this very morning, begin making her plans. Clothes – he would have to have new clothes, something more suited to his new station in life. And books. Everything should be fitting for the son of a parson who held a rich living. And of course the boy must learn to speak properly, with a more genteel accent.

She wouldn't say anything of this to Justin today, though. Best to wait until after the funeral. That would be more seemly. She might not have borne him, but she would *make* him her son, make him love her. That woman didn't deserve a boy like that.

Rachel had intended to go down to see the parson about the funeral, because the Thorpes were always buried in Setherby churchyard, not in the newer church in Upper Clough, but by the time she had walked up the hill again, she was feeling bone weary after her disturbed and almost sleepless night, so she went to lie down on her bed 'just for an hour'.

She woke to the sound of voices and hurriedly straightened her clothing before going downstairs to see who had called.

Justin turned to greet her, startled at how drawn and tired she looked. 'My dear Rachel, I was so sad to hear of your loss.'

'Yes.' She swallowed hard, not wanting to weep in front of him or anyone else.

'How are you feeling?' Nathaniel had already sent him a note, informing him of the sad, confused state of the widow's mind and her conviction that her husband had been murdered.

She shrugged. What did it matter how she was feeling? Without Thomas, there was little that really mattered, only – her eyes sought her son – only Adam, the tangible proof of Thomas's love for her, and hers for him.

'Shall we go and pray over the body?'

She inclined her head and led the way into the front parlour, stopping beside the sofa to look down at the still white face so unlike her ruddy, vigorous Thomas.

Justin was surprised. 'Have you got no coffin yet?'

'No. I've been trying to get some justice first.' But she frowned. Why had Mordrew Bates not brought up a coffin? She had sent word to him yesterday, and he was not usually remiss.

He said gently, 'Mr Armstrong told me what you said – accused folk of. You're letting your imagination run away with you, Rachel, my dear. No one murdered your husband. It was just an accident, a very sad accident.'

She gave a scornful snort. 'No doubt folk will say so. They're always ready to call me a liar. But I know what I saw, and one day I'll prove it.'

'Rachel—'

'We have to decide about the funeral,' she said, cutting him off. 'And perhaps when you go down the hill, you'll see Mordrew for me and ask what's keeping that coffin.'

She began to talk so sensibly that Justin was relieved. He did not yet ask her what she intended to do with herself and her family. He would not do that until after the funeral. Their landowner was a kindly man and would not throw her out of the house. Besides, she and Thomas must have some savings put by. They were affluent working folk, not paupers, and with her weaving, Rachel would not need much help once she had moved into a smaller house.

He called in to see Mordrew Bates. 'Why have you not sent a coffin up to Mrs Thorpe?'

Mordrew, a skilled carpenter and a cabinet maker, was in his workshop. 'I got word she didn't need one.'

'Who told you that?' asked Justin, puzzled.

'It was a lad. I didn't see his face. He just stood in the doorway an' called out.' Mordrew grinned. 'Some of 'em don't like to come in here among the coffins. Think it's bad luck.'

'But she's waiting for you to send one.'

'She must have changed her mind, then. They told me the accident had turned her brain.' He laid down his saw. 'I'll go and get out the coffin I had in mind and take it up the hill, then. I have one just the right size for a man like Thomas.'

'She seemed in full possession of her senses when I saw her this morning.'

Mordrew shrugged. 'Well, I'm glad she's all right. Hoy, Phil lad, go and harness up Smokey.' Whistling, he began to move some pieces of wood to get at the coffin he had in mind, for he had a stock of them ready made. There was always a demand, especially for smaller ones.

Justin frowned as he walked across to the parsonage. He could not understand who would have sent such a message and he was sure it had not been Rachel.

Maggie was waiting for him at home, eager to hear all the details.

He gave her only the bare facts, finishing, 'And I hope you'll be present at the funeral tomorrow morning, my dear.'

'Well, of course I shall be there. I shall wear my black merino, I think. It's still too cold for silk.'

'Is this the time to discuss clothes, Maggie?'

She bit back a sharp rejoinder. She must not antagonise him. 'Poor Rachel. We must do everything we can to lighten her burden from now on, must we not?'

He was pleased at her concern, though mildly puzzled at how happy she looked when only yesterday she had been complaining yet again that he neglected her, never spent time with her.

That evening, the talk in the alehouse turned once again to the need for a new putter-out.

'I reckon Walter Smedling could do it,' Bill said – he had deliberately chosen to drink in the front room that evening.

His companions looked through the doorway into the back room where Walter and Tam Barker were speaking earnestly, with pots of ale stilled halfway to their lips.

'Dost think so?' asked one doubtfully.

'Why not?' Bill replied. 'He knows his weaving, Walter does. None better.'

'Yes, I'll grant you that, but how is he going to afford to buy the cart off Mrs Thorpe and rent North Beck Cottage? He's never been one to save his pennies. And if he starts doing the job, then goes back to his boozing ways, he'll be no use to us.'

Bill tried to speak casually. 'I thought I might go in with him, to help out. An' I'll see he doesn't drink too much. I've a bit of brass saved up an' so has he. This is a good chance for us to better oursen. We don't want someone from outside doing it, do we? Us men from Whin Vale should stick together on this.'

More head-shaking, muttering and sideways glances, but no one suggested an alternative or contradicted him. He could be a mean bugger, Bill Withers. But he was sharp, too, so maybe it'd be better to have him working for them.

When men started talking of seeking their beds, Walter and Bill left the alehouse separately, but met outside.

'Well, how did they take it?' Walter asked.

'They looked thoughtful like. Give 'em time. We need to let the idea sink in afore we do owt.' Bill grinned, teeth gleaming in the moonlight.

'Yes, but are you absolutely sure about the money?'

'Aye. O' course I am. I know where Thomas kept it, too. I spied him through the window once, pulling up the floorboards and putting some coins in a box. It looked nice an' heavy.'

'And you're sure no one has noticed anything about last night?'

'No, course not. I took that old rock away and chucked it back where I got it from. I couldn't find it again if I wanted to, let alone anyone else finding it.' He clapped Walter on the shoulder. 'Now, you stop worriting, lad, an' get yoursen off to bed. You'll need to have your wits about you tomorrow.' He chuckled. 'Mind, you'll have to work harder from now on. No more boozy nights, or they won't trust you.'

'Aye. I suppose so.' Walter scowled into the darkness. 'Is it worth it? I mean, I make enough for my needs now.'

'It bloody is worth it. Besides, there's no one else steppin' forward to do the job, is there?' He chuckled and thumped one fist into the other, then smacked his hand again for emphasis. 'And there won't be.'

Walter winced and turned to make his way home.

Bill pulled him back. 'Just make sure that wife of yours doesn't say owt.'

'Oh, she's the least of my worries. She's that keen to move to North Beck Cottage, she'd swear the moon fell into the water butt if I told her to, she would.'

Without another word, Bill swung off into the darkness, exultation singing through him. Ha! Rachel Thorpe would soon find out who was the clever one now. And she'd find life a lot harder from now on, by hell she would. He and Tam would make sure of that.

His smile faded as he reached his house and found Mary asleep already, with the baby grizzling in its cot. Damned childer! They dragged a man down, allus needing food or clothes. That's what made you old – childer. Unless you had a bit of money behind you, that was. He kicked his wife awake and said curtly, 'See to that noisy brat, you! A man needs his sleep.'

'Oh, and I suppose a woman doesn't?'

And they were off quarrelling again. When he raised his hand to her, she thumped it aside with a fist just as large as his. She had grown stout now. And to think how trim she'd been when he wed her! Eh, all women were cheats.

As he turned his back to her and settled to sleep, a grin curved his lips briefly. It only remained to get *her* out of the valley, then there'd be nowt to hold him back. He was going to make money, a lot of money, before he was through.

The next day, the funeral took place in Setherby. It was well attended. Those of Thomas's friends still living were present to a man. Gracie Berris came from Todmorden on the carrier's cart with Ruth, who had hardly stopped weeping since she'd heard about her father's death.

In spite of being ill, Auntie Susan insisted on attending the funeral, so Rachel hired a gig from the livery stables in Setherby to take her and the old lady down the hill and bring them back up again afterwards. They could afford it, after all.

She sent the children off early to walk down to the church, and when Adam pestered to take Dusty with them, she agreed. 'Only take a rope to tie him up during the service. He can't come inside the church, you know.' But Thomas would have liked the dog to be there, she was sure. She waited in grim silence for Mordrew's cart which would carry the coffin down the hill, a great creaking vehicle used to carry all sorts of things. Only the poorer folk carried their own dead to the church in Whin Vale.

'You might have cleaned that cart out properly!' Rachel snapped at the men when they arrived, and went to get her broom and a blanket for the coffin to lie on. Only when she was satisfied that the cart was clean did she allow the waiting group of his friends to carry Thomas out.

As she and Auntie Susan rode slowly down the hill, folk came to their doors and bowed their heads in respect. Rachel stared straight ahead, concentrating on not weeping, because if once she started, she did not know how she would stop.

The previous night, she had gone to sit beside the coffin for a while and whisper her own farewell to Thomas, laying her hand on the shiny wood and letting a few tears fall on him in the darkness where no one could see her weakness. Now, she would just endure all the fuss that had to be got through. Nothing anyone said or did could make up for the fact that she had lost not only her man, but her only real friend, too.

Outside the church she helped Auntie Susan down from the gig, worried at how white the old woman was, and how racking the cough that bent her double for a few moments. All three of Thomas's children were standing at the gate, waiting.

'Aunt Gracie is inside,' Ruth whispered, giving Rachel a quick hug. 'She said the cold air was getting to her chest.'

Rachel pulled the girl back and held her close for a moment, a gesture so unlike her that Ruth stared up at her stepmother in astonishment.

Slowly, matching their pace to Auntie Susan's, the small group made their way across to the church porch, where the parson was waiting for them. Maggie Kellett was there too, very elegant in black, and wearing a milkmaid hat freshly trimmed with black ribbons.

'Eh, our Thomas were well loved,' Auntie Susan whispered. 'He were that. Look at all these folk come to see him off.'

Adam walked behind his mother and when Maggie tried to get him to stay with her, he shook her hand off. 'I mun be near my mam,' he said loudly.

Maggie frowned as she waited to walk inside the church behind the family, and looked scornfully at Thomas's two daughters who were clinging to one another. They sobbed throughout the ceremony.

The widow did not sob. She stood and sat as required, looking fierce and angry. But she clasped Adam's hand now and then and was glad of its warmth. She hardly heard what the parson said. Her grief was so sharp it seemed to fill every inch of her and she was longing for the service to end. What good did it do, all these people coming to gape? She hated to be a public spectacle, absolutely hated it.

When she got back home, she would have to carry on, look after Thomas's children, make some sort of life for herself. And she *would* do it! She would do whatever was necessary to give her son a good start. And Thomas's daughters, of course. Though Ruth seemed settled now with Gracie. But things would never be the same for her, and she could not see herself ever being truly happy again.

When the ceremony came to an end, she was so lost in her thoughts that Auntie Susan had to prod her to leave the pew and follow the coffin out to the grave that had been dug in the hard ground.

Rachel scattered earth into the hole, hating to think of her Thomas shut away down there. She put one hand on Adam's shoulder and the other on Kitty's and the simple warmth of their young bodies was the best comfort.

As they were all leaving the grave, Gracie pulled Rachel aside, away from the group of silent children. 'Ill look after the older lass, Rachel. You've no need to worry about Ruth. I've already made a will, leaving her the shop. She's a good little worker, so she'll be fixed for life.'

'That's kind of you, Gracie.'

'But I can't offer to have the other lass, I'm afraid. My place is too small. The shop makes enough to feed me an' Ruthie, but it'd be hard to stretch it to another.'

'There's no need to worry about Kitty. I shall still have my weaving. I can support us all.'

'Who'll be doing the putting-out now?' Gracie asked.

Rachel could only stare at her, amazed that she had not thought about that.

'Don't you know yet?'

She shrugged. 'No.' She could do it, she knew that. In fact, now she came to think of it, it'd be good to keep the business for Adam when he grew older. Then she remembered how Walter and his cronies had refused to deal with her, even when Thomas was alive, and sighed. Would they let her even try? Would Mr Harrison in Rochdale agree to deal with a woman? She doubted it. And if she stood here any longer in this cold wind, she'd be catching a cough herself, then who would look after Auntie Susan and the children?

When they got back to North Beck Cottage, Rachel jumped down from the gig without anyone's help. She took out the heavy key from the pocket hanging on its tapes under her skirt.

The driver of the gig, in a hurry to get out of the cold wind and having already been paid, tipped his hat to them and clicked to his horse, which trotted off down towards the valley.

Adam, who had run ahead of them up the path, stopped in shock and called, 'Mam! Someone's broken the door. *Mam, come quick!*'

For a moment Rachel could not move, then Kitty began to weep and the old lady to cough, so she shooed them all inside, past the broken door. She cast a quick glance around to make sure nothing had been touched in the kitchen and then settled Auntie Susan in front of the fire. 'Swing that kettle over the flames, Kitty, and me and Adam will have a good look round.'

Adam rushed to open the door of the front parlour and cried out in shock. Rachel went to stand beside him in the doorway, staring into the room that had been left immaculate when they carried Thomas out.

The rag rug had been thrown into a corner and the furniture shoved back anyhow. Holes gaped in the floor where the boards had been prised up and someone had swept the ornaments off the mantelpiece, so that the floor was covered with pieces of broken pottery from her best dishes and the few things she had had left from her mother.

'No! Oh, no!' She didn't even realise that she had cried out, for the faint wailing sound seemed to come from a long way away.

The thieves must have known where to look, though they'd

damaged several boards as they levered them up. How had they known about the tin box with nearly all their savings in it? Rachel had never liked leaving all the money in one spot, but Thomas had just laughed at her indulgently and said he reckoned it'd be quite safe to leave the pot on the mantelpiece in Upper Clough, because none of his neighbours would ever rob him.

Rachel fell to her knees beside the gaping empty hole, pain slicing through her. Nearly a hundred guineas gone. All their savings, all their years of hard work. The nest egg that had been meant to give Adam a good start in life. Who could have done this?

'Walter Smedling.' She'd spoken the words before she knew it, then she clapped a hand over her mouth to stop herself from screaming them again and again. For a moment she could not move, just kneel there, trying to think what to do.

Adam stood beside her, not knowing what to say or do, only knowing that his mam was upset, that someone had stolen their money.

So quiet was it that they could hear the quavering old voice from the kitchen quite clearly. 'Our Rachel? Is everything all right, love?'

Rachel pushed herself to her feet and went into the kitchen. 'Someone's broken into the house, Auntie. They've taken all our money, everything we had saved.' Well, not quite everything, because she'd always kept a few coins hidden elsewhere. But that was nothing compared to what they'd lost.

Auntie Susan's face wrinkled up and tears filled her eyes. 'Eh, no! No! Who could have done that?'

Kitty began to weep, Adam stood beside his mother, scowling, and Auntie Susan sobbed into her handkerchief, in between coughing.

In the end Rachel said numbly, 'I mun go down and see the village constable in Setherby. And – and maybe the parson, too.' She turned to the children. 'Look after your auntie, and don't let anyone in while I'm away. Slide the bolts inside the door.'

It was Adam who said, 'All right, Mam.'

At the front door, she turned to add, 'And don't touch owt in the front room. Leave it like we found it.'

Then she set off to walk down the hill again, not noticing who she passed or who tried to speak to her. But they noticed her and wondered where she was off to now, murmured to one another that she looked strange, wild even.

'It's turned her brain,' they said. Everyone was saying that.

Rachel plodded on, her thoughts going round and round inside her head like angry bees. It couldn't have been Walter Smedling, surely. He hated her, but he wasn't a thief. It'd be men on the tramp who'd broken into her house. You got them passing through every now and then. Men who cared for nothing and nobody. They'd never catch them.

But it was Walter Smedling's image she kept seeing in her mind. And Bill Withers, too. It had taken two men to strike down her Thomas. What more likely than that the same two men had stolen her money?

As she reached the outskirts of Setherby it suddenly occurred to her to wonder why passing thieves would have broken her ornaments. Surely they'd have taken them to sell or else ignored them. But Walter would have recognised some of the ornaments, the ones which had belonged to her mother, anyway. She could just picture him sweeping them off the mantelpiece in a rage. It was exactly the kind of thing he'd do.

She wanted to throw herself on the ground and wail like a child, but instead she kept setting one foot in front of the other, forcing herself to go on. She'd lost everything now, not just Thomas, but all her money. Without that, how was she going to make a new life for them all? Adam, Kitty, Auntie Susan – they were all her responsibility, and she had never felt less capable in her whole life.

CHAPTER TWELVE

Rodney Furson, the cobbler and village constable, stared at Rachel in shock. 'Someone's broke into your house?'

'Didn't I just say so?'

'Eh! Eh, I never! An' while you were burying your Thomas, too. Who'd ever have done such a dreadful thing?'

She breathed deeply, impatient with his slow ways. 'Well? Are you coming to look? You *are* the constable for Whin Vale.'

'Yes, yes of course. Only there's – but no, that can wait. I must – let me see now. How much did you say has been took?'

'All our savings. Near a hundred guineas.'

He goggled at her, unable to believe that anyone could possibly have saved so much. 'A hundred guineas! Nay, lass, that's a lot of money. Are you sure it were so much?'

'Of course I'm sure! Me and Thomas have worked hard for years, saved hard, too, and—' Her voice faltered for a moment, then she took refuge in anger. 'Are you going to do something or not?'

'Have you sent word about this to Mr Armstrong?'

'No. That's for you to do, surely.'

'Yes, well, I suppose it is. I'd better come and look first, though what I can do now, I don't know. But yes, I'll come and have a look.'

On the way through town, they passed the parsonage.

She hesitated. 'Maybe we should tell Mr Kellett what's happened.'

Rodney seized on this idea gratefully. 'Oh, yes, I think we should. I do indeed. He'll know what's best to do.' Before she could change her mind, he led the way smartly up the garden path and knocked on the door.

Inside, Justin was listening in horror to Maggie's suggestion that they offer to adopt Adam Thorpe. When the door knocker went, he held up one hand. 'We can't discuss this now, Maggie. But I don't like the idea at all. It's heartless at a time like this. I don't know how you can be so cruel.'

He went out into the hall, but the maid was before him and was already opening the front door. The last person he'd expected to see was Rachel Thorpe and by the expression on her face there was more trouble. He hurried forward.

'My dear Rachel, what's the matter?'

She explained in a few terse phrases what had happened.

'Oh, no! Rachel, I'm so sorry. I'll go and get my cloak, come home with you, see what I can do.'

Rodney sighed in relief.

In the parlour Justin quickly explained what had happened to Maggie. 'Send the maid with a note to let Mr Armstrong know what's happened.'

'Yes. Of course.'

But when he had gone, she smiled at herself in the mirror and patted her hair before she did anything. 'Now she'll have to let us adopt him. She won't be able to feed him, let alone look after him. And it serves her right. She doesn't deserve a lad like him.'

At North Beck Cottage, Justin examined the front room in grim silence, then asked, 'How did they know where to look if they were strangers? How did they even guess there'd be money here?'

Rodney gaped at him, because this aspect of the crime had not occurred to him. He'd decided as they walked up the hill that it must be some tramping folk. 'You mean – you think it's someone from *our* valley, Parson?' he gasped. 'Eh, never! Who'd do such a thing?'

'It'll be the same people who murdered my Thomas,' Rachel said dully.

Rodney was so stunned he could hardly form a word. 'You mean – you think – nay, you can't think someone killed your Thomas – not a-purpose? Oh, never, Rachel lass!'

'I know for *certain* someone killed him and I can guess who. One day I shall prove it, too, and see justice done.' Her voice was so quiet and sure that both men stared at her, then Justin turned to the constable.

'Mr Armstrong doesn't want this – this accusation talking about. He feels Mrs Thorpe is mistaken.'

'*I'm not mistaken!*' Rachel shouted, frustated at being fobbed off. 'I *know* what I saw. Next you'll be telling me I'm mistaken about this.' She gestured to the broken floorboards.

'I saw a stone near the cart as well,' Adam said. 'The one Dad hit his head on.'

Rachel looked at Justin, who said quietly, 'This is not the time to pursue that. We have to see if we can catch the thieves.'

But she knew already they wouldn't catch anyone. Because no one would want to believe that it could be someone from Whin Vale who'd done it. Because her enemies had been very clever – and she hadn't.

That afternoon, Nathaniel rode up the hill to inspect the damage in person, making angry muttering noises at the sight of the broken floorboards. 'I shall myself offer a reward for the capture of the thief, Mrs Thorpe.' He fumbled in his pocket. 'In the meantime, you will need some money to buy food. Let me—'

She took a step backwards, putting her hands behind her back. The last thing she wanted was anyone's charity. 'No, thank you, sir. I have a bit put by elsewhere, and I shall have more when I take the piece I'm weaving in to Rochdale. I'll finish Thomas's piece, too.' She had to breathe deeply before she could continue speaking. 'No, I can manage for the time being, as long as I can do my weaving.'

He frowned as he walked away from the house. Too proud for her own good, that one. Not even a tear from her today, just this white face and bitter anger. It was dreadful about the money being stolen, though. But a hundred guineas? He rather doubted the amount she'd named, for he could not see how a working fellow like Thorpe could ever have saved so much. Still, it must have been a substantial amount and he hated to see such a poor reward for honest folk's industry and frugality, absolutely hated it.

As for her finishing the weaving, he was very dubious about that. Tam Barker had reminded him that very afternoon that she'd never woven on her own, only under the supervision of a man. Without help, she'd never be able to finish the pieces to a decent standard. It was a pity, but there you were. You had to face facts. Weaving was a man's job and no one was going to pay Rachel Thorpe much for poor quality work. She'd have to be helped to find some other way of earning her bread.

The days following the funeral were stormy, rain and sleet lashing against the windows, wind howling around North Beck Cottage, water running down the rutted track that linked the three villages. All those who could stayed indoors, and even the parson went out only when he had to. Auntie Susan was no better and was coughing so badly, Rachel insisted on lighting a fire in her room. 'It'll be easier for you to breathe if we keep it warm in here,' she said gently, brushing the sparse white hair back from the hot forehead. Then she sent Adam down to the apothecary to get a bottle of cordial to ease the cough.

'I'm just – a burden – for you, lass,' said Auntie Susan. 'And in your time of trouble, too.'

'You're family, an' family's never a burden,' Rachel repeated, as she had been doing all morning. 'Stop worriting and have a good sleep. There's naught so healing as sleep.'

Sadly Rachel watched the paper-thin old eyelids close over the faded blue eyes. She did not think Auntie Susan would last much longer. She had seen that look on old people's faces before, a sort of transparency, as if they were no longer made of solid flesh. Eh, she wished she could take her own advice and get a good sleep, but she hadn't slept properly since Thomas died. Going to bed, she would feel exhausted, but would toss and turn all night, dozing, then waking with a start to find the big bed empty. You grew used to a man's warm, solid body beside you.

She cleared Thomas's things out, a sad business, which had her in tears several times, despite her resolve not to weep any more. But she still hadn't worked out what she was going to do with the rest of her life. Looking up the stairs, she wondered if she could get some weaving done this morning. She'd still not finished her piece. Although she had a few guineas left, they wouldn't last for ever.

When someone knocked on the door, she sagged in annoyance, then went to open it. She could do without people calling in today. They'd come every day since he died, rain or no rain, to see if she was all right, Thomas's old friends. Their neighbours. And though they meant it kindly, she'd just wanted time on her own, peace and quiet to pull herself together. But all she'd done today was think about the money that had been stolen, wonder what Walter was going to do with it. Waste it on drink, no doubt. Oh, it made her so angry! And she felt so helpless!

Banging the door open, heedless of the rain and cold, she scowled to see Tam Barker. She did not invite him in, for she hated his sneering, superior ways. 'Yes? What can I do for you, Mr Barker?'

'Can I come inside, Mrs Thorpe? We have things to talk about.'

She let out a sigh of exasperation. 'I suppose so. Mind you wipe your feet properly, though.'

He did as she asked, mocking her by going on for too long with the feet wiping, then followed her into the living room. He looked round, assessing what she had, then looked equally thoughtfully at her, standing with her arms folded, waiting for him to speak. Any other woman would be hovering over him, offering him a warm drink, but not Rachel Thorpe. She was getting above herself. Well, he'd soon pull her down, by heck he would.

Yet now that it had come to it, he was feeling somewhat uneasy about what he and Bill had planned. His employer would not be pleased, but with a bit of luck, the Thorpes would be gone from the valley before Mr Armstrong even found out about this. He had just left to visit his family in Todmorden, and was to stay there for a week to see his niece wed. They did such things in style, the Armstrongs.

'It's a big house, this.'

She just stared at him.

'Too big for a woman,' he added emphatically.

'That depends on the woman, surely. Tell me straight out what you want with me today, Tam Barker. The rent isn't due yet, so it can't be that. And I've got a hard day's work ahead of me, what with—'

'I need to know when you're moving out of here.'

'What? I'm not moving. Not yet, anyway.'

He gave a scornful snort. 'You'll have to, you fool. You can't afford to pay the rent on a big place like this now you've lost all your money.'

'I have enough left still to pay the rent, if that's what's worrying you. And what's more, if the men will agree, I can carry on with the putting-out, as long as I can get someone to take the pieces into Rochdale for me.' She'd lain awake trying to work it all out, and she knew she could do it, because she'd done all the accounts and calculations for Thomas. She wasn't sure they'd agree, but she'd try to persuade them, at least.

'A woman do the putting-out!' He exclaimed. 'You've run mad, Rachel Thorpe, if you think the men will stand for that.'

She'd guessed they wouldn't let her do it but she wasn't going to let him say she *couldn't*. 'Why couldn't I? I'm the one who organised everything before, did all the calculations. Thomas took the stuff into Rochdale, but I did everything else. Everything.' But she could see he wasn't even listening. He was just grinning at her, so she shut her mouth and waited for him to go on.

He leaned forward, enjoying himself. 'Mr Armstrong needs this house. Now.'

'But I—'

'There's someone else going to be doing the putting-out and he'll need this place. It's all arranged.'

'Who?' She'd hardly spoken to a soul since the funeral, but surely someone would have let her know if they'd decided this already.

'Never you mind.'

'Where am I to go, then?'

'How should I know?'

She clutched one hand to her breast in shock. 'You mean Mr Armstrong won't even let me have a cottage?'

'I'm the one as won't let you have a cottage. It's me as is the land agent round here, me what chooses the tenants. An' a woman on her own takin' a house, well, I reckon that's just asking for trouble.' He waited for her to plead with him, but she just stared.

Eventually she said in a hoarse whisper, 'But I can pay rent on a cottage same as a man can.'

'Oh, yes? How?'

'From my weaving.'

'No one's going to take your pieces into Rochdale. Women can't make a decent job of it. We'd be ashamed to take your stuff.' That was the story he'd told Mr Armstrong and that was what Bill and Walter were telling other folk, too. 'You had a man to keep an eye on you afore and help you with your work. Now you've no one. An' the new putter-out doesn't want to bother with your rubbish.'

At the expression on her face, he took an involuntary step backwards. She looked absolutely terrifying, with rage boiling in her eyes and spewing out of her mouth as she yelled and pushed him out of the door.

'Get out! Get out of my house, you! You're lying! Mr Armstrong wouldn't turn me out. He *wouldn't*.'

She slammed the door in his face, but he called out loudly, 'Mr Armstrong's a kindly man and he's not rushing things. He'll give you a few days to get yourself somewhere to live. But I want you out by Friday. *Friday, mind!* And there's nowhere else for you in the valley because folk don't want you living here, if you must know. So you'd better get started on your packing because if you're not out by then, we'll *throw* you out.'

He waited a minute, but no sound came from inside the house, so he set off back to Setherby, whistling cheerfully. That'd told her, the uppity creature! Eh, how he and Bill would laugh over this!

When Auntie Susan called out, Rachel took a few deep breaths, forcing back the sobs and the anger. Then she went to tend the old woman, who was feverish.

'Who was that, love?'

'Just someone to see we were all right.'

'Folks are kind.' Susan's eyes closed again, but her breath rasped in her chest.

Rachel went into the kitchen and looked at Kitty. 'Did you hear what Tam Barker said?'

'Yes.' Kitty's eyes filled with tears. 'Shall we really have to leave?'

'I don't know. I need to go and talk to Parson. Will you see to Auntie while I'm gone?'

'Yes.'

'And lock the door. Don't let anyone in till I get back. No one at all. You understand?'

'Yes.'

Sitting by herself next to Auntie Susan, Kitty shivered and could not prevent tears from rolling down her cheeks. Terrible things were going to happen to them, she knew it. Tam Barker had shouted that he'd come and throw them out. He'd said they couldn't even stay in the valley. But where else could they go? Would they have to go into the poorhouse?

Rachel knocked on the parsonage door. It was a while before

anyone opened it. 'I have to see Parson,' she told the young maid.

'He's out.'

'Is your mistress in?'

The maid blushed. 'Er – no, she isn't.'

'Then I'll wait for him.'

'Er, we're cleaning the place today. There's nowhere for you to sit.'

Rachel stared at her in astonishment. It was well known that you could sit in the hall to wait for Parson. Everyone did it. Maggie didn't like it, she knew, but Justin allowed it. Why had the maid refused to let her in? Was the whole world going mad today? Was Parson also plotting to get rid of her? Surely not.

Embarrassed, Lal closed the door and rushed back to the kitchen to confide in Mrs Charnley that it was a poor look-out when you couldn't invite a widow in to sit and wait for the parson. The housekeeper agreed, but she knew it was as much as her place here was worth to go against her mistress who might pretend to be a weak female but who had her own methods of getting what she wanted.

'Eh, it's not right, though,' she muttered into her bread and began to knead it ferociously. She looked across at the maid. 'Get on with your work, then, Lal.'

Rachel stood outside the front door, wondering what to do. As rain began to fall, she decided to go into the church porch and wait for Justin Kellett there. She huddled on the stone bench near the big church doors, not wanting to go inside in case she missed him coming back.

It was two hours before he came into sight and she rushed out at once to intercept him before he could get into the house and shut her out. 'I've been waiting to see you.'

'My dear Rachel, why did you not go inside and sit with Maggie?'

'I knocked. The maid said I couldn't wait in the house.'

'You must have mistaken what she said.' He put one arm round her to draw her across the road and Maggie, watching from the upstairs window, felt a surge of anger that he should touch that woman so familiarly and never lay a finger on his wife nowadays.

Inside Justin stared at Rachel anxiously. Her face was bone-white, her hands were like ice and she was shivering. He led her into his study, sat her beside the fire and rang the bell. 'Fetch a pot of tea at once, Lal, and something to eat.' Then he followed the maid out of the room and asked in a low voice, 'Did you really deny entrance to Mrs Thorpe?'

Lal lost herself in a morass of explanations, but he realised from what she said that she had only been following orders.

'Where is your mistress?'

She glanced upstairs, frightened to say it aloud.

He nodded and pushed her gently in the direction of the kitchen before striding up the stairs to the bedroom where he found Maggie reclining on her sofa, a damp cloth across her forehead, one hand shading her eyes. 'Why did you deny entrance to Rachel Thorpe?'

'I have a megrim.' She groaned and added, 'Oh, Justin, my poor head is aching so.'

He looked scornfully across the room at her. 'I don't know what you are thinking of to deny Rachel entrance. Get dressed and come downstairs at once. Our friend is in great distress.'

Maggie began to sob. 'I can't. My poor head hurts. How can you even ask it of me?'

He came to stand over her. 'If you ever do this again, Maggie Kellett, if you ever deny entrance to a person in need, I'll whip you myself. I'm ashamed of you. And deeply disgusted. I can't think what's got into you lately.'

'You know what's got into me, and you'll do nothing to help me.'

'That boy is her son. I'll have no hand in parting them.'

She jerked upright to argue with him, but he had gone out, banging the door behind him, so she slumped down again and began to sob in earnest.

In the parlour, Rachel stood by the fire, holding her hands out and trying to get warm, but still shivering, for the cold and rawness of the day seemed to have penetrated her very bones.

When the door opened, the maid followed the parson in with a tea tray.

'My wife is not feeling well, I'm afraid,' said Justin. 'It was all a mistake. The maid misunderstood her directions.' He turned to frown at Lal and added loudly and clearly, 'Everyone here is aware now that I'll not have anyone denied entrance to my home, *ever*!'

Lal flushed and decided she'd look for a new place come the summer hiring fair. She wasn't working for folk who blamed you for what they had themselves told you to do. And anyway, the mistress was getting sharper and sharper lately, shouting at folk for no reason.

Rachel just continued to gaze at Justin, not moving.

He spoke gently, frightened by the wild, staring look on her face. What else could possibly have happened to her? 'Will you pour us some tea, my dear, and then you shall tell me how I can help you.'

She did not even attempt to touch the teapot, just said baldly, 'I'm to be turned out of North Beck Cottage.'

He knew Mr Armstrong had intended to ask her to leave, but not yet. 'Well, it will be too big for you now, won't it? Mr Barker will find you another cottage and—'

She thumped her hand on the table, causing a piece of cake to fall off the plate, though she didn't notice that. 'Tam Barker says there isn't another cottage. He says,' her voice became thick with tears, 'he says I've to leave the valley, find somewhere else to live.'

It was a moment before Justin could take this in. 'No, no! There must be some mistake. I have spoken to Mr Armstrong myself and he intends to find you another cottage and—'

She stared at him. 'A weaver's cottage?'

'I – don't know.' But he was aware that Nathaniel Armstrong did not approve of women weaving, knew too that Tam Barker kept saying Rachel couldn't weave on her own without a man to help her – though Justin didn't believe that. He could remember folk saying when he first came to the valley that she was a better weaver than her father. He could also remember Thomas Thorpe's pride in the high quality of his wife's work.

'How am I to earn my bread if I'm not to weave?' she asked him, hands outstretched in unconscious appeal. 'And why cannot I weave? I'm as good as a man. Better than most.'

'Um – I'm afraid Tam says you're not a good weaver.'

'Then Tam Barker is lying.'

'Walter Smedling says the same thing.'

'He would. He hates me.'

'I'm afraid Mr Armstrong believes them.' Justin hesitated. There was another aspect to it that would prevent her from weaving. 'In any case, if you cannot get your pieces into Rochdale and cannot get Mr Harrison to deal with you, you will not be able to continue doing that sort of work, I'm afraid.'

She had lost the urge to weep and her eyes were fixed on him with a burning intensity. 'Why should I not be able to get my pieces into Rochdale?'

'Because the new putter-out says he will not carry a woman's work.'

She was wringing her hands, not even realising it. 'Who is he? Tam Barker would not say.'

'The new putter-out is to be – well, it's Walter Smedling.'

She sat very still. 'But how will he find the money to do it? 'Tis well known he never has a penny to spare, for he spends it all on ale.'

'He has a little money saved. And Bill Withers is to go in with him. Together they think they can just manage it.'

She looked at him then, a scornful look. 'And you believe that?'

'What do you mean?'

'This proves who took our savings and why. Surely you can see that's the only way those sots could have found the money to take over. Save! They've never saved a penny in their lives!'

He blinked at her in shock. 'No, no! I'm afraid you're wrong there. And Tam Barker has lent Smedling and Withers some of the money, I believe, as he feels they are the best men for the job. He says we should keep the putting-out in the valley and not have outsiders taking things over.'

She could not hold back an angry sob. 'Those two took my money. I know it.'

He patted her shoulder, feeling helpless. 'Look, about finding you somewhere to live – I shall go and see Mr Armstrong myself as soon as he gets back. I'm sure he doesn't intend you to be put out of house and home.'

'He might not intend it, but others do. And I've been told to get out by Friday. He's not coming back till next week, is he?' She stood up and walked out then, numb with shock and anguish, and hating to see the pity on Justin's face.

Blindly she stumbled up the hill and went to stand at her weaving, but she got little done because her thoughts twisted round and round inside her aching head. Wasn't it enough that she had lost her husband? Was she to lose her home and livelihood too? When would this all end? Would they murder her as well if they couldn't send her away? Would they murder her children? She must think, work out something to do. Only she couldn't seem to think straight since Thomas had died. If only she could sleep! If only she had more time before the date for moving out to find a solution to her problems.

CHAPTER THIRTEEN

The next day Rachel realised she would have to go into Setherby, for they were running short of food. She would call in and see the apothecary, too, to ask if he could think of anything else to help Auntie Susan. And come Thursday, she would go to market and try to sell the cart. She refused to think about Friday and Tam Barker's threat that she must be out of the house by then. Surely Mr Kellett would persuade Mr Armstrong to allow her more time.

Three men stepped into her path just beyond Lower Clough. She had been so lost in thought she hadn't even noticed them lying in wait for her.

'Well, *daughter*, so you're leaving Whin Vale, are you?' Walter Smedling jeered.

'By Friday,' Tam Barker said. 'In two days' time.'

She closed her eyes for a moment and prayed for strength to endure their jeering, but as Bill Withers grinned and moved closer, she began to feel nervous. She tried not to show her fear but there was no one else in sight and she did not like the look on Bill's face.

'What do you want?' She took a step backwards, but he followed.

Walter came closer on her other side. 'It's me as wants summat – your cart and donkey. And I'm prepared to pay you,' he paused, smiled and said, 'a whole guinea for them.'

'They're worth far more than that!' She felt outraged by his offer.

'Not if there isn't anyone else offering to buy 'em, they aren't,' Bill said. 'And we've put out word that we want 'em, that we won't look kindly on anyone as tries to stop us, so there won't be any other offers. Why,' he exchanged smiles with his two companions, 'we might not even take pieces into Rochdale for anyone as tried to help you.'

A sick feeling settled in her stomach and she tried to walk on, but they moved to and fro, blocking her path and giving her little shoves that sent her stumbling from one to the other. Were they going to beat her? Ravish her? What had the world come to when three bullies behaved like this in full view of a village?

She stopped trying to move. 'I'll not sell them. If no one will pay me what the cart is worth, I might as well keep it for myself.'

They all guffawed, slapping one another on the backs and wiping tears from their eyes. But that didn't prevent them from continuing to block her path.

She told herself to wait quietly till they'd finished tormenting her, but Bill suddenly reached out and squeezed her breast.

'Eh, I didn't think she had titties like other women,' he said and grabbed at her again.

She batted his hand away, but found her arm held by Tam Barker, so she rounded on him and tried to shove him away. She was a tall woman and strong, but she was no match for two men who held her fast.

As they swung her round to face the man she had once called 'father', Bill gave her arm a shake. 'Stand still, you fool woman, an' listen to what we're telling you! We haven't finished with you yet.'

'Mam would be really proud of what you're doing,' she flung at Walter.

He turned red. 'Don't you even mention her name to me, you heartless trollop! If it hadn't been for you, we'd have been happy together, me and Alice.'

'No woman could be happy with a bully like you.' She made a huge effort to get free, but the other two men held on fast, mocking her fruitless efforts.

Suddenly, there was a quavering voice behind them. 'Shame on you!' Thomas's old friend, Rob, moved forward, his hand shaking as he leaned on his walking stick. 'Shame on you all!'

Tam changed his stance at once, pretending that he was trying to pull Rachel free. 'Now, you two, leave go of this poor woman. She's lost her senses and doesn't know what she's doing, so it's not fair to torment her.'

The old man, whose eyesight was bad now, stopped and squinted at them all, as if he wasn't sure what to believe.

Tam turned to Rachel and gestured to her to pass on. 'And don't you tease these hardworking men again, wench! Just get about your business.'

She did not dare risk stopping to tell Rob what had really happened, for he was too feeble to protect her, so she ran off down the track as fast as she could, breath sobbing in her throat.

Just before she got to Setherby, she stopped and tried to set her clothing to rights, but her hands were trembling and she knew she must look strange – passers-by were staring at her.

She bought her provisions quickly, not saying anything unless she had to. When she saw a group of women from Upper Clough, she greeted them by name and moved forward to join them, thankful to have found some protection for the walk back.

'We don't want you walking with us,' one of them said at once with a furtive look over her shoulder, as if afraid.

Another whispered, 'Sorry! But they're watching us.' Then she made a flapping gesture with one hand, as if to shoo Rachel away.

Rachel hesitated, then began to walk up the hill a little behind them, hoping this would give her enough protection against the bullying. Not once did any of the women speak to her, though they occasionally turned round as if to check that she was still following them.

She saw the three men waiting for her near Lower Clough and her heart began to thump in her chest. She had never been afraid like this before in her whole life. Perhaps she should have gone and asked Justin Kellett's help. But she was tired of going to him, tired of all the struggling. If it hadn't been for Auntie Susan and the children, she thought she might just have left Whin Vale and sought a job in service. But she had three people depending on her, so she had to be strong, had to make some sort of life for them.

It seemed to her that once they had walked past the three men, the other women slowed down deliberately, one pretending to stumble and spill things from her basket, another clutching her side and complaining they'd been walking too fast and it had given her a stitch.

Rachel hurried to catch up with them and although Bill pretended to grab her and laughed as she flinched away, the audience prevented the men from touching her.

'Thank you,' she whispered as she passed the women, not able to stop the tears tracking down her cheeks. Even a quick sideways glance showed her that some of them looked upset, others frightened, but none spoke to her.

As she hurried up the hill, she kept looking back over her shoulder, but the men didn't pursue her, just stood and watched. And there was something menacing even in the watching.

She went straight into the kitchen, sighing in relief to find Adam and Kitty both there. 'Stay here!' she ordered and rushed round the house, locking the doors and closing the windows.

'What's wrong, Mam?' Adam asked.

'I'll tell you in a minute. Where's Dusty?'

'Out at the back.'

'Well, bring him in quickly, then lock the door again.'

Only when every door and window was shut fast did she sit down, bury her head in her shaking hands for a moment, then pull herself together and tell the children what had happened.

Kitty began to weep. 'I don't like Bill Withers.'

'I don't think they'll hurt you, love. It's me they're after. Just make sure you don't go out alone until I sort all this out.'

'But I don't want them to hurt you either,' Kitty sobbed.

Rachel gave her a quick hug, then changed the subject. 'How's Auntie Susan?'

'She keeps coughing,' Kitty said sadly. 'She's — she's not getting any better, is she?'

Rachel could only shake her head, her eyes filled with tears.

Adam slipped his hand in hers and the three of them sat there together for a while, then Rachel dragged herself to her feet and went to see to her aunt, before cooking the children some food. But she couldn't eat much herself. And she couldn't sleep that night either. She kept waking and thinking she heard someone trying to break in.

Before it was light the following morning Rachel roused her son and asked him if he could take a note down to the parson's house in Setherby without anyone seeing him. During the long hours of darkness she had decided that this was not a time to stand on her pride. She had to get word to Justin Kellett. She made the boy promise not to use the main track, but to slip through the nearby fields and go down into Setherby the back way. In the note she explained what had happened and admitted that she was now afraid even to leave her house, having been set upon the previous day on her way home.

She was afraid for her son, too, apprehension skittering along her veins the whole time he was away. She began to look out of the windows long before he could be expected back and she sobbed in relief when he crept into the garden the back way and tapped on the kitchen window.

No one from the village had been near the house all day, and very few people seemed to have been moving about either. It was as if normal life had stopped with Thomas's death, as if everyone was waiting for something else to happen, something bad.

'Was Parson home?' she asked at once when Adam was safely inside.

'Yes.'

'Did you give him the note?'

'Yes.'

'What did he say?'

Adam wriggled. Mr Kellett had asked him a lot of questions about how his mother was bearing up and whether she was acting strangely. He hadn't liked the questions. His mother wasn't acting strangely. It was other people who were trying to hurt her. He had had to admit that he hadn't seen this happening himself, but if she said it had then he believed her.

Mrs Kellett had come in while they were talking and had asked him to stay for a while, but Mr Kellett had said the boy had to get back at once. They'd seemed to be angry at one another and Adam had been glad to leave the house.

'What did the parson say to do, Adam?'

'He said he'd come and see you.'

'Didn't he give you a note for me?'

'No. He said he'd be up the hill as soon as he could.'

That afternoon, there was a knock on the door and when Rachel peeped out of the window, hating herself for feeling so afraid, she sobbed in relief to see Justin Kellett standing there.

She flung the door open and surprised them both by bursting into tears. She tried to stop weeping, but could not.

Justin pushed her gently towards the kitchen and whispered, 'I'll go and see your aunt first, then come and talk to you.'

She sent the children out into the back garden to get some fresh air, feeling they'd be safe while Parson was there, and waited impatiently in the kitchen. By the time he joined her she had regained control of herself, though her head was aching fiercely for lack of sleep.

'I'm sorry,' she said, gesturing to a chair. 'I just – don't know what to do.'

'Rachel, I find it hard to believe what you wrote in your letter.'

She stared at him open-mouthed.

'I went to see Tam Barker this morning, but he wasn't in. When I met Smedling on my way here, he admitted he and Withers had been teasing you and that perhaps they'd gone a bit far. He said Barker was trying to stop them.'

'And you believed him?'

He shook his head helplessly. 'How can I tell what to believe, Rachel?' She did look strange, wild even.

She went to get Thomas's big Bible, thumped it down in front of him and laid her hand on it. 'I swear by this Bible that every word I told you was true.'

But still he did not meet her eyes. 'It is possible to tell the truth and yet be mistaken, Rachel.'

'And the offer to buy my cart and donkey for only a guinea? Was I mistaken about that as well?'

'They said the donkey was old and the cart damaged after your husband's accident.'

She grabbed his arm then and dragged him out to the shed, to show him the cart whose paintwork was scratched, certainly, but whose body was in sound enough condition with the new wheel the men had fitted before they brought it back to her. 'A guinea?' she demanded. 'For this cart? I'd as soon burn it as give it them for that. Sooner. And Sukey's *not* old.' She waved one hand at the donkey. 'Look at her! She's a fine animal, good for years yet. And they,' she had to stop for a moment to prevent herself from weeping in sheer rage, 'they offered me a guinea – one guinea.'

'I'll speak to them. It's definitely worth more. How much would you be prepared to take?'

'Not less than ten guineas.'

'I'll see what I can do.'

When she said nothing, he hesitated, then said, 'I suppose I should be getting back. I have someone to see, only I was worried about you.' But although she looked tired and anxious, she was unhurt and she'd be safe inside her house till he had sorted something out.

She took hold of his arm to prevent him leaving. 'How do I get into Setherby on Friday for the market if I'm to be waylaid?'

'Rachel, you're seeing trouble where there is none.'

'I suppose I saw savings where there were none, too. I suppose I imagined the broken floorboards, the stealing, the smashing of my ornaments?' She was weeping openly now. 'And I suppose I imagined Tam Barker saying I had to be out of this house by Friday?'

He frowned at that. 'I'm sure you are mistaken. Mr Armstrong would not turn you out.'

'I'm *not* mistaken!'

'I'll have a word with Tam myself.' He'd already tried once or twice, but Barker had been out both times he'd called and had not responded to his message.

'But—'

'It's all a mistake. It must be. Nathaniel Armstrong would never treat a tenant like this.'

When he had gone, she sat down and put her head in her arms, dozing for a while, then waking with a start. She felt so muddled and tired. Had she really been mistaken? No, Tam had said it most clearly. But Parson would sort things out, get them to give her more time. Surely he would.

Justin went to see Tam Barker, who insisted he had to get the woman out of the house by Friday.

'Mr Armstrong told you to do that?'

'He didn't need to. We want that house for the new putter-out. It's urgent.'

'You're acting too hastily. You can wait for a few more days to get her out. I'll see Mr Armstrong myself when he gets back and we'll sort something out for Mrs Thorpe.'

'Look, Parson, my master is a busy man. He won't want disturbing by this little affair. And he leaves renting out the cottages to me.'

Justin walked out.

As Tam said to Walter that night in the Weaver's Arms, they'd be lucky now to get the thing done before Mr Armstrong came back.

'Damn the parson for interfering!' Bill said. 'You don't think he'll go into Todmorden to fetch Mr Armstrong, do you?'

'I hope not. No, he said he'd see him when he got back.' But

Tam was getting really worried now. Why had he let himself be persuaded into this?

Bill nudged him. 'Look, we'll have to load her stuff on the cart ourselves tomorrow morning, drive her out of the valley and dump her and her family somewhere. We can say we took her to stay with relatives of her husband.'

'It'll not work,' Walter worried. 'He hadn't got no relatives, except for the old woman.'

'It might just.' Tam chewed his lip. 'Mr Armstrong won't know that, will he?'

Bill slapped one hand down on the table. 'Look, we'll *make* it work. Well, we will as long as we get that cart. Mr Armstrong won't be back until Saturday, because of that wedding. You see if we don't get rid of her before then.'

On Friday morning, Rachel left the children at home, protected, she hoped, by Dusty, then drove the cart slowly down the hill, her heart thudding with fear all the way in case someone leaped out at her. She had decided to try to sell it herself at market, or at least she'd put the word out that it was for sale. A guinea indeed! Did they think she was stupid?

She had done nothing about moving out because she couldn't think what to do. She'd just have to trust that Justin would arrange for them to stay at North Beck Cottage for a while longer.

She didn't see Bill Withers peering out of his window, or notice him trailing down the hill behind her. She felt so exhausted, everything seemed to be coming and going around her.

The market was as busy as ever, so she made a few purchases, then settled herself beside the cart with a sign saying 'CART AND DONKEY FOR SALE TEN GUINEAS'. She'd written the words herself in charcoal on one of her good sheets and she hung it over the cart so that they showed clearly.

People looked at the cart as they passed, but no one offered to buy it or even stopped to bargain with her for a lower price.

She sat there wondering if she would have to take the cart into Todmorden and sell it there.

Then a man she'd never seen before, a farmer by the looks of him, came up and asked, 'How much?'

'I thought ten guineas.'

He stood back and made sucking noises with his mouth as he thought about it. 'Eight.'

'Nine.'

He shook his head. 'Eight and that's my top offer.'

'Very well. I'll take it.'

'I'll be back in an hour with the money.'

Heart lighter, she waited, patting Sukey and wishing she didn't have to sell Thomas's beloved donkey. When an hour had passed by the church clock, she started to look round, wondering what was keeping the man.

Half an hour later, someone whispered 'Psst!' from behind her.

She turned round and saw a woman she knew slightly. 'Eh, I'm sorry love.' The woman kept well back and said hurriedly, 'I overheard them telling that fellow it weren't your cart to sell. They said you were a madwoman who's done this afore. He's a stranger in town and he believed them.'

Rachel bent her head, unable to prevent tears from flowing. 'Has he left town now, then?'

'Aye, he has. Eh, you'll have to sell to 'em, love, or they'll hurt you. They've threatened to set fire to the cart if anyone else buys it, or there's one or two others would have offered.'

'Th-thank you.' When she looked up, the woman had gone.

For the whole of the morning, Rachel sat there, at first because she didn't know what else to do, then because she had grown stubborn.

When the stalls were mostly empty and folk began to pack up, Bill sauntered over. 'A guinea,' he said, slapping the coin down, 'and I'll take the sheet, too.'

That was the final straw for Rachel. She got down from

the cart, unhitched the donkey and tethered Sukey with her purchases a little way off.

Bill followed her. 'What do you think you're doing?'

'Watch me and you'll find out!' Rage hummed along her veins, thumped behind her forehead, the hottest rage she had ever known.

The only thing left on the cart was a small bale of hay she used as part of Sukey's feed. She spread it in a corner, rubbed some butter she'd purchased into it, then she went back to confront Bill.

'I heard you've threatened to burn the cart if anyone else bought it,' she said loudly, and saw with savage satisfaction that people had stopped to listen.

He just looked sideways to some cronies who were waiting nearby, ready to swear anything he wanted, and grinned, utterly confident. 'Well, it's not much use to you now. We're being kind, really, taking it off your hands. It's a rackety old thing, too, and will have to be repaired.'

From across the market square, Caleb, who had just arrived to take home any unsold produce from his stall, noticed the stir and wondered what was happening.

Rachel raised her voice to a shout. 'You've only offered me a guinea for both the cart and the donkey, you cheat! It's worth a lot more than that, and you know it.'

Caleb recognised the voice, but he had never heard her sound so strained and angry. What was going on? Had someone really only offered Rachel Thorpe a mere guinea for a donkey *and* cart? Surely not.

Someone near him muttered, 'Shame!'

Someone else on the far side of the crowd, called, 'Leave her alone! It's her cart.'

Bill ignored the voices, but two of his cronies moved through the crowd towards the sounds and though they couldn't tell who had spoken, their fierce looks and bunched fists stopped any more remarks like that.

Caleb was astounded at the sudden menace in the air. He'd seen Bill Withers bullying folk before and had taken a dislike to him, but the fellow had never come near him or his stall. He said urgently to an old woman next to him, 'Has this been going on for long?'

She glanced over her shoulder before whispering, 'Aye. All day. A fellow offered to buy the cart an' they told him it weren't hers. They're trying to cheat that poor woman. Mester Armstrong's away an' the parson's not at home neither so there's no one dares help her. They thumped a couple of fellows who were going to try, an' they're lyin' at home now with broken heads.' Then she looked round, as if afraid she'd said too much, and moved away from him.

Horrified, Caleb began to shove forward towards Rachel but he made slow progress through the crowd.

'Now stop telling lies, you fool woman,' Bill said loudly. 'You know we've offered you five guineas.' In a low voice, he added, 'Though you'll only get one and you'll keep your mouth shut about it if you value your precious son's safety.'

The threat against Adam tipped Rachel over into a red haze of anger. 'One guinea was all you offered me, you liar!' she yelled. 'You've stopped anyone else from buying my cart and now you're threatening my son. So if this cart is so rotten it isn't worth more than one guinea, I reckon the best thing for me to do is burn it.' So quickly that she took them all by surprise, she wrapped her cloak round her hands, grabbed the nearby brazier of a hot chestnut seller and flung it on to her cart, scattering the glowing coals over the pile of butter and straw.

Bill roared in anger and tried to stop her, but she had the extra strength extreme anger sometimes lends and she used the chestnut seller's shovel to keep him at bay.

'Help me, lads!' Bill yelled and five men began to move towards him.

Caleb shouted 'Help her, someone!' but his voice was lost in the noise.

The straw caught light instantly and Rachel held Bill off for long enough for the flames to catch the dry old wood. By the time Caleb got to the front of the crowd, the cart was blazing furiously.

Rachel dropped the shovel, put her head in her hands and began to sob.

Bill moved forward, his expression ugly, his fist raised to thump her.

Caleb ran across, yelling, 'Get away from her, you!' He was only one man, but he was dressed more like gentry and though they outnumbered him, the bullies hesitated.

'She's a madwoman,' Bill roared. 'She should be took up and locked away in the bedlam. Everyone here's just heard me offer her five guineas.'

Caleb approached Rachel and put his arm round her. When she struck out at him, he said quickly, 'I'm not one of them.'

She looked up and saw it was the parson's cousin. This time when Caleb put his arm round her, she collapsed against him, sobbing bitterly, unable to think straight, unable to do anything but let him guide her across the square towards the parsonage.

Behind her one stallholder, ashamed that he had not done more to help her, went to pick up her things, and when Bill and the bullies tried to take them away from him, other stallholders gathered round.

The constable came up to the group. 'That's enough. You're not stealing her things as well.'

Bill turned an innocent face on Rodney. 'I weren't stealing them. I were goin' to take them across to her.'

'I'll do that. An' I'll take her donkey, too.'

Bill looked at the cart, furious that she had done this. 'She should be locked away. Only a madwoman would do a thing like that.'

Rodney also looked at the blazing cart. 'You should have offered her a fair price for it, then.'

'I did. I offered her five guineas. Didn't I?'

But when he looked round for corroboration, the people nearby turned their backs to him, ashamed now that they had let him and his bullies drive Thomas Thorpe's widow to desperation.

'Eh, they're a bad lot, them buggers are,' one woman murmured to another. 'After he'd said five guineas, I saw him whisper summat in her ear an' I saw how mad she got.'

'I reckon she were telling the truth.'

'Aye, but it were them bullies as broke John Hunter's leg that time when he tried to stop 'em taking stuff off his stall. I don't want my Robert attacking one night, nor a lighted brand thrown into my kitchen.'

'Me neither.'

They both turned to look at the flames as the cart crackled and burned.

'But to burn the cart!' one whispered.

'She were driven to desperation, that's what. Eh, poor woman. Whatever will she do now?'

CHAPTER FOURTEEN

Caleb was half carrying Rachel towards the parsonage when a carriage drove into town and he saw with relief that it contained Mr Armstrong. Surely the landowner did not intend to just stand aside and let folk ill use her? If he would not help, Caleb's face tightened on the thought, then he would take her to his own home and ask his mother to help her, then go back to her house for her children and possessions. Injustice and cruelty, in whatever form, always made his anger rise hotly.

With his arm round the weeping woman, he stood and waited for the carriage to draw up. As it came closer, he saw trotting behind it, on a long tether, Justin's horse, then his friend sitting beside his patron in the carriage. Caleb exhaled in relief and patted Rachel on the back. 'We'll be all right now. Justin will know what to do.' But she was beyond reason or thought. Each sob she uttered tore at his heart. What had it taken to bring a strong woman to this?

Nathaniel looked out of the window at the conflagration in the market square. 'What has been happening here? If I'm not mistaken, that's a cart burning.'

Justin noticed Rachel's donkey tethered in one corner and his heart sank. 'I believe,' he hesitated, then said slowly, 'I think it might be Mrs Thorpe's cart.'

'Is that woman to cause us nothing but trouble!' Nathaniel exclaimed, still annoyed at having been brought away from the family gathering, but his parson had absolutely insisted.

'I do believe she is more sinned against than sinning, sir,' Justin said quietly. Then he noticed Caleb supporting a woman. It was a moment before he realised who she was, then he tugged at the check string of the carriage, not waiting till it had stopped to leap out.

He rushed over to his cousin and helped him support Rachel. 'What happened?'

By now, she was only half conscious.

'She set fire to the cart herself rather than let those villains rob her of it.' Caleb stared down at the head so close to his own, feeling the familiar feelings tugging at his heart and wishing desperately that he had the right to comfort her and look after her.

Nathaniel's voice behind them exclaimed, 'She set fire to her own cart! Has she run completely mad?'

'Hear me out, sir,' Caleb begged, 'and you will see how grievously wronged Mrs Thorpe has been today. They drove her to it and I believe I should have taken a similar step myself in the circumstances.' He made no attempt to remove his arm from round Rachel's shoulders, fearing she would collapse if he did.

Nathaniel looked down his nose, made a snorting sound, then said, 'Help her into the carriage and we'll take her to Cleving for my aunt to deal with. I wish to find out exactly what has happened. Exactly!'

Caleb hesitated.

'Is there some problem to that?'

''Tis *your* land agent, sir, who has told her she must leave her house by today at the latest. And refused to find her another house.' A woman had whispered this information from behind a stall as he helped Rachel but had not come to his aid.

He saw the shock on the landowner's face and felt hope surge in him. Perhaps there had been some mistake. 'And some other men have offered her only a guinea for a cart and donkey – and they seized hold of her in the market square and used her shamefully. I witnessed that myself.'

Nathaniel goggled at him for a moment, then looked grimly across at the charred skeleton of the cart, nearly consumed now by the flames. 'If Barker has done this, it is without my authorisation. I hope you will believe that I would never drive a widow from her home or refuse her somewhere else to live.'

'I do believe it, sir. Nor would you, I'm sure, allow men to rob her of her cart for a mere guinea.'

'I find that very hard to believe.'

'They'll no doubt have their own tale – men like that always do.' Caleb had his own memories of being bullied when he was younger, and being helpless to protect himself when a group of other boys told lies about him. 'Bastard!' they had yelled after him in the street, before he was even old enough to understand its meaning, though he had understood from an early age that there was something shameful about the word and therefore about himself, something that made even grown people whisper to one another as he passed, and eye his mother and himself with disapproval.

He bent to say quietly to Rachel, 'Let us get into the carriage, my dear. Mr Armstrong will see that you are not ill-treated again. And,' he looked at Nathaniel for confirmation, 'he will not throw you out of your house.'

She opened her eyes and when Nathaniel nodded, she murmured something indistinct and let him help her into the carriage. Justin followed and sat down beside her. So wan did she look that the men exchanged shocked glances, for she looked twenty years older than she had before Thomas's death. Guilt that this should happen on his land made Nathaniel clear his throat and shake his head, fumbling for words. Justin was silent, facing his own guilt that he had failed so badly in his care of one of his parishioners.

Caleb hesitated, then looked towards his own cart. 'I must be about my business soon, but I think Mrs Thorpe trusts me, so perhaps I could come with you until you have worked out what to do. She cannot go home in safety, sir, and her family are still in Upper Clough. They will be worried and they will need help as well.'

'She can stay at Cleving for the moment,' Nathaniel decided.

'We can be sure she's safe there, and I have enough servants to look after her. I shall send someone to stay with her family.'

So Caleb got in, sitting next to Rachel as the carriage rolled slowly towards the big house. He saw how she lay against the padded seat back, utterly spent now, her eyes closed, as if she could only let them do what they would with her. He wished he could take her in his arms and give her the sort of comfort she needed, the comfort of a human touch, a soothing voice speaking gently. He had thought he was cured of caring about her, but now he knew he wasn't – and perhaps would never be.

Only when they got to the front door of the large house and the carriage stopped did she rouse enough to ask faintly, 'The donkey? My things?'

'The donkey is being looked after,' Caleb told her quietly, daring to pat her hand, 'and your other things are quite safe. The constable has them.'

'He can't – they might . . .'

He clasped her hand for a moment. 'Nothing will happen to them, I promise you. Mr Armstrong will know what to do. Let me help you out of the carriage. We cannot talk here.'

Only then did she look across at the landowner, a quiet, hopeless look of someone who expected nothing but more trouble.

It cut straight to Nathaniel's heart. He was sure he had read something in the Bible about visiting the widows and the fatherless in their affliction, and he had failed in his duty to protect them – a sacred duty in his mind. But he would find a way to make amends to this woman, he vowed. And see that she was properly cared for.

'Come inside, Mrs Thorpe,' he urged. 'Mr Hesketh is quite right. We cannot talk here.'

She walked slowly, still clutching Caleb's arm, moving like someone at the utter end of her strength.

As the ill-assorted group entered the house, a maid wheeled Hannah out of her rooms, for she lodged on the ground floor now to make matters easier for the servants who cared for her.

When she had seen the woman being helped from the carriage, obviously in distress, she had instantly demanded to be taken out to help.

While Nathaniel led Caleb and Justin into the library to find out exactly what had happened and decide what to do about it, the housekeeper and maid helped Rachel into the old lady's rooms. There, she allowed them to seat her in a chair near the fire, for she was still unable to think clearly, so dizzy and distant did she feel.

'A dish of tea first,' Hannah decided. 'The warmth will be a comfort. Matty, will you go and fetch a tray yourself?'

The housekeeper nodded and hurried off.

'Dorcas, please bring a shawl to put round Mrs Thorpe's shoulders.'

Hannah sat beside Rachel and patted her hand, it being all she could think of to do. How cold the hand was and how limp! And how pale the poor woman was!

Shivering, Rachel stared at the fire and gave a long sigh of relief as she stretched out her free hand to its warmth. 'I'm frozen,' she said in tones of surprise. 'It's so cold.'

The maid brought the shawl and when Rachel made no effort to help herself, Dorcas placed it round her shoulders, then looked at Mrs Hannah for further instructions.

'Leave us for a while, but stay within sound of my bell.'

For a few moments, there was silence in the bright, airy room, which was cheerful even on this dull day, with its yellow silk hangings and embroidered firescreen.

Rachel let out another long sigh and Hannah said quietly, 'When you feel better, you shall tell me what has happened, but there is no hurry, my dear. We'll take a dish of tea together, shall we? I am a firm believer in a nice warm drink when one is feeling low.'

Rachel gave a laugh that turned into a hiccup, then had to fight against the urge to start weeping again. 'Feeling low!' she said at last, in a voice that cracked with emotion. 'I think I have never felt so low in all my life, not even when my mother died.'

There was a knock on the door and the housekeeper came in with a tea tray and a platter of scones. She set it down by her mistress and in response to a jerk of Hannah's head, went quietly out without saying anything.

Hannah busied herself with pouring the tea, and snipped a good lump of sugar off the cone to sweeten it with, though normally she felt sugar spoiled the taste. With her twisted hands, she made heavy weather of the task and, without thinking, Rachel reached out to complete it for her.

'I'm afraid I'm not much use these days,' Hannah said quietly, staring down at her hands. 'Age is very cruel.' She watched Rachel sip the hot liquid and sigh with pleasure. Not until the dish was empty did she say, 'Pour yourself another and then, when you feel ready, tell me what has happened to upset you so.'

It was a moment before Rachel could speak, but as she began haltingly to tell what had happened to her since Thomas's death, and her conviction that he had been murdered, the words tumbled out faster and faster. Before the tale was completed, she was sobbing again, and somehow found herself on the floor with her head in the old lady's lap as she finished her story.

The harsh sound of weeping penetrated into the bedroom where the maid was waiting and Dorcas risked a peep into the sitting room, but a shake of her mistress's head sent her outside again.

In the hall, the housekeeper was also waiting and she, too, peeped into the room to see if she could help, for Hannah was well loved and served by the staff. But Matty closed the door quietly again in response to a wave of her mistress's hand, feeling upset to hear anyone so distraught.

A little later, Mr Armstrong came to the library door and raised his eyebrows questioningly. Matty trod quietly across the shining marble floor to say, 'The lady is sitting with her head in Mrs Hannah's lap, weeping, and your aunt is stroking her hair.'

'Ah. Yes. Well, my aunt will know what to do.' He retreated back into the library and listened in indignation as the other two men pieced together what they knew of events. After a while, he rang the bell and told the footman who answered it to send for Tam Barker, 'on the instant'.

Justin looked out of the window to see the short winter's day drawing to a close. 'There are two children waiting for Mrs Thorpe in Upper Clough, and an old lady who is, I believe, quite ill.'

'Hmm. We'd better send someone to see to them.' He looked at Justin. 'Your housekeeper, perhaps, and ask her to stay there overnight.'

'Yes. I'll – um, go and see to that.'

Left alone with the landowner, Caleb stared round. He had never been inside this house before, but although it was much larger than Mrs Bretherton's home, it had the same air of comfort and affluence. Carpets underfoot in all the rooms, hall floor tiled with smooth, shining marble, gilt-framed pictures on the walls.

'Do you think Mrs Thorpe is telling the truth?' Nathaniel asked abruptly. 'Kellett feels she may have mistaken the matter, be seeing things as worse than they are.'

'I don't agree with him. Mrs Thorpe is an intelligent woman and I have never heard her called a liar – rather the contrary, for she is sometimes too blunt for her own good.' Though Maggie had phrased that rather less tactfully. 'Besides . . .' Caleb hesitated.

'Go on! Go on!'

'Your land agent is not known for dealing kindly with those in trouble. You may not have realised that, but I have myself seen people put out of cottages in the outlying districts for no reason other than that they offended him.'

'*What?*'

Caleb gave him a long, level look. 'And your land agent is also known as a tippler. He spends many an evening drinking with a certain group of men whom I should neither employ nor invite to my house. Walter Smedling and Bill Withers are the main ones, both of whom bear Mrs Thorpe great ill will.'

Nathaniel felt aggrieved as well as angry about this. He

had prided himself on knowing his people, on keeping a firm hand on the reins, and now this fellow from Hepstone, who only came into Whin Vale on market days, was telling him that Barker had been pulling the wool over his eyes. He remembered cottages coming empty from time to time – but Barker had said that death or old age was the cause, explaining that the remaining family had decided to live with relatives.

Suddenly he wondered what else Barker had been keeping from him. 'Tell me everything you know,' he said sharply. 'Else I cannot set things right.'

'You believe me, sir?'

He studied Caleb's face and nodded. 'Aye.' He suspected that this man, like Mistress Thorpe, would err on the side of bluntness.

'Unfortunately, sir, what I know is only hearsay and I can prove nothing, but I did see Withers taunting Mrs Thorpe today, and holding her roughly, too. She shouted out quite clearly that he had offered her only a guinea for the donkey and cart before she set fire to it.' He sighed. 'I would have paid her eight or nine guineas myself for them, had I known. The animal has been well looked after and the cart was sound, in spite of the recent accident.'

'It's a bad business. Thorpe's death has left us with the problem of getting another putter-out and Smedling is the only one who has offered to take over.' Nathaniel frowned. 'And Mrs Thorpe was robbed while the funeral was taking place. Did you know that?'

Caleb gasped. 'What did they take?'

'She says they took all her savings, over a hundred guineas. I find that – hard to believe.'

'I would believe her.'

Nathaniel looked at him in surprise, so vehement was his tone.

Caleb flushed slightly. 'I cannot think she would lie to you about something so important.'

'You seem to think very highly of her.'

'I've met her quite often when visiting my cousin Justin.'

'He is your cousin?'

'On the wrong side of the blanket.'

'Ah. Well, that's as may be, but it makes you a distant connection of mine as well.'

Caleb would never have claimed a relationship, but he could see that Nathaniel Armstrong was the sort of man to value things like that, so he did not contradict him.

Silence filled the room, with only the wood crackling on the fire and the gilt ormolu clock ticking on the mantelpiece to break it. The owner of the house was, from his expression, feeling upset at what had happened and Caleb waited for him to take the lead.

In the end Nathaniel said thoughtfully, 'I shall have to think about these matters and speak to Barker, but rest assured that I shall deal with this and that Mrs Thorpe will not be left without a home.' And he'd check over his own rent accounts, too, while he was at it, he decided grimly, and all the other accounts involved in running a large estate like this one. If Barker would behave badly in this, what else would he do?

Caleb gave a snort. 'Oh, Barker will have a tale to explain it all to you, Mr Armstrong. He usually does.' But Tam had never been able to explain the small flock of sheep on the distant farm on the moor's edge, among which Caleb had recognised several of his own beasts. Barker had strenuously denied taking them and professed himself happy to return them when confronted.

'You do not like my agent?'

Caleb shrugged. ''Tis not my place to like or dislike, but I definitely do not trust him.' He looked across at the clock. 'If Mrs Thorpe is recovered, I should like to take my leave of her. My mother will be worrying that I'm so late getting home.'

'Yes. Yes, of course.' Nathaniel went out into the hall and asked the housekeeper to find out how things were in Mrs Hannah's room.

Matty peeped into the small sitting room again, then came back shaking her head. 'Mrs Hannah waved me away again. The other lady is still lying with her head in your aunt's lap, sir, though she is not now sobbing.'

ANNA JACOBS

Caleb sighed. 'Then perhaps you will tell Mrs Thorpe farewell for me and – and say that if she finds herself in any further difficulties, she can always come to stay with me and my mother. We would not turn her away – and that includes all her family, too.' He looked at the housekeeper to make sure she had understood this and when she nodded her head, he turned to his host. 'Then I'll take my leave of you, sir, and get about my business.'

'I'll send word to you tomorrow about what happens.'

From the front door, Nathaniel watched Caleb stride off down the drive and stayed there for a while, lost in thought, heedless of the icy air that was blowing in. Then he looked at the housekeeper, hovering in the hall. 'Is Mr Barker here?'

'I believe so, sir.'

'Kindly ask my groom to come and wait outside the estate office. I may have need of Timothy's services.' Barker was a burly man and he might prove difficult to handle.

'Yes, sir.' She hurried away.

Squaring his shoulders, Nathaniel strode towards the offices at the rear of the house. Best to have it out with the fellow at once. Whatever the rights of the matter, Tam Barker should not have been involved in the matter of the cart, nor should he have harassed Mrs Thorpe like that.

When Justin arrived home, Maggie pounced on him as soon as he entered the house. 'Did you hear about what happened today? My friend Lydia came to tell me about it. Rachel Thorpe ran mad and burned her own cart in the market place. Can you believe that? *Her own cart!* And to think I missed seeing it!' She was angry about that; she had been lying down with another of her headaches when it all happened and had scolded the maids roundly for not coming to tell her what was going on.

'Mrs Thorpe is not to blame for what happened. She had been driven to desperation by a group of greedy and wicked men who wished to rob her. But those men will soon find that Mr Armstrong does not look kindly on those who try to take advantage of widows.' He turned to ring the bell.

210

Maggie could have shaken him. 'What happened, then? Tell me this instant!'

'In a moment. First I must send Jane up to look after the children and the old lady at North Beck Cottage.'

'Why?'

He ignored her and explained the situation to the house-keeper, who agreed to spend the night in Upper Clough, if necessary.

'Only, sir, it's a bit lonely up there. I'd feel better if I had Lal with me.'

'Very well. Send to the livery stables for a trap to drive you both up the hill. And you are to write a note to me when you get there, telling me whether anything is amiss.' Then he looked at Maggie as if he hardly saw her and added, 'I must return to Cleving now, to confer with Mr Armstrong about this.'

'But—' Maggie stared in indignation as he ran up the stairs, then came running down again a minute later and left the house without a word to her. Feeling angry, she went to catch the housekeeper. 'I'm coming with you to Upper Clough.'

'Madam?'

'Those children know me better than you. They will be afraid. I may even bring young Adam back with me tonight.'

Jane Charnley looked outside. 'It's getting dark, madam. And it's coming on to rain. You've not been well all day. Should you really venture out?'

Maggie joined her by the window, frowning. Wind shook it and a flurry of rain pattered against it. 'Hmm. Oh, very well. But if the little lad needs comforting, you must send him down the hill with the driver. I could look after him far better here. Yes, that is what we should do. You must send him back here at once.'

'Mr Kellett told me to stay up there with the children, madam.'

The two women looked at one another. When Maggie saw that Jane had no intention of doing as she asked, she gave an angry sniff and stormed off to the parlour.

The two servants left the daughters of the house sitting in

the warmth of the kitchen, keeping an eye on the food that was cooking. They were driven up the hill together in the gig from the inn, carrying a basket of food.

'It's a strange business, this,' Jane said thoughtfully as they jolted along.

'Very strange,' Lal agreed, enjoying the sudden departure from routine.

When they got to North Beck Cottage, they found the old lady desperately ill, struggling for each breath, and the two children anxious about their mother.

'Your mother's being looked after,' Jane said firmly. 'Now, go and sit with your auntie and Lal and I will get some food ready.'

Then the driver banged on the front door and said he must be leaving, which made them realise that they had not yet written a note for their employer. Jane went to find a scrap of paper and a quill, and wrote to say how ill the old lady was. She gave strict instructions to the driver of the trap that it was not to be handed to Mrs Kellett, but taken to her master at Cleving Park, if necessary. Then she and Lal went to make the old lady comfortable and feed the two children.

'She keeps a clean house here, I will say that,' Jane said later as she bent to wipe the forehead of the poor old lady, who was gasping for breath and only half aware of what was happening around her. An hour after that they had to change the stained sheets, as they would for a baby.

'We all come to it,' Jane said quietly as Lal pulled a face at the mess.

Tam Barker was haled out of the inn in Lower Clough by a groom and ordered to go and see his employer immediately. He walked back down the hill slowly, worrying about what this might mean. The groom had got back on the horse and galloped off, without answering Tam's questions, and he had looked at him scornfully as if he knew something but wasn't telling.

He and Bill had let things go too far today, Tam knew. They'd shown their hand, treating Rachel Thorpe like that in full view of the citizens of Setherby Bridge. Not clever, that. It was Bill who'd pushed him into it. By hell, Bill hated that woman. Tam had never seen anyone hate as viciously as his friend did.

The trouble was, he sucked thoughtfully on a rotten tooth as he mulled it over, you couldn't exactly deny something so public. And what had brought Mr Armstrong home when he'd not been expected for another day or two? Bit of bad luck, that.

At the big house, he was kept out of the estate office by Timothy until Mr Armstrong opened the door and gestured to him to come inside.

He tried to put a good face on it. 'You're back early, sir. I hope nothing is wrong.'

'You know very well that something is wrong, Barker,' Nathaniel snapped. 'What happened to Mrs Thorpe at the market today?'

'The woman ran mad and burned her own cart.'

Nathaniel didn't offer him a chair, just stumped round behind his desk and sat down. He could smell the ale on his agent's breath. He had had misgivings about Tam Barker when he first came here. He should have heeded them, but there had been so much to do and it had seemed unfair to judge the man purely on feelings, with no logical reason to dismiss him, especially when the estate had such a good steady rent roll, with no bad payers. 'Why did you not stop it?'

'She acted so quickly no one could have stopped it.' Tam explained about the hot chestnut seller's brazier and the straw catching light.

'I'm talking about Withers. Stop him. Half the town saw him bullying her, and I'm told he had friends in the crowd who were preventing anyone else from helping her, fellows from outside the valley.'

How the hell had Mr Armstrong found out about that?

'I am most displeased. I will not have women ill-treated like that in Whin Vale. And,' he shouted as Tam tried to say something, 'I am told that you, Tam Barker, ordered her to leave her house by today! I gave you no such instructions. What did you think you were doing, acting without my leave?'

'I was trying to get the house free for the next putter-out, sir. The whole valley will suffer if there is no one to take the finished pieces into Rochdale and bring the yarn back.'

Nathaniel's voice became quieter, but his words echoed with anger behind the measured tones. 'And which cottage had you found for her to move into?'

'She – she did not wish to stay in the valley, sir.'

Nathaniel bounced to his feet. 'Liar! I have heard the whole story and I say you're a liar, sir! Mrs Thorpe has an old aunt living with her and two children. She had no wish whatsoever to move away.'

'But she would not sell us the—'

'*Us?*' The voice was very soft indeed. 'What do you mean by "us"?'

Tam realised he had betrayed his own interest in the matter and wondered desperately how to amend that.

Nathaniel sat down again, breathing deeply and balancing his chair on its two back legs as he stared at his agent. He stared so long that the silence grew uncomfortable and Tam began to fidget visibly. 'Do not lie to me any more, Barker. You had intended to feather your own nest at the expense of *my* tenants – a matter which would have touched upon my honour – and I have consequently decided we shall do better if we part company.'

'*What?*'

'You heard me. I intend to find myself another land agent and I shall be glad if you will vacate your house as quickly as possible. I shall not put you out until you have somewhere to go, of course,' the scorn in his voice was heavy, 'but I would prefer you to leave as soon as possible.'

Tam stared at him in horror. 'But sir, I . . . Sir, please—'

Nathaniel held up one hand. 'I do not intend to discuss this matter further. Nor shall I change my mind. In the meantime, do you have the keys to the cupboards in this room on you?'

'N-no, sir.'

'Then I shall send one of the maids across to your house with you to fetch them back. You need not come into this office again.'

'But sir, I have things of my own here.'

'Make me out a list and if I can't find something, I'll bring you here to find it yourself later.'

Tam drew himself up and nodded, but his heart was thudding. Best not to pursue matters in case Mr Armstrong examined the account books too closely. Best just to do as he was asked. And at least he had somewhere to go until— He cut that thought off. He might have to postpone his other plans for a while. And what his wife would say about moving up to his family's scrubby little farm on the tops – if you could call it a farm – he did not know.

As he walked back across the rear gardens to his own snug little house, anger roiled in him. This was all due to *that woman*. Walter was right. By hell he was! Rachel Thorpe brought a jinx upon anyone who associated with her, whether willingly or unwillingly. In Tam's great-grandfather's time, she would have been accused of witchcraft and probably been burnt at the stake for one. Pity they didn't still do that to women like her.

Well, if he ever found a way to pay her back, he'd seize it. Oh, indeed he would. Bill Withers was right about that. You didn't let folk harm you without taking your revenge.

Back in the office, Nathaniel began a long, methodical search, checking each book, each item entered and remembering each detail, as he always did. Step by step he built up a picture. He said nothing to anyone about what he was doing, not even when he found things that did not seem to match with what he knew. He could not accuse a man on a mere suspicion.

He would continue to investigate matters until he had proved to his own satisfaction what he now only suspected. And when he did, he would take action. In the meantime, he would allow Smedling to become putter-out, because the weavers must have some way of getting their pieces into Rochdale. Meanwhile, he would say nothing to anyone of his plans.

CHAPTER FIFTEEN

The following morning tempers were still high all over the district. Nathaniel Armstrong woke early to the bitter knowledge that he had failed in his role as responsible landowner. He got dressed in a glum silence that had his man whispering to the other servants to watch out for storms today. Since they all knew that Tam Barker had been dismissed the previous day ('And good riddance, too!' the head groom had said) they set about their duties with extreme care.

Nathaniel ate breakfast in his usual solitary state, but today he would have preferred company. 'It's definitely time I took a wife,' he told the ham gloomily. He needed to talk to somebody, a woman, about dealing with another woman. His aunt was never up until later so he nerved himself to ask Matty whether Mrs Thorpe had risen yet.

The housekeeper just shook her head. 'Dorcas says the bell hasn't been rung, sir.'

So Nathaniel went into the agent's office to start going through the books and papers.

When Matty tapped on the door to say his aunt was now up and wished to see him, she was startled to see how black was his frown, for the master was usually very even-tempered.

He stared at her as if he did not really see her, then said curtly, 'Kindly ask one of the gardeners or grooms to come and sit in here while I'm gone, and tell everyone to remember that Mr Barker is to be denied entrance to the house, and most especially to this office.'

She goggled at him.

'Go on, woman!'

She hurried off.

He waited, fingers tapping impatiently on the desk, until she came back with the first male servant she had found – a gardener. Alfred Tubbins, beaming broadly because he had never penetrated beyond the kitchens or hall before, intimated that he would be delighted to sit in the office until Mr Armstrong came back instead of digging over the vegetable patch.

'And that's all, sir? I mean, you don't want me to *do* anything?'

'I don't want you to do or touch anything at all. But you are to see that no one else comes in here, especially not Mr Barker. You understand me?'

'No, sir. I mean, yes, sir.'

Nathaniel found a pale but composed Mrs Thorpe in his aunt's sitting room beside Hannah, who was looking brighter than usual today. He kissed her on the cheek and noted how fondly she was looking at Rachel Thorpe, and how she had hold of one of the guest's hands, as if to give the young woman courage. He could remember her treating him the same way when he came here as a lad and fell over, cutting his leg so badly the doctor had insisted on stitching the flesh together. How it had hurt! But he had not cried out, because she had given him courage. He still had the scar.

He cleared his throat. 'I, hope you are feeling brighter today, Mrs Thorpe.'

'Yes, thank you, sir.' But Rachel was feeling guilty at neglecting her family. 'You're sure that – that someone went up to my house last night?'

'Certain of it. Parson sent me word that his housekeeper and maid were looking after your children and aunt. And after you and I have talked, I shall send you home in my carriage so that you may be with them yourself.'

'Thank you, sir. And – and I do most truly thank you for all your help.' Rachel still could not quite believe that she had been so foolish as to burn her cart yesterday. She remembered flames leaping up, then her memories were rather blurred, but she did remember Caleb Hesketh and how he had helped her, held her, soothed her.

'I feel I must make up to you for the fact that my land agent has dealt unjustly with you.'

She clutched Hannah Armstrong's hand even more tightly. 'So I – I don't need to leave North Beck Cottage?'

He decided it was better to be frank from the start. 'Eventually, you will need to leave. I'm afraid I shall require that cottage for the next putter-out. It is by far the most suitable place. But you need not leave until you're quite ready, and of course we shall find you somewhere else to live.'

She blinked away a tear and felt Mrs Armstrong pat her hand. She had loved living at North Beck Cottage and it held so many memories of Thomas – but it was best not to dwell on that. She took a deep breath to steady herself. 'Is there another cottage I can have, sir? One with a weaver's attic?'

He frowned. 'I have been wondering about that. My dear young woman, the men of this valley have said your weaving is not good enough,' he heard her gasp in shock and remembered that it was Tam Barker who had said it and added, 'but whether it is or not, they refuse categorically to carry your pieces into Rochdale, nor will they bring you back the necessary yarn, so I'm afraid you will have to find another way to earn your bread. Be sensible about this, my dear.'

Rachel bent her head, despair flooding through her. What else did she know but weaving? And why were the men of Whin Vale being so cruel? No, most of them were just being weak – it was Walter Smedling who held a grudge against her, and Bill Withers. It was they who were preventing her from earning her bread. 'I cannot change how they feel, sir, but I tell you now that I weave *better* than most men, and that is the real reason certain of them refuse to deal with me.'

He could see no guile in her face and he felt she might be

telling the truth, but it would cause a lot of trouble if she tried to continue weaving, so it was better she did not. He would have to find something else for her to do, though what he could not think.

'I have an idea,' Hannah said quietly, still holding Rachel's shaking hand in hers. Her heart went out to the poor young woman who was being so cruelly treated, and she thought, not for the first time, that women were just as good as men, only men were afraid to let that be seen. Although Hannah's own husband had treated her kindly, he had always spoken and acted as though she was a lesser being. And his nephew held similar beliefs.

'Dorcas wishes to leave Cleving, to marry, and I shall be needing a maid – not just a maid, but someone of sense who is strong enough to lift me and who will help me in my daily tasks.' She stared down at her twisted hands, then set aside her anger at what was happening to her body, which had once been as young and straight-limbed as that of this young woman. 'I thought Rachel might make a good replacement for her.' Hannah looked at Rachel. 'Would you do that, my dear? Come and look after me?'

Rachel smiled at Mrs Armstrong, who reminded her a little of her own mother in her gentleness. 'I'd be happy to help you, madam, but,' her face clouded over again, 'I'm afraid I have other responsibilities. My husband's aunt is dying, and I have two children to look after, my son and stepdaughter. I must find another way to support them.' Her face became stern for a moment and she looked very directly at her host. 'I should not like to rely on your charity for that, sir, or anyone else's.'

Nathaniel nodded. He had expected no less from her.

Hannah was still frowning. She was going to miss Dorcas and she really liked the idea of having Rachel to help her. No, she definitely did not want to look for another maid. She had taken to this young woman, not just because she was in trouble, but because she was brave and sensible. 'There may be a way around that. How old is your stepdaughter?'

'Nearly twelve, madam.'

'And your son?'

Rachel could not help smiling at the thought of Adam. 'Going on six, and very large for his age. Intelligent, too, though perhaps I should not be the one to say that.'

'Hmm.' Nathaniel looked from one woman to the other. He had not thought of this solution to the problem of replacing Dorcas, but he liked the idea of it. A good strong woman, Mrs Thorpe, and would be able to help his aunt in any way necessary. He would discuss it with Hannah later. Maybe there would be a way to arrange matters.

'Well, we shall send you home to see that your children are all right and care for your aunt, Mrs Thorpe, then we can discuss your future when next we meet. In the meantime the new putter-out can use your shed for his things.'

'I do not wish to deal with Walter Smedling,' she said sharply.

Nathaniel stifled a sigh. 'He need only use your shed.'

Rachel did not feel up to arguing about this. 'And your agent, Mr Barker – he is aware that I can stay on?'

'Mr Barker is no longer my land agent. Until I can find someone else, I shall be dealing with these matters myself, so you need have no fear that anyone will try to make you move while your aunt is ill.'

Her face brightened. 'And – Bill Withers?' For she feared him more than the others, felt he meant to do her actual harm if he could.

'I shall send word to Withers this very morning that he is to keep right away from you.'

'Then I should go home now, I think.' She turned to smile tremulously at Hannah. 'And I cannot thank you enough for your kindness, Mrs Armstrong. I don't know what I would have done without your wise counsel.'

Nathaniel nodded approvingly. Prettily said.

Rachel turned back to him. 'And I thank you, too, sir. Taking me into your own home. I know not how I can repay your kindness, but be sure I am deeply grateful, and if there is ever anything I can do for you, I shall.'

ANNA JACOBS

He blinked in surprise at this. He was not used to the lower classes thinking of repaying him.

When the young woman had left, Hannah said wistfully, 'It's a pity she is not free. I should really have liked Mrs Thorpe to tend me and be my companion. I don't feel embarrassed in front of her. She makes it all seem quite natural when she helps me. And she is more intelligent than Dorcas, who is a kind girl, but not – not a thinking person. Oh, well, I dare say we'll find someone else.'

He nodded, but made up his mind to grant her her wish. She had been a good aunt to him in the days of her health, and now that she was growing more frail, he would look after her.

Caleb was in a bad mood that day, still angry that Rachel had been treated so cruelly and worried about what was happening to her. When his mother made light of the matter and said *that woman* was playing on the situation to gain sympathy, he turned on her.

'I don't want to hear such talk again, Mother!'

Joanna scowled at him, but when he spoke in that tone, he looked so like his Singleton grandmother that she did not even try to argue.

He waited a moment to emphasise how important this was to him. 'Rachel Thorpe has been treated very badly indeed, and it pained me to see her so upset.'

Joanna breathed deeply. She thought he had got over his old attraction to that woman, but now that Thomas Thorpe was dead, his widow was free to marry again. Why could Caleb not like Amy Birtle, who was as nice a lass as you could hope to meet? Why did he have to set his mind on that tall, ugly female? She had seen Rachel Thorpe once or twice and had not liked the look of her. Not at all the sort of wife she wanted for her son. Besides, a woman as managing in her ways as that one would take over everything here and would probably send her mother-in-law to live in the poorhouse. She realised Caleb was speaking again.

'I shall go into Setherby again this afternoon, Mother. I must find out what they are doing to help her.' Another determined look pinned Joanna in her place. 'And if they are not protecting her as they ought, then I shall invite her to come and stay with us until she can find some way of earning her bread.'

'*What?*'

'You heard me.'

'Caleb, *please* don't get mixed up with that woman!'

'If I see someone in such sore need, I cannot stand by and let them be treated cruelly.' He couldn't even stand by when the village boys tormented a kitten. 'And don't bring any more young women round to tea. When the time comes, I shall choose my own wife.'

'Her, I suppose.'

He was silent, then admitted for the first time, 'If she will have me. But it's far too early yet for me to say anything. She's still grieving for her husband – and he was a fine man, by all accounts.'

'Oh, Caleb, think what you're doing! She'll only mean trouble for you.'

'Strange, you've been urging me to marry for a while now.'

'And I've introduced you to some lovely lasses. Why could you not take one of them? What's wrong with Jemima Green?'

He gave a scornful sniff. 'She's an empty-headed fool who'd let you rule the roost here still. I do not intend to breed my children from a woman like that.' You bred your sheep for strength, intelligence and other qualities. In his opinion you should take as much care with your own children.

Joanna made a muffled sound of exasperation and marched out into the scullery, her back rigid.

He sighed and went to stand by the window for a moment, looking out across the moors he loved so much, watching the last of the morning mist swirl up from a small depression at the far side of his land, a hollow with a small pond in it where he had paddled as a lad.

'There is only her,' he said softly. Rachel Thorpe had been

figuring in his dreams for so long now that she seemed almost a part of him. 'I am not like my father,' he added. 'I am faithful to the one I love.'

In the parsonage, Justin and his wife were arguing across the breakfast table which she had had to set and prepare food for herself, since the housekeeper and maid had not yet returned from Upper Clough. Maggie had sent her daughters to eat in the kitchen so that she could talk to Justin and persuade him to do as she wished.

'We need to discuss the boy,' she said as calmly as she could manage, though she could feel how fast her pulse was beating.

He groaned. 'I have said all I intend to say about Adam Thorpe.'

'Well, I have not!' She glared at him across the table. 'His mother will not be able to look after him now and you know how much more we can offer him.'

'We do *not* know that his mother won't be able to look after him.'

'She won't be able to put a roof over her head even. How can she possibly care for him as he deserves?'

Justin closed his eyes and prayed for patience, as he often did when Maggie got one of her fusses on – except that this was not just a fuss and he had to admit to himself that since she had planted the seed in his mind, he, too, would like nothing more than to adopt young Adam Thorpe as his son. His internal prayer changed to a plea to his Lord to help him avoid temptation. 'She is his mother, Maggie. You are not.'

'You don't care about me any more!' She buried her head in her hands and began to weep.

He sat there for as long as he could, trying not to give in to her tears. But even though he knew how easily she cried, he could also see how much she cared about this. 'My dear, please do not get yourself so upset.'

She only cried the harder.

He stood up and went to put one arm round her shoulders.

'Justin, at least promise me you'll a-ask?' she begged, her voice breaking on the last word.

'Very well. If an opportunity arises, I'll ask. But she'll not agree to it, I know. And I won't force the issue.'

She sighed and allowed him to comfort her and wipe away her tears. When he went out to the kitchen for more hot water for a fresh pot of tea, she allowed herself a smile, then quickly composed her face into a wistful expression. She had made a start. See if she didn't get what she wanted from him in the end!

When the carriage drew up at North Beck Cottage, Rachel jumped out at once, not waiting to be helped. Even before she reached the front door, Adam and Kitty flung it open and rushed to throw their arms round her.

Behind them Jane and Lal exchanged glances. The children had been fretting since they'd woken up, wanting their mother. 'I don't care what folk say about her,' the housekeeper murmured, 'she loves them dearly.'

'And they her. Eh, it does your heart good to see them, doesn't it?'

When Rachel went inside, it was to find the house spotless, the latest batch of washing hanging near the fire to dry, and Auntie Susan changed into a clean nightdress. The old lady was still weak and feverish, but roused to whisper how glad she was to see Rachel back.

'What happened yesterday, Mam?' Adam asked when the parson's servants had been driven back down the hill. 'Mrs Charnley said there'd been trouble at the market but she wouldn't tell us what.'

So Rachel told the two youngsters the plain unvarnished truth, about how silly she'd been, how her temper had led her into trouble. 'Don't ever let your temper get the better of you, Adam my boy,' she finished. 'I know you've inherited it from my side of the family, but keep it in better check than I have done. Things done in hot anger are never right.' She looked down at her hands for a moment, then managed to smile at gentle Kitty, who was looking distressed. 'You don't have the worry of a hot temper, my lass, and should be thankful for that. You're like your father, with a steady head on you.'

'But what's going to happen to us now?' Adam persisted. 'Shall we still have to leave this house?'

Rachel could hear her voice wobble as she said, 'I'm afraid so. But not – not yet.'

She talked to them for a little longer, then went to check on her aunt, pausing outside the door for a moment to pull herself together. The future looked bleak for them all, but at least they would still have a roof over their heads for a while longer.

If it wasn't for the children, she'd take up Mrs Armstrong's kind offer once Auntie Susan died – for the time being, anyway. But she wasn't giving her son to anyone else to look after, she definitely wasn't.

She took a deep breath and opened the door. First, though, there was Auntie Susan to nurse through her final days. Another grief for the children – and for her. She laid a gentle hand on the old lady's cheek and sat down beside the bed, smiling. 'Have they been looking after you all right, then, Auntie?'

Tam Barker's wife did not stop scolding and shouting and weeping all the time she was packing their things. He tried clouting her and she grabbed the nearest solid object to clout him back.

'Taking me away from all I know to that nasty little hovel on the moors! How *could* you behave like that? I never thought I'd married a thief and a cheat.'

'It was an opportunity to do something for myself so I'd not spend my whole life saying yes, sir, no, sir, to someone else.'

'But it was such a good position here,' she mourned. 'Worth saying yes, sir, no, sir for. I could hold my head up in Setherby. Wife of the land agent to Mr Armstrong of Cleving Park! And now what will you be? A sheepherder on the moors? We'll be snowed up half the winter. I'll not have a new bonnet from one year to the next. There'll be no one to talk to. How could you be so *stupid*, Tam Barker? And so dishonest, too.'

In the end, he took refuge in the outhouse where he kept his personal tools, pretending to sort them out. He'd better go up to Crag End tomorrow and check that the house was habitable. Thank heavens Jen didn't know about the money they'd stolen from Rachel Thorpe! Well, he wasn't intending to live up at Crag End for ever. Oh, no. He'd keep the money safe with the other funds he'd amassed over the past few years and live quietly till he found a way to get a proper place of his own, not a poor place on the moors.

He had a few things planned to get more money and would bring them forward now that he no longer worked for that stuffed shirt. Who'd see what he was doing when he lived up at Crag End? He'd be much freer there. He began to whistle. Maybe this wasn't such a bad thing after all.

CHAPTER SIXTEEN

The following day Nathaniel summoned Justin to the big house and explained how much his aunt wanted to have Rachel Thorpe as maid and companion. 'I haven't seen her so taken by an idea for a long time, and I am very eager to fulfil her wish.'

'And Rachel, is she taken by the idea?'

'I think she would not be averse to it were it not for her family responsibilities.' He chewed on his lip for a moment, then tapped his fingers on the solid oak desk which had been his uncle's and which he refused to replace with one of the new mahogany pieces much in vogue. 'But she has a young son of whom she is very fond.'

'Yes. Adam.' Justin breathed very slowly, trying to avoid temptation.

'You are godfather to this child, I believe,' Nathaniel went on, in his measured way.

'Yes. Yes, I am.'

'And I am told that your wife is very fond of the lad, too.'

'Yes. Very fond. We both are. He's a lively child, very – very engaging.' He looked up at his patron and said in a rush of guilty words, 'But I know how dearly his mother loves him and I would not wish to separate her from him.'

'If he were living nearby, she need not be separated, but could go and see him every week.'

Silence hung heavy between them, but Justin would not

be the first to speak the words that would deprive Rachel of her son.

Nathaniel said them for him. 'Could you not foster the lad for a while? Take him into your home? Sadly, I don't think my aunt will make old bones, so it'll only be for a year or two at most.'

Foster! Justin seized on this idea gratefully. 'Foster him? Well, yes, of course we could do that. Then he could go back to his mother again if her circumstances changed. You would no doubt offer her a cottage to rent if anything happened to your aunt?'

'Naturally.'

And so it was settled, in Nathaniel's mind, at least.

But guilt still lingered in Justin's. He knew how his wife would take this, and if – no, *when* they came to give Adam back to his mother, he knew how Maggie would react. He winced at the mere thought of the hysterics that would give rise to.

And what about his own daughters? His wife had been neglecting them lately, he knew. He tried to pay them more attention to make up for that, but it wasn't the same, coming from a man. They needed a woman sometimes. Thank goodness for Jane Charnley and her good sense. He didn't know what his daughters would do without her. He didn't know what he would do without her, either, for she somehow contrived to stay on good terms with Maggie while still managing his household efficiently. An admirable woman, Jane. He wished Maggie was more like her.

Later that day, Nathaniel drove over to Todmorden to visit his mother and the young woman who was staying with her. Now that he had decided to wed, he saw no reason to delay and was quite willing to inspect the candidates she continued to present. But he intended to make his own decision about whom he would marry.

'Miss Hartley.' He bowed over a firm white hand and looked into a face more sensible than pretty – not an ugly face, but one where the essential nature was painted very clearly.

He approved of that. Beautiful women made him nervous. He didn't trust them. Nor did he want a wife whom other men would covet, or who would expect too much attention and fuss from him.

He must have held the hand for too long because his mother, watching with great interest, said, 'Ahhh!' very softly and directed them to sit together on the sofa opposite her, smiling benignly as they did so.

He set himself to converse, introducing a range of topics which were of interest to him to elicit Miss Hartley's opinions – and found to his delight that she shared his concerns about the education of children and the difficulties of the daily lives of the poor. Not only shared, but had good points to contribute to the discussion. He could see that his mother was heartily bored by the topic but after a while he forgot her. Eyes met eyes. Smiles were exchanged, and nods, and frequent murmurs of agreement. Conversation never flagged between the two of them. And it was not difficult to find other topics when one had been fully explored, though with some young women, Nathaniel had found conversation an almost impossible hurdle. With this one it was actually a pleasure.

When he looked at the clock, he clicked his tongue in amazement. He had been here for far longer than he had realised. He brought the discussion gently to an end, then stood up. 'It has been a great pleasure to meet you, Miss Hartley.' He bowed over her hand, and a nice firm hand it was, too.

Turning to his mother, he invited her to bring her young guest to visit him at Cleving Park before Miss Hartley returned home.

Dorothy Armstrong beamed at him. 'In two days' time?'

'That would be delightful, Mother,' he responded.

After her son had left, Dorothy spoke frankly to Miss Hartley. 'You seemed to get on well with my Nathaniel, Catherine.'

'I found him a very conscientious landowner, feeling as he ought about serious matters.' A slight blush coloured cheeks not normally given to blushing. 'Yes. I feel we – we did get on well.'

Nothing more was said openly. They both knew why Catherine had been invited to visit. Miss Hartley came from a good family and would have a respectable portion to bring to the marriage, even if it was not as large as an ambitious mother would have wished.

Walter Smedling came to the door of North Beck Cottage, very stiff, staring somewhere past Rachel's right shoulder as he spoke, to avoid meeting her eyes. 'Mr Armstrong says I'm to use the shed till you move.'

She was equally stiff. 'Yes. So he told me. I've taken our things out of it. If you wish to buy any of them, you can come and discuss that with me.'

'I'll have a look at what's left first.'

He came to the kitchen door within minutes. 'Where is everything?'

'In here.'

He was fairly sputtering with indignation. 'Those things belonged to the putter-out! You had no right.'

'I had every right. They belonged to my husband, who bought them in the first place, and now they belong to me. But I'm prepared to sell them to you – and will charge you less than it would cost to buy or make new gear, since it is convenient to both of us. After all, it is a way to get some of my money back, is it not? The money that was stolen from me.'

Breath whistled into his mouth and anger twisted his face. They stared at one another and neither said a word as the seconds ticked past.

It was definitely he who had done it, she thought angrily. Guilt was written all over his face. But she had promised herself not to let anger get the better of her again, so she said nothing. What could she do without proof anyway?

Walter wondered desperately what to do about her accusation, then reason told him she could prove nothing, so he shrugged and ignored her words. 'Show me what you have to sell, then.'

Very reluctantly, she let him into the kitchen and showed him the equipment, naming a price for each piece, correcting him when he added up the total to his own advantage, then folding her arms and refusing to discuss it further.

'It's too much.' He left, hoping that time would soften her attitude.

She could not resist calling after him, 'I'll burn it before I'll give it to you for nothing.'

He stopped moving for a moment, fists clenched by his sides, then continued walking without looking back.

She waited, sure he'd be back. In the meantime, she tended to the old lady's needs, worrying that each breath Auntie Susan took was a triumph, knowing death to be very near now. And then she would be alone in the world, with just the children for comfort, children who would rely on her for everything.

It was two days before Walter returned to North Beck Cottage, having waited in vain for Rachel to send word that she'd lower her price. He and Bill had discussed her offer and had come to the conclusion that it was still a cheaper way to get the equipment than buying it all new.

'Offer her half what she asks,' said Bill at last.

'She won't take it,' Walter said, supping his ale slowly to make it last. 'Allus was a stubborn wench.'

'And what about that donkey? Did you ask about that?'

'No. Went clean out of my head.'

'You're not thinking straight, you aren't, lately.' Bill leaned closer and whispered, 'Forget him. He's dead.'

'I keep seein' him a-lyin' in the road, with his blood all over that stone.' Walter shivered, then looked up and called, 'Hoy! Another pot of ale, Jude!'

'Shh!' Bill took it upon himself to countermand the order and scold his friend. 'You can't drink any more ale tonight, lad. Mr Armstrong said he'd watch how you went, and he warned you he wasn't having no drunkard acting as putter-out. I think if he'd had anyone else, he'd not have let you try it.'

He smiled. 'But I made sure no one else would step forward, didn't I?'

Walter scowled at his empty pot. 'What's the world coming to if a man can't get hisself a drink of an evening?'

'It's coming to money, that's what it's coming to. You listen to me and you'll wind up comfortable in your old age. And me with you.' Heaven knew, he certainly needed more money. Children and babbies might be small, but they cost you a fortune till they grew old enough to bring in some money themselves. One of his sons had died a few months ago and his wife had moped around the house like a cow whose calf had been taken away from it. Only now that she was carrying another baby had she got back to her old self, in bed and out of it.

Walter went to knock on the door of North Beck Cottage and made a higher offer, but still lower than what Rachel had asked.

She refused. 'Not even a farthing less,' she declared, folding her arms and leaning against the door, not inviting him inside this time.

He breathed in deeply. 'Well, what about the donkey, then? We'll pay your full price if you throw in the donkey.'

She laughed in his face. 'Mr Armstrong says he'll help me sell Sukey elsewhere if I can't come to terms with anyone round here.'

'Why, you—' He broke off as Dusty growled from behind her. 'You should keep that dog tied up. It's a dangerous brute, that one is.'

'Only with people who mean me harm, and he's a good watchdog, too, our Dusty.' Rachel leaned forward, smiling sweetly. 'I'm quite prepared to have another bonfire,' she said again. Then she started to close the door. She didn't mean it, of course. She would never do such a stupid thing again, but he clearly believed her, because he put out a foot to hold the door open.

'All right, all right! We'll pay you your money, you cheating doxy! Show me where the things are and I'll carry them out to the shed again.'

'Not till after you've paid me for them, you won't.'

He pressed his lips together and breathed deeply. 'You're too sharp for your own comfort, you are. I don't know how Thorpe put up with your grasping ways.'

She was suddenly suffused with rage. 'Don't you even mention his name to me, you murderer!'

He fell back a step, his face going pale.

She saw her suspicions confirmed again by the guilt written so clearly on his face, but although she had to dig her nails into the palms of her hands to prevent herself from hitting him, from screaming the accusations aloud, she did not let her anger escape. She had vowed never to give way to it again, whatever the provocation. But one day she would make sure he paid for what he had done. She had vowed that, as well. Slowly and emphatically she said, 'Don't ever – *ever* – mention my Thomas's name again.'

Quietness beat around them, filled only with small sounds, the wind teasing round their bodies, a bird calling from some-where far away, and the high but muffled tones of children's voices from inside the house.

Walter shivered and tried to pull himself together, but he was afraid, desperately afraid. He had a sudden urge to tell her it had been an accident, that it hadn't been him who threw the rock, that he hadn't meant anything like that to happen to Thomas – but he swallowed the words and continued the conversation with a safer topic. 'I'll bring your money round this afternoon.'

'The things will be ready for you as soon as I've counted it.'

'And the donkey?'

'You can buy it from me if you want.'

'How much?'

She was less certain here. 'Ask Caleb Hesketh,' she said in the end. 'He'll name a fair price for me. I'll see him myself come market day or you can speak to him before if you want.' And wondered at herself afterwards for thinking instinctively of a man she hardly knew.

'Got your eye on another fellow already, have you?' he sneered.

'There *are* no others like my Thomas.'

Suddenly she could not stand the sight of him for a moment longer, so slammed the door in his face and leaned against it, repressed anger growling in her throat and making her limbs tremble. It was several minutes before she was calm enough to go in and sit with the old lady.

Auntie Susan died the next day. She was holding Rachel's hand when she suddenly stiffened and stared at the corner as if she saw someone standing there. A faint smile crossed her face, then her head rolled to one side and her hand went slack.

Rachel sat beside the body for a few moments, tears running down her cheeks, then went to tell the children. They all wept, knowing they would miss the old lady.

The simple funeral was attended by a sparse gathering, elderly folk mostly, those who had known Susan in her childhood, or who had been friends of Thomas. After Auntie Susan had been laid to rest beside her husband in Setherby graveyard, Justin insisted on taking Rachel back to the parsonage to eat dinner with them, but it was an awkward meal, with Maggie fussing over Adam but ignoring Kitty and her own children.

Justin turned to his guest when the meal ended. 'I'd like to speak to you privately in my study before you go, if you don't mind, Rachel.'

Maggie said quickly, 'I'll keep an eye on Adam.'

Rachel did not say that her son needed no eye keeping on him but could be trusted to behave himself, but she thought it. She followed Justin suspiciously, wondering what was to come that he had to take her aside to speak of it.

When she had sat down, he spoke of Mrs Armstrong, her great need for a maid and companion, and of his patron's desire to gratify his aunt's wishes.

Rachel stared at him in puzzlement. 'But I told him I could not do it. With two children to look after, I cannot possibly go as Mrs Hannah's maid.'

'But if you did not have the children, would you consider the offer then?'

'What do you mean? Why should I not have the children?'

It was difficult to find the words to tell her. 'You need to find a way to earn your bread, Rachel, so I would be prepared – we both would, for Maggie loves the boy too – to foster Adam for a while. You could come and see him every week and—'

'*See him every week?* I want to see him every day, be with him, look after him! I'm his *mother*!'

'It isn't always possible to have what we want, Rachel.'

She said slowly, 'Mr Armstrong has asked you to do this?'

'Yes.'

Breath caught in her throat, anger simmered in her belly, but she held them back and just said, 'No!' very firmly.

He opened his mouth to say something.

She remembered how Maggie doted on young Adam and said it again, more loudly, 'No, Justin Kellett! I'll not give up my son to you or anyone!'

'But how shall you earn your bread otherwise?'

'I'll find something.'

'What?'

'I don't know! And besides, there is Kitty to think of. What am I to do with her?' Her voice became scornful. 'Or is your wife prepared to have her as well?'

'Mr Armstrong has offered to take Kitty on as a maidservant at Cleving. She would have a fine life there, learn about a wider world than just Whin Vale.'

'I still say no. I will not give up my son.' Then she got up and walked out, going to the kitchen to collect the two children. She found only Kitty, looking out into the garden, and followed her gaze to see Maggie walking along with her hand possessively on the shoulder of Adam.

They were *not* going to take him from her. She went to the back door. 'Adam! We're leaving.'

Maggie turned round, her hand tightening on the lad's shoulder. 'Is – has Justin not spoken to you, Rachel?'

'What about?'

'Why, about us adopting Adam?'

'*Adopting!* He spoke only of you looking after my son for a while, fostering him.'

Maggie shrugged. ''Tis the same thing, surely.'

'No. It isn't. And anyway, my Adam doesn't need fostering while he has his own mother to look after him.'

The boy chose that moment to pull away and run across to Rachel, standing beside her and staring back at Mrs Kellett with a frown. 'What does she mean, Mam?' he asked, sensing the hostility that underlay their voices.

'I'll tell you as we walk home.'

Maggie stepped forward to block their path. She had been hoping to keep him here, had the bed aired ready.

Rachel simply walked round her and left the garden. Why could folk not leave her alone? Why did they keep interfering in her life?

The children followed her without a word until they were out of Setherby.

'What's fostering?' Adam asked again as they began the long pull up the hill.

'It means looking after a child whose mother cannot look after him herself. Parson and his wife want to look after you, Adam, because Mr Armstrong wants me to go as maid to his aunt.'

Kitty walked beside them, her brow creased in thought. 'What is to become of me, then?'

Rachel gave her a quick hug. 'I told them no. You will stay with me and Adam, of course. You're my daughter, love, and always will be.'

'But – if we have to leave our house, if Mr Armstrong won't let you have a weaver's cottage, where can we all live?' That worry was haunting Kitty.

'I'll find somewhere.' But Rachel was worried about that, for all her defiant words. Desperately worried. Mr Armstrong was a very powerful man. He owned nearly all the houses round here.

★ ★ ★

When she took Miss Hartley to visit Cleving Park, Nathaniel's mother pleaded tiredness and left him to show the visitor round his house and its extensive grounds himself, while she sat with Aunt Hannah.

'Will she not make a fine wife for him?' Dorothy demanded as soon as they were alone.

'He has said nothing to me of courting anyone,' Hannah observed mildly.

'They have only met once so far, two days ago. But I saw immediately that he and Catherine were well suited.'

Hannah thought about how the two of them had looked as they walked away. 'Aye. I think you're right. They seemed,' she searched for a word, 'comfortable together.'

From attics to cellars, Nathaniel showed his guest the house, telling her his plans for improving it. She nodded and made the occasional suggestion. And sensible suggestions they were too. They went on to walk round the gardens.

'Cleving has a pleasant situation,' she allowed, staring down the slope at the little town of Setherby Bridge, nestled in the valley below them, just a pleasant stroll away.

He looked back at the house with a proprietorial air. 'The house is sheltered from the worst of the weather, being on a south-facing slope, but I would wish to plant more trees around it.'

'You must leave vistas through them, however. Here, for instance . . .'

Before they realised it, two hours had passed. She didn't exclaim in pretended shock as he remarked on the time, just looked at him sideways, a long, thoughtful look.

He decided to put the matter to the test there and then. There was, after all, no reason to wait. 'Are you aware of my mother's reason for introducing you to me?'

She inclined her head.

'And – would you be averse to – to what she wishes?'

A slight flush mantled her cheeks, but she said quietly, 'No. Not at all averse.'

'Then would you do me the honour of becoming my wife, Miss Hartley – Catherine?'

'I should be pleased to marry you, Nathaniel Armstrong.' At four and twenty she could not afford to be choosy, having been disappointed before. Besides, he was a well-set sort of man, with a steady, dependable look to him, which was far more important in her opinion than being handsome or fashionable.

He wondered whether he ought to kiss her but could not make up his mind about it, and the moment passed as she turned back towards the house.

'We should tell your mother, I think, Nathaniel,' she said composedly. 'Then you must come to Rochdale to speak to my father – though he will not refuse you, I'm sure.'

'That will please me very much – Catherine. And – and I hope there is no reason to delay the wedding.'

'None at all.' She would be glad to have her own house, glad to get away from her prettier and younger sisters. Exultation filled her, but she did not let it show. She had learned to hide her feelings over the past few years. It was better not to let other folk know all that went on inside her head. It was better to manage life gently and unobtrusively.

For the next two weeks, Rachel tramped everywhere in Whin Vale and beyond it, going anywhere she thought might offer a chance of finding work and a cottage to rent. She even went to Todmorden and spoke to Gracie, who was very discouraging. Life was hard for a woman on her own. It wasn't just a question of Rachel finding a house. She might well be able to do that, but how was she to earn the money to pay her rent and buy food?

'By weaving, I thought,' Rachel said.

Gracie frowned. 'If Mr Armstrong wishes you to look after his aunt, he will stop you from doing any weaving. The family has a lot of influence in this town. They stick together, the gentry do, so it's best to do as they want.'

'I have spoken to Harrison's in Rochdale. They will be happy to take my work.' It had warmed Rachel's heart that they had remembered her and her husband, and spoke highly of the work they had received from both the Thorpes in the past.

In a burst of renewed energy, she finished the piece she had been working on intermittently, then rode into Rochdale on the carrier's cart to deliver it, smiling as they rumbled along. Why, she could manage everything perfectly well, if only Mr Armstrong would rent her a weaver's cottage. She didn't need a putter-out. She would go and see the landowner herself when she got back, make him see that she could earn her bread without any help. Tell him to ask Harrison's if he didn't believe her.

But this time Simon Harrison took her into his office and said bluntly, 'I can't take your work, after all, I'm afraid, Mrs Thorpe.'

She stood very still, and it was a moment before she spoke, her voice coming out harshly. 'Why not? What's wrong with it?'

'Nothing. There's nothing at all wrong with it. In fact, it's a fine piece of work.'

'Then why? *Why* won't you take it?'

Hating to see the happy look fade from her face, he decided to tell her the truth, then at least she would know this wasn't his doing. 'It isn't approved of that you should weave like a man, Mrs Thorpe. Not now you're on your own in the world.'

He had received a visit from Nathaniel Armstrong the previous day, explaining the situation, the way the other weavers of Whin Vale refused to work with this woman, how it would cause trouble among them if she were allowed to do a man's job. And when Simon had said he didn't like to take a woman's living away from her, Mr Armstrong had informed him that Rachel had a job waiting for her at Cleving, looking after his old aunt. Without another word being said, let alone threats being made, Simon had realised where his own best interests lay.

Rachel bowed her head, unable to stop the tears from falling.

'Look, I'll buy this piece from you, give you a good price, so you won't go back empty-handed. But I can't buy any more. It's

– not wise to give offence to those with property and influence.' He let the words sink in, then added, 'You take my point?'

She was still unable to speak, so deep was her disappointment.

'Mrs Thorpe, I will speak frankly, for your own good. You cannot go against those who have money and power. They will break you if you try. Best to bend before the wind. After all, you have been offered another job, have you not?'

'Aye. And they will take my son away from me so that I can do it. Is that fair?'

She walked out without a farewell and tramped back to Setherby, not waiting for the carrier's cart. It was a long, weary trail home, but she needed to think, to come to terms with the pain of what was happening to her. It seemed as if the whole world was conspiring to take her son away from her, her only son. How could they do this? How could she bear it? Only – she had to bear it if there was no other solution, and help Adam bear it, too.

Determination grew in her, however, as the miles blurred beneath her feet. She might have to accept this for the moment, let them take Adam away from her for a while, but she needn't accept it for ever. If she went to work at Cleving she would have time to think about the future and plan for a life with her son. And she would find a way to achieve that, too.

When she got back, she sat with the two children and talked about what had happened, what they all had to face. 'They've forced me into this, but it won't be for ever. I shall save my money and look about me for other things to do. And – and I shall be able to come and see you, Adam love. Every week I'll come, rain or shine.'

He struggled to understand. 'But I don't want to go and live with Mrs Kellett. She's strange and I don't like her.'

Rachel could not help being glad he had not succumbed to Maggie's blandishments. 'We have no choice about this, son.'

'What about Dusty? I'll not go without him.'

'I think Mr Kellett will let you keep him. I'll ask.' She would also make it plain that she considered this state of affairs only temporary, that she was not giving up her son for long.

Kitty was the only one to be pleased by the situation. She was looking forward to working at the big house. Now, when Ruth boasted about her life in Todmorden, Kitty would also have something to boast about.

'Eh,' Rachel said that night as they all got ready for bed, 'I don't like to think of living shut up in that great dark house. I shall miss the moors and the fresh air on my face.'

'It'll be interesting, though,' Kitty said.

Adam didn't say anything. He didn't at all want to live with Mrs Kellett. He wanted his own dad back, and if he couldn't have that, at least he ought to have his mam. It wasn't right for them to take her away from him. He wept bitterly into his pillow once he was alone.

Rachel heard him but could think of no words of comfort to offer. If she'd gone in to speak to him, she'd have wept with him. And that would do no good. From now on she had to be strong, think and plan carefully. She had to make sure they didn't take her son away from her permanently.

'Have you heard?' Walter demanded two nights later in the alehouse.

'Heard what?'

'*She* is to go as a maid at Cleving Park.'

Bill froze, tankard halfway to his mouth. No need to ask who his friend was talking about. 'The cunning doxy! She's found a way to get round Mr Armstrong then. Probably sleeping in his bed. Though he has strange tastes if he fancies someone like her.'

'No, no! I doubt it's that. Where have you been all day that you haven't heard the news?'

'Out on the moors. Mary was birthing today. It's best to get right out of the way while a babe is being born or you get caught up in a mort of fuss and botheration. See how easily a sheep has a young 'un, then see the fuss my wife creates about it all. Makes you want to puke, it does. What are women for but havin' babes, when all's said and done?'

Walter didn't answer that. His present wife had never quickened. Only Alice had borne a child to him— He pushed that thought to the back of his mind. What point was there in worriting about all that now? 'Well, you missed a good day's gossip at the markets, that's for sure. Our Mr Armstrong is to wed a young lady from over Rochdale way, it seems. About time he got wed. I were beginning to think he didn't fancy the lasses.' Walter winked at his friend, trying to jolly him up.

'And *she* is to go to the house to look after Mrs Hannah Armstrong.' Bill sat frowning into his ale. 'What about her childer, then?'

'The little lass is old enough to work for her bread and is to go to the big house as a maid. And Parson is to take the lad.' He grinned. 'Only 'tis Parson's wife as is keen to have him, so I hear. Wants him for a son, she does. Dotes on him. Wants to keep him.'

As they were walking home together, Bill said abruptly, 'I were hoping she'd leave the valley.'

Walter sighed. 'Aye. I were, too.'

'You're sure she knows how Thorpe died?'

'Aye. There's no doubt she's guessed. And she knows who took the money as well.'

'Then we'll have to make sure she does leave here, one way or the other. We don't want no one around to point a finger at us.' Bill was utterly determined to better himself. It had become an obsession with him now.

'How can we send her away if she's working at the big house?' Walter stopped dead, looked at his friend's face, grim in the moonlight, and said in a hoarse voice, 'I'll not be involved in no more murders, Bill Withers. Nor in any more stealing, neither. I still can't get it out of my mind how Thorpe looked a-lying there in all that blood.'

Bill spat on the ground. 'Ach, don't be so soft, you fool. That were an accident, not a murder. And anyway, no one knew about it.'

'They'd hang us if they found out.'

'Well, they won't find out,' Bill repeated impatiently.

'What does Tam say? Last time I saw him, he were mad as a young tup in spring, vowing to get back at her.'

'I'll keep him in check, don't you worry.' Bill feigned a punch at his friend's arm. 'Ach, you're allus worriting about summat or other, you are. Things'll work themselves out all right, you'll see.'

'Aye, I suppose so.' Walter turned off towards his own home, looking forward to the day he'd move into North Beck Cottage.

Bill watched him go, then gave a snort of laughter. Walter was getting soft in his old age. Well, he and Tam weren't soft, and they planned to make sure *she* could never betray them. But they'd have to wait a while. Couldn't risk doing anything else till all the present fuss had died down. They'd settle her hash for her one day, though, they were agreed about that. And he looked forward to that day. He'd had enough of her staring at him in that scornful, knowing way. More than enough.

CHAPTER SEVENTEEN

Rachel took a deep breath and hesitated, then berated herself for a coward and rapped on the back door of Cleving Park. 'I wish to speak to Mr Armstrong,' she told the maid who opened it.

They tried to make her speak to the housekeeper, then made her wait for nearly an hour before they took her through to their master.

The landowner was waiting for her in a room full of books. She had never seen so many in her whole life and wondered how one man could possibly have read them all. He didn't ask her to sit down, which she thought ill-mannered of him, so she remained standing, head up, shoulders back, arms folded. She stared straight back at him, too.

'You wished to speak to me, Mrs Thorpe?' He wondered if he should have asked the housekeeper to stay with him. He was not sure how to deal with this woman; her manner was too forward for someone of her station and yet somehow he could not reprimand her as he would a servant. 'Well?'

'It's about coming to work here.'

'Yes?'

She would have liked to accuse him of forcing her to work here, of stopping her from doing as she wished, but seeing him here in his fine clothes, with a big soft carpet on the polished wooden floor and velvet curtains at the windows, she understood for the first time something of what it was like to be rich. Instead, she softened her demands to, 'I need to ask a favour of you before I accept, sir.'

He waited, once again surprised at her boldness, but nodded to her to continue.

'When I come to look after Mrs Hannah, I don't want to lose my furniture or my bits and pieces, which I'll need afterwards. I thought you might have somewhere I could store them till – till I leave again.'

He frowned. 'You are already thinking of leaving?'

'Nay, sir, just thinking to the future. Mrs Armstrong is an old lady. Speaks you fair, she does, and I hope she lives for a very long time, but well, it's not likely, is it? And then where would I be? I'd want to go and set up my own home again. I shan't spend my life in service. It wouldn't suit me at all. It's just – for her, this. So I shall need my bits and pieces afterwards. They'll not mean much to a rich gentleman like you, but they mean a lot to me.' She had to take a deep breath before she could continue and she was ashamed of how wavery her voice sounded. 'All my memories of my marriage are in them, you see.'

He pursed his lips, touched in spite of himself. She was being very sensible, really, planning ahead. Not at all a stupid woman, this. 'Very well. We have plenty of sheds and attics. I'll tell the housekeeper to find you somewhere.'

She let out a whoosh of breath. 'Thank you. I'm that grateful.' She could see him already looking down at his papers, as if expecting her to leave, so she added quickly, 'And there's one other thing, sir. My son.'

'He is to live with Mr Kellett, is he not? You surely have no worries about that?'

'I've no doubt he'll be well looked after there but,' she looked him right in the eyes, great landowner or not, 'I wish to make it plain from the start – to you and to Mr Kellett – that Adam is *my* son and I'll not let Parson and his wife adopt him. Not for anything. When I leave here, my lad is coming with me.' She could see him opening his mouth to speak and added desperately, 'He's the only child I have and he means more to me than life itself. So I thought if I made it all plain to you now,

I could trust you to see that no one tries to stop him coming back to me. Afterwards. You being the magistrate.'

He stared at her in astonishment, amazed at her impertinence, then seeing the desperate expression on her face, he realised she did not mean to be impertinent. And how could he fault a mother for loving her son? If he had a son – as he hoped soon to have – he would not want the child taken from him either. 'Very well. I understand what you are asking.'

'You won't – let them take him from me? Afterwards?'

'Not if you are in a position to care for him yourself.'

His words were not an absolute guarantee of support, but they were, she supposed, as much as she could hope for. 'Then, sir, I will come and look after your aunt, and you may be sure she'll have no reason to complain about me.' She walked out without him dismissing her.

He was torn between amusement and irritation as he watched her go. Servants did not usually dictate terms to their masters. Or leave a room before they were told to. But then, she was not like any other servant he had ever employed. She had not meant to be impertinent, but was just – determined, yes, that was the word, determined to keep her son. Amusement won over the irritation. And he felt a sneaking admiration for her courage, too.

He went to share news of this morning's visit with his aunt, who frowned at the thought of the boy being taken from his mother and said when he had finished, 'Promise me you'll not let them take her son away from her after I'm gone, Nathaniel.'

'Aunt, there is no need for you to concern yourself about that. I'm sure you will live for many years yet.'

'Nevertheless, I ask you to make me that solemn promise.' She understood what they were doing to Rachel, and yet she could not resist having the woman come to look after her now. Old age was a fearsome thing, even for an Armstrong of Cleving Park. It had made her selfish. 'Promise me, Nathaniel!' she repeated.

He saw that she needed it, so he said, 'I promise.' But he

made a mental proviso that he would only help Rachel if she looked after his aunt well.

Caleb leaned on a gate at the far end of his farm and stared across the hills. There would be rain before nightfall, perhaps sooner. The air had that damp, clinging feel to it and clouds were massing in the south-west. He saw the familiar carriage approaching along the road to Todmorden and moved over to the road to wait for it. She usually stopped to chat. When the carriage door was opened by the footman, he stepped forward smiling. 'Mrs Bretherton! What brings you this way?'

'I'm driving into Todmorden to buy some material for a new gown. Mr Armstrong is to get married soon and I am invited to the wedding in Rochdale.'

''Twill be a large gathering, I believe.'

'It will indeed.' Georgiana Bretherton paused, looking at him shrewdly. 'You haven't been to see me for a while, Caleb.'

'No. I've been – busy.' He returned her look and realised she was not fooled. 'I've been feeling somewhat dispirited, if you must know, Mrs Bretherton.'

'You should marry, get yourself children,' she said, as she had done several times before.

'My mother and I cannot agree on the sort of woman I should marry, I'm afraid.' He did not tell her who his choice was. He did not intend to tell anyone till he had spoken to Rachel. But he must let her get over her grief first.

'Will you come and take tea with me on Saturday, Caleb? I have something to discuss.'

'It'll be my pleasure.'

'Then close this door for me – that's a cold, damp wind! – and tell my coachman to drive on.'

He did as she asked and watched the carriage jolt away over the tops and down towards Todmorden. It was a poor sort of road and often impassable in winter. At last the cold drove him back to the house, reluctant to face any more arguments and fussations, for his mother could be tenacious when she set her mind on something. Well, so could he. He was not marrying a woman like Jemima Green and that was that!

When he got to the farmhouse, however, he found the wench already settled at the tea table with his mother, and looking at him expectantly. And yes, she was pretty, but it made no difference to him. This had to be stopped once and for all. So he did what he had threatened and told Jemima plainly, 'You're wasting your time here if you're looking to find a husband. When I want to wed, I'll do my own courting, not ask my mother to find me a wife.'

Then he walked out to the sound of weeping and his mother's angry voice calling to him to come back this instant and apologise.

Not until he had seen Jemima leave did he return to the house, and when his mother began to berate him, he lost his patience and shouted back at her, speaking so unkindly that he was ashamed of his hasty words when he thought about them later in the darkness of his bedchamber.

But it stopped his mother's attempts at matchmaking, thank goodness.

The day before they were to leave North Beck Cottage, Rachel got all ready, then in the afternoon she went for a tramp across the tops on her own. It was Friday, market day, and it felt strange not to have to go and buy food for the following week. Why, there was hardly a bite left in the house.

She didn't want to go and live down in the valley. One day, she vowed, she'd get her own home again, somewhere up near the moors, where the breezes blew clean and fresh, and where people didn't have to live so close to one another. Even a small town like Setherby was too crowded for her.

She went up to sit up on Whin Ridge, having promised herself this last treat. And there she sat and stared her fill, ignoring the chill breeze, just letting the peace fill her. Yet when the setting sun warned her that it was time to return to Whin Vale, she suddenly found herself weeping helplessly, soft tears flowing down her cheeks, blurring the world around her.

ANNA JACOBS

'Oh, Thomas,' she murmured brokenly, 'why did you have to die? We were so happy together.' She was suddenly reminded of the time she had come up here with Bill Withers and ended up weeping just as bitterly. How long ago all that seemed. How much had happened since then! And not all of it bad, by any means.

Eh, she should just count her blessings. She'd been married to a fine man, she had a son any woman would be proud of and one day she would make a home for him again.

As she slowly made her way back towards Upper Clough, she saw a man striding up the path towards her. Surely that was – yes, it was – Caleb Hesketh. What was he doing up here on the tops? Her heart started to thump in her chest as she worried that something might be wrong. She couldn't take another step, just froze where she stood and waited for him to reach her.

He stopped a pace or two away and nodded a greeting. 'They said you'd be up here.'

'Who did?'

'Your children.'

'Oh.'

'I called at the house. I wanted to – to speak to you. Can you spare me a few moments?' He gestured to some rocks and when she sat down, he came to sit beside her.

For a while, they stared across the moors, neither making any move to break the silence.

'I love to feel the wind in my face,' he said at last, his voice softer than she had ever heard it before.

'Yes. So do I. And I never thanked you for setting a price on the donkey. They'd not have taken my word for anything.'

'I was glad to help.' Another silence, then he said abruptly, 'You've been weeping.'

She closed her eyes in sudden embarrassment and drew in a shaky breath, but another tear or two trickled down her cheeks.

'I'm sorry. I didn't mean to distress you. I'm too blunt in my ways.'

'It's nothing to do with you.' But her voice wasn't sharp.

'They said at the market that you're to work at Cleving looking after the old lady.'

'Yes.'

'Are you happy to do that, Rachel?'

'No. They're forcing me to it. And – and they're taking my son away from me. That's why I was weeping. He's going to live with the parson and his wife. But I won't let them keep him. One day I'll find a way to make a home for us again.'

'Life can be cruel.' The only answer he received was an angry little choking sound, so he rushed into what had brought him here. 'I wanted to say – to tell you . . .' Devil take it, how hard it was to say this! He took another deep breath and said rapidly before he should lose the courage, 'I wanted to say that if you're ever in trouble, you should come to me. I'd help you.'

Rachel could not think what to say to that. Caleb Hesketh was known as a stern, taciturn sort of man, fair in his dealings, but not over-generous. He was a confirmed bachelor, had never even tried to court a woman that she had heard. And since he had not been a friend of Thomas nor was he related to her in any way, why should he care about her now?

He could feel that he was flushing but had promised himself to explain this to her, so he continued. 'You will be wondering why I say this.'

'Well, yes, I am.'

He could not tell her that he loved her and had done for a long time, for fear of driving her away. 'I think,' he frowned over his words and spoke them haltingly, 'it is because I feel they have treated you harshly. I know – know what it's like to be different, to be shouted after and tormented.' He saw her look of surprise and said curtly, 'I am bastard born. My father was already wed and could not marry my mother. After he died, it was his family who provided for us, gave us a little land. Out of pride they did that, not because they cared about me. So,' he swallowed, hoping he had not offended her, 'so I can understand how it is for you. A little, anyway.'

She gave a bitter laugh. 'Aye, you have the right of it. I *am* different. I'm a good weaver and they won't let me earn my bread that way because I'm a woman. I can think out business matters better than most men, but they won't let me be the putter-out either.'

'I thought it was more because of Bill Withers and Walter Smedling that you couldn't work at your weaving.'

'Partly. But I could have got round that, only – only it's Mr Armstrong who is stopping me now. He won't rent me a weaver's cottage and he won't let Harrison's buy from me.' An angry sob escaped her before she could stop it and briefly Caleb's hand rested on hers, so that she stared down at it, wonderingly. It felt so warm and comforting, as Thomas's hand had done.

He flushed and removed the hand. 'Will you tell me exactly what happened?'

'I had made an arrangement with Harrison's. They were going to deal with me, take my cloth – because I'm a good weaver! – but Mr Armstrong told them not to. He said it would cause too much trouble among the men in Whin Vale but I know it's because he wants me to look after his aunt instead.'

'Mrs Bretherton says Hannah Armstrong is failing.'

'I would not mind too much if it were not for Adam,' Rachel said. 'For a time, anyway. Mrs Armstrong is a kindly woman, but—' Sobs thickened her throat, so she could not continue.

His voice was very gentle. 'You don't want to be separated from your son.'

'No, I don't.'

'I've seen him with you at market. He's a fine lad.'

She could only nod because she did not trust her voice, but the compliment pleased her.

Silence stretched over long minutes, but neither of them tried to break it. Only as a mist of light rain came sighing across the moors to caress them did he start to speak again.

'I meant what I said, Rachel. If you are ever in trouble, you can turn to me for help. And since I own my farm, Mr Armstrong has no way of threatening me.'

'I thank you for that.' It warmed some chill place within

her that he had bothered to make the offer, that someone understood how alone she was.

'And your boy – if you like, I could make the opportunity to speak to him on market days, keep an eye on him. I know Maggie Kellett can be a foolish woman, but I think she will look after him well enough.'

Rachel could not hold back a scornful laugh. 'Oh, yes. I have no doubt she will look after him. She wants to take him away from me completely, you see. "Adopt him", she said. She wants to make him into *her* son. But he's all I have left of my Thomas,' her voice broke as she said her husband's name, 'and I shall *not* let her have him!'

Silence folded around them again. The rain had passed and only the wind was paying attention to them, lifting the edges of their garments, touching their skin gently, making free with their hair.

As the chill bit into her bones, Rachel suddenly felt very weary. She could not take in any more today. She felt as though her heart was ready to burst from her chest with the pain of it all. And underlying that was the nervousness about how she would go on in a big house like Cleving. She had no airs and graces, and she knew only too well how blunt her tongue could be.

Caleb touched her shoulder. 'Shall we start walking back now? I think it is going to rain much harder before nightfall.'

'Yes.'

When she stood up, her foot slipped on the damp rocky surface and she would have tumbled backwards but he caught her, and for a moment they stood there, pressed together. But he did not attempt to take any liberties, as other men might have, simply waited till she had her balance and then released her.

'Thank you.' She turned and began to stride along the path beside him.

He glanced sideways, admiring her sturdy body, the strength that radiated from her, even now when the world seemed set against her. He wished he could do more than offer help, but this woman was still grieving for her husband and it was not yet time to court her.

'I meant what I said,' he repeated as they parted company. 'Remember that.'

'Thank you.'

Rachel was touched by his offer but thought no more of it other than to wonder once or twice that he had understood what it was like to be different. He was a kind man under that stern exterior.

The next morning a dray from Cleving Park arrived in Upper Clough soon after daybreak.

Walter Smedling's wife came bustling up to the attic where he was weaving and keeping an eye on the goings-on in the village. 'It's here,' she announced.

When he didn't reply, she repeated her remark. He'd been so strange lately and she was tired of his scornful attitude, tired of the way Bill Withers seemed to lead him around by the nose as well. She wished she'd never married him. He hadn't even been able to give her a child.

'The dray's come to take her stuff down to Cleving.' She scowled as she stared out of the window. ''Tis a pity, that. I'd hoped she'd be selling up. I'd have liked to buy some of her pieces. That dresser she had in the kitchen is much nicer than our old thing.'

'Aye. An' why should she need those things again? She's set for life at the big house. Trust her to land on her feet!'

She tittered. 'Go and ask her. She used to be your daughter, after all.'

His voice grew harsh. 'She's no daughter of mine, that one isn't, as well you know. You only say that to annoy me.'

'It takes nowt to annoy you lately, Walter Smedling! There's no pleasing you.' And they were off on one of their quarrels.

In Setherby, Maggie went rushing down to Justin's study when she saw the dray. 'Why is the dray from Cleving Park carrying Rachel's things? I might have liked to buy some of her pieces.'

Justin had delayed telling her, knowing she would not be pleased. 'Mr Armstrong is to have her things stored in the attic for the day when she can make a home for herself and her son again.'

'What? Why did you not stop this, Justin Kellett?'

'Why should I stop it?'

''Tis obvious! If she sets up home again, she'll want Adam back, and I'm not having that. He'll be ours from today, like you promised me.'

'I promised you nothing of the sort, Maggie. We are not adopting him, only fostering him.' He had said this many times already, to no avail. She refused to accept it.

She set her hands on her hips and stared at him. 'You'd better understand now, Justin Kellett, that I'm not giving him back. He's going to be my son – *our* son! I'm quite determined on that.' She paused at the door. 'And why you agreed to have that dirty great dog here as well I cannot understand. It's not coming inside my house, bringing mud and fleas and who knows what else with it.' She would find someone else to take it or – she paused on the thought – simply get rid of it. She did not want anything from the boy's past here. She was going to make a completely new life for him, so that he would forget his old one.

When the dray had left, Rachel walked slowly round the house, mentally saying goodbye. It didn't look like her home now, all empty and echoing. 'Come on then, you two!' she called. 'No use staying here any longer. Go and get Dusty's leash.'

'I'll hate it at the parsonage,' Adam muttered as they walked along. 'Who wants to be fussed over by that silly woman?'

Rachel could not bring herself to chastise him for his disrespectful words.

'Well, I shall enjoy living in the big house,' Kitty declared. Once she had realised that her future was secure, she had brightened considerably and was looking forward to her new life.

'I don't know why I can't come to Cleving with you two,' Adam muttered, though it had been explained to him time and time again. 'It's not fair! They've got plenty of space there. Me an' Dusty could sleep in the stables. I could run messages for them, do little jobs.'

'Life isn't fair,' Rachel told him yet again. 'So don't complain, just get on with it.' But she gave him a hug to soften her words.

When they got into Setherby, they all three stopped, then Rachel marched forward and rapped on the front door of the parsonage. It was thrown open before she had finished knocking, and by Maggie herself.

'Come in, dear boy! Come in!' She pulled Adam towards her and moved to bar the way.

Rachel stared at her, hurt by this, and set one hand on the door to keep it open. 'I would like to see his bedchamber,' she said firmly, not moving. If she knew what his room was like, she'd be able to imagine him there. It'd help.

'See his bedchamber? Do you not trust me to house him properly?' Maggie tossed her head. 'He'll be a deal better housed here than he ever has been before.' She tried again to close the door but another hand pulled it back from inside the house and she gasped in shock. 'Justin! I thought you'd gone out.'

'It's a good thing I hadn't.' He turned to Rachel. 'Come in, my dear. Of course you'll want to see where Adam is to lie. I'll take you up myself.' Which left Maggie to trail sulkily after them.

Kitty stared after them uncertainly and remained in the hall.

Rachel stood in the doorway of the small bedchamber with her arm round her son's shoulders. Justin held Maggie back, to prevent her from interfering.

Rachel went inside the room, moving from one piece of furniture to another. She touched the polished surface of the chest of drawers, fingered the fine material of the bed curtains, and then went to check the exact view from the window.

'You can see Cleving Park from here,' she said, relieved. 'See, Adam love, just the corner of the house beyond the trees. That's where I'll be.'

He nestled against her comfortably, as he had done a thousand times before.

Watching the two of them together, Justin felt guilt increase within him. Their love for one another was so visible. How could Maggie ever expect to make him into her son when he had a mother like this?

'Well, now,' Rachel said after a while, forcing herself to push Adam away. 'I'll have to be going, love. Make sure you behave for Mrs Kellett.'

He nodded, trying hard not to cry.

Then, because she was feeling the same and didn't want Maggie to see her weeping, Rachel muttered something that could have been a farewell, clattered off down the stairs and strode round the side of the square to the lane that led to Cleving, with Kitty panting along behind her. Dusty, tied to the gatepost, sat and howled till Justin came down with Adam to take him round to the back garden, give him a bowl of fresh water and show him the straw where he was to lie in the shed, things Justin had organised, since his wife said she had better things to do than fuss over a stupid dog.

'I don't like that animal,' Maggie grumbled, for of course she had followed them outside. 'I don't know what you want with it.'

Adam glared at her. 'He's *my* dog now that Dad's dead and he's my friend, too.'

She shut her mouth on a further complaint.

The boy turned to Justin. 'Dusty won't like sleeping out here and he'll get cold in winter.' His lips were trembling.

'We'll work something else out before then.' He looked at Maggie as he added, 'You'll not lose your dog as well as your home, I promise you.'

At the gates to Cleving Park, Rachel stopped to look back once. 'I don't like to leave him in that house,' she muttered. 'I don't know why, I just don't. She gets sillier with keeping, Parson's wife does.'

'He'll be all right, I'm sure.' Kitty laid a hesitant hand on her stepmother's arm.

Rachel looked at the girl. 'I'm glad you're going to be at

Cleving too, love. It'll make things seem a bit – a bit more homelike.' She turned her face towards the big, sprawling house. 'Well, come on, then. We mustn't be late.' She would not think about Adam any more till she was alone in her bed – dared not or she would weep. She would just get on with what had to be done.

Part Three

CHAPTER EIGHTEEN

Rachel was surprised to be shown into Mr Armstrong's study, for she had not expected to see much of the master of the house once she started work there. Again he did not ask her to sit down and again she wondered at how ill-mannered rich folk were.

Frowning, he shuffled his papers. 'I wish to make it plain before you start that my aunt's welfare is very important to me. If you think of anything – anything at all – which will make her life easier, then you are to tell me – not the housekeeper, me personally. Is that clear?'

'Yes, sir.'

'And I want no complaints to my aunt about missing your son. You will be able to see him every Sunday, so you will have nothing to complain of.'

How could anyone think that? To see Adam for only a couple of hours a week! She had to force the expected response out. 'Yes, sir. I shall make Mrs Armstrong's welfare my first concern while I'm here,' she affirmed quietly.

He stared at her, surprised at how this woman had been on his mind, at a time when he should be thinking only of his wedding plans. But he knew he had forced her to give up her son and that did not sit easily with him, especially after what his aunt had said – though the lad would learn better manners and improve his understanding of the world at the parson's house as he could never hope to do while living in a weaver's cottage.

He stretched out one hand and with his usual deliberation rang the bell that stood on his desk, setting it down in exactly the same place. The door opened and Matty came in, bobbing a curtsy.

'Take Rachel to Mrs Hannah now.'

In the hall, Matty stopped and stared up at Rachel. 'I hadn't realised how tall you are. Must be useful when there's a crowd. I'm too little to see anything when folk stand in front of me.'

Rachel realised in surprise that this was not said in rancour, just spoken casually, and she took heart as she followed Matty across the black and white tiles of the huge hall. She was so used to meeting hostility she had been half expecting it here. 'I'd rather be shorter,' she admitted. 'I'm taller than most of the men, even.'

Matty chuckled. 'And they don't like that, I'm sure. But it won't matter here. It'll be good that you're strong. It hurts Mrs Hannah when someone bumps her, poor lady. But she never complains.' She stopped at a door and tapped on it, pressing her ear close to hear the response.

Once inside, she bobbed another curtsy. 'I've brought Rachel to you, Mrs Hannah.'

'Good, good. And I hope you'll all look after her, Matty. She'll be feeling a bit strange at first.'

'Oh, we will, madam, don't you worry.'

Hannah lifted her twisted hand and beckoned Rachel over. 'Come and sit down by me, child, and tell me how the move went. I've told them to put your things in the attic and you can go and check them later, but you must be feeling sad at leaving your home.' She indicated a chair beside her. 'Here, come and sit by me. If you're to look after me, I'd like to know you better. Dorcas will show you your duties later, but for now I wish to talk.'

Rachel went forward hesitantly. 'Just – sit and talk?'

Hannah saw the strain on Rachel's face. 'My dear, I know you've been pushed into this position, but it may be a good thing for you to get away from,' she hesitated, seeking for a word, but finding only, 'your troubles.' The maids had told her how some men had bullied poor Mrs Thorpe after her husband died. Nathaniel should have done something about that, but he said there was no proof, and like all men he didn't take women's complaints seriously.

This sympathy was so unexpected that Rachel had to blink away moisture from her eyes and dig her fingernails into the palms of her hands, or she would have embarrassed herself by bursting into tears. 'G-good for me?' she managed in a husky voice as she sat down. 'How is it good for me to leave my son?'

'He'll learn a lot at the parsonage, things you could not teach him. And it won't be for ever.' Hannah pulled up her skirts to reveal legs as twisted as her hands. 'I'm unable to walk more than a few paces – and even that hurts. I shall not be sorry to leave the pain behind.'

Rachel stared at her, amazed at such frankness.

'My dear, if I cannot be honest with my own maid, how can anyone help me? It hurts me even to stand upright now.'

'That must be hard to bear.'

Hannah grimaced. 'Yes. I dislike being carried about like a child. I have to be lifted into my bed at night and helped up in the mornings, for I wake very stiff. And – and someone must help me to the chamber pot. That will be part of your duties now, I'm afraid. Please do not be angry at me for benefiting from your trouble to get help for myself. It's hard indeed to find a maid I can trust, and I was drawn to you from the first. I will see that you do not lose by it. And – and I will protect you from those men for a while, at least.'

Rachel was to be constantly surprised during those first few days at how frank Mrs Hannah was about her condition, and about Adam, but she knew Mr Armstrong did not wish her to mention her son, so she mostly held her tongue. She was further surprised to find her new mistress making detailed plans for her to see Adam every Sunday after church.

'Two whole hours,' she said, beaming at her maid as if this was a great treat.

Rachel realised she was supposed to be grateful for this,

so forced some words out. 'That's very kind of you, Mrs Hannah.'

But as the days passed, all of them spent inside the house, it seemed a very long time till Sunday, and Rachel missed Adam even more than she had expected. She would think of him before she went to sleep, wondering how his day had been, and often lay awake half the night, worrying about where all this would lead. She saw Kitty every day, at least, and had no worries about her, for the child seemed happy in the big house, helping out with whatever task she was given and soon winning friends with her cheerful manner and willingness to work hard.

But however safe she was and however kind a mistress she had, Rachel could not like being in service and she hated – absolutely hated – having to bob curtsies. It made her feel as if she was not free any more. Well, she wasn't, was she?

Adam stared at Maggie mutinously. 'I have to go out and see to Dusty first.'

'Oh, the dog's all right. We put him in the shed.'

'I still have to see he's all right. It's my duty to care for him. Like Dad did.'

'Sit down and eat your breakfast first.'

He considered this briefly, tempted by the good food, then shook his head.

The two girls tittered and Maggie stared at the boy in shock. In all her imaginings, she had not expected him to refuse to do as she told him. She had expected him to be grateful for her kindness, happy to be in such a comfortable house. Only – she had heard him weeping into his pillow last night and this morning he had done nothing but scowl at her. She debated ordering him to sit down, but what if he refused?

'Oh, very well! Go and see to the stupid animal, then perhaps you'll believe me when I say that he's well housed.'

Adam went out and found Dusty tied up in the dark shed, with the door closed. He was lying down, looking utterly dejected. The boy glanced back towards the house and, deciding that no one could see him, sat down on the ground and put his arms round the animal. Despite his efforts, tears flowed down his face.

A shadow passed across him and he looked up to see Peg standing beside him. He wiped one arm across his eyes and scowled down at the ground, hating to be caught crying.

Peg, who had been sent out to fetch him and who was feeling resentful at all the fuss her mother was making about the newcomer, suddenly felt sorry for Adam. He was only a little lad, after all, much younger than her fourteen years. She went over to sit on a wooden box near him. 'You'll be finding it strange here, I expect.'

He nodded and risked another quick swipe at his eyes. 'Dusty doesn't like being tied up. He's feeling strange too.'

'Is he fierce?'

'Not if he knows you.'

'Can I touch him?' They had never had a dog. Her mother said dogs were dirty things, but this one had a nice face, and Adam was right, the poor creature did look unhappy.

'Aye, you can touch him.' He turned to Dusty and said firmly, 'Friend!' Then he beckoned her closer. Patting her arm, he said, 'Friend!' again once or twice, then whispered, 'Let him sniff your hand. Dogs like to sniff folk. They understand smells better than words, I reckon.'

So she held out her arm and let the huge dog sniff at it, giggling suddenly as Dusty's breath and face hair tickled her skin. When the dog gave her hand a quick lick, then settled back on his haunches with a sigh, she looked at Adam inquiringly. 'What does he want?'

'To go for a walk. He's not used to being shut up like this.'

The dog's ears pricked up.

'I'll ask Father for you, if you like,' she said suddenly. 'He'll sort it all out. It's usually better to ask him about such things than mother.' Already Peg could organise matters better than her mother, but her father said you had to be kind to people since not everyone could be clever, like her. Her sister Lizbet was a bit like Mother, always messing things up and forgetting to finish a task, but so pretty that everyone seemed to forgive her.

Adam looked at her hopefully. 'Will you really ask your father?' He was still a bit in awe of the parson.

'Yes.' Then a voice called sharply from the house and she said hurriedly, 'We'd better get back inside or she'll be angry with us. Here, let me brush you down. She hates people to get dirty.'

So began a bewildering day.

After Peg had a quiet word with her father, Justin decreed that Adam should have the duty of taking Dusty out for walks morning and evening.

'But he'll get dirty!' Maggie protested. 'And what if it rains?'

'If it rains, he can take his cloak. A dog has to have exercise, Maggie, and Dusty is Adam's responsibility. When the dog is more used to living here, he can have the run of the back garden.'

'He'll dig up the vegetables. He'll—' She saw Adam scowling at her and bit back further protests. She would definitely get rid of that animal, she decided, and the sooner the better.

At last Sunday came round. As Rachel got her mistress up that morning, Hannah said, 'You look brighter today.'

'I'll be seeing my son.'

'You must bring him back here one day so that I can meet him. I'd like that. I don't see any children nowadays and I miss them.'

Rachel nodded, but if truth be told, she didn't want to share Adam with anyone during her precious two hours.

When she was ready, she left Matty sitting with Mrs Hannah and went to fling her cloak round her shoulders and hurry down to the village.

She knocked on the front door of the parsonage, and Maggie opened it herself. 'Oh. It's you.'

Rachel stared at her in silence, then said, 'Is Adam ready?'

'Not yet.'

'What?'

The boy came clattering down the stairs, pushed past Maggie, and threw himself into his mother's arms. 'Mam! Oh, Mam, I've missed you so!'

Rachel felt tears welling in her eyes and hugged him close to her. It was a moment or two before she realised how angrily the other woman was staring at her.

'I told you to tidy your room up,' Maggie said to Adam. 'I'm sure you can't have finished it yet.'

'I'll do it after I get back.'

Peg, who had been listening from another room, hurried into the hall. 'Mother, Lizbet has just spilled some water on your best Turkey rug.'

With a shriek, Maggie flew into her parlour, and as Peg made shooing motions with her hands, Rachel and Adam hurried off down the path.

'Peg's nice,' he confided. 'But I don't like living with Mrs Kellett.'

Rachel could not help feeling glad about that.

When Maggie returned to the hall, she found them gone and went storming into the kitchen. 'Why did you not stop them?' she demanded of her elder daughter. 'You knew I wanted him to tidy his room.'

'She only has two hours with him. He can clear up his room later.'

Maggie breathed deeply. 'I forbid you to interfere.'

Peg sighed. Yet again, she would have to mention this to her father. She didn't like spying on her own mother, but she didn't like the way her mother was behaving either. In fact, her mother was getting very strange lately. As soon as she could, Peg escaped into the back garden to go and sit next to the dog, of whom she'd quickly become fond, though her mother complained they would get fleas from the animal.

It was there her father found her half an hour later when he came back from church.

Justin smiled at the picture they presented, Dusty leaning

against the girl and she stroking his ear absent-mindedly. 'You like the dog now you've got used to him, Peg?'

She nodded.

'Did – did Adam get off all right today? With his mother?'

They looked at one another and although neither put it into words, they knew instantly that they would have to form an alliance on this matter, as they had over the dog.

'Yes, but she tried to stop him.'

He sighed.

'Father, why does she behave like that?'

'I don't know.'

'I like Adam, but – but he's not our brother, whatever she says.'

'No, he isn't, Peg.'

'And he refuses to call her Aunt. I – I don't think he likes her much.'

'No.' Justin had quickly realised this himself. And who would want to keep a child away from its mother? Now that he saw how close the bond was between Adam and Rachel, he certainly didn't. But Maggie would not listen to reason. And at the present time, the boy needed a home.

Rachel and Adam walked slowly through Setherby, then into the grounds of Cleving Park by a side gate.

'I wish we were still at North Beck Cottage,' he said. 'I miss the moors.'

'Aye, so do I.'

'Tell me what it's like at the big house. And how is Kitty? Is she liking it there?'

They walked to and fro, absorbed in one another, but eventually Rachel said, 'We'd better go and see what time it is by the church clock.'

They stood in the churchyard together. 'Nearly time for me to go back,' she said, trying to speak cheerfully though her throat felt full of sobs that she must hold back.

He flung himself into her arms. 'I don't want you to! I don't, I don't!'

'Nay, lad. We cannot always have what we want. You know that.'

He sniffed and looked up at her. 'Yes, but – Mrs Kellett is – she's funny.'

'What do you mean by that?'

'She acts funny. A bit like Goody Palmer sometimes.'

'What? Surely not.'

He nodded vigorously. 'She does. Oh, not as bad as Goody Palmer,' for that old lady was mad as a hatter, though harmless with it, 'but still she has a look in her eyes sometimes that makes me feel funny.' He looked at her solemnly, an expression older than his years. 'And I'm feared for Dusty. She tries to stop me spending time with him, wants me to sit with her instead. But when I do, she just stares at me.' He was glad he still went up to the curate for his lessons, for that got him out of the house for several hours each day.

Rachel didn't like the sound of this.

'I like Peg, though,' he went on. 'She's been kind to me. And Dusty likes her too.'

'That's good. What about Lizbet?'

He wrinkled his nose. 'She's silly. Like her mother.'

'That's no way to speak of Mrs Kellett. You must be respectful.'

'I only say it to you, Mam.'

She sighed and glanced again at the clock. 'I must go back now, love.'

'I'll come to meet you next week.'

It hurt Justin to see the loving way they walked back across the market square together, and the anguish in Rachel's face as she turned away from her son. He still could not see what else he could have done but take the boy in, given the circumstances, however.

When Justin went into the house, he found himself in the middle of a row, with Maggie screaming at Adam that he was late, and he wasn't to stay out so long next Sunday, and Peg trying to distract her mother. Justin cleared his throat and they all turned to look at him. 'What is wrong?'

When they all tried to speak at once, he took Maggie into his study and questioned her, sighing at her stupidity. 'You cannot keep the lad back when it's his day with his mother.'

'I don't want him spending all that time with her.'

'You are not to try to stop him. Promise me that!'

But she just looked at him mutinously and said, 'I must do the best I can for our adopted son.'

'He is *not* our adopted son, Maggie.'

But she wasn't listening. She never did when it was something she didn't want to hear.

In the Weaver's Arms, Walter sat morosely surveying his empty pot. He didn't want to go home. Well, North Beck Cottage didn't seem like home and he didn't really like living there. It still seemed full of Rachel's presence and he half expected her to be there waiting for him whenever he returned. And upstairs in the weaving attic the feeling was far worse, for there he felt the presence of Thomas Thorpe too, come to haunt him, come to blame him for the stone Bill Withers had thrown. He had dreamed of the man more than once, dreamed of him shaking his fist, demanding justice against his murderers.

Bill nudged him. 'What's got into you lately, lad? Things are going well for us, don't you think?'

Walter scowled. 'How am I to know? There are so many things to think about, and with all the pieces of cloth to take into Rochdale, I never seem to have a minute to spare.' And his wife wasn't any use. She liked their new home but was giving herself airs and graces since they'd moved in, wanting a silk gown, of all things, and new furniture too. They had had sharp words this very evening about it. He sighed.

'Eh, you're a proper misery, you are.' Bill smiled. 'I'm enjoying our trips into Rochdale.' For though Walter was nominally the putter-out, and had to remain so for the time being, he could not manage the job without help.

But whatever he said or did, Bill could not make his friend

cheer up, and was relieved to see Tam Barker come in – surprised, too, because Tam didn't often drink here nowadays, it being too far away from his little hill farm.

'You're a long way from home, lad,' Bill said. 'What's brought you over to Whin Vale?'

'Oh, a bit of business. I'm staying overnight with my wife's cousin.' He glanced round, scowling when he saw how everyone was staring at him. 'What's wrong with that lot? Have they nothing better to do than gawk at folk?'

'Ah, ignore them. Let me get you some ale.' Bill waved a hand to the potman, who hurried to bring another jug of ale across. He watched his friend take a long sup, then asked genially, 'So, how are things going?'

'How the hell do you think? Stuck up in that hovel, wind whistling round you all the time, nothing to see but sheep and moors and more cursed sheep.'

'You're lucky to have a place of your own.'

Tam grunted and took another long pull at the drink. 'Ah, well, I'll be luckier still before I'm through, I tell you.'

Bill leaned forward. 'Found something interesting to do?'

A wink was his only answer, so he held his peace till they could speak privately.

When they left the inn, they strolled up the hill to Walter's new house, it being the largest and most comfortable. He sent his wife off to bed, ignoring her protests, and settled his friends in the warm kitchen.

'Nice big place, this,' Tam said. 'You need some more chairs, though.'

'Aye, well, it may be nice, but I can't get *her* out of my mind. I keep thinking I see her standing in the doorway, like she used to.'

The other two exchanged long-suffering glances.

'She still working at Mr Armstrong's place?' Tam asked.

'Course she is. A month she's been there now and Matty told my Mary she's settled in well. Wouldn't even listen when my Mary told her not to trust Rachel Thorpe, said she could tell an honest person from a cheat any day.'

'Worming her way in,' Bill said gloomily. 'Beats me how she does it.'

'I want her out of the valley.' Tam thumped one clenched fist on the table. 'I'd be happiest of all if she were six feet under the ground.'

Walter jerked and spilled some ale. 'Nay, don't talk like that.'

'Why not? We'll never be safe as long as she's alive. She knows we took her money and she won't forget it. Do you want to hang for that? I don't.'

There was silence for several moments, the men avoiding each other's eyes. Bill nodded. 'You're right there. But she's going to that fancy wedding over in Rochdale next week, so we can't do owt till all the fuss is over. They say Mester Armstrong is to take his new wife down to Buxton afterwards for a week or two. That'll be the time to act, while he's away.'

Walter looked from one to the other, his jaw dropping. 'You don't mean it!'

'I do. We have to deal with her. Get rid of her. It's her or us.'

'I'll not be party to murder. I'll not.'

Tam leaned forward. 'You *have* been party to murder, an' if we don't get rid of that woman, it'll come out sooner or later, you mark my words, and then they'll hang us all.'

But however much they argued and reasoned, Walter Smedling could not be persuaded to act against his dead wife's lass.

'Ah, we'll have to do it without him,' Bill said as the two men walked down the hill together.

'Well, start thinking what.'

'No use rushing into anything. It'd be better if it could look like an accident. Trouble is, she never goes anywhere now that she's working at the house. But we'll think of something.'

CHAPTER NINETEEN

The Armstrong wedding was to be a fine occasion and all the servants were very proud of that. Nonetheless, they were glad to wave their master goodbye two days before the event, wish him well, then enjoy a bit of peace. Mr Armstrong had been very chancy-tempered lately, picking fault with anything and everything. Which just went to show that even rich folk could get nervous.

Hannah had questioned whether she should even try to go to Rochdale for the wedding, which had made Nathaniel say with one of his disapproving looks, 'I would prefer you to come, Aunt.'

She sighed. 'The journey will try me sorely.'

'Won't you want to see everyone?' He didn't say it might be her last chance to attend a big family gathering, but they both knew that.

What won her over was the hesitant way he added, 'I – I would like you to be there, Aunt. Truly I would. You're like a second mother to me.'

It was unusual for him to plead, so she stifled a sigh. Like the servants, she had realised how nervous he was. 'Very well, Nathaniel. I will go if you wish it.' And had her reward in the beaming smile he gave her.

So she and Rachel had to sort through her gowns and find something fine enough for a wedding, then alter it, for the hoops of the past had placed the fullness of the skirt to the sides, while ladies now wore short rounded hoops, Hannah informed her wondering maid.

Rachel picked up the wired and padded canvas petticoat. 'It seems silly to make your shape different.'

Hannah laughed. 'It is silly, but the other ladies will notice how old-fashioned my things are. Oh, well. It can't be helped, and I am too old to waste money on new gowns.'

'Could you not – change this one?'

Hannah held out her twisted hands. 'How?'

'I don't know. I'm not good at sewing, but,' an idea occurred to her, 'Mrs Kellett is. Could we not ask her help in this?' Rachel was quite sure Maggie would help, if only for the pleasure of rubbing shoulders with the Armstrongs.

So the parson's wife came up the next day and stayed at the big house till evening, altering the hopped petticoat and then the skirts that went with it. And she suggested adding new ribbons to form an échelle of bows down the front of the bodice. Her friend, Mrs Payne, had some ribbon for sale which would look good with this colour.

Hannah nodded agreement. 'But I wonder if I could ask you to choose the ribbons for me before you come tomorrow, Mrs Kellett – if you don't mind continuing to help me, that is?'

While Maggie sewed and talked, enjoying being the focus of Mrs Armstrong's attention, Rachel threaded needles and did some of the plain sewing, helping in any way she could.

Hannah sat and watched them, occasionally contributing to the conversation. There was a tension between the two women – because of young Adam, no doubt. And some of Maggie Kellett's remarks were very spiteful. Hannah never had liked the woman, but expressed her gratitude without betraying that. 'If you can come again tomorrow, we may be able to finish it. You'll take your dinner here afterwards, of course? And perhaps your husband could join us?'

Maggie threw a triumphant glance towards Rachel, who did not take dinner with the Armstrongs. 'That would be delightful.'

When she had gone, Hannah leaned her head back and let

out a murmur of exhaustion. It had been a long day for her, and she had missed her usual afternoon rest.

'You should dine in your room and get to bed early tonight, madam,' Rachel suggested. 'Your nephew will understand.'

Hannah was too weary to argue and allowed Rachel to help her to bed. 'You'll like Rochdale,' she said suddenly as she leaned back against the pillows. 'It lies in a valley and there is a pleasant river running through it. Many of the buildings are of stone, and very elegant they look, too.'

Rachel nodded and pressed her lips together to prevent herself from protesting at what this would mean to her personally, for they were to leave on a Saturday and the wedding was on the Monday. Anyway, she'd been to Rochdale before.

Hannah looked sideways, saw her expression and guessed at her concern. 'You will not be able to see your son on Sunday. Is that what's troubling you?'

Rachel nodded, miserably aware that Mr Armstrong would not like her worrying his aunt about such details.

'There is no reason why you cannot see young Adam another day. I'll speak of it to Mrs Kellett tomorrow.'

'She won't like it. She – she doesn't want me to see him at all.' It was out before she could prevent it, her voice breaking on a sob as she said it. 'She wants to adopt him as her son.'

'Ah.'

'She can't have any more children of her own, you see.'

Silence, then, 'Perhaps he could come up to the house for a change before we leave?' Hannah beamed at Rachel, pleased by this idea. 'Yes, that's it. He can take tea with me. I've been wanting to meet him.'

It seemed unfair to complain, because though it would mean seeing him, Rachel wouldn't have her son to herself, wouldn't be able to ask him how things were really going.

On the appointed day, Rachel went to meet Adam at the gates of Cleving Park, noticing with a pang that he was growing taller and was wearing a new shirt. 'Did Mrs Kellett make you that?' she asked, fingering the material, which was of an excellent quality.

He looked down at it indifferently. 'Yes. What's the big house like inside, Mam? I want to see everything.'

'We have to see Mrs Hannah first and we shall probably stay in her rooms.'

His face fell. 'But I wanted to see the house. I've never been inside one so big before. Mrs Kellett says it's splendid.'

'I'm only a servant there, love. The house belongs to Mr Armstrong and – and servants don't have the freedom to wander round it at will.'

'Oh. Shall I not be able to see Kitty either?' He had so much to tell his half-sister.

'Mrs Hannah has arranged for Kitty to come and sit with us for an hour.'

At first, the small tea party was very stiff, with the two children on their best behaviour and Rachel anxiously keeping an eye on them. Kitty was so overawed by this honour that she could hardly be got to say a word, while Adam had so many questions to ask he could hardly be persuaded to stop speaking. Fortunately, the old lady was amused rather than offended by this.

Then Hannah had the happy idea of showing the children the contents of her black and red lacquer cabinet, which had come all the way from far-away China and that broke the ice nicely, for the strange trinkets fascinated both children. When Adam mentioned that he'd love to see the rest of the house, Hannah said why not and asked Rachel to wheel her round the ground floor. 'My nephew is out, so we'll disturb no one.'

'It's very kind of you to allow this, madam.'

'It's kind of you to share your boy with me.'

While they were looking at the library, Nathaniel returned home, surprised to find the small party in the room he regarded as his own. But as the first thing he heard was his aunt's laughter, he did not complain, just watched them indulgently, noting how well-mannered Rachel's son was. A fine lad, that. He was looking forward to having a sturdy son of his own.

★   ★   ★

Georgiana Bretherton looked across the table at her guest. 'You're very quiet today, Caleb.'

'I have a lot on my mind, ma'am.'

'Could you not share your troubles with me?'

'Some of my sheep have gone missing. Some of yours, too, I gather.'

'They'll be hidden in a gully somewhere, like last time. You'll find them.'

'Aye, that's what I thought. But they've been missing for two weeks now. And I found some of them last time on Tam Barker's land.'

She raised one eyebrow. 'You think they have been stolen?'

He pursed his lips, opened his mouth to speak, then shut it again. He did think they had been stolen, was convinced of it, in fact, but how to prove that? He had been across the tops and looked at Tam Barker's sorry little farm while the owner was absent, and the missing sheep were definitely not being kept there this time. He would have to make inquiries in Todmorden and Rochdale next, see if Tam had been selling any sheep for meat lately.

He was very angry to lose these particular animals, for he had bred them carefully and had wanted to breed more out of them, for himself and for Mrs Bretherton. Most of their offspring were plumper animals than usual, with sweeter and more tender meat, not stringy, hardy beasts that nearly broke your teeth to chew them.

'I'm going to Nathaniel's wedding,' Georgiana said in an abrupt change of subject, 'and am invited to travel over to Rochdale with them.' She chuckled. 'Nathaniel is trotting out all his relatives to add to his own consequence. The Hartleys will be hard put to house everyone.'

'And are you pleased to go?'

'Why not? I shall enjoy the change.'

'Is,' he tried to speak casually, but had to clear his throat before he could continue, 'is Rachel Thorpe going with her mistress?'

'I believe so. My cousin Hannah can no longer manage without help.' She looked down at her own hands regretfully. The skin was liver-spotted with age, but her joints were still functioning reasonably well, thank the Lord. Poor Hannah, who at seventy was ten years older, was totally dependent upon her servants now. She had visited her only a few days previously and had been sad to see how weak she looked.

'I wonder how Rachel is enjoying life at Cleving Park,' Caleb said, not realising how he was betraying his feelings.

Georgiana glanced quickly in his direction, intrigued. 'My cousin tells me she has settled in well and become a valued member of the household. Hannah speaks very highly of her and would not know how to manage without her now.'

'She'll be missing her son, though.'

'They let her see him every Sunday.'

He snorted. 'Once a week! Fine doings that, to take a woman away from her child. She grieves over it, you know. And so does he.'

Georgiana was very alert now. Was it possible he had an interest there? She hoped so. It would be good to see him wed to a decent woman. 'I shall be able to tell you how your friend is faring when I come back,' she said with seeming casualness. 'She is to act as maid to me, too, while we're in Rochdale.'

His face became suddenly closed tight, even his eyes expressionless. 'Is she, then?'

She was wise enough to change the subject. He was a very private person, Caleb was. But she would take a good look at this young woman who had been at the centre of so much trouble, and if she liked what she saw, then maybe she would do something about bringing the two of them together.

When Georgiana arrived at Cleving, from where she was to travel to the wedding, she stopped dead at the sight of Rachel, the colour draining from her face.

Rachel wondered what had upset her. Since the visitor's eyes were almost devouring her, she risked a quick glance in the mirror to see if anything was amiss with her own person, but her new clothes were as neat as ever, and she saw no dirty marks on face or pinafore.

The moment passed and Mrs Bretherton recovered her composure. The two ladies sat down for a gossip before the time appointed for their departure, but it had seemed to Rachel, who was in and out of the sitting room on little errands or to answer Mrs Hannah's queries about the packing, that *both* ladies were now staring at her rather intently. She was greatly relieved when it was time to leave.

Squashed in the second coach with the other servants, with her mistress's wheeled chair strapped on the back, Rachel enjoyed the drive over to Rochdale. She chatted with the others as they drove, for unlike the folk of Upper and Lower Clough, her fellow workers at Cleving seemed to have accepted her from the start and now included her in all the gossip and doings of their cosy little world.

If it were not for her son, she might even have considered staying in service, because waiting on others was not nearly as bad as she'd expected and there was no denying that life could be hard for a woman on her own. But there was her son to consider. She still missed Adam dreadfully and was determined to get him back.

The Hartleys came out under the portico to welcome Nathaniel and the two elderly ladies. Catherine waited behind her father, but could not keep her eyes off her betrothed, who was looking particularly fine today in a coat of dark green broadcloth with black braid round the edges and matching green breeches. The coat had silver buttons and was worn over a brocade waistcoat. He wore his own hair, not a wig, and it was plentiful, of a light brown colour. She was glad not to have to face a bald pate like her father's in private. Or the domestic problems of keeping wigs clean and lice-free.

Triumph swelled through her as she smoothed her open-fronted skirt, which showed off the glossy ruby damask of her underskirt to perfection. She had found herself a husband, even though she wasn't pretty, and he was very much to her taste. She glanced at the two elderly ladies who had accompanied him and nodded. Even more important, he was a man who dealt kindly with his old aunt, so he would not be likely to treat his wife unkindly either.

But all she said as she inclined her head to him was, 'Nathaniel.'

And he repeated her name just as quietly. 'Catherine.' But smiled warmly as he said it.

Then her mother bustled forward and they had no more time to be alone.

The wedding in St Chad's Parish Church the following day went very well, Nathaniel felt, and afterwards he drove back in a carriage with his new wife, she in a blue silk gown and he in darker blue to complement it.

'I hope we shall be happy together, my dear,' he offered, taking her hand in his and patting it.

'We must make sure of that,' she responded, smiling. 'You will not find me hard to live with, Nathaniel.'

He smiled. 'You may find me a little harder, I'm afraid. I'm used to being master and having my every word obeyed, I am aware of that. But I shall try not to give you too many orders.' This was as near a joke as he could get.

'And I shall try to obey most of your orders,' she responded quietly with another smile. 'I shall enjoy being mistress of my own house and you need not fear that I shall make your aunt uncomfortable. I like Mrs Hannah and I'm sure she and I will deal very comfortably together. Though that is a strange sort of maidservant for her to have. Such a tall woman, with a fierce expression sometimes.'

'Rachel Thorpe is not in the usual mould,' he agreed, 'but she has many good qualities, not the least of which is that she is strong and can lift my aunt with ease. Also, she is very honest, and I find I value that above servility.'

She made a note of that, but vowed to keep an eye on the woman. Her own maid said Rachel was proving very helpful in the servants' quarters, turning her hand to whatever was asked of her, so that was in the woman's favour, at least. But it was never wise to take other people's opinions without testing them out.

When a gargantuan meal had been consumed and all the post-nuptial fuss was over, Nathaniel distributed gifts of gloves to all the ladies present, for the old-fashioned custom pleased him. Then he and his bride set off for a small tour of the Peak District and a visit to Buxton Spa, where the baths had recently been refurbished and where the water, apparently, had curative properties, as well as springing forth from the ground warm, something he would be interested to see.

The following day, the Hartleys sent the two old ladies home in their own carriage, and, Rachel went with them.

On the way home, Mrs Bretherton kept staring at her and asking her questions about her mother and her upbringing, which did nothing to lessen her embarrassment. She was puzzled by it. Why would this rich lady be interested in her?

'Well, Rachel, how did you like your visit?' Mrs Hannah asked as she prepared for bed that night.

'I liked it very well, thank you. But I'm glad to be back.' She had had the pleasure of seeing her son waving to her from the garden of the parsonage as the carriage rumbled through the village. That had gladdened her heart more than anything.

'I think Mrs Catherine will be a good mistress for Cleving,' Hannah mused, not feeling like sleep just yet. 'Don't you? She is such a sensible young woman.'

Rachel knew better by now than to comment on that. 'Me? I have no opinions about that, madam.'

The old lady just smiled. 'Very tactful, but I'm sure you have opinions about everything, Rachel Thorpe.'

And have learned to keep them to myself here, thought Rachel, feeling stifled and rebellious.

'She's back, then,' Bill said that night.

'Who's back?' Walter asked, though he could guess.

'Her. That gowky owd maypole. Come back riding inside the carriage with the two old ladies, they tell me. Did I not say she was worming her way in? We'll have to act before she gets them to throw us out of our houses.'

Walter goggled at him. 'Why do you say that?'

'Because,' Bill tapped his nose, 'I'm a bit smarter than you about these things.'

'Not smart enough to get made putter-out, though.'

Bill stared at him coldly. 'It were better for you to do that, you bein' older like. When you get too old, I'll take over from you.'

'Hah! An' maybe it were also because you're known as a brawler that they wanted me.'

Bill breathed in deeply and concentrated on his ale. Walter was getting a bit touchy and was reluctant to do the sensible thing about that woman. He and Tam might have to act without him. Then he shook his head on the thought. No, they'd not act without him. He had to be in on everything, then there'd be no chance of him giving them away afterwards.

He dug an elbow in his friend's ribs. 'Ah, don't be so daft. You know we have to get rid of her.'

But Walter remained stubborn. 'No. I don't. She's out of our way where she is, an' she's doin' us no harm. Why should we take any more risks?' Or burden their consciences with more sinful acts? He still could not get the memory of Thomas Thorpe's death out of his mind, and had nightmares regularly about that night.

Bill prayed for patience. 'I keep *tellin'* you. Because she knows too much.'

'She's too busy lookin' after the old lady to worry about us now.'

'You're wrong. And Tam agrees with me.'

Walter took a loud slurp of ale and glowered down at his pot.

Bill judged it best to leave the matter there for the time being.

When she got back to her house in Hepstone, Georgiana went to stand and stare at a portrait of her husband, painted when he was about thirty. 'Why did you never tell me?' she asked it, for when she was troubled, she sometimes talked to the painting.

Such a tall, handsome man he had been, and how sad she had been not to bear him a child. She had been quite ill for a few years with women's problems when she was in her late thirties, so that they had not even been able to make love easily. Not that he'd ever reproached her about that. No. Ralph had been very kind always. But she had wondered sometimes if he found comfort elsewhere, for he was a man who needed women and wanted congress often.

'You should have told me about her,' she repeated to the portrait. 'And done something for her.' For Rachel was so like Ralph that Georgiana had been shocked rigid when she saw her and had no doubt whatsoever about the relationship.

She would, she decided, find out more about Rachel Thorpe, about her life, her childhood – and about her mother. It hurt to think of another woman loving Ralph – but perhaps it had been just a practical arrangement.

She clicked her tongue in exasperation at the tears in her eyes. Why was she getting so upset now, after all these years?

Later, as she lay in her bed, unable to sleep, it came to her that if Rachel was Ralph's daughter, then she owed it to him to protect the poor woman. She seemed to have been ill-treated by the man who had acted as her father, and by some of the other men in Whin Vale too.

She would change her will the very next day to leave Ralph's daughter something. And – she smiled in the friendly darkness – she would definitely foster a match with Caleb Hesketh. Why not? He was already attracted and he would know how to care for and protect Ralph's daughter.

But Ralph's daughter was as like him as two peas, and when Rachel came to live in this district, tongues would certainly wag about the resemblance. Georgiana would not let that stop her from doing the right thing, though. And anyway, she was too old to worry about gossip. And too lonely. She would continue to befriend them and, if God spared her, enjoy watching their children grow up.

CHAPTER TWENTY

While Mr Armstrong was away on his wedding tour, life at Cleving went along very quietly. The servants knew their work, had all been there for years except for Rachel and Kitty, and had Mrs Hannah to refer to if in doubt about something. But with the reduced duties and absence of a demanding master, there was a holiday air about the place and they had more hours free.

On the Sunday following their return from Rochdale, Hannah suggested, 'Why don't you take a little longer with Adam today?'

Rachel beamed at her. 'That would be lovely. Thank you, madam.'

When she went to collect her son, she mentioned to Maggie that Mrs Hannah had given her extra time off, so they wouldn't be back until later.

'What? But he's to come to church with us! No, he can't stay any longer with you. He can't possibly.'

Adam was already scowling at her and just as Rachel opened her mouth to protest, a voice behind them said, 'Maggie!'

She jumped at the sound of Justin's quiet but reproving voice and one hand fluttered up to fiddle with the bows on her bodice. 'Oh, you startled me. I did not know you were back.'

'I returned for a book and was surprised to hear what you said. I can see no reason why Adam should not spend more time with his mother. *Now or at any other time.*'

Maggie said nothing, just shot a venomous glance at Rachel.

'Well, my dear?' Justin prompted.

She saw he was still looking at her, but behind his smile lay determination. Anger at his obtuseness where his own interests were concerned made her burst out with, 'But it won't look well for your son to—'

'I think you mean "godson", do you not?'

She flounced one shoulder at him. ''Tis the same thing, near enough. And it *won't* look well if the boy does not attend church with his family.'

'That's easily remedied, then. He can attend with his mother.' Which would show people in the village that Rachel still was his mother and that the lad loved her greatly – for that love shone out of both of them every time they were together.

Rachel, who had planned to take Adam walking on the tops, stifled a sigh and accepted the inevitable. 'Thank you, Mr Kellett. We'll do that.'

Maggie stormed off to the kitchen without another word.

Adam looked up from one remaining adult to the other. 'Why does Mrs Kellett get so angry every time Mam comes to see me?' And why, he wondered yet again, though he did not ask, did she keep calling the parson his father? He remembered his father well, still cried for him sometimes in bed where no one could see. No other man could ever take his father's place.

'Oh, Maggie is upset about something else, Adam,' Justin said quietly when he saw that Rachel was at a loss for words. 'She'll be herself again soon.'

Rachel nodded her head in unspoken thanks for his stepping in and took Adam outside with her. They walked round the streets for a while, then went to sit on the low wall at the back of the churchyard.

'Mam, what are we going to do on Sundays when it rains or snows?' he asked, shivering a little in the cool breeze. 'We can't walk round and round the streets then.'

'We'll find somewhere to go. The church porch, maybe.' She would ask Justin Kellett later about that. She was sure he would help them. 'Now, tell me how your lessons are going.'

That set him off on a long tale of how he and Richard Payne had quarrelled, for he was sure of his audience's interest. No one listened to his tales like his mother did. In fact, there was no one quite like his mother and he wished he could still live with her, and poor old Dusty, too.

'Why doesn't Mrs Kellett like Dusty?' he asked on the thought.

'Doesn't she?'

'No. She says he's dirty, and he isn't because Mr Kellett has given me a brush and I brush him with it every day. She says he gets under her feet, but he won't go near her, so how can that be? And he hates being shut up in the shed. I wish we had a place of our own again.'

She stifled a sigh. 'Well, this is the best we can do for the moment, love.'

He sat very quietly for a few minutes, then said softly, 'It all changed when Dad died, didn't it?'

'Yes.' Tears thickened in her throat and she couldn't say more for a minute.

'Will we ever be able to live together again, Mam? Sometimes at night I want you so badly! I can't talk to anyone like I can to you, not now Dad's dead.'

Suddenly she felt fierce determination pierce her and gave him a hug. 'Yes, we will live together again. I'll find a way, Adam, I promise you.' And she would. She had stopped thinking and planning for her own future as she settled in at Cleving, for she had grown fond of Mrs Hannah. But no one was as important to her as her son. Anyway, Mrs Hannah was not a well woman, even though she rarely complained. Rachel had seen that look before, in Auntie Susan. And she knew, too, that her mistress was getting tired of the pain and found it hard sometimes to put on a cheerful face.

On her way back to Cleving Park, Rachel met Bill Withers, lounging just round the corner from the front gates of the house, in a place where he was hidden from both the town and the gatekeeper's cottage. This made her feel apprehensive, so she quickened her pace and tried to walk straight past him.

However, he moved to bar her path, and when she tried to step round him, he grabbed her arm, a nasty grin on his face.

'Leave go of me!' She pushed him away from her.

He let go of her and moved back a step, but stayed between her and the gates, still with that sneering look to him. 'I need to talk to you.'

'I can't see what you want with me, Bill Withers. And I certainly don't want to talk to you.'

He came straight to the point. 'We want you out of our valley.'

'Since when has it been *your* valley?'

'Since me and Walter took over the putting-out.'

Still feeling upset at saying goodbye to her son for another whole week, she was unguarded enough to ask, 'Isn't it enough that you've driven me from Upper Clough, denied me a home of my own?'

He threw back his head and laughed. 'No, it's not enough. Not nearly enough. We don't like you and we want you gone.'

'Well, I'm not going. I have work here at Cleving and have a son in Setherby, so I'm staying.'

'I thought you'd say that.' But Walter had insisted on her being warned first, so Bill had agreed to approach her. The mere sight of her made Walter nervous since they'd taken her money. He was a fool. Soft. But Bill needed his help still, so he put up with him. He wouldn't always, though. He'd have his day.

'Then why did you even bother to tell me to go away?' she asked.

'To see if you'd learned a bit o' sense yet.'

She gave a bitter laugh. 'Oh, yes. I've learned a lot of sense. I've learned to hide my money more carefully, for a start. And not to go near such as you if I can help it. And I've learned what it's like to lose a husband, too, a husband who should still be alive.'

Anger growled in his throat at what was hidden behind these words. She had just proved how dangerous it was to leave her around. If she kept saying such things, someone might listen. 'If you had any sense, you'd leave. And the sooner the better.'

'I shan't go. Not for anything. And you'd better leave me alone from now on, or I'll complain to Mr Armstrong about you when he gets back.'

For a moment or two, they stood eyeing one another, anger on both their faces, then she drew a deep breath. 'Now are you going to let me pass or do I have to shout for help? They'll hear me from the gatehouse, I'm sure. I've got a loud voice when I want.' But she was beginning to feel nervous because he'd put weight on lately and he looked much stronger since he'd given up boozing all the time. She wasn't at all sure she could best him now, or even defend herself adequately. It made you soft, living in such luxury did.

He stepped aside, but as she walked past him, he feinted towards her, laughing uproariously when she jerked away and started running towards the gates.

'I'll make you run!' he shouted after her. But when she had disappeared from view, he stopped smiling. She obviously wasn't going to leave Whin Vale of her own accord. That one was as stubborn as they came. Well, at least Walter would be satisfied they'd tried to persuade her to go peacefully. And no one had seen Bill speaking to her today, so there was no harm done. He left the path and went along by the back of the river, keeping out of sight till he got beyond Setherby.

At the gatekeeper's cottage, Tilda was out in the garden, hoeing.

'Who was that speaking to you?' she asked as Rachel walked past.

'Bill Withers.'

'Oh, him! I saw him hanging around some time ago while I was fluffing up the feather mattress. We don't want his sort at Cleving.' People from the village often forgot there was an upstairs at the gatehouse cottage. Tilda could see a lot from her window, and spent an occasional idle moment there watching the road that led into the village.

★　　★　　★

The next day Hannah noticed that Rachel seemed to be bursting with energy and it occurred to her that she might be fretting at this inactive life, so she asked her if she'd mind going into the village to buy a few bits and pieces. Rachel was unguarded enough to say, 'Oh, I should enjoy getting out sometimes.'

When she thought it over, however, she wondered whether she might get waylaid again. The lane from the village was bordered by shrubs and hedges, and it made her feel a bit nervous to walk alone along it after the encounter with Bill Withers. Still, he would be safe in Upper Clough most of the time, surely, for he still had his weaving to do. Though she'd keep an eye open for strangers from now on whenever she used the lane.

So Rachel began to walk into the village two or three times a week, sometimes being lucky enough to catch a glimpse of Adam, sometimes just enjoying the open air and a brief period of liberty. She felt sad that many folk still eyed her askance. They had clearly not forgotten how she'd burned the cart. She wanted to go up to them and say, 'I was driven to it, driven!' But of course she couldn't. And even if she did, they wouldn't believe her.

Mrs Payne in the linen draper's shop was the most hostile of all the people she encountered, though Rachel could not understand why until one day she found Maggie Kellett sitting in the shop on the chair provided for the better class of customer, chatting to the owner's wife with all the appearance of an old and very close friend.

The two women stopped talking to stare at her, then Maggie leaned forward to whisper something to Mrs Payne, after which both ladies tittered.

Rachel waited a long time but Mrs Payne made no attempt to serve her, so in the end she said loudly, 'I'm here to buy some things for Mrs Hannah Armstrong. Shall I go back and tell her you won't serve me?' There was an exclamation from the back room and Mr Payne came out, frowned at his wife and started fussing over Rachel.

But Maggie Kellett didn't even attempt to greet Rachel,

just scowled across the shop at her. And Lydia Payne ignored her husband's displeasure, turned her back and busied herself straightening some ribbons.

Parson's wife is determined to take my Adam away from me, Rachel thought as she walked back to Cleving. Well, I can be just as determined and she's not having him. Not for anything. Not unless she kills me first.

Caleb Hesketh went further and further afield, asking around and searching for his missing sheep. A day or two later, he found four of them in a rough pen in a small depression on the moors. He examined the ground nearby, finding a soft muddy patch which showed footprints of at least two men, possibly three, and the pawprints of a dog, too. Not his dog, for he had not walked this way. But unfortunately, although he went in the direction they had come from, there was no way of tracing the owners of those footprints because except for this low-lying marshy patch most of the ground up here was too hard to show any tracks.

The next day he went into Todmorden to put out word that he was looking for another shepherd's lad or two, for he and his shepherd, Joseph, had decided to set a couple more lads on to watch the flocks at night. After that, knowing he had done all he could for the time being, he went home for his dinner.

As soon as he walked into the house, however, he saw that his mother was in one of her moods.

'If I'd known you were going into Todmorden today,' she complained as he walked through the kitchen door, 'I'd have come with you. I enjoy a little trip out now and then, you know I do.'

'I didn't have time to wait around for you to do your shopping. I went there on business. And anyway, you can catch the carrier's cart into Tod any time you like.'

'Oh, yes. On my own. And how would the work get done here if I went rushing off to Tod all the time?' She loved going there because it was so quiet out here she thought she'd go mad sometimes, though she'd never admitted that to anyone. This isolated farm had been her one chance of independence for herself and her son, so she'd set her mind to living here and that was that.

'The work would get done well enough for me,' he said indifferently. 'An odd day out wouldn't make that much difference. Things are going well for us these days – though I'll make sure those scoundrels don't take any more of my sheep.' He went across to sit at the table expectantly.

She began to serve him some stew. 'Have you seen any more of that woman?' she asked suddenly.

'If you mean Rachel Thorpe, aye, I've met her a couple of times.'

'Oh, Caleb, people say such things about her and her temper.'

He stopped eating to say, 'You shouldn't listen to gossip.'

'But what if I don't like her, don't get on with her? What shall I do when you marry?'

He'd been thinking about that for a while now. 'You won't need to get on with her. I'll find you somewhere else to live when I get wed. I'd not ask you to play second fiddle here to a younger woman. I mean to set you up in your own home.'

But that didn't please her either. 'That's right, push me off into some hovel of a cottage and leave me all on my own with nothing to do from dawn till dusk, no money, no one to talk to. Well, I won't leave here. It was me as got this farm for you and don't you ever forget it. I have a *right* to live here. Just as much right as you.'

It annoyed him that when they quarrelled, she always threw at him what she'd once done for him, as well as speaking as if they were poor. 'Mother, you'll do as I say in such matters. And I'll make sure you have a nice place to live in and enough money to live on comfortably, so you don't need to worry. We're not short of a bob or two these days.'

Her voice wobbled as she said, 'But Caleb—'

'Mam, nothing's going to happen for a long time yet.' But he knew he'd hurt her, explained things badly. Why, he wondered, as he got on with his work, did he behave like this towards his mother? What had changed him? And of course the answer was obvious. Association with Mrs Bretherton had changed him, was still changing him and – he closed his eyes and sighed – meeting Rachel Thorpe had changed him too. So many years ago now since he'd first seen her and still she was the only woman he had ever wanted to marry.

He'd give her time to get over losing her husband and while he waited he'd try to get to know her and her son better. Then, within the year, he'd put his desires to the test, ask her to marry him. Surely she would not turn him down. Surely what he could offer her was better than any other prospect, even if she didn't care for him as he cared for her? For he was like a hungry man who would eat anything given to him. He would take Rachel Thorpe to wife on any terms.

But he couldn't even be sure of her paying heed to how sensible it'd be to wed him, for she was a fierce, independent creature. A bit like him, really. And she'd never shown any signs of being attracted to him. Not once.

It was not like him to be afraid of anything, but he was afraid of her rejecting him – absolutely terrified of that. What would his future be like if she did? Bleak, that's what. Too bleak to contemplate.

Mr Armstrong and his new wife came home looking happy and at ease with one another. Rachel watched them and sighed for her days with Thomas. It had been so wonderful not to be alone. She seemed to have spent her whole life alone, apart from those few precious years. She made a little exasperated sound in her throat. Oh, she was a fool to fret like this! Even though Thomas had gone, she was not alone, how could she be with a son like Adam? And she had a dear stepdaughter in Kitty, too, though the girl was getting very grown-up since she'd started working here.

The next morning Mr Armstrong disappeared into his office and the new Mrs Armstrong took hold of the household reins in no uncertain manner. One by one she called the indoor servants into the small but comfortable room she had designated as her private parlour, asking about their work, their family backgrounds, asking all sorts of questions and seeming genuinely interested in their answers.

Rachel was one of the last to go in to see her.

'Sit down, please, Rachel, and tell me about yourself.'

'I'm Mrs Hannah's maid.'

'Yes, I know that. I want to know something about you, not what you do here.'

Rachel frowned and tried to think what to say. 'I'm a widow. I have a son and Kitty is my stepdaughter.'

Catherine knew that already, so she asked about something that had intrigued her. 'My husband tells me that you used to weave like a man. Is that possible?'

'I was as good as any man, too!' Rachel snapped.

Catherine looked sharply at her but decided not to take offence. Nathaniel had said the woman had a brusque way with her at times, but that at least you could be sure she would never deceive anyone or behave dishonestly. 'Do you miss the weaving?'

'Sometimes. But I miss more how it was with my husband and myself. He used to be putter-out, and I used to do all the calculations for him.' She sighed. 'I really enjoyed that. I have a good head on me for ciphering.'

'And now? Do you enjoy working here, looking after Mrs Hannah?'

A sigh was her only answer.

Catherine was a little surprised by that. 'You don't enjoy it?'

'I do in part. I've grown very fond of Mrs Hannah. She's a dear, kind lady. But I miss my son.' In spite of herself, tears filled Rachel's eyes. 'I'm g-grateful for the place here, don't think that I'm not, madam, and I promise you I do my best at all times, but,' another sigh, a wobble in her voice, 'my Adam's growing so fast. And I'm not there to see it most of the time.'

It was a cry from the heart and Catherine was not an insensitive woman. 'Aunt Hannah is looking very tired lately. Nathaniel was shocked when we came home. I don't think she'll be with us for long.'

'Yes. I'm sorry for that.'

Catherine frowned. Nathaniel had made one thing very plain. He would not allow Rachel to set up as a weaver again. That had caused too much trouble in the valley. 'But after Mrs Hannah dies, what shall you do with yourself?'

Rachel shook her head, unable to answer. The same question had been keeping her awake at night since her last meeting with her son. 'I don't know. I have a little money saved, and I'd like to have my own home again, bring my son up and keep an eye on my stepdaughters, but it isn't easy being a woman on your own. Especially if they won't let me weave.'

Catherine felt an unexpected surge of sympathy. It was cruel to keep a mother away from her son. Without realising what she was doing, she set one hand on her own belly. Already she had hopes, for she'd never been late with her monthly courses before. And if she was spared and the child thrived, she knew she wouldn't want to give it up to anyone else. She had hungered secretly for a family for a while now. This woman also had a look of hunger on her face when she spoke of her son. 'If we lose Mrs Hannah, I shall make sure you are not set adrift in the world, Rachel, I promise you.'

'And my Adam?'

'I'll do my best for you there, too.' Though Nathaniel seemed to favour the boy being adopted outright by the parson, said it'd be in the lad's best interests. Catherine decided she would have to see the mother and son together before she came to a conclusion about that. If there was a strong bond of love between the two of them, it would not be fair to separate them, whatever Nathaniel said. Her husband could be very set in his ways. Kindly, yes, but autocratic. If she ever had to act against his wishes, she'd take care how she set about it. If she had been able to manage her father, she should be able to manage Nathaniel – well, most of the time, anyway.

'Thank you. You may leave me now. I hope we shall work well together.'

'Yes, madam. You can be sure I'll always do my best.'

Rachel bobbed one of the hated curtsies and left, wishing now that she had not spoken so frankly about herself.

Catherine sat on alone for a while, pondering the situation. She enjoyed helping folk, and if ever a woman needed help, it was Rachel Thorpe. But would her husband allow it? And would Rachel herself accept any help?

CHAPTER TWENTY-ONE

The following Sunday, the master and mistress drove over to Todmorden to visit his family, and Hannah, who had started taking a long nap every afternoon, told Rachel she could again spend longer with her son.

Rachel looked at her, feeling worried at how transparent her mistress had been looking lately, how other-worldly the look in her eyes. Without even realising what she was doing, she smoothed back the grey hair as she asked, 'Are you sure? You seem so – tired. Perhaps I should stay here with you today and see Adam another time.'

'No. I'll ask Matty to come and sit with me later. Tell her I've given you permission to stay out for longer. And put my handbell within reach.'

Feeling her heart lift as it always did at the thought of seeing Adam, Rachel donned her best clothes and walked briskly across to the parsonage. There the joy faded a little as she had another confrontation with Maggie, who complained yet again about the boy being taken away from 'his family' every Sunday.

'I'm his family. His only real family.' Rachel put an arm round her son's shoulder. 'Perhaps you should remember that, Mrs Kellett.'

'You can't look after him!' Maggie burst out, her face contorted with anger. 'How can you even call yourself a mother?'

Adam edged closer to his mam, scowling at the woman who

had said this dreadful thing. 'She *is* my mother!' he shouted. 'And you're not.'

Seeing the resentment in his eyes, Maggie said nothing more and stepped backwards into the house. Now was not the time to make a stand. But she wasn't going to wait much longer for the boy. She wasn't! She was going to cut him away from everything to do with his old life. Eyes still burning with anger, she went slowly up the stairs, not even noticing her daughter, Peg, standing at the back of the hall with tears in her eyes.

Maggie came down again almost immediately, knowing the kitchen was unoccupied. She found some pieces of meat and mixed in with them some powder her friend Lydia had bought for her, then went outside and approached Dusty cautiously. 'Here, boy!'

The dog raised his muzzle and looked at her, but did not move.

Maggie set down the dish of meat and nudged it forward with her toe. 'Here you are!'

Dusty ignored it completely.

She decided the dog would be more likely to eat if she was not there and went inside again.

When she saw through the window that Adam and his mother were still standing talking in the village square, she stared at them for a moment or two, then went storming into Justin's study, banging open the door and rushing across to stand in front of the heavy desk loaded with books and papers. 'She's doing it again.'

Justin looked up, still lost in thoughts of his next sermon for the day. 'I beg your pardon?'

She put her hands flat on his desk, covering his papers, and leaned forward. 'I said, she's doing it again.'

'Who is doing what?' Though he could guess.

'*That woman* is taking Adam away from us for longer and longer each week.'

'I thought we had settled the matter once and for all. She is his mother and has a right to see him.'

Maggie tossed her head. 'Fine mother who can't make a

home for her son and look after him herself. Well, I won't put up with it, indeed I won't. It's too bad.'

He stared at her, searching for the gentle, pretty girl he had married but unable to find her in this vituperative shrew. Poor Peg was having to take on more and more the duties of mother to Lizbet as Maggie neglected her own children in her obsession for another woman's son. He sighed and pinched the top of his nose in an attempt to stop the headache he seemed always to get on a Sunday these days. He didn't know what he was going to do about the situation, but he would have to do something, that was sure. This could not go on.

A gust of wind rattled the windows and as he looked outside again, he thought how cold Rachel looked with her arms clasped tightly across her breast, the cloak billowing out around her. The dark clouds scudding across the sky promised rain later. He hoped for their sake it would hold off.

'Just look at her, lolling around like that! I don't know why she has so much free time, I don't indeed. She's cheating that poor old lady, taking advantage.'

He turned back to his wife. 'Mrs Hannah gives Rachel the time to be with her son and I forbid you to do anything to stop her seeing him. Nor do I wish to be disturbed each Sunday by these fusses. He is *not* our son, Maggie, and,' he paused and looked at her, to make sure she was listening, 'he never will be.'

He had grown very fond of the lad, of course he had, but it would not be good for Adam to be brought up by this foolish woman. If Mrs Hannah had not been looking so frail, or did not speak so warmly of how well Rachel was looking after her, he would have asked Nathaniel to let Adam's mother go, would have helped her somehow to find a home of her own.

Seeing that he had forgotten her already, Maggie let out a mew of disappointment and went off towards the kitchen, banging the study door behind her.

Rachel and Adam, happy simply to be together again, stood at the side of the market square, she with her arm round his shoulders, he leaning his head against her. After discussing where to go, they decided to walk up the hill to Lower Clough, then come back through the fields.

'Can we take Dusty with us?' he begged.

'Why not?'

'I'll go round and get him.' He crept round to the back of the house and Dusty rushed over to him, only to be dragged back by the rope. The dish full of food went skittering to one side and Adam never even noticed it. He untied the animal quickly, keeping one eye on the kitchen window, then crept out to the square again.

The dog went into paroxysms of joy at seeing Rachel, jumping up and trying to lick her face, and when he could not reach it, licking her hand instead. She laughed and petted him, then they all set off on their walk.

'Eh, Thomas did love that dog,' she said as Dusty bounded along happily beside them. 'An' no wonder. He's a loyal fellow.'

'I love Dusty too. I go and talk to him sometimes.' The dog was a comfort to Adam on days when the air inside the parsonage seemed to be full of an unspoken anger that bewildered him, on days when even Peg didn't seem to want to speak to him and Lizbet was openly hostile.

Half an hour after Adam had taken Dusty, the air at the parsonage was pierced by a child's scream, followed by another and cries of, 'Father! Father, come quickly!'

Justin jumped up and ran out to the back of the house where Lizbet was still screaming and begging someone to come and help. On the ground beside her the cat was having a fit and rolling around frothing at the mouth, obviously in extreme pain.

Wondering what could have caused this, he looked round to see Maggie standing at the kitchen door, one hand to her mouth, guilt written all over her face. Then he looked down at the dish of food lying in the part of the garden where Dusty was usually tied up. It was one of the kitchen dishes, not the old broken platter they usually placed the dog's food in. It was obvious what she had done. Disgust made him feel physically sick for a moment, then he said, 'Go inside, Lizbet.'

'But Tibby is—'

He had seen animals die of poisoning before and knew he had to put the poor creature out of its misery as quickly as possible. '*Go inside at once!*'

Crying loudly, Lizbet went.

Peg, who was standing at the side of the house, watched him take a shovel and kill the poor agonised creature, watched him shade his face with one hand and shudder afterwards, then go and dig a hole at the back of the garden. He put the dish of poisoned meat into it first, then the cat's body, then filled it with earth, stamping to firm it up.

As he walked back to the house, he saw her watching him. 'It had to be done, my dear.'

She went rushing to hug him. 'I know, Father. How – how did the cat get poisoned?'

He kept his arm round her as he walked inside, but said nothing.

'It was Mother, wasn't it?' she whispered in horror.

He didn't answer that either.

Maggie was in the kitchen, talking to Jane Charnley, and did not turn round as he came in, so he let go of his daughter, went across and took his wife's arm.

'Did you put out a dish of meat for Dusty, Jane?' he asked the housekeeper.

Jane looked at him, puzzlement on her face. 'No, sir. I always leave that to young Adam.' She smiled. 'Besides, the dog won't take food from anyone but him.'

Maggie made a choking sound and tried to pull away from Justin, but he kept a firm hold of her.

'Did you give Dusty some meat, Peg?'

'No, Father.'

'Lizbet?'

'N-no. But,' tears trickled down her face, 'I saw the cat

eating from the dog's dish. And then,' she gulped loudly, 'and then she fell down.'

He looked at Maggie and said nothing for a few long minutes, and so stern was his expression, so marked the revulsion on his face that no one else spoke either.

'I need to talk to you privately, I think, wife.' He had to pull her with him across the room. She was sobbing loudly before they were halfway down the hall, protesting she had to go and lie down, was ill with a megrim. But this time her tears didn't move him. He simply shoved her ahead of him into his study and slammed the door behind him.

Jane Charnley looked from one child to the other, realising what must have happened. She said nothing, but her expression was grim as she went about her work. Shameful thing to do, that. The mistress was getting more difficult by the day. But to kill a poor animal – that sickened her. If it weren't for the little lasses, she'd be thinking of finding another place, she would that. She felt sorry for the master. He had his trials, poor man.

By setting a brisk pace, Rachel and Adam kept warm and as usual they had plenty to say to one another. She was interested in every detail of his life and with the dog beside them, she did not feel as afraid of meeting Bill Withers.

When it was time to return to Setherby, they both grew quieter and she said goodbye to Adam at the parsonage gate in a husky voice. As she walked away, her eyes were blind with tears and she bumped into a tall figure. She choked out an apology. 'I'm sorry! I wasn't looking where I was going.'

She felt hands steadying her and looked up into Caleb Hesketh's concerned eyes. Feeling embarrassed by the tears on her cheeks, she tried to turn away, but he did not let go of her straightaway.

'Are you all right, Rachel?'

She spoke the simple truth, sure he would not mock her for it. 'I just – I miss my son, hate leaving him each week.'

'You're returning to Cleving now?'

'Aye.' Her voice was bitter. 'I have no choice about that, do I?'

'Allow me to escort you to the gates, then.'

'Oh. Well. All right. Thank you very much.' She didn't refuse his offer because she still worried that Bill Withers might be lying in wait for her, and each time she walked that short stretch of lane where she was out of sight of both the town and the gatehouse she was on edge, ready to run for her life. She glanced sideways at Caleb, wondering why he was doing this, but she felt safe with him so did not ask.

He caught her eye and smiled, the slow smile that lit up his sombre features and made him almost handsome. 'Have you enjoyed being with your son today?'

She nodded, too full of emotion to speak about that.

'It must be hard for you, seeing him only once a week.'

'Yes.' Her voice came out thick and choked with unshed tears still. She swallowed hard and concentrated on choosing her path carefully.

He watched her in concern, hating to see her distress, not feeling able to offer her any real comfort, so began to talk of his farm instead.

Gradually she calmed down a little and listened with interest to his plans.

Neither of them noticed the two figures lying in wait in the bushes, men whose faces were full of anger and disappointment that their plans to ambush her had come to nothing.

At the gatehouse she stopped. 'Thank you for your company. I don't enjoy walking along this lane. I was accosted by a – a man here once.' Then she hurried inside the grounds before he could say anything else, because she still felt like weeping. Today the parting had hurt her more than ever, for while they were out, Adam had wept and pleaded with her to take him away from the parsonage.

Caleb stood and watched her, then sighed and went back to visit Justin, as planned.

He could feel the tense atmosphere as soon as he entered the house, and as he stood in the hall with the maid who

had opened the door, he heard a shrill voice scolding from
upstairs.

Justin was sitting in his study, trying to block out the sound
of Maggie shouting at Adam and wondering whether he should
go and intervene. She had refused even to admit what she had
done and he was beginning to wonder whether she was in her
right mind, so obsessed was she with Adam, so sure of the rights
of her case. The lad had done nothing to deserve a scolding, but
the same thing happened every Sunday, and he'd seen how the
boy's feet dragged today as he walked slowly back down the
garden path with his dog. But it'd make her even angrier if he
intervened and he could not be there every minute of the day
to protect the poor lad.

When he heard Caleb's voice, Justin came out of his study
and greeted his friend thankfully. Turning to Lal, he said, 'Tell
your mistress we have a visitor, will you?'

Caleb didn't pretend about the noise from upstairs. 'Is
Maggie upset?'

'Yes.' Justin hesitated, then, feeling a need to confide in
someone, added, 'About Rachel seeing her son, actually.'

'But whatever's wrong with that?'

Justin was too upset himself to hide his feelings. 'She wants
us to adopt the boy, won't take no for an answer, seems obsessed
by it. And yet I never saw a more loving mother than Rachel
Thorpe, nor a child so fond of its parent, and I would *never* take
her son from her.'

'That's not right.'

'There's worse. Today she tried to poison his dog, only she
poisoned our cat instead.'

Standing at the door of the parlour, Maggie set her hands on
her hips and said, '*Well!*' in a tone of shrill outrage. 'How dare
you say such a thing. It's not true! *Not true!* She's set you against
me now, your own wife scorned for a woman like that.'

Justin closed his eyes for a moment, then took a deep breath
and said as mildly as he could manage, 'Could we offer our
visitor some tea, do you think, Maggie?'

'*You* offer it! Then you can go out and blacken my name

to all our friends. Just because I care about a child who needs a proper mother and home! You're not fair to me, Justin. You don't love me any more. No one cares whether I live or die.' Sobbing loudly, she ran upstairs again.

Adam, who had crept to the top of the stairs, from where he often listened to what they were saying downstairs, stepped quickly back into his room and closed the door. When the weeping woman had passed, he tiptoed down to take refuge in the kitchen. At least if he sat in there she couldn't come and whisper bad things to him about his mother.

The maid and housekeeper made the mistake of assuming he was too young to understand their allusions and continued to discuss the situation in an undertone, for they were all too well aware of the tensions in the house and the reasons for them, tensions which grew worse each week. And today's episode with the cat had shaken them all.

'I'm going to hide the rat poison,' Mrs Charnley said. 'I'm not having poor animals killed.'

'It's a good thing that dog won't eat from anyone's hand but the lad's or—'

Jane nudged Lal and she closed her mouth on the rest of the sentence.

Adam stared from one to another, but knew they wouldn't tell him anything even if he asked. Only his mother told him things, told him the truth – and Mr Kellett sometimes.

He scowled down at his hot milk and they began whispering again. If Mrs Kellett really had tried to kill his dog, he would not speak to her ever again.

Which caused more trouble the following day.

'Why will you not answer me?' Maggie demanded at breakfast.

'Because you tried to kill my dog.' He suddenly resembled his mother so much that she gasped in shock.

There was dead silence in the dining room, then Justin said quietly, 'Eat your food, Adam.'

But the damage was done. Maggie blamed this change of attitude on Rachel and told her friend Lydia how that woman had been poisoning the child's mind against her, telling him lies. Lydia passed it on to two or three customers who were also friends, and they, of course, did not keep it to themselves.

Suddenly the town was full of rumours about Rachel Thorpe causing trouble again.

Nathaniel heard the gossip from his new land agent.

'What did you say?' He frowned as the situation was explained, but made no comment.

Later that day, he sent for Rachel.

She came, all unsuspecting, dropping him a curtsy and waiting to see what he wanted.

He came straight to the point. 'I believe you have been causing trouble for Mrs Kellett, setting the lad against her.' He steepled his fingers and looked at her sternly over them.

'I – I don't understand, sir.'

'I am told that you have been setting your son against Mrs Kellett.'

'I've done no such thing.'

'Oh? Then why is she so upset?'

She folded her arms. 'I have no idea, sir.' It was not her place to speak about someone behind their back. In her opinion, Maggie Kellett had turned strange lately. Maybe she should try to find somewhere else for Adam to lodge until Mrs Hannah no longer needed her. But would they let her?

'If you cannot stop causing trouble between them, I shall forbid you to see him so often.'

'But sir—'

'Do not answer me back!' he thundered. 'You forget your place.'

Very fortunately, Catherine had walked into the room while they were speaking and she set one hand on Rachel's arm, squeezing it a little and shaking her head.

With a huge effort, Rachel bit back her hasty response. Everyone knew the master hated to be contradicted in any way, and since she had been in this house, she had had many lessons in biting her tongue. When Nathaniel flapped one hand irritably in dismissal, she turned away, but was unable to hold back a sob as she rushed out.

Catherine waited for an explanation but it did not come. Seeing the anger on her husband's face, she decided not to ask him outright, which he would probably resent, but see if Mrs Hannah knew anything about this matter.

Back in her mistress's overheated room, Rachel stood just inside the door, flattened against it, fighting for self-control and not succeeding as well as usual.

Hannah could not understand what had happened, but she could recognise distress when she saw it, so simply held out one twisted hand and said, 'Come and tell me what's wrong, my dear.'

With her head buried in her mistress's lap, Rachel sobbed out the story of the unjust accusation and her terror of being kept from her son.

Hannah frowned down at her, stroking the fine, soft hair and wondering what had happened to make Nathaniel do this.

By the time Catherine came in, Rachel had recovered a little, though her face still bore signs of weeping.

When Rachel had left the room, both women pooled their knowledge of what had happened, then decided that Catherine should pursue the matter over dinner, a time of day when Nathaniel was usually at his most mellow.

At first he declined to discuss the matter, so she said in a matter-of-fact tone, 'I should prefer to know what has upset you, my dear. After all, it is my duty to supervise the servants, so really I should be the one to deal with any troublesome maidservants, should I not?'

He opened his mouth to protest but realised that she was right and bit back a reproof. The servants were indeed her province and he should have left her deal with it. In a calm, reasoned voice, he passed on the gist of what his land agent had told him.

She considered this, then risked saying, 'My dear, the man is merely repeating gossip. Clearly something has happened but would it not be better to find out what before upsetting the poor woman with accusations? After all, gossip is not always right. And we don't want to be unjust to someone who serves your aunt unstintingly, do we?'

First he frowned, then he looked at her and slowly nodded, acknowledging her good sense in this matter. 'Yes. You're right, Catherine. I did indeed act too hastily. In fact, my dear, I shall request you to look into the matter for me. Perhaps you could go and see Mrs Kellett, ask her what is wrong.'

'I should be happy to do so, my dear.'

They smiled at one another, he satisfied with his sensible wife, who did not fuss and fret about things, and she pleased that she was learning to manage him.

In the middle of that same Sunday night, Caleb was awakened by someone hammering on his door, shouting, 'Come quickly, Master, come quickly!'

He struggled into his breeches and crammed his bare feet into his shoes, then went rushing down to find his shepherd's wife leaning panting against the doorpost.

'They've attacked young Matt and knocked him senseless,' Dinah gasped.

Joanna came down the stairs to join them. 'Who have?'

'Them thieves. And Joseph says more sheep are missing, Mester Hesketh.'

'Tell him I'm coming.' Caleb ran back upstairs to don some warm clothes over his nightshirt.

Joanna went to get the fire blazing. She did not think she would sleep again this night. Who was stealing their sheep? She hoped Caleb would catch the thieves and beat them senseless, she did indeed.

He hurried along the lane to the shepherd's cottage and what he found made fury sizzle in him. The lad was lying in front of the fire, shivering and only half conscious, with a battered and bloody head. Joseph was out with the sheep.

'What exactly happened?' he asked Dinah.

'The dogs began to bark, but Joseph said Matt would come for us if aught were wrong. Then later the dogs started barking again, on and on. So Joseph went out to see what was happening. He found Matt lying on the ground, and if he hadn't gone out to check, the poor lad might have perished, 'deed he might, in the cold and rain.'

Caleb went to discuss the matter with Joseph and keep him company in the fields for the rest of the night, but they could do nothing until daylight except patrol the boundaries and keep watch over the remaining sheep. In the cold light of dawn, they took stock. Not only were more sheep missing, but the lad's young dog had been killed, its throat cut.

'What sort of folk would kill a poor animal like that?' Joseph asked in horror, stroking the dead head and closing the animal's staring eyes. 'Eh, you didn't deserve that, Rusty.'

'They're getting too bold,' Caleb said, equally sickened. 'And they've taken too many sheep this time. We shall catch them, Joseph. See if we don't.'

'But we won't get them sheep back.'

'No.' More of his fine breeding ewes gone, and some of the younger sheep, too, plump meat animals, just ready for the market. Black anger settled in him, and he knew it would not fade until he had caught the thieves.

Even his mother forgot her hostility towards him in her fury at what had happened and for a time they worked together in their old way, each knowing what to expect from the other without telling. She didn't raise the question of finding him a wife or invite any other young women to tea, and she worried that he was looking older lately, with such a grim look to his mouth.

The following morning, Tam Barker was very cheerful over breakfast, though his wife sat mute and pale opposite him. 'Aw, mend your face, woman, do! I've just made mysen a few golden guineas by this night's work.'

'Or you've set yourself up for the gallows,' she muttered, for once not minding her tongue.

He jumped up and clouted her, so that she fell off the rough bench on to the floor. 'If you breathe a word of this, even hint at it, I'll give you a right old peppering. It's only right that I set myself up properly, after being unjustly dismissed. It's all *her* fault it happened. They'd have burned her on a bonfire for a witch in my grandad's time.' Like Bill and Walter, he had got into the habit of blaming Rachel for everything. They were going to get rid of her, one way or another. He could keep his wife quiet, but no one could trust *that woman* to keep her mouth shut – and next time someone might believe her accusations.

If it hadn't been for Caleb Hesketh, they would have caught her the other Sunday, so it was doubly just that they'd taken some more of Hesketh's sheep. Sod the man for interfering! The carcasses would sell well at Todmorden meat market. He frowned. Or maybe they should be taken over to Halifax. After all, no one could identify a carcass, could they, as long as you cut off the ears, with their tell-tale clip marks that showed who the animal belonged to.

He sat down again and thumped the table. 'Get me some more of that small ale. And see you keep your mouth shut about my business from now on, woman, or you'll have no one to earn your bread for you.' Which made her shiver and go very quiet, for it was her worst nightmare.

The following Sunday Adam had bruises on his face and confessed reluctantly that he had been fighting.

'But what about? Eh, that's not like you, lad,' Rachel said.

He scowled down at the ground.

'Adam, love. Tell me what it was about.'

He shook his head.

Then she realised it must be about her. 'Oh, child, don't start fighting over me!'

He flung his arms round her. 'But they say such terrible things about you, and none of it's true.' They said she was a bad mother, and he knew she wasn't. It was Mrs Kellett who was a bad mother, he'd decided, watching how often the two girls were scolded for nothing and how Mrs Kellett never cuddled them.

'Eh, lad. We're both in the wars lately, we are that!' Rachel held him close for a moment, then pushed him to arm's length, looked into his eyes and begged, 'Don't fight over me any more. Tell them they don't know what they're talking about and walk away. It does no good to fight.'

But he knew he wouldn't obey her. None of the other lads was going to say such things about his mam. Not even if they were bigger than him. Not even if they all ganged up on him.

Within a few days, Catherine Armstrong had proved to her own satisfaction that it was nothing but idle gossip blackening Rachel's good name. What was more, she suspected it had come from the parson's wife, a woman for whom she had no time, a woman who neglected her parish duties and lounged around her house much of the time, leaving everything to the housekeeper and maid – who were good women, but who should not have the responsibility for everything.

Nor did she like Mrs Payne, who was altogether too servile and flattering and who had tried to pass on to her some malicious gossip about Rachel. She had called Mr Payne over and told him straight out to make sure his wife kept such lies to herself if he wanted to keep her custom. As she left, she had had the satisfaction of hearing them shouting at one another.

Catherine carried her conclusions to her husband, but he listened with only half an ear because he was still so delighted by her other news. Well, so was she. Thrilled to be with child and hoping very much for a son this first time. But that wouldn't stop her doing her duty as mistress of Cleving, she hoped.

She called Rachel in to see her one afternoon while Mrs Hannah was having her nap. 'I have told my husband that people have been maligning you.'

Rachel stared at her in amazement.

'I can see for myself how fond you are of your son and he of you, and I'm sorry we're keeping you from him. But Mrs Hannah does rely on you. Can you stay with us until – until you're not needed?'

The thought that her new mistress believed in her innocence

made the hurt inside Rachel lessen and she looked up to say, 'Thank you.'

'I'm grateful for your hard work, Rachel, and your tender care of Mrs Hannah.' She waited expectantly, but Rachel made no promise to stay and, indeed, continued to look grim and thoughtful over the next few days as she went about her duties.

The following Sunday Rachel could see that Adam had been fighting again, but he got that stubborn set to his mouth when she tried to talk about it, and his expression reminded her so much of Thomas that it brought a lump to her throat.

Thank goodness Parson was allowing her and her son to sit in the vestry now on Sundays, for it had been raining all day and she did not want Adam to catch a chill. Not that it had been exactly warm in the vestry, but at least they'd not got wet there – and had been safe from prying eyes, too, for it was very quiet between services.

When they were walking, she occasionally felt as though someone was spying on them, though she had never seen anyone. It was just a feeling she got sometimes, as if there were hidden watchers. So she took care now not to go anywhere there would not be people within call.

When Caleb Hesketh turned up again just in time to walk her back to the gates of Cleving, she was relieved, then angry with herself. Eh, it was a poor thing when you were afraid to go out and about, it was that! But he was a kindly man and talked good sense, and she enjoyed his company. The servants at Cleving seemed interested only in the doings at the big house, while she was yearning to hear about the world outside, for she missed Thomas and his newssheets.

She lingered to chat for a few minutes and Caleb told her about his farm and the sheep that had been stolen.

'There is only one set of thieves in Whin Vale,' she said before she could prevent herself.

He nodded. 'I know. And I share your suspicions. But it's finding the proof that's the problem.' His face grew grim. 'But

I shall not give up until I have done so.' Then he took his leave and walked off.

She watched him until he was out of sight. What a fine strong man he was. And how kind.

CHAPTER TWENTY-TWO

Next market day, Caleb went into Todmorden, not wearing his usual neat, dark clothing but dressed as a working man, with dust and cobwebs rubbed into his hair to add a greyish tinge and make him look unkempt. Taking care to keep the brim of his old round felt hat pulled low and to slouch along so that he did not look as tall, he walked past the butchers' stalls at the market, noting their contents with a careful eye. At the last stall in the row, he paused, studying the meat carefully.

'Dost want something?' the woman behind it asked. 'My man'll be back shortly, but I can cut you a piece if you're in a hurry.' She gestured towards some pieces of mutton hanging up. 'See what fine young meat this is?'

He mumbled something and made a pretence of studying it. Yes, it was fine meat, markedly plumper than the usual lamb and mutton sold at market. Something told him this came from his sheep, but he could not see any way to prove that.

In the end, he shook his head and strolled on. Harry Brent was the owner of this stall, and Caleb would not have expected him to be buying stolen carcasses. But then, even good men could be weak sometimes where money was concerned and Harry had a large family to support.

Caleb slouched into the inn where the stallholders usually drank and sucked in his breath in shock, for Tam Barker was there, sitting in a corner with Harry Brent, the two of them with their heads together over pots of ale, nodding and smiling like men well satisfied. Another piece of evidence, to Caleb's mind, though again this would not prove anything.

Before anyone could recognise him, he ambled outside again, then hurried to retrieve his horse from where he had tethered it just outside town. Halfway home, he changed his mind and turned on to a side track, riding furiously up towards the poorer land near the tops. He had to find proof. He just had to. There must be some sign of his other sheep!

He tied up his horse in a sheltered place and climbed up the rising ground that overlooked the rear of Tam Barker's farm. A heavy shower drenched him before he was halfway to the top, but he ignored that. Taking care to keep out of sight of the house, he found a place from where he could examine the sheep in the fields. There were more of them than he'd expected, certainly, but none of them were his, he could see that at a glance.

After a few minutes, he clicked his tongue in exasperation and walked back down to his horse, worrying over the problem from every angle and stumbling on the slippery ground a couple of times, so lost in thought was he. Where were they keeping the rest of his sheep? And who was helping Tam Barker to steal them? Were any other nearby farmers affected? There seemed no end to the questions – and no beginning to the answers.

When Rachel got back from seeing her son, chilled to the marrow, Mrs Hannah was in one of her brighter moods. She sent her companion to fetch a tea tray, then insisted Rachel sit down and share it.

'Eh, sit down, do,' said Hannah, 'and tell me what's putting the frown on your forehead now, my lass. I want the truth, mind. Surely there isn't any new trouble.'

Rachel hesitated, then said in a rush, 'It's my Adam. He's been fighting again – and over me. Even the children are saying things about me!' She gulped back a sob.

The old lady made little noises of dismay, then drifted off into talk of her own childhood, which she was thinking about more and more nowadays. When she dozed off, Rachel got up and cleared away the tea things.

But from then on, Hannah could not stop thinking about

that little lad, separated from his mother by her own selfishness – there was no getting round that – a lad too small to defend his mother's good name, but still trying and getting hurt doing it. He was only – what? Six-years old, however big he was for his age. It didn't seem right. She ought to do something about it, make amends for separating them. But what could she do?

The following Sunday was stormy again, and after she had taken Adam back to the parsonage, Rachel hurried along the lane to Cleving Park, her head down and her cloak wrapped tightly round her. There was no sign of Caleb Hesketh today, hardly anyone out and about. People had come to church for the service but had not lingered.

Maybe it was because of the rain and howling wind, but she didn't keep her usual sharp watch and before she knew it a man had jumped out in front of her. And for all he had a mask over his face, she recognised Walter Smedling at once. How could she not after living with him for so many years?

Before she could turn to run, she felt a blow to her head and cried out in pain, trying to fend off her assailant. But that blow was followed by others, to many parts of her body, delivered by a stout stick. Pain upon pain that made her cry out. As she tried to protect herself, she searched for an opening so that she could flee towards the gatehouse.

Then a stronger blow than before knocked her to the ground and a foot connected to her ribs, driving the breath from her body.

'Nay, that's enough,' said a voice she recognised clearly as belonging to the man she had called Father for so many years.

As consciousness was fading, she heard another voice, Bill Withers, saying, 'Let go of me. If she's dead, she can't tell any more tales about us.' Then a blow to the head knocked her into a darkness she believed to be eternal.

When Rachel came to, she was lying in a big soft bed and could do nothing but moan. Her mouth was so swollen that the sounds coming out of it were not recognisable as words and her whole body seemed a mass of pain.

'Here, lass, drink this,' said a man's voice and gentle hands lifted her up.

When a beaker was set to her lips she could do nothing but sip, though the liquid had a bitter greasy taste to it and stung the cuts. It was a relief when he let her lie down again.

'She'll sleep for a good many hours now,' said the same voice.

She tried to frame words, tell them who had attacked her, but her muscles would not respond and she felt sleep sucking her down into a grey warmth that pushed away the pain. But she was alive, at least. Adam would not be left alone in the world.

That was her last thought for a while.

Downstairs, Nathaniel Armstrong received the doctor in his study. 'How is she?'

'In a dreadful state. She has been beaten near to death. If your gatekeeper's wife hadn't heard the noise and called her husband, the scoundrels might have killed her.' He shook his head and clicked his tongue in disapproval.

Furious that this could happen so near his own gates, Nathaniel said in a tight, clipped voice, 'You are to spare no expense to get her better.' For he was responsible for the welfare of his servants, as well as for law and order in his valley.

'I'm afraid it's time will be the healer now. Fortunately she has no broken bones, but she is severely bruised. 'Tis a shocking thing.'

'Indeed, yes.'

When the doctor had gone, Nathaniel sat thinking, remembering the accusations Rachel had made after her husband's death. He drew in a long slow breath as he contemplated the matter. Both the men she'd accused had risen in the world lately, and had profited from Thomas Thorpe's death. Surely he could not have been so mistaken about them? Why, Smedling had stopped getting drunk and Withers had pulled himself together. And the two of them were doing the putter-out's job well enough. Not as well as Thorpe had, by all accounts, but still well enough.

After some more thought, for he never liked to act pre-cipitately, he rang the bell and asked for his groom. He sent Timothy to find out where Withers and Smedling had been when Rachel was attacked. 'And tell no one about this,' he added. 'No one at all.'

When Justin called Adam into his study and told him his mother had been injured, the boy turned white and demanded to go and see her at once.

'She's not conscious, lad. They've given her a sleeping draught. We'll find out how she is tomorrow and then I'll take you over to see her as soon as she's awake, I promise.'

But Adam slipped out of the house secretly soon afterwards and made his way to Cleving, knocking on the back door and begging the maid who opened it to let him see his mother. 'Just to see she's still alive! *Please.*'

'Eh, lad, I don't know.' Then she saw how he was fighting against tears and her heart went out to him. 'Look, come inside by the fire – eh, it's a raw day, isn't it? I'll go and ask the mistress.'

She found Mrs Armstrong in Mrs Hannah's room and bobbed a curtsy. 'Sorry to disturb you, madam, but Rachel's son is in the kitchen, begging to see his mother.'

The two ladies exchanged glances.

'There is a great deal of love between the two of them,' Hannah said quietly. 'We are wrong to separate them – see what has come of it. I think we should let him see her, my dear.'

So Catherine went to the kitchens herself and paused in the doorway to stare across at the lad with the white, anxious face, sitting hunched up by the fire. Nodding a greeting to Cook, she went across the room.

As soon as he noticed her, Adam stood up politely and waited for her to speak.

'I'm Mrs Armstrong.' Goodness, he was already as tall as her shoulder and his expression had something very unchildlike in it, a steadiness and responsibility, for all that he was clearly upset. What would he be like as a man? Impressive, she was sure.

He nodded impatiently. He knew who she was, as did everyone in the valley. 'Can I see my mother? *Please?*'

'Of course you can. I'll take you to her now.'

He followed her to the door and through the large, quiet house, not even looking round him, so desperate was he to see for himself that his mother was all right.

When they took him into the bedroom, he could not hold back a sob at the sight of his mother's bruised, swollen face and ran to the bed, kneeling beside it, clutching the limp hand in his and covering it with kisses. Other sobs followed and he buried his face in the bedcovers, trying to muffle the sound of his weeping.

Catherine rushed to put her arm round him, her heart aching for the lad who had bravely defended his mother's name and still wore his own bruises from that. 'She's going to be all right,' she whispered. 'I promise you she is.'

Without thinking, he burrowed into the warmth of the kind lady with the soft voice, sobbing out his fears that he'd lose his mam like he'd lost his dad.

'We're caring for her and the doctor says she'll recover,' Catherine murmured again and again until the words had sunk in and the tears stopped.

A noise from the bed made them both turn round and they saw that Rachel's eyes were open.

Catherine drew her arms away from the child with the whispered warning to mind his mother's bruises.

He flung himself on his knees beside her. 'Mam! Oh, Mam! You're hurt.'

The voice was a mere croak. 'I'm – all right. Don't – fret yourself.'

Catherine touched the boy's shoulder. 'Let me give her a drink.'

When she had sipped some water, Rachel tried to smile at her mistress. 'That's – good.' She still felt sleepy, but had to tell them, 'It was Bill Withers – and Walter Smedling – who did it.'

Catherine stared at her. 'You're sure of that?'

'Oh, yes. Very – sure.'

'I'll tell Mr Armstrong.'

Only then did Rachel turn to her son again, fumbling with one badly grazed and swollen hand in an attempt to hold his. 'As long – as you're – all right, love. Take care how you go – down that lane.' She fell asleep almost immediately.

Still holding his mother's hand, Adam turned to look anxiously at the lady.

'She's been given a sleeping draught. She can't feel the pain when she's asleep, you see. It'll help her get better.'

He turned back to his mother, gulping audibly. After a while, Catherine touched him on the shoulder to get his attention. 'It would be better if you didn't tell anyone what she said about who did it.'

'I'll make them sorry when I grow up. See if I don't!' For a moment his young face seemed to take on the look of the strong man he would one day become.

'I hope we can make them sorry long before then. But we must keep it a secret until we have proof. I shall talk to Mr Armstrong, who is the magistrate, and he will attend to this matter. Now, I think you must leave your mother to sleep and come back to see her tomorrow.'

His face clouded. '*She* won't let me.'

'Who won't let you?'

'Mrs Kellett won't let me come. She doesn't like me seeing Mam.'

Catherine frowned. If that was true, it made matters even worse. Aunt Hannah was right, they had to do something about this situation. 'I'll write a little note to Mrs Kellett. You'll find she will let you from now on.'

He looked at her unwinkingly. 'She'll make a fuss when you're not there, though.'

She sighed. 'I'm afraid you must bear that for the moment, child.'

He grimaced and nodded, but did not protest any more, just went and sat by his mother's bed. And Catherine decided to leave him there for a while.

★   ★   ★

When Caleb heard from his mother that Rachel Thorpe had been beaten 'nigh unto death' in the lane leading to Cleving Park, he was both shocked and angry.

'Who did it?'

She shrugged. 'Thieves, I expect, after her purse.'

'And – how badly is she injured?'

'Beaten black and blue, they say. Hardly able to move.'

'Where is she now?' His voice was so sharp that his mother stared at him, but forbore to comment.

An hour later, Caleb slowed down as he rode into Setherby, realising suddenly that he could not just go and knock on the door of Cleving demanding to see Rachel. So he turned towards the parsonage, hoping to glean some information there. Fortunately he found Justin coming back from a visit to a sick parishioner and the two men entered the house together, to sit in the study, shutting the door on the sound of Maggie's scolding. A message had been sent down from the big house to say the boy was safe there and would be sent back later in the care of one of the servants, but that had only exacerbated her ill temper and made her take out her feelings on the maids, who were both very wooden-faced today.

Caleb looked at his friend. 'Who did it, do you think?'

Justin shrugged. 'That can only be a matter for conjecture.'

'Has she – said anything about who it was?'

'I gather she was unconscious when they carried her to the house. They feared for her life when they found her.'

Caleb groaned and buried his face in his hands.

Justin looked at him in astonishment. 'Are you – that upset?'

His cousin let his hands fall and nodded.

'I didn't know you still had an interest there.'

Caleb stared blindly towards the fire. 'I hope to have. One day. When she has finished grieving.'

'She won't make an easy wife.'

'No. But then,' he managed a wry smile, 'I doubt I'll make an easy husband. Or at least, so my mother tells me. Both Rachel and I are of an independent turn of mind. Still, I feel drawn to her as to no other. She's very special to me. I thought so the first time I met her – only she married Thomas Thorpe before I could speak out. And I had my way to make in the world in those days, was only just starting to earn decent money. But now, surely she'll listen to an offer of marriage from me. Will you – stand my friend in this?'

'If I can.' Justin let silence reign for a few minutes, then asked in a brisker tone, 'Have you found out anything about your missing sheep?'

'Nothing certain.'

'But . . .'

'I shall keep my thoughts to myself, I think, till I can find proof. Then you may be sure I'll act.'

'And if you need help . . .'

Caleb nodded. 'I'll call on you.' He stood up, unable to sit still. 'I must get back. You'll let me know if – if anything happens?'

Just then there was a clopping sound outside and the carriage from Cleving drew up. Through the window they could see Mrs Armstrong herself step out of it, followed by Adam. She said something to the lad and he nodded, walking beside her.

Caleb was close behind his cousin as they hurried towards the front door.

Maggie came rushing down the stairs, her voice high with excitement. 'Did you see who's brought him back? Mrs Armstrong herself.' Then her voice grew tight with anger. 'Upsetting everyone like that! He's a naughty wretch! I'll—' She bit off further threats when she saw Caleb, but sent him an unfriendly glance.

Footsteps sounded on the path and the doorknocker thumped out its message, so she whirled round and gestured to her husband urgently to attend to it.

Justin opened the door. 'Mrs Armstrong. Please come in.' Already he felt at ease with his patron's lady, who took a kindly interest in the sick and troubled folk from the poorer families, and was both generous and practical in her help.

She came inside, smiling with her usual composure, one hand resting lightly on the boy's shoulder. 'I thought I'd bring Adam back myself. I shall send my carriage to fetch him every afternoon from now on, if you agree, Mrs Kellett. We cannot let him come alone up the lane where his mother was set upon, can we?'

Maggie muttered something indistinguishable, scowled at Adam and gestured to her guest to come into the parlour. 'Do come inside. And let me send for a tea tray.'

Catherine held up one hand to halt her. 'I'm afraid I haven't time for a visit just now, but I shall come to call upon you another day, if I may.' She bent to hug Adam and say quietly, 'We'll look after her, don't worry.'

And he hugged her back without thinking, unaware of the social gulf between them, knowing only that this lady had been kind to him.

When Mrs Armstrong had left, Maggie turned to Adam and said curtly, 'Go and wait for me in your bedroom.'

Justin stepped forward. 'A moment, if you please. I should like to speak to the boy myself.' He gestured towards his study and when Maggie would have followed them into it, barred the way. 'I think we shall do this best without you here, my dear. Perhaps you could go and get the boy some food.'

'He does not deserve any dinner! He *disobeyed* me.'

He could not hide his shock. 'You forbade him to go and ask after his mother?'

'Of course I did. I keep telling you she's not a good mother. She doesn't *deserve* a boy like him!'

Hearing this further proof of her antipathy towards Rachel, Caleb had trouble holding his tongue. He glanced down at the boy and saw how rigid he had gone, so said in a low voice, 'Pay no attention to her, lad. She's in a sour mood today. I think you were right to go and ask after your mother. Any good son would have done the same.'

Adam looked up at the tall, dark man and whispered back, 'Mrs Kellett is always saying that about my mother. But she's wrong. My mam's good to me and cares about me and I w-wish I was living with her still.'

'No doubt you will do again one day.'

The boy nodded, but his shoulders were drooping. He knew Mrs Kellett would punish him in some way or other for going to Cleving. She made life uncomfortable for him after every meeting with his mother.

Justin came back into the room, shutting the door carefully behind him. 'Now, Adam, come and sit by the fire. There. Will you tell us first how you found your mother?'

The two men questioned the boy gently and he told them how badly bruised and hurt she was, tears trembling in his eyes at the memory.

'But she was in her rightful mind?'

'Oh, yes, and she—' He remembered that Mrs Armstrong had commanded him to say nothing about who had done it and closed his mouth on the words he had been going to say, staring down at his feet.

'She what?' Caleb prompted.

Adam shook his head.

'She told you who had done it?' Justin hazarded.

Adam looked from one to the other uncertainly. 'Mrs Armstrong said I wasn't to tell anyone what Mam said.'

'Let me guess then. Was it someone your mother knows?' At a nod from the boy, he continued, 'Someone who has treated her badly before?'

Another nod.

'Walter Smedling?'

Adam looked at him apprehensively.

'I'm right, am I not?'

'Yes. And . . .' Adam counted off two fingers to show how many men were involved.

'Bill Withers, no doubt. The two of them are as thick as the thieves they are.' Justin smiled reassuringly at the anxious child. 'Don't worry. You didn't tell us; we guessed. And we won't tell anyone else. But maybe we can do something to help bring them to justice – look into the matter, at least.'

'Mrs Armstrong said Mr Armstrong would do that. She said it was his duty, because of being the magistrate.'

The men exchanged glances, both sure that they could find out far more than a rich landowner.

That evening over dinner, Catherine shared the information about who had attacked Rachel with her husband. He stopped eating to consider it.

'I wondered myself and asked Timothy to find out what the two of them were doing yesterday.'

'And?'

'He says they left town together in the morning to go over to Tam Barker's house, and were not seen again until the evening, coming back from the same direction.'

'Is Barker not the land agent you had to dismiss?'

He nodded.

She pursed her lips, looking at him sideways, wondering if she dared say more, but he spoke before she did.

'I am not completely satisfied about all that,' he announced. 'It was Tam Barker they were with the other times there was trouble – or so all three of them say.'

'Other times?'

'When Mr Thorpe was killed and later, when a large sum of money was stolen from Mrs Thorpe's house.'

'Oh.'

'I shall give the matter my further consideration. I am not satisfied that I know enough yet to make a judgement. Tomorrow I shall speak to the gatekeeper, see if anyone has been seen lurking near the lane.'

Catherine addressed herself to her food, knowing when to leave her husband to find his own way.

'So I shall be obliged if you would say nothing of this to anyone else, my dear.'

She inclined her head in agreement.

'Now tell me how you are feeling today. You have not experienced any more sickness? We must look after our heir, must we not?' He glanced fondly at her belly.

CHAPTER TWENTY-THREE

Rachel recovered from the attack more quickly than anyone had expected, but her battered face was disturbing to all who saw it. She did not go into the village, and Catherine continued to send a servant to escort Adam to Cleving to see his mother once a day, and he was allowed to curtail his studies with the curate to do this.

Hannah Armstrong, seriously worried by this attack on her companion and fearing another, began to cast about for a way to keep Rachel safe, even at the cost of her own comfort. After some consideration, she wrote to beg her cousin Georgiana to come across to Cleving and confer with her.

'Why do I not take Rachel into my own household as a maid for a time?' Georgiana offered, hating to see Hannah's distress and guilt.

'But that will place her further away from her son.'

'I can send my carriage to fetch him on Sundays. She'll still be able to see him. And he can stay for the whole day.'

'Yes, oh, yes, that will help. Oh, thank you, Georgiana.' Hannah sagged against the chairback. 'I shall miss her greatly, though. She is an excellent maid.'

'Well, I could lend you my own Jenny in her place.' Georgiana smiled. 'She's a strong girl, and as she's walking out with a young man from Setherby, she will no doubt be happy to be closer to him. I expect they will be getting married in a year or two.' By which time Hannah would no longer be there to need help. Both of them knew that without needing to put it into words.

'What is she like?'

'A plain, sensible girl, conscientious and of a cheerful nature, though,' Georgiana screwed up her face expressively, 'her mind runs mainly on matters domestic.'

Hannah pulled a rueful face.

Rachel, still restricted to easy duties, was folding linen in the bedroom which opened off Mrs Hannah's sitting room and could not help overhearing snippets of this conversation. She sat motionless, a nightgown half folded in her hands. They were doing it again! Disposing of her without asking her opinion, as if she had no more will of her own than a piece of cloth. However good their intentions, going further away from Adam was not what she wanted. She felt anger welling up inside her. She had only stayed on so long at Cleving because she had grown fond of Mrs Hannah, but she refused, absolutely refused to be sent further away from her son!

At that moment she decided to do what she had wondered about several times: leave Whin Vale entirely and take her lad with her. She and Adam would go somewhere far away – London, perhaps. They said it was a big place, so they could surely hide there. She had enough money to manage on for quite a while and did not doubt her ability to find work of some sort or other.

But what about Kitty? The girl was happy working here at Cleving and Rachel was sure she wouldn't want to leave. She did not dare confide her intentions to Kitty, who could not keep anything secret for more than five minutes. She would have to leave a note for her stepdaughter, explaining what she was doing, and another note for Mrs Armstrong, begging her to keep an eye on the girl, not to mention one for Mrs Hannah, thanking her for her many kindnesses.

She felt fairly sure that Mrs Armstrong would not get angry with Kitty, but if the worst came to the worst, her stepdaughter could go to stay with Cousin Gracie in Todmorden till she found another position. At least Kitty was not without other relatives, as she herself and Adam were.

Should she just tell her employers straight out what she intended? It was what she would have preferred to do. But Mr Armstrong was not only her master, he was also the local magistrate and he might prevent her from leaving. No, she did not dare take the risk.

Only when Georgiana Bretherton began to take her leave did Rachel realise she had been sitting there doing nothing for quite a while. But no one would notice. She spent a lot of hours on her own while Mrs Hannah was resting. It was easy work, this, but not the sort of life she enjoyed. She much preferred to be busy.

Later that same day, when Catherine came in to visit her, Hannah explained what she had arranged and her niece expressed approval.

'You're right, my dear aunt. We don't want her within reach of them. They might kill her next time.'

'Do you think Nathaniel will prove who it was?'

'He will try.'

'She's sure it was Smedling and Withers.'

'Yes. And I think she's probably right, but you know Nathaniel. He will not act unless he has proof. So we'll say nothing to her yet.'

In bed that night, Rachel began to make more definite plans. She would need to take some of her clothes with her and bestow her remaining money safely about her person, in her petticoat, perhaps.

The following morning she got up very early and made a start. She lit her candle and though the cold made her fingers stiff and clumsy, she sewed the coins into her petticoat and bodice before anyone else was astir.

When Adam came to see her the next afternoon, she took him for a walk in the grounds and explained the situation to him. 'Do you want to come with me?' she ended hesitantly. She would not do anything against his wishes, even though she had a parent's right to make decisions about his future.

'Yes. Oh, yes, yes!' He flung himself into her arms. 'If you only knew how hard it is to live with Mrs Kellett. I hate it there.' He hesitated, looking at her, then burst out with, 'She says terrible things about you, Mam, and although she says she loves me and wants to be my mother, she's not like a mother. She never hugs Peg and Lizbet and she's always scolding. And – and she tried to poison Dusty. I hate her.'

This final disclosure set the seal on Rachel's decision. 'We shall leave next Sunday, then. I'm sure we won't be missed for an hour or two, so we should be able to get well away from the valley before they wonder about us. But we'll need to take some clothes with us. I thought I could smuggle some of my things out of the house because Mrs Hannah is still insisting I go out for a stroll each day, but I shall need to find somewhere to hide them.'

They walked along in silence for a few moments, both frowning as they tried to think of a place. She gazed into the distance, loving the beauty of Cleving Park, and at that moment caught sight of an old summerhouse down near the river. 'Look! Maybe . . .' They moved towards it, finding it musty-smelling and in need of repair, but with a weathertight roof still.

'It's obvious no one comes here in winter,' she said thoughtfully. 'Look at the dust and dirt on that floor. I can pile my things behind these chairs. But how to retrieve them?'

They went exploring further and found a small gate in the wall not too far away. 'No one will even notice if we come this way to pick up my things,' she said in satisfaction. For once, chance was helping her.

'It'll be great fun!' Adam said, eyes asparkle.

She looked at him solemnly. 'I doubt that. It'll be hard and uncomfortable at first – and maybe dangerous at times, son. I wouldn't run away at all if I could think of any other way of us being together. I *hate* the idea of leaving Whin Vale.'

He looked back at her just as solemnly. 'Perhaps we'll be able to come back here one day.'

But she could not believe that. 'There is just the question of your clothes,' she said as they started walking back to the house. 'On Sunday can you wear two of everything, three even?'

He laughed at the thought of this and entered into the spirit of the planning. 'I could do that when I come to see you as well, and then you could take my things out to the summerhouse with yours.'

'You're a clever lad.'

But when he'd gone she felt very down-hearted. It went against her nature to run away from anything. And how would she feel, away from her beloved moors? Worst of all, what if running away put her son in danger?

Caleb was summoned to see Georgiana one afternoon that week.

Over a cup of tea she said casually, 'I thought you would like to know that Rachel Thorpe is to come to me as maid.'

He froze where he was, staring at her in amazement, then frowning as he tried to take in the implications.

She was very satisfied with this reaction. 'Well, have you nothing to say about that?'

'When was this decided? Justin has said nothing to me of it.'

She stirred in her chair. 'It was not his idea, but my cousin Hannah's. She wants to keep the woman safe, even at the cost of her own comfort – though I am to send Jenny to her in Rachel's place. I dare say she will do almost as well.'

Caleb tried to hide his pleasure at the prospect of having Rachel living so near. 'Is Mrs Thorpe pleased about this?'

'We have said nothing to her or any of the other servants. We don't want news of where she's going to be spread around the valley, for her own safety's sake.'

He became very still. 'She doesn't know? Hasn't given her consent?'

Georgiana shrugged, annoyed that he did not seem happy with her fine scheme. ''Tis for her own good. What will she have to complain of?'

'She'll be further away from her son here. That will upset her.'

'I shall send the carriage for him every Sunday.'

'In the snow? When the roads are impassable?' In winter they could be very isolated up here at Hepstone, and the roads were poor, full of great ruts that made them a trial even in the driest of summers.

There was silence for a moment, then she said, 'I had thought you'd be pleased, Caleb. It'll bring her nearer. You can court her properly.'

'I can find ways to do my own courting when the time is ripe, Mrs Bretherton, but I cannot like taking Rachel to live so far away from her son. And without even asking her.'

She made a sniffing noise and twitched her head to one side pettishly. 'Well, 'tis settled now and she is to come to me on Monday next.'

That Sunday, Rachel woke feeling as though she were starting a cold, but ignored that. She put on as many layers of clothing as she thought would not show, placed her letters of explanation and apology on the rickety chair beside her bed in the tiny attic bedroom she had been given for herself since the attack, and then left the house without looking back. She had persuaded them to let her visit Adam today, though Mrs Hannah had insisted she was to stay in Setherby.

One of the grooms was waiting for her outside the house at the rear, to see her safely into the village, a sign of her master's care for her safety which only added to her feelings of guilt about running away like this.

'I s'll come for thee in two hours, then, lass,' he said on parting from her outside the parsonage.

'Oh, didn't they tell you? Mrs Hannah says I can stay longer today. Come in four hours instead, Tom.' She tried to sound casual but did not dare look at him as she spoke.

He nodded. 'Eh, she's a kind lady, that one is. She'll be sorely missed when she dies.'

Which made Rachel want to weep.

Adam was waiting for her at the side gate of the parsonage, his face so bright with suppressed mischief it was a wonder no one suspected something was going on.

'I'll just go and get Dusty,' he whispered.

'Nay, we can't take the dog with us!'

His face fell. 'But she'll kill him. And he won't eat food from anyone else. Dad would *want* us to take him, I know he would.'

Rachel hesitated, then said, 'All right, then.' Like her son, she couldn't bear to think of Thomas's dog being ill-treated.

They set out walking with Dusty trotting happily beside them. Nothing to show we're running away, Rachel kept telling herself, but she still kept wanting to glance over her shoulder to check they weren't being followed. People they passed stared openly at her face, which still bore signs of the beating, she knew, but she just stared back at them. Some nodded a greeting, some didn't. I shan't care about it, she told herself firmly, when a man whom Thomas had called 'friend' passed her by without a nod. But it hurt all the same.

They walked first along a lane that led only to some outlying farms. This route, a bare cart's width wide, followed the high walls surrounding Cleving Park for a time. Rachel breathed a sigh of relief when they found the small gate still unlocked. After making sure there were no gardeners around, they hurried across the grass towards the summerhouse to pick up their things. She looked down at the bundle for a moment, eyes blurred by unshed tears. It seemed a very small collection to show for a lifetime's work from her and Thomas.

Just before they left the grounds again, she stopped and stared back at the house. Large and solid, it seemed. So much land around it and all for the use of one family. It didn't seem fair, when she could not even find a cottage to live in. And yet they meant well, these rich folk – only you always had to do things their way and she wasn't going to let them take her further away from her son, whatever they said about it being for her own good!

The two of them took a small path that curved back up

the hill towards Lower Clough, and then turned on to the road which led out of the valley. By unspoken consent, they stopped for a moment at the place where Thomas had been killed. 'He'd have understood us leaving,' she said in a husky voice, 'though he'd have been saddened by it. He loved this valley, your father did.'

Adam looked round and remembered with a shiver that cold winter's evening. Then he looked back towards Whin Vale. 'I don't want to leave either,' he said, surprised by that realisation. 'And I'll come back here one day, Mam. You see if I don't.'

'When you're a man, you can do what you please. Life is easier for men, it is that!' She pulled herself together and began walking again. 'Come on, love. Let's get as far away as we can while it's still light.'

They met no one, since most folk were at home resting comfortably after church and a hearty dinner at this time of day. At the end of the lane they turned left, going towards Todmorden, but intending to turn off the road before they got there and make their way across the tops into Yorkshire. Surely no one would expect them to take this route.

'It'll be a long, hard walk, and we'll have to sleep at night in a barn or some such place,' she warned Adam needlessly.

'It'll be fun,' he replied but spoke more quietly now. Even this much walking had brought home to him how cold it could get and how alone they were in the world. He had seen homeless folk on the tramp – who had not? – and now he was like them. But he was with his mam, at least, and together they would find another home somewhere. He bent to pat Dusty and then tried to stride forward as briskly as she did.

An hour later light rain began to fall, but they paid no attention to it, just continuing to move on at a steady pace, speaking from time to time, smiling at one another when they stopped to catch their breath, with the dog loping along beside them, no longer tied to the end of a rope.

They stopped for a few minutes on a rise which gave them a view behind of the whole valley.

'I *shall* come back to Whin Vale,' Adam vowed, looking suspiciously bright-eyed.

Rachel said in a gruff voice, 'Of course you will. Now, come on, love. We have to get as far away as we can, in case they come looking for us.' For she could not rid herself of the notion that someone would pursue them.

Caleb decided to go into Setherby that Sunday to call on Justin. Maggie no longer made him welcome, but he simply had to check that Rachel was all right. He had been feeling uneasy about her ever since Mrs Bretherton told him she was to come and live in Hepstone.

He arrived in Setherby in the early afternoon, between church services, left his horse at the livery stables because the weather was so cold, and went straight to the parsonage where he was taken by his host into the cosy study without any pretence of greeting the mistress of the house.

'How is she?' he asked without preamble.

Justin smiled, knowing perfectly well who 'she' was. 'Doing well, by all accounts, though they say her face is still very bruised.'

'Is she visiting her son today?' Caleb was hoping to see her.

'Yes. They went out for a walk an hour or two ago. In fact,' Justin glanced at the clock, 'they ought to have been back by now.'

Both men turned to one another, the same apprehension making them frown.

'No,' said Justin. 'They wouldn't have dared attack her again – and anyway, she has the boy and the dog with her. She's not on her own.'

They continued to chat of this and that, but Caleb looked at the clock every minute or two and as time passed without a sign of Rachel and her son he could not hide how worried he was.

There were footsteps in the hall and Maggie came in without knocking. 'He hasn't come back,' she announced, arms akimbo. 'He's late *again*.'

'What is he late *for*?' Justin asked wearily.

'He's just late. He shouldn't stay out for so long. And on a Sunday, too.'

'I'm glad they can spend some time together. They are mother and son, you know.'

Justin watched her fling out of the room, slamming the door behind her, and shaded his eyes for a moment, wishing she would not embarrass him like this. People were beginning to talk about her strange behaviour. And no wonder. Her conversation was disjointed and often switched from one subject to another without reason. And she kept mentioning Adam, talking of him openly as 'my son'.

'Is Maggie all right?' Caleb asked hesitantly.

'What do you mean?'

'Well, she looks very thin and – and feverish.'

Justin frowned. 'Do you think so?'

'Yes. She's changed a lot in the last few weeks.' But Caleb did not pursue the matter. He had never thought his cousin wise to marry such a foolish, frivolous woman, however pretty she had been in her youth. She was not pretty now, too thin and with lines of discontent as well as age engraved on her face.

Ten minutes later, Maggie flung open the study door again. 'The servant is here from Cleving. He's been waiting in the kitchen this past half-hour and no one told me. It's too bad! It really is! Over four hours they've been gone now.'

Caleb stood up. 'It's not like her to be this late, is it?'

'No. Definitely not.' Justin went to look out of the window. 'And it'll soon be dark.'

'Send the servant back to Cleving with a message that we're worried how late she is,' Caleb urged. 'I'll get my horse from the stables and ask if anyone saw which way she went.' He was gone almost before he had finished speaking.

Justin bent over his desk to scribble a note, ignoring his wife's shrilling complaints and having to push her aside to get out to the kitchen.

Timothy sighed when the gardener brought the note from the

parson. 'He won't like it. He always sits with the ladies of a Sunday.'

Nathaniel came to the door of the parlour, looking annoyed. 'What's the matter?'

'Sorry to disturb you, sir, but Tom just came back from the parsonage. That maid of Mrs Hannah's hasn't returned from her walk. And the boy is with her. Parson sent up this note for you. Tom says he and Caleb Hesketh have gone out to look for her, they're that worried she might have been set on again.'

Nathaniel breathed deeply. Was he never to have a minute's peace? He opened the note, read it and turned over the facts it presented in his mind. 'She may just be late back.'

Timothy nodded, but his expression showed his doubt about that all too clearly.

'On the other hand, we cannot take any risks, with the villains who attacked her not yet apprehended.' Nathaniel went back into the parlour where the two ladies had been listening unashamedly to what was being said.

Hannah had one hand to her breast, her face bloodless. 'She should not be out so long in this weather. She's not yet fully recovered.'

Struck by a sudden thought, Catherine stood up. 'Wait. I'll go and check her room.'

She was down again within a couple of minutes, holding three letters. 'One is addressed to me, one to Kitty and one to you, Aunt Hannah.'

While the two ladies busied themselves with their notes, Nathaniel stood waiting, foot tapping the floor impatiently.

Catherine looked up first. 'Mine begs pardon for leaving without warning, but says she cannot bear to be separated from her son again. She asks me to look after Kitty.'

'Mine also says she's sorry to leave so suddenly and – and thanks me for being a kind mistress.' Tears began tracking down Hannah's cheeks. 'So kind I am that I have separated her from her son and caused her to run away!' She covered her face with one shaking hand.

'I looked into her trunk and I'd guess she's taken some of her clothes with her,' Catherine said.

'And the other letter? The one for her stepdaughter?' Nathaniel twitched it out of her hand and without the slightest hesitation unfolded it and read the contents, his face growing angry. 'She has indeed run away – simply taken her son and run away! I am seriously displeased about this.'

Hannah spoke up. 'We have treated her badly, Nathaniel. She's a good and loving mother. Would you like your son to be taken away from you?'

That caught his attention and his eyes went to his wife's belly, still showing no signs of the child when she was dressed, but nicely rounded now beneath his hand in bed at night.

'Nonetheless, it is ungrateful,' he muttered.

'I thought I was helping her, sending her to Georgiana's,' Hannah mourned. 'But I wasn't. That's what's done it. It's my fault she's run away. Blame me if you must blame someone.'

Catherine went to pat her arm. 'Don't upset yourself, Aunt. I doubt anything we could have done would have suited Rachel unless we gave her back her son and a life of her own.' Even though her own child was unborn, even though her mother and aunts wrote to advise her not to grow too attached to it until she was sure it would live, she had grown very happy about the idea of having a child, talked to it inside her head sometimes, promising to love it and cherish it – and so she could understand Rachel's feelings better than she would have done before.

She turned to her husband. 'She must be found. And helped to make a new life with her son. Not scolded. Not taken away from him. It's only just.'

Nathaniel sighed and stood up. 'I shall ride out to look for her myself, I think.' He turned to his groom, still standing at the back of the hall. 'Timothy, will you tell them to saddle my horse and yours, too, for you'd better come with me. We must make sure she's all right.'

But although they searched high and low for as long as daylight lasted, they did not find Rachel or Adam that night.

*   *   *

'Hast heard?' Bill muttered to Walter in the inn that evening. 'She's up an' run away, that one has.'

'Good riddance to her, say I!'

'I'll drink to that.'

Both men raised their glasses and made a solemn toast.

'So we're safe now,' Walter said quietly. 'Don't need to do owt else about her.'

'Unless she comes back.'

'Eh, I don't reckon she'll do that. We're shut of her now.'

But as he walked home to the comfortable house he'd taken over from Rachel in Upper Clough, Walter could not stop himself from feeling guilty. His first wife would be angry and hurt at the way he'd treated her daughter, driving her away from her home like this, allowing Bill to hurt her so badly. He imagined he saw Alice sometimes, speaking to him, scolding him, saying he'd pay for his wickedness. And he often woke sweating and spent from trying to flee the ghost and its recriminations.

He dreamed of his dead wife again that night.

'Not long now,' Alice crooned to him. 'You've done wrong, Walter Smedling, but you'll soon start paying for it.'

Which was a strange thing to dream when he'd just heard that he was safe.

CHAPTER TWENTY-FOUR

Rachel found it harder and harder to keep going. She could not remember ever feeling so dreadful, ill and feverish and weak. But she was determined to take her son away so she continued along a road that seemed to get steeper and steeper – if you could call it a road now. It was more like a cart track, and one not often used, at that. It wound up towards the moors, twisting and turning in a way she found bewildering, because she had never been this way before. It was hard to keep your bearings when you were one minute facing into the setting sun and the next minute turning your back to it. And when you couldn't seem to think straight.

Her ribs were hurting her, for Bill Withers had kicked her hard. She was feeling faint, too, and very distant from everything. But she and Adam had to get away, so all she could do was set her head down and plod on. She would not, could not, give in to her body's weakness.

As it grew darker, she began to worry about where they would sleep that night. She stopped for a rest in the lee of some rocks and gave Adam the remainder of the bread she'd taken from her mistress's tray of unwanted food.

'What about you, Mam? What are you going to eat?'

'I'm not hungry.'

He stared at her, then at the bread. Licking his lips, he shook his head. 'Neither am I, then.'

'We'll share it.' For in truth she was as hungry as he. But

she didn't complain when he broke off a piece for Dusty and she did the same herself. She worried at how tired her son was looking.

To wash down their scant meal, they found a stream and scooped up water with their hands, icy cold and yet sweet, too. For a time this seemed to refresh her and Rachel strode along with better heart. But it was nearly dark now and she'd no idea where they were, nor could she see any dwellings. And Adam had been silent for some time. It was hard going for a lad his age.

The wind grew stronger and it began to rain. Despair filled her. What had she done? Run away like a foolish child and put her son's life at risk, that's what. And although they were both warmly dressed in several layers of clothing, they were soaking wet by now, and that made the cold even harder to bear.

Just as she was wondering whether to go back, she saw a building in the distance and her heart lifted. It seemed a long time until they got close enough to find out that it was only a tumble-down barn, but up a small rise was the farm itself. Rachel stopped to get her breath and debated going to ask for help. She could, after all, afford to pay for a bed for the night. But she was anxious not to be seen until they got well away from Setherby, so she decided not to approach the farmer, but just creep into the barn. She whispered her plan to Adam and he nodded.

'Me an' Dusty are tired. I'm glad we've found somewhere to stop.'

But he hadn't complained, so she gave him a quick hug and moved on with her arm round his shoulders.

They found the door closed, but not locked. Inside, the barn seemed warm and cosy after the cold wind outside and they both sighed in relief. It took a few minutes for them to see their way around, for it was nearly dark now, but as their eyes adjusted to the dimness, they saw in one corner the heaped remains of the summer's hay.

'We can sleep on that hay,' Rachel whispered. 'But we mustn't damage anything.' She led the way across the beaten earth floor. 'Move to the back of the pile, love, where we'll be out of sight.'

He giggled and did as she bade him.

As they settled themselves into a scratchy nest hidden from the door, Dusty came and flopped down with them. Rachel was glad of the extra warmth of the dog's body on Adam's other side, because after the first few minutes of relief from the wind outside, the barn began to seem chilly and she kept shivering in her wet clothes.

She had no idea whose farm this was and worried about the sort of reception they would receive in the morning. Tramping folk were badly treated sometimes. 'Best we leave before the farmer starts his day,' she told her son, hugging him close.

'I like it here,' he said sleepily. 'And I like being with you again, too.'

Tucked cosily between her and the dog, he was soon asleep. Rachel smiled as she listened to his soft, steady breathing, but didn't expect to sleep much herself. However, in spite of the damp and the wind that blew through cracks in the barn walls, exhaustion claimed her almost immediately.

Caleb was very late getting home to Hepstone that night.

'Eh, I thought you were never coming back!' his mother exclaimed at the sight of him. 'And what's given you that long face? It seems nothing can please you lately.'

He was tired of her scolding ways and answered her sharply. 'I must be out again early next morning.'

'Whatever for? It's set in to rain. You'd be best staying round the farm tomorrow.'

'I have to help search for someone,' he admitted reluctantly.

Joanna stiffened. 'Who?'

'Rachel Thorpe. She and her son are missing. They've run away from Cleving because Mr Armstrong was sending her to work for Mrs Bretherton.'

'Eh, what's she running away for? Your Mrs Bretherton is a kind lady.'

'Rachel doesn't want to be even further away from her son.'

And looking at her own strong, fine son, Joanna could understand that, however reluctant she was to sympathise with a woman who seemed to have set everyone's back up in Setherby. If anyone had tried to take Caleb away from her when he was a lad, she'd have fought them tooth and nail. Even the Singletons hadn't tried to do that. And Rachel Thorpe had been badly beaten recently. Even out here in Hepstone, they'd heard how bruised and battered she was.

She glanced sideways again and saw how miserable Caleb was looking. He must be very fond of this Rachel Thorpe to look like that. He had never shown the slightest interest in any other woman. He looked up to see her staring and she said quickly, 'Eh, well, these fine gentlemen don't understand a woman's heart, that's for sure. Have they found out who attacked the poor woman yet?'

'No.'

Caleb seemed so low in spirit that for once she didn't scold, just insisted he make a hearty meal. 'You'll need to keep your strength up if you're to tramp across the moors tomorrow hunting for her.'

Halfway through the meal, he pushed his plate away. 'I'm not hungry, Mam.'

'Eh, eat it up. It's good food, that is.'

'Aye, but I can't help thinking of Rachel, wondering if – if she's eaten – if she's got somewhere warm to sleep. And how the lad is keeping up. He's a grand little lad. You'd like him.'

Joanna's expression was thoughtful as she cleared up and went to sit in front of the fire. If she wanted grandchildren, maybe she should meet this woman and judge for herself what she was like. At least Rachel Thorpe had shown that she could bear healthy children, and that was not to be sneezed at. In fact, Joanna decided suddenly, she'd better find some way to mend her fences with her son. She could not bear the thought of being estranged from him.

★   ★   ★

At Cleving the family was very quiet over supper. Nathaniel was still displeased about Rachel's running away, so Catherine sensibly refrained from trying to make conversation.

As the wind grew stronger and rain began to lash against the windowpanes, however, she said involuntarily, 'Oh, I do hope Rachel has found somewhere safe and warm to shelter tonight! Think of that poor little boy!'

Nathaniel snorted into his glass of port but he, too, looked sideways at the windows as the rain beat against them and shook his head.

Hannah pushed her plate away with very little eaten, saying, 'She wasn't well, Rachel wasn't. She hadn't recovered from that attack.' A minute or two later, she murmured to herself, 'She shouldn't have left. If only she'd *told* me how she felt!'

'She should have been grateful for what you were trying to do,' Nathaniel snapped, hating to see her so upset.

'Would you have been grateful to be sent away from your child?' Hannah threw back at him.

He looked at Catherine, well-fed and plump with their child, and even he sighed. 'Well, we'll try to find her tomorrow as soon as it's light, Aunt, I promise you. But there's nothing more we can do tonight.'

In the morning, Rachel jerked awake as she heard someone approach the barn. It wasn't light yet, but she could see the glow of a lantern. She grabbed Dusty's muzzle and stopped him from barking as a man came in and began to grumble under his breath, fumbling around near the door. Beside her Adam stirred and woke up, so she made a faint shushing noise and was relieved when he kept quiet.

As the man came into the light of the lantern he had hung upon a nail, she nearly gasped aloud. Tam Barker! They had taken shelter under the roof of one of their enemies! What would he do if he found them? It was a wonder he hadn't seen them already. It could only be a matter of time.

When he stumped out of the barn again, taking the lantern with him, she whispered, 'Keep hold of Dusty and don't let him

347

bark. We must get away as fast as we can. That's Tam Barker and he's a close friend of Bill Withers.'

They crept to the door and saw a light shining from inside the house, but no one in sight. The morning was still dark, but there was enough starlight for them to find their way out of the yard.

Just as Rachel thought they were safe, a dog behind them started barking and Dusty dragged himself away from Adam to return the compliment with lusty enthusiasm.

There was the sound of running footsteps and voices calling to one another behind them.

'Quick, run!' she commanded and took her son's hand.

'But Dusty!'

'He'll follow.'

As fast as they safely could, they stumbled and slithered along the track. Rain had deposited water in the ruts and hollows and soon Rachel's feet were soaking. Her son's feet must be the same. At one point, Adam insisted on stopping and gave a loud whistle, which Dusty usually obeyed. They waited, but nothing happened, so the boy whistled again.

There was some more loud barking from the direction of the farm, then a confusion of yelping and cursing. When Adam whistled a third time, they heard a pattering sound and shortly afterwards Dusty joined them, panting mightily and still making low growling noises from time to time as he looked backwards.

'We won't run, because we'll only fall over, but we must hurry.' Rachel took Adam's hand to help him along. As the sound of voices faded behind them, she felt it safe to slow down a little. She had felt tired before she began today, but at least it wasn't raining.

'Where are we?' Adam asked.

'I don't know which direction we're heading now,' she admitted after a moment's thought. 'But Tam Barker's farm lies near Hepstone. I didn't realise we'd come so far.'

'Well, we'll soon find out where we are, won't we? This track must lead somewhere.'

'Aye, I suppose so.' But although she was glad to hear him sounding quite cheerful, she was worried they would be pursued. And out here there would be no one to see what went on if someone attacked them. 'Look, if they come after us, love, you must run away.'

'No! I'm not leaving you!'

'It'd be the best thing to do. We can't fight more than one and you could fetch help.'

'*No!*'

'There'd be nothing you could do against grown men, Adam. You're to run for help if they find us and I'll try to stop them following you.' When he didn't answer, she said, 'Promise me!' and after a moment's silence, he did.

So they continued to stumble along, with Rachel looking over her shoulder and stopping at intervals to listen for pursuit.

Back at Crag End Farm, Tam Barker examined the barn angrily. 'Someone slept here last night – see, look at my clean straw, squashed. The cheeky devils!'

'Aw, they haven't done any harm,' his wife protested. 'They must have been tramping folk. And it was a nasty old night.'

'Well, harm or not, I don't like having strangers sleeping in my barn without so much as a by your leave. They could at least have knocked on the door and asked permission. I've a good mind to saddle Queenie and go after them, I have that!'

'Oh, leave 'em be, Tam. We've enough on our plates getting our living without chasing across the moors after poor folk who've done us no harm. What would you do when you found them, anyway?'

'I'd set about them with my stick, to teach them to stay away from my place in future.'

Jen clicked her tongue in exasperation but didn't argue with him.

When he came in from the barn demanding a pot of mulled ale, she made it quickly, hoping it would sweeten his temper. As she handed it to him, she ventured to ask, 'Have you got rid of those sheep yet, Tam?'

'What's it to you?'

'I was just asking.'

'Well, don't ask. I'll tell you what you need to know. And what I do with them sheep is my own concern. Yours is to look after the house, the children and the poultry.'

An hour later, he said suddenly, 'I think I'll take Queenie out and check that those tramping folk have left the district. We don't want anyone spying on us. The only good thing about living here is that there's no one to see what we do.' As he left, he said in a vicious tone, 'And if I find them, I'll make sure they never come this way again. Aye, I will that.'

She sighed and held her peace. You could never tell Tam anything. He always knew it all. Tears came into her eyes as she remembered the fine house they had lived in at Cleving, the way they'd been respected and comfortable, with a maid and another woman to do the rough work. And now look at them! Stuck out here in this draughty hovel on the edge of the moors, with her working every daylight hour just to keep food on the table. And no help around the place – no thanks from Tam for all she was doing, either. Just curses and complaints, and him in a foul temper most of the time.

And yet he had some money. She'd found his hiding place one day and been astounded to see how much there was in it. He could well have afforded to buy them a few more comforts, or even to rent a good farm. But she didn't dare suggest that. Hadn't even let him know she'd found his secret hoard. She couldn't think where he'd got so much money. He'd never been one to save. So she worried about that as well.

Caleb rode into Setherby again the next day, setting off before it was light. In the hall of the parsonage, Maggie walked past him with a sniff, looking in the other direction.

'Ignore her. She's alternating between hysterics and furious scolding,' Justin murmured wearily.

'She looks ill.'

'Mrs Charnley says she's not eating much at all. But she won't see the doctor. I don't know what to do about her, and that's the truth. But that's neither here nor there at the moment. It's Rachel and Adam we have to think about.'

'There's no word?'

'None.' Justin was desperately worried about them as well. If he could just hear that they were safe, maybe he'd be able to think more clearly about his own situation. 'I've got some men organised to search in every direction, but we thought you could maybe take the moor track back to Hepstone, going up the lanes and asking at the farms whether anyone's seen them. You could keep your eyes open as you ride.'

'Is that all?' Caleb wanted to stay here in the thick of things.

Justin shrugged. 'What else do you suggest? If she and Adam got a lift on a cart, Rachel could be over in Yorkshire by now, or down in Manchester. It's just – well, I feel we ought to keep searching, at least for today. Mr Armstrong has sent word that two of his grooms will be available to help, so it's just a question of dividing up the district. I'm to arrange that. And it makes sense for you to cover Hepstone. No one knows that part of the district as well as you do.'

'All right. But you'll let me know if anything happens? Whatever it is? Just send the lad from the livery stables with a message. I'll pay the expenses.'

About two hours after they had left the farm, Rachel stumbled and fell. For a minute she could not get up and just lay there with her eyes closed.

'Mam! Mam! What's wrong?' Adam tugged at her arm.

'I'm just – catching my breath a bit.' But she could hardly speak for wheezing and the wind seemed to be sticking sharp knives into her chest. However, after another minute or two, she dragged herself to her feet and stumbled on.

Twice more she fell and each time it took her longer to pull herself together and start moving again.

When Adam said, 'Let's sit down for a minute behind

that wall,' she let him guide her towards it and sank to the ground.

'Let me go for help, Mam.'

She looked at him, feeling muddle-headed.

'I have to get help,' he repeated.

She closed her eyes and had to force the words out. 'Yes. But keep – keep to the – the road, love.' A minute later when she opened her eyes again, he was running along the track with Dusty racing beside him.

She had never been so cold in her life. They said hell was hot, but for her hell would be a place as cold as this. She could not stop her teeth chattering, could do nothing but huddle in the lee of the wall and shed useless tears that she had managed this venture so ill. They would take her son from her now, for sure. She deserved to have him taken away, putting his life at risk like this.

On the way home, Caleb decided to ride round by a little-used track that led towards Crag End Farm.

When he saw a figure stumbling towards him, he reined in to narrow his eyes and try to make out who it was. A lad and a dog! It was Adam Thorpe! But – he scanned the horizon – where was Rachel?

Desperately afraid for her, he rode forward at a fast trot and when he got nearer, the lad stopped and waited for him, one hand on the dog's collar.

'Mr Hesketh! Oh, I'm so glad it's you. Mr Hesketh, she's ill. She can't walk any further. Can you help us, please?' Adam was sobbing openly.

'Get up behind me, lad, and tell me which way to go.' Caleb reached down one hand and hauled the boy up, hardly giving him time to settle before he nudged the horse into movement again. Dusty turned and trotted along behind them, but he looked exhausted and footsore.

When they saw Rachel, she was not moving. Even when they stopped beside her, she did not open her eyes.

'Mam! Mam, it's Mr Hesketh!' Adam called, sliding off

the back of the horse so quickly it was startled and edged sideways.

She only muttered something and shivered uncontrollably.

Caleb dismounted and knelt down. It was immediately clear to him that she was very ill indeed and would not be able to sit on a horse. Nor could his poor mare carry two adults. 'You stay here with her, lad. I'll go and get my cart.' He took off his cloak. 'Here, huddle up to her to keep her warm and get the dog to lie on her other side. I'll be back in less than an hour.'

He tucked the cloak round them, then got on the horse and rode as fast as he safely could, wishing there was somewhere closer to ask for help. He didn't notice the cold and lack of a cloak, and when it began to drizzle, he didn't notice that, either. All his thoughts were for Rachel. People died of exposure. But he wouldn't let her die!

Adam lay beside his mother, glad of the cloak. It seemed to him that she was a little easier, now that they were both warmer, for her teeth had stopped chattering and she was no longer muttering in the way that had so terrified him.

He didn't notice the man coming towards them until Dusty began to growl, then he grabbed his dog's collar and shouted to him to stay.

'Was it you who slept in my barn?' Tam began, then edged his horse a little closer. 'Well, I'll be damned. It's *her*.' A nasty smile curved his lips. 'Would you believe it? Falling right into our hands like this.'

Adam jumped to his feet. 'You leave my mother alone.'

Tam turned to study him. Too knowing by far, that lad. They'd have to get rid of him, as well. 'She needs help. We'll have to set her on my horse and take her to my house.'

Something about his manner made Adam feel afraid. 'Mr Hesketh's already found us and gone for help. He'll be back in a minute with a cart.'

'I don't believe you.'

Adam felt more afraid than he ever had done. 'I'm telling the truth. It was Mr Hesketh. And he gave us this cloak, so he *will* be coming back.'

Tam decided that soft words would win him more than threats. 'He should've set her on his horse and brought her over to my farm. It's the nearest. We'll take her there now and I'll send a message to him. She shouldn't be left lying here in the cold.'

'No. We're not coming with you. Mr Hesketh said to wait for him here.'

Tam prepared to dismount.

Terrified, Adam picked up a stone and chucked it at him. It missed the man but hit the horse on the rump. The animal neighed and jerked backwards, so that its rider had to settle back into the saddle until it had calmed down.

Adam picked up another stone and Dusty growled. Tam cursed them and fumbled for his knife.

At that moment they heard the rumble of wheels in the distance.

'See! We don't need your help!' Adam repeated, but he didn't let go of his second stone. '*Go away!*'

Tam cursed again and waited till the cart drew up beside them, nodding to Caleb, furious that it would be this man, with whom he'd had one or two disagreements about boundaries and sheep. 'We could take her to my farm,' he offered. 'It's closest.'

'Don't let him! He's a bad man!' Adam shouted, terrified Caleb would agree to this. 'Mam wouldn't want to go to *his* farm.'

'Quiet, lad.' Caleb looked at Tam and his expression was scornful. 'I'll look after her from now on.' He got down from the cart and looked the other man in the eyes for a long minute before he added, 'And I'll make very sure none of you ever hurts her again, believe me.'

Tam ignored the last remark and forced a smile to his face. 'Well, that's good to hear. She needs someone to look after her, that one does. Hasn't got the sense she was born with.' His eyes flickered towards the cart, then towards the unconscious woman and his scowl deepened. 'I'll get back to my day's work, then.'

Caleb watched him for a minute, not surprised when Barker did not offer to help lift Rachel into the cart, then turned back to the task at hand. 'Here, lad, let me pick her up. You bring that cloak to cover her with.' He lifted Rachel into the cart, surprised at how thin and bony she felt. After that, he helped the boy to get on the back of it beside her. 'Your dog looks tired, too. Tell it to get up with you. And try to keep your mam from bouncing around.'

Adam nodded. He found himself weeping as they drove off, the relief was so great, but luckily Mr Hesketh got on the front of the cart and clicked to the horse to start moving, so he didn't see the tears.

'We'll take her to Mrs Bretherton's,' Caleb called over his shoulder. It was just as close as his place and Rachel would be safe there, even from Nathaniel Armstrong.

Adam knuckled the tears away and tucked the horse blanket round his mother, sitting with one hand protectively on her shoulder.

But she didn't open her eyes, didn't even stir. Was she going to die like his father had? In spite of himself more tears tracked down his dirty face. And still more.

CHAPTER TWENTY-FIVE

On his way to Upper Clough, Tam met several parties out searching for Rachel and made an effort to ingratiate himself with them.

'She's been found!' he called to the first group. 'Caleb
Hesketh has found her.'

'Are you sure?'

'Course I'm sure!'

'Did he send you to tell us?'

'He was too busy taking her home to think of anything, so
I reckoned I should come and save you all a cold day out on
the tops.'

'Thanks.'

They stared at him as he tramped on towards the valley,
and their glances were not friendly.

'I never thought that one would be helping Hesketh,' one
said to another. 'I'd have thought—' He broke off and did not
finish his sentence.

One of his companions nodded. 'Aye, well, misfortune
makes strange bedfellows, it does an' all.'

They turned to tramp back towards Setherby, glad to get
out of this bitter weather.

Tam met another party nearer to Whin Vale and gave them
the same message, then carried on riding, thinking over what
had happened. He dismounted and hammered impatiently on
Bill Withers' door. When Bill's wife answered, Tam pushed
her aside with an 'Out of my way, you.'

He found Bill working at his loom. 'Not out searching for
her, then? All the rest of 'em from Whin Vale seem to be,
the fools.'

'Wasn't asked. Wouldn't have gone if I had been asked. I
hope she falls down one of them rocky bits and breaks her neck,
or better still breaks her leg an' rots slowly.'

'Well, you won't get your wish. She's been found.'

'Damn the woman! Who found her, then?'

'Hesketh.'

'It would be him.'

'An' he's been nosin' around my farm. One of the children
saw him.'

'Did he find owt?'

'No. Course not. But I haven't been able to get the last lot
of sheep away. I will soon.'

'Sooner the better.'

They both stood staring out of the big weaver's window at
the valley which looked dark and unfriendly as a strong wind
chased black clouds across the sky and shook some more rain
out of them. 'Eh, the wet weather has set in,' Bill said at last.
'Look at that rain.'

'Good night to get rid of them sheep, I'm thinking.'

'You'd never see your way in the dark.'

'I know them moors well enough to find my way blindfold,
but I'm going to need some help. No time to get my other
friends across to pick up the sheep, so you'll have to help me.'

'Nay, them sheep were your idea. An' who wants to—'

Tam grabbed Bill's shirt front and hauled him forward. He
was no bigger than Bill, but he radiated determination and
something different, something more powerful, so when he
repeated, 'I need help and soon,' Bill agreed to join him.

Maggie stared at Justin in dismay. 'She's been found? Alive?'

'You don't sound pleased about it.'

She pursed her lips but did not speak her thoughts aloud.
'What about Adam?'

'He's fine. With his mother.'

'You must go and bring him back straightaway, make it plain that she can't keep him.'

He just looked at her, sick of arguing the point.

'Where is she?' Maggie persisted.

'At Mrs Bretherton's. They'll look after the boy as well.'

'They won't want the trouble. Tell them we'll have him back.' She had hold of his arm and was shaking it, her eyes feverishly brilliant and her cheekbones flushed like those of a painted wooden doll.

He unclasped her fingers and put his hands on her shoulders. 'Maggie, that boy is not coming back here. Not ever. It was time he went back to his mother. He's never stopped missing her.'

She just stared at him blindly. 'He'll miss *me*. He loves *me*, not her!'

'You have children of your own.'

'They're only girls. They'll be perfectly all right with Mrs Charnley.'

He felt so angry at this indifference that he turned and left her. He had never felt like hitting a woman before, but he did now. And yet at the same time he was worried by the increasingly wild light in her eyes.

She trailed up the stairs to stand in the doorway of Adam's room, looking at his things. After that she moved on to her own room and stood in her favourite position near the window, looking out across the town. Groups of men were coming back, a few at a time, as the word went out that Rachel had been found. And they looked pleased, too.

Well, she wasn't pleased. And she was going to do something about it. Muttering to herself, she went to get her cloak and then slipped quietly out of the house.

Two hours later one of Mr Armstrong's grooms turned up to say that Maggie had been found walking towards the moors, soaking wet and seeming to have very little idea of where she was going or why.

Jane Charnley exchanged worried glances with her master but said nothing as he went to fetch his wife.

And when they got back, Maggie kept weeping and protesting that she had to go and find Adam, so that it took both
Justin and Mrs Charnley to put her to bed.

'She's turned very strange,' Lal commented to Jane.

'You can keep thoughts like that to yourself, my girl. It's not
your place to comment on your betters.' Not that Jane Charnley
did not agree with Lal. But she had seen Justin's worried face,
had heard Peg cry herself to sleep – and was wondering where all
this would lead. 'Least said, soonest mended,' she added sharply.
'Think on, you're not to say owt about this.'

When Rachel recovered consciousness, she found herself in a
big soft bed in a room that was furnished with every luxury you
could need. Bed hangings in colourful chintz, soft blankets, a
mirror on the wall and a big square of carpet covering the
polished boards of the floor.

She heard footsteps approach the room, so she turned her
eyes towards the door, wondering where she was.

The woman who entered looked like a maid. Rachel waited
for her to speak, but she didn't. Instead she gaped down at the
bed and gasped, 'Eh, I'd never have thought it, but it's true.'

'What's true?' Rachel's voice was husky and she wasn't at
first sure if the woman had heard her.

The woman took a deep breath and said hurriedly, 'I'd
better go and tell the mistress that you're awake. She said to
tell her straightaway.' She bustled out before the sick woman
could speak, not wanting to be the one to answer any awkward
questions.

Rachel tried to sit up but the room spun around her, so
she let her head drop back on the soft pillows and waited to
be enlightened.

The next person walked more slowly along the corridor and
paused in the doorway, also staring at Rachel. Then she smiled
and moved forward towards the bed. 'Well, you did give us all
a fright, my dear.'

'Where am I, Mrs Bretherton?'

'You're at my house. It was closer than Hepstone and Caleb

knew I had plenty of room.' He'd also said he thought Rachel Thorpe would be safer there than out at his lonely little farm. And Georgiana had agreed. But it was bittersweet to see her husband's face looking up at her from the pillow and she knew that the older servants had seen the resemblance too.

In a sudden panic, Rachel found the strength to sit up. 'Adam?'

'He's in the kitchen eating a hearty meal. We have even found him some dry clothes. I'll send him up to see you when he's finished.'

It was too much trouble to hold her head up, so Rachel slid down into the wonderful softness of the pillows. 'I won't be separated from him again. He's my son.' Her voice was husky and it was hard to find enough breath to speak, but she forced more words out. 'We belong together.'

Georgiana came closer and patted her hand. 'We shall keep both of you here until we decide what to do with you.'

Her words absolutely terrified Rachel.

'Oh, my dear, don't look at me like that. If I give you my word not to try to separate you and your son, will you believe me?'

'Yes. Thank you.' Rachel let out a long, shuddering sigh, gave a croaky little laugh and relaxed again. The bed linen was so smooth . . . and the bed so nice and warm . . .

Georgiana watched her for a minute, then flicked away a tear and got to her feet. Rachel looked so very much like her father.

She went out and summoned a maid to sit with the sick woman. 'If we keep her warm and feed her up with good beef tea, I think we may see her recovering in a few days.'

The next time Rachel drifted out of sleep, it was to find Adam sitting in a big chair beside the bed, sound asleep with his head on a soft cushion. She felt reassured to see him there, just as Georgiana had meant her to be, and sighed with relief and pleasure that he was looking rosy again. She watched him for a while, then she fell asleep again with a half-smile on her own face.

They were together again. Mrs Bretherton was keeping her promise.

That day, cold as it was, Nathaniel made a journey over to Halifax because he had received some disturbing news from the man whom he was employing to investigate certain matters. What he found out there filled him with anger, but he kept it in check, merely authorising a continued watch, then going to find a lawyer with whom he had dealt before.

William Hughes was horrified at what Nathaniel revealed, but readily agreed to keep silent about this until they should have more proof.

Nathaniel smiled grimly as he was driven back home. It was taking a while, but he was getting to the bottom of things. Tam Barker had been greedy — and careless lately. It would be his undoing.

After he had delivered Rachel to Mrs Bretherton's house, Caleb drove his cart home, his face thoughtful. He squinted up at the sky, trying to ignore the drops of rain falling into his eyes for long enough to estimate how the weather would set for the rest of the day.

Rain. And another storm, probably. No, not worth keeping watch tonight. No one would go out in this weather. Thunder rumbled across the hills and seemed to add its agreement to that decision.

And at least Rachel was safe now. He hugged that satisfaction to himself.

His mother was waiting for him, sitting idly in the kitchen, which was unusual for her. She looked up. 'Well, did you find her?'

'Yes.'

'I thought you were going to bring her here.'

'I took her to Mrs Bretherton's. She'll be safer there. And she'll be looked after more willingly, too. She's ill. Not fully recovered from the beating and has now taken a chill. She needs tending carefully.'

Tears came into Joanna's eyes. 'How could you think I'd not look after a sick woman.'

He came across to the fire and sank down on the settle. 'We need to talk, Mam.'

She nodded. 'I'll just set a poker in the fire to mull you some ale.' She suited the action to the words, then sat down in her rocking chair opposite him, looking apprehensive.

'Mother, I love Rachel. I intend to persuade her to marry me.'

'Oh.' She stared down at her lap. When he said nothing, she raised her eyes and asked, 'You want me to leave, then?'

'I don't know.'

She bent her head again to hide her tears.

'You've been on at me to marry for years, Mam. Why will you not accept my choice of a wife?'

And suddenly she was so afraid of losing him that she had to clasp her hands together to stop them trembling – and knew from his glance that he had seen it anyway. 'I've only ever wanted the best for you, son.'

He sighed and after a long pause said, 'I know. But I'm the one who'd have to live with a wife, so you can't choose one for me. I'm not an easy man to suit. And anyway, I've been thinking of her, of Rachel, for a long time now.' Another pause, then he added quietly, 'I was thinking of building you a cottage in Hepstone, perhaps, and letting you handle the spinners from there. You'd have plenty to keep you busy.'

'Yes. I suppose so.'

'You could get a maid to keep you company, maybe a girl from the orphanage, or an older woman, a widow, anyone you like – so you'd not be on your own.'

'You'd come and see me sometimes though?'

'Of course I would!' He got up and pulled her to her feet, putting his arms round her. 'Mam, Mam, I shan't stop loving you or looking after you, but I reckon if Rachel will take me, we shall do better on our own here.'

'Oh, she'll take you all right. She's not stupid.'

He shook his head. 'I'm not at all sure about that.'

She pulled back to stare up at him. 'Why ever should she not?'

'She's not like other women. She's very independent.' He gave her a rueful smile. 'A bit like you in some ways. But even worse.'

Her heart was breaking at the thought of leaving him, but she managed a smile. 'I shall try to get on with her for your sake.'

'That's all I ask, Mam.' And he gave her another cracking hug, just holding her close for a few minutes. Which made her feel a little better. At least she had not driven him to hate her.

The following day there was a great commotion outside High Fell House and Georgiana, who was sitting with Rachel, bounced to her feet and hurried over to the window. 'It's Nathaniel Armstrong.'

Rachel, who had been enjoying their quiet chat, jerked upright in the bed. 'He's come to take me back! Or to take my son. Oh, please, Mrs Bretherton, hide Adam! Don't let them take him away from me again.'

Georgiana came across and pushed her down on the pillows, clicking her tongue in irritation at the sudden look of panic on her guest's face. 'There's no need to hide anyone. I've known Nathaniel since he was a boy and he will do as I say about Adam, believe me.'

'You're – sure?'

'Of course I am, my dear. Just leave this to me.'

'I can't understand why you're doing this, Mrs Bretherton.'

Georgiana looked down on her solemnly. 'I shall tell you about that in a day or two. I do have a very good reason, as you will see.'

Downstairs she found Nathaniel waiting for her in the parlour.

'Is she still here? Or has she run away again?' he asked.

'Of course she's still here.'

'And the boy?'

'He's here, too.'

'I've come to take him back to Setherby. He will be much better off with Justin Kellett than with a foolish woman who runs off in the middle of a storm and nearly gets him killed.' Though the parson's wife hadn't much more sense. Still, a man's presence made all the difference when it came to bringing up a boy.

'Nonsense.'

He blinked at her.

'Sit down, Nathaniel Armstrong, and listen to me.' Upon which she gave him a lecture on a mother's love which had him squirming like a schoolboy being chastised.

But in the end he was still scowling. 'I will admit that she loves her son, but she still cannot provide for him.'

Georgiana looked at him thoughtfully. 'But I think she can – and offer him a home, too.'

'What do you mean?'

'Caleb Hesketh is going to ask her to marry him.'

He goggled at her.

'And I shall tell her to accept his offer.'

'But – why should he do that? I know Hesketh. He's an able young fellow and could look much higher for a wife.'

'But he doesn't want anyone else.' She waited a moment to let the idea sink in, then said, 'So I shall keep Rachel and her son here with me and when she is better I shall see her safely wed.'

'It's not right.' He thought for a minute, then shook his head. 'No, it's definitely not right. And Rachel Thorpe is not your responsibility. I'm annoyed that my aunt bothered you with our problem.' He chewed his fingertip for a moment and said decisively, 'Tell Hesketh, if you have any influence with him, not to rush into such an unwise marriage. The woman is to come back to Cleving when she's better. My wife will know how to handle her. And if she will not behave, I shall speak to her severely. The lad can return to the parsonage where he will have the benefit of a man's influence.'

Georgiana could see that he was in one of his stubborn moods, so decided that as Rachel's looks would betray the truth eventually, she had better reveal it herself. 'Nathaniel, I believe Rachel to be Ralph's natural daughter and therefore in some degree my responsibility. I'm sure he would want me to look after her.'

Nathaniel opened and shut his mouth, unable to speak for a moment or two. 'Are you certain of that?'

She took him into her small parlour and gestured to the picture hanging up there, a picture she kept for herself and did not show to many people. It showed Ralph as a young man – young and strong, smiling confidently – and it did indeed show who must have fathered Rachel Thorpe.

'You do not mind?' he asked at last.

'Well, of course I do. But it's a bit late to be objecting now, isn't it?'

'She's not really your responsibility, though. You're behaving with your usual generosity.'

Georgiana gave a wry smile. 'Well, since I have no family worth speaking of, I shall be making myself a family by doing this. And that pleases me. So you see, I'm acting quite selfishly.' She let that sink in, then asked, 'Now, do you still wish to see Rachel? She's terrified of you taking her son from her.'

'We-ell . . .'

'But since Caleb is definitely going to offer for her, I think this whole matter can safely be left in my hands.'

He frowned. 'I will consider the matter. And speak to her another time. And see what Hesketh has to say.'

But she knew she had won her point. By tomorrow, he'd be agreeing.

Walter was sitting in his kitchen at North Beck Cottage, his eyes vague and unfocused, rocking slightly and staring into the fire. Hetty kept glancing sideways at him, worried at his pallor and the way breath was catching in his chest. He'd been out during the night – he'd refused to tell her where – and had come back soaked and shivering with an ague.

'Shall I go and get you my other shawl to wrap round your shoulders?' she asked. 'You still look cold.'

He stared at her as if he had never seen her before. 'I'm not shivering; I'm too hot, Alice. Leave me alone, will you?'

Hetty scowled into the fire but did not correct him. A few times lately he had called her Alice, and when she had protested, he had shouted at her like a madman. And if he caught his death of cold, it would be that Bill Withers' fault. In fact, if Bill had only left them alone in the first place, they'd have been a lot happier as a plain weaver and his wife, they would indeed. Walter wasn't meant for this responsibility. It didn't suit his nature.

She sighed. But it was no use saying anything, or trying to reason with him. Walter never listened to her. She could not think now why she had ever married him and had regretted it many a time. He might be a good provider, but he was a sour and carping person to live with – and he mixed with bad company.

CHAPTER TWENTY-SIX

When Rachel was feeling better and ready to go downstairs for the first time, Georgiana said abruptly, 'Sit down on the bed for a minute before we go down. There is something you need to know.' She hesitated but could think of no easy way to introduce the subject. 'My dear, I believe you to be the natural child of my husband.'

One hand covering her mouth, as if to hold back an exclamation of shock, Rachel stared at her.

'You are very like him and,' Georgiana stared bleakly into the distance, hating to admit this to anyone, 'I knew he had – sought comfort elsewhere. You see, I was – I was not well for several years, women's troubles. Then, as I grew older, my health improved greatly. Strange, is it not? Only then – it was too late for us to have children.'

Tears of joy welled up in Rachel's eyes, for it seemed too wonderful to be true that she should find out who her real father was. 'Am I so like him?'

'Yes, my dear. Very like indeed.' Georgiana stood up. 'When you come down, you will see his portrait and you will understand why I have no doubt about this matter.'

So Rachel came face to face with her real father at last, and was glad when her kind hostess left her alone to study his face and weep a little. She felt happy, yet sad as well, to think she had never met him when he was alive, never even watched him walk past, though he had lived so close to Whin Vale. But, she raised her head and stared at the portrait again, you could be proud of a father like this, proud even of looking like him.

★   ★   ★

Caleb stared at Georgiana in shock. 'You think I should just – just speak to her – *now*?'

'Why not?'

'But – she hardly knows me yet and – and . . .' His voice trailed away as he realised he was terrified of asking Rachel to be his wife.

Georgiana smiled at him. 'Ask her tomorrow. She'll be up and about by then, though I shan't let her overdo things. She must have an excellent constitution to recover so quickly.'

'She's a strong woman,' he said, with a smile that softened his whole face in a way few people ever saw. 'I don't think you've ever seen her looking happy. She's very different then. Thomas Thorpe made her happy.' His frown came back. 'I don't know if I can do as well. I don't know if she'll even want me to try.' He stared fixedly at the leaping flames in the fireplace. 'I'm not good at dealing with people, you see.'

Her heart went out to him, this big, incoherent man with a loving heart concealed beneath his stern exterior. 'If you keep trying to make someone happy, you'll succeed in the end, Caleb.'

'Only if the person will let you.' He looked up and said simply, 'Well, then. I'll put it to the test tomorrow.'

'I'll speak to her for you today, if you like, to prepare her.'

'No!' His voice was sharp. 'I can do my own asking.'

Her voice was softly persuasive. 'Of course you can, but a wise commander prepares the ground before he attacks.'

He looked at her dubiously, then shrugged his shoulders very slightly. 'Well, all right. If you say so. I don't – have much experience at this.'

When he had left, Georgiana went upstairs, reflecting that life was a lot more interesting when she was not living in solitary state. She paused on the landing, smiling. She had a few surprises planned for both members of what she considered her adopted family. Caleb and Rachel deserved something good to happen, for both had led hard lives – but she wasn't going to tell them about her plans yet.

On that thought she knocked on the door of her guest's room and marched inside. 'So, my dear, no need to ask how you are – you're looking much better now.'

'I'm feeling much better, ma'am. But I'm worried . . .' Rachel hesitated, then blurted out, 'What if Mr Armstrong comes and *insists* on taking my son away from me? He is a magistrate, after all.'

Georgiana sat down by the bed and took the big capable hand, pressing it between her two wrinkled ones. 'He did come here. And wanted to take the boy back to the parsonage, I'm afraid.'

Rachel gasped and clutched at her chest. 'Adam?'

'Is still here.'

Rachel groaned.

Georgiana shot a quick glance sideways beneath her lashes and added slyly, 'But I'm afraid Nathaniel is still convinced the boy's best chance in life is to live with Parson Kellett. However, I think I know a way to prevent that.'

'Oh?' Rachel was wary of solutions offered to her by the gentry, which always seemed to involve taking her son away from her.

'If you had a home of your own, somewhere you could care for Adam properly, and a husband who was providing for you both, no one would even think of taking Adam from you.'

'Well, I don't have a husband,' Rachel's throat grew thick with grief, 'or even a home of my own. They took *everything* away from me when Thomas died.'

Georgiana took a deep breath. 'That could all be changed. Listen . . .'

At High Fell House the next day Caleb was greeted in the hall by Georgiana, who saw at a glance how nervous he was and patted his cheek in encouragement. She didn't give him any time to change his mind, but showed him into the library with a quick, 'Here's Caleb to see you, my dear!' before closing the door firmly on them.

Rachel was sitting in front of a cosy fire, dressed in a gown of her hostess's, hastily let down by one of the maids for this occasion but still too short for her.

She looked up in confusion, feeling a blush steal across her cheeks. She had not yet decided whether to do as Mrs Bretherton said and accept Caleb Hesketh's proposal – always supposing he really did wish her to wed him, for she found that hard to believe.

He paused by the door and they studied one another in silence across the room.

Rachel thought he looked stern, but then he usually did. He was a fine figure of a man, though, and was wearing his Sunday best today. He was looked up to as a leader in these parts, Mrs Bretherton had told her the previous day, and the maid who'd helped her get ready had whispered that he was the best-looking man in the district and sighed as she said it.

For a moment, Caleb found himself unable to move forward into the room, for he felt almost frozen with fear that she might repulse him. Nothing had ever terrified him as this did. And yet, Rachel did not look angry or annoyed with him, just thoughtful. He liked the colour of her hair, for it reminded him of honey, and he liked its silkiness, so much at odds with the strength of her face and body. It seemed to suggest that beneath it all, she was a woman like any other, a woman who would welcome a man into the softness of her body and who could love a man, as she had clearly loved Thomas Thorpe.

He cleared his throat and took a step forward, trying to think how to begin.

'Come and sit down, Mr Hesketh,' she said at last, wishing she could read his face better, but he had a way of keeping his features very still which hid his feelings from the world. She had always been able to tell what Thomas was thinking, but with this man, she would not know how to start understanding the thoughts behind the face. And that worried her.

He came across the room but did not take a seat, just stood in front of the fire, gazing down at her. 'I'm glad to see you looking a lot better today, Rachel.'

She nodded. 'Thanks to you, Mr Hesketh.'

'Caleb.'

'Caleb, then.' A nice, sturdy name. 'I think you saved my life that day on the moors.'

'I was out looking for you. We all were.'

That surprised her. 'All?'

'Aye, half of Whin Vale was out looking for you, and Mr Armstrong sent his grooms along to help too.'

'*Looking for me?*'

'Did I not say so?'

'But – no one even likes me – they – they . . .' Her voice trailed away.

'Well, there were some anxious folk out in the rain looking for you, so they must have thought you worth the trouble. And you're wrong there. Some folk speak very well of you and are sorry for your troubles. Only they're afraid of those bullies.'

She stared down at the soft Turkey carpet beneath her feet, trying to take in that idea. As the silence lengthened, she began to wonder why Caleb was not saying what he had come here for. Had he changed his mind? Had Mrs Bretherton been wrong about his intentions?

He cleared his throat and she looked up to see him trying to frame some words. And suddenly he reminded her of Thomas, who had also been a man to find words difficult, and she guessed that he was nervous behind that still, mask-like face. As she would have done with her husband, she said simply, 'Come and sit down by me, Caleb, and speak when you're ready.'

He did as she asked and sat on the sofa, half facing her, feeling her eyes steady on him. Suddenly it seemed foolish to have got himself into such a state that he could not even speak. 'I came here today to ask if you would marry me, Rachel. I know you loved your husband greatly and – and not a lot of time has passed since you lost him, but you need a home, a father for the lad and – and I – I need a wife.'

'Why do you need a wife so suddenly?'

He was taken aback and fumbled for words again. 'Why, because – because I am of the right age and have got myself set up in life.'

'Why me, then? There are other young women more – more – who might be easier to live with.'

He sought for words to tell her how much he loved her and could not find them, could only say gruffly, 'I do not want them. They are empty-headed fools.' He hesitated, wishing he had more skill with words. 'I am a serious sort of man. I do not like empty-headed babble. And you – you are a woman of sense. That would suit me better, I believe.'

It sounded such a cold reason for marriage. 'And shall *you* suit me, do you think?'

He thought about it for a minute. 'I would try very hard to make you happy. I am thought to be a – a fair man, I believe.'

She nodded. He meant that, she could see. But she had to make sure they understood one another on all counts. 'I have a son. I will not be parted from him.'

He could not hide his surprise. 'Why should you be? I have a farmhouse with plenty of room for him and – and for other children, if we should have them.' He dared to take her hand in his and gaze earnestly into her eyes, which were the colour of brook water running over stones, grey with just a tinge of blue. 'I would care for Adam as if he were my own son, Rachel. Indeed, he and I have spoken a few times now and got along well. I think him a fine lad.'

'It seems a s-sensible arrangement, then.'

'Does that mean – you are saying yes?'

'I am. But there is one thing.' She took a deep breath. 'I would not wish to share a bed with you until we know one another better. It is all too sudden for me.' She had known Thomas for years when she married him. This man was a near stranger, about whose habits and feelings she knew very little. Perhaps he would grow to care about her, as Thomas had. But perhaps – she caught her breath on the thought – perhaps he did not wish to encourage such feelings. He had said he wanted a sensible wife. *Sensible!* Sudden anger filled her at her own stupidity today, at the way she had hoped he would say he liked her, at least, as Thomas had done. Why should Caleb

Hesketh say that? She was not the sort of woman whom men liked in that way, and she never would be.

He stared at her as if trying to read her thoughts, then smiled at her.

She blinked in surprise, for the smile lit up his face, made him look younger and – and rather handsome, too. The maid had been right. He was a fine figure of a man.

He held out one hand to her and when she placed her own in his, said simply, 'I'm pleased you have accepted my offer, Rachel. Really pleased. It will be a – a very suitable match.'

And though that smile puzzled her a little, for it suggested he was happy at her response, the word 'suitable' did not please her. What a cold word! she thought desolately, remembering how Thomas had been wont to call her 'my lass' in fond tones, how he had cuddled her and cared for her. It was too soon to remarry. Far too soon. If she had not needed a way to keep her son safe, she would have refused him.

One thing more worried her, so she brought that out into the open too. 'Did Mrs Bretherton tell you she – she thinks I am the child of her husband. That means I am bastard born.'

'I'm bastard born as well. It matters naught to me.'

She could not hold back a sigh of relief. 'So, then,' her voice shook for a minute, 'we shall be wed. And – and I shall try to make you a s-sensible wife, Caleb, if that is what you want.'

What he wanted was to take her in his arms, hold her close, kiss her, but he did not dare. She looked so unhappy. Did she feel forced into this marriage?

She had a sudden longing for a man's embrace, but although he continued to hold her hand in his, it was a light grasp only and she knew him so little that she did not dare do anything but meet his quiet comments with calm responses.

He stared down at their joined hands, his expression unreadable, then raised one of hers to his lips and kissed it lightly before letting go. 'I shall seek Mrs Bretherton, then, to tell her that we have agreed to wed,' he said, for the silence had grown too heavy to be borne and he did not know how to lighten the mood.

Mrs Bretherton came back with him, congratulated them both and sent the maid to search for Adam. But when she had done that, she too fell silent, sitting opposite them, watchful.

It was left to the boy to bring a lighter mood to the gathering. Adam beamed at Caleb when told the news and said instantly, 'I shall like you to be my stepfather, Mr Hesketh. You'll be able to look after my mother properly.' For young as he was, he had been very worried about what would become of them now. He thought about it some more and let out a little crow of joy. 'And that means I shan't have to go back to live at the parsonage, doesn't it?'

Caleb nodded, smiling slightly.

'Oh, good. I like Peg — and Lizbet is all right, too, but I don't like living with Mrs Kellett.'

'Well, I hope you will like living at Black Top Farm,' Caleb said. 'I think it a grand place.'

Adam went to lean against the sofa next to his mother. 'I'm sure I shall like it — I shall be with my mother, you see.'

Tears of joy and pride came into Rachel's eyes at that artless speech. Such a fine son. She found Caleb nodding at her, as if to say the same thing and beamed back at him.

Georgiana broke the emotion-charged silence that followed by ringing the bell and ordering a bottle of wine and her best glasses to be brought to celebrate the betrothal. The maid smiled at them all, then hurried to spread the word and do her mistress's bidding.

But although Caleb and Rachel each drank a glass of claret dutifully, he because he knew Mrs Bretherton liked the stuff, Rachel out of curiosity to taste this drink of the gentry, they would both have preferred to drink small ale or cider. And although they glanced at one another from time to time, they did not try to touch again, each nervous of doing something to upset the other.

The door of North Beck Cottage slammed open and both Tam and Bill Withers stormed into the house, pounding up the stairs to the weaving attic without so much as a word to Hetty, who was sitting spinning by the kitchen fire. She got up to close the door with a mutter of annoyance.

'Hast heard the news?' Bill demanded.

'Heard what?' Walter turned from his loom to stare at him. 'What are you on about now?' But he said it without force, for something seemed to have gone out of him lately, and he did nothing with fire or anger, only sullenly and slowly, as if it was all too much effort.

It was Tam who said it. '*She* is to wed Caleb Hesketh out at Hepstone.'

'*What?*'

'Ah, I thought that'd shock you.'

'Nay, it doesn't shock me, just surprises me he'd want her. But Alice will be pleased.'

Bill decided Walter's dead wife's name was just a slip of the tongue. 'Well, I don't like it,' he said, scowling. 'I don't like it at all.'

Walter stared at him. 'But what does that matter to us? It means she won't be living in Whin Vale, so we shan't have to see her or deal with her, an' that's what you wanted, isn't it?'

Tam gave a growl of impatience. 'It's that fellow's sheep as my associates are interested in.'

Walter blinked in bewilderment. 'They've getten the sheep now. We delivered 'em for you 'tother night.'

Bill began to pace up and down, annoyed at how slow Walter was to comprehend everything today. 'Aye, but Tam's agreement was to get *all* the fellow's sheep. He told you that afore. Those fellows don't want Hesketh setting up against them in breeding better sheep. In fact, they'd be glad to see him at the Devil.'

'Well, I don't think you should take 'em all. Let alone it's risky, it's not fair.' Walter didn't mind taking a bit here and there, but to strip a man of all he possessed seemed to be going too far. And Alice agreed with him.

'Well, these folk want all those sheep,' Bill continued to scowl at his friend, 'and they aren't going to be happy if we don't deliver 'em as promised.'

Walter turned to Tam. 'But why did you agree to take so many? Apart from owt else, you must ha' known it'd be risky going back for more. He'll be keeping better watch now. Nor I didn't like that shepherd lad gettin' hurt. There were no need for you to hit him so hard. Or to kill that poor dog.'

Tam shrugged. 'We didn't want him waking up and recognising us. And besides, they're paying me well to do this, which means I'll pay you well.'

'You'll have to tell them it's got too risky.'

'You don't tell men like them you won't do something they want, not if you value your life.' He was in a bit too deep to rock the boat, if truth be told, for these same men had been buying produce and stock from Cleving from him for years on the side. And besides, he had the added incentive of wanting very much to spite Caleb Hesketh, who had once lost his brother his job with Mrs Bretherton. The Barkers never forgot a grudge.

And there was the extra money. He kept his back turned to Walter to hide the exultation he could feel creeping on to his face at the thought of it. Once he got that, he'd get right away from this place. He'd make himself a new life in the south somewhere, buy a bit of land, proper land, not a sour little farm on the edge of the moors. And he'd never, ever come back here to Whin Vale again.

He didn't speak for a moment or two, as he gloated over his plans. He'd purchase a decent sized farm, find himself a new wife and raise some children who'd be as near gentry as made no difference. He had it all planned. Jen was a shrew, always complaining, never satisfied whatever you gave her, and she had lost her looks completely. She could keep Crag End Farm, sell it and set herself up somewhere with the whining brats she had produced. The place would bring enough money for that if she was careful. He'd send word he'd been killed then she'd be able to marry again. She wasn't the sort to live happily on her own.

Oh yes, he had it all planned, every last detail. But he needed to satisfy his partners in crime before he left. They could be mean buggers, them lot could. He turned round and said firmly,

'We'll give Hesketh a week or two to lull his suspicions, then we'll strike. I'll send you word when it's to be.'

Walter shook his head immediately. 'Nay, I'll have no part of it. Alice would skelp me alive if I did. She's angry at me, Alice is, says I haven't treated her daughter right.'

Tam stared at him, open-mouthed. This wasn't a slip of the tongue. 'But your Alice has been dead these many a year.'

Walter ignored his words. 'You and Bill will have to do it on your own.' He turned back to his weaving. 'Me an' Alice don't want to be part of such wrong-doing any more, do we, lass?' He smiled at a shadowed corner, then went back to his weaving as if Tam wasn't even there, humming to himself, and after a moment or two began to converse with his dead wife.

A shiver ran down Tam's spine and seemed to leave a chill in his whole body. He exchanged glances with Bill and they backed out of the room. But Walter's voice followed them down the stairs, still talking to Alice.

In the kitchen, Hetty looked up, saw their expressions and gave a grim smile. 'He's talking to her again, then?'

'You – know about it?'

'Aye. He's been like this for a few weeks, but getting soaked to the skin the other night didn't do him any good. You leave him be from now on, Tam Barker. And you too, Bill Withers. If you come round here again, I shall tell Parson what I know.'

At that, Tam's expression turned ugly and he grabbed her by her bodice, shaking her like a rat. 'If you say one word of this to anyone . . .'

She cried out hastily, 'I won't, I won't! But *please* leave Walter be. He gets worse every time he goes out with you.'

He threw her aside and stormed out of the house.

Bill stayed behind a moment to stare round the kitchen, unable to hide his gloating expression. If Walter was going crazy, he'd soon be able to take over as putter-out and then this place would be his. And he deserved it, too. He'd worked hard, scheming to make things go right for him. He smiled at Hetty, nodding as he saw she understood what he was thinking, and walked out, pausing at the door for another look round.

When the two men had gone, Hetty sat down at the table, buried her head in her hands and sobbed bitterly. Nothing was going right. Nothing. And her husband was getting stranger by the day. People were starting to notice.

When he told her the news, Maggie stared at Justin, her eyes wide in horror. 'Caleb is to marry that woman? *Your cousin Caleb!* But why? He's a fine-looking man and could have anyone. And she's nothing. Worse than nothing. She's a bad mother. Why, her own son doesn't even love her. How can your cousin tie himself to *her*?'

'Maggie, Rachel's son does love her. Why will you keep saying this?'

'Because it's the truth.'

'You know better. Adam loves his mother and she loves him.'

'She doesn't, she doesn't!'

'The boy won't be coming back here again, so I want you to pack his clothes and send them over to Hepstone.'

At that Maggie pushed him away and fled upstairs, sobbing. 'You're lying! I won't listen to you. I won't!'

He stood at the foot of the stairs for a moment, then went to ask Jane to pack the boy's things. 'And don't let my wife stop you doing it. She's, um, too upset to think clearly.'

Jane nodded, feeling sorry for him. Maggie Kellett was more than upset, she was getting stranger by the day. And looking ill, too, pressing her hand against her belly sometimes as if it hurt her. Hadn't he noticed that? The girls had.

Justin went into his study but could not settle to anything, could only sit there with his head buried in his hands, worry churning round and round inside him. What was he going to do? He could not hide from his patron for much longer what Maggie was like. He was beginning to worry that she might do something foolish – might even try to harm Rachel. Or herself.

Luckily he heard her creep down the stairs after everyone had gone to bed and was able to bring her back before she got out of the garden. But he had to lock her in her bedroom to keep her in the house and then listen to her sobbing and ranting at him for hours. No doubt the servants heard her too – well, they must have – but he was sure Jane Charnley would say nothing and would not let Lal speak of what was going on either. He'd have to have a word with the girls in the morning, tell them their mother wasn't well.

At Cleving Park, Hannah sat with Catherine and read the letter from Georgiana with great satisfaction. 'How glad I am for Rachel! With your help I have made up for my selfishness, so I can die with a clear conscience.'

'Oh, Aunt, don't say that.'

Hannah stared at her solemnly. 'It's true and you know it, my dear. I very selfishly let them take Rachel's son away from her so that I could have a companion. And I have regretted my action many a time. She was so good to me, too, never reproached me, served me faithfully.'

'Well, it is all coming out right now,' Catherine said soothingly.

'Yes. Yes, it is. I shall go to the wedding, as Georgiana suggests. It will make folk think better of Rachel, help her settle down again.'

'Aunt Hannah, I don't think Nathaniel would want that.'

The older woman's voice took on a pleading tone. 'Don't try to stop me, Catherine. I haven't long to live and I want to see them safely wed.'

After a short struggle with her own loyalties, Catherine said, 'Very well. I shall come with you.'

'And little Kitty shall come as well.'

Hannah grew so animated in thinking about the wedding that Catherine had not the heart to stop her, though Nathaniel had already made his displeasure quite plain at what he called 'this improvident and hasty match'. Catherine had to use all her ingenuity that evening to persuade him that she needed to go to the wedding with his aunt to see that the old lady did not overexert herself.

ANNA JACOBS

'It is you I care about most,' he replied, looking disapproving. 'You must take great care of yourself and our child. I'm
not at all sure you should be going.'

'Why don't you come too? Mrs Bretherton has invited us
all.'

He drew back. 'I shall do no such thing. I may not be able to
prevent the marriage but I do not intend to condone it publicly.
She is marrying above her station and *he* has always been overly
ambitious. My aunt should not encourage them in their folly.
Nor should my cousin Georgiana. People ought to know their
place in the world and keep to it.'

Catherine sighed. He was a good husband, but so fixed in
his views of the world that she found it difficult to hold her
tongue at times.

When Georgiana informed her guest that they were to have
such fine company attending the wedding, Rachel stared at
her in dismay and blurted out, 'Oh no! Please ask them not
to – to make a fuss. I want it all to be very quiet. Just – just
me and Caleb – and you and Adam, of course.'

'Well, Justin is Caleb's cousin and you come from his parish.
It is only fitting that he marry you in Setherby. And we can't
tell Hannah she's not wanted when she's so pleased about the
match. She's bringing Kitty with her too. And do you really
wish to insult Catherine by refusing to let her attend?'

Rachel felt no one would listen to her. It seemed as if she
was once again being pushed down a slippery slope whether
she wanted to go in that direction or not. She lay awake at
night worrying about the future, worrying about everything.

Was it right to marry Caleb Hesketh just for her own selfish
purposes? But then, if he only wanted a 'sensible wife' – and
how those words kept coming back to haunt her! – why should
her reasons for marrying bother him? She was certainly sensible.
Most of the time, anyway. A good housewife, hard-working,
prudent with money. And it would be a fine thing for Adam
to have a father again, especially since he seemed to like Caleb.
But to do their marrying in public, to be the target of fuss and

382

congratulations on marriage to a man she hardly knew – why, the very idea of that made her feel uncomfortable.

But they continued to rush her along, making her a fine new gown of blue paduasoy in which to be wed and pestering her to say how she wanted it styling. Fashion! Dressmaker's moppets from London! What did such things matter to her as long as the garment was warm and serviceable? And this was a heavy silk, so it would *not* be as serviceable as wool, which she greatly regretted.

But Mrs Bretherton would not listen to a word she said about that either, so they made her a lady's garment, an open gown with a loosely pleated sack back hanging down from her shoulders. The bodice was cut so low Rachel blushed to see the top of her breasts showing and was grateful when her smiling hostess permitted her to wear a fichu over the open neckline. Why, she would catch her death of cold in such a garment if she did not!

When the gown was finished, she tried it on and stared at herself in the mirror, so astounded at how well she looked that she could not speak. The colour really suited her hair, even if dark blue would have been more practical, and Mrs Bretherton's maid had promised to arrange the soft tresses in a special style that would not fall down halfway through the ceremony.

'You look lovely,' Georgiana said softly.

'I don't feel like myself at all.' Rachel twisted round to see how the pleats hung down the back, then lifted her skirts to inspect the layers of fine linen petticoats, stiff with newness – though the bottom one, thank goodness, was of honest Rochdale flannel, soft next to the skin. No need to beat that to make it wearable as you did with linen. She looked up again to study her face under the butter-fly cap of finest muslin edged with lace, which was to be worn under the hood of a new long cloak of soft wool in a darker blue.

'Why are you doing all this?' she begged her hostess. 'I feel so – so *burdened* with your kindness.'

Georgiana tried to smile, but it was a poor effort. 'Perhaps because I never had a daughter to fuss over and am enjoying myself.'

'Oh.' Rachel was tempted to go and hug her as a daughter would, but did not quite dare. After that, she tried not to complain, for she could see that Mrs Bretherton really was enjoying herself. If only Caleb had loved her, had wanted her and no other, she might even have enjoyed it herself. But he didn't really care about her at all. She was just 'suitable' and 'sensible'. Perhaps he was just doing this to oblige Mrs Bretherton.

'Can we not wait a little?' she begged him one day. 'It all seems to be happening in such a rush I can't keep up.'

'It would be more sensible to wed now, before the lambing starts.' Even though he would have so few lambs this year after all the thefts.

That word again. Sensible! She was beginning to hate the very sound of it. 'Yes. I suppose so.'

'Have you changed your mind?' He looked at her fiercely.

She was reminded of a hawk hovering over its prey, but at the same time there was a gentleness in his touch, in the hesitant way his hand rested on hers for a moment. She looked down at that hand and tried not to cling to its warm, solid strength. 'No.' And realised in surprise that she meant it. 'Only – I'm being foolish, I know – so much has happened. I can't – can't change easily. I would have preferred to take things more slowly.'

He looked her earnestly in the eyes. 'Once we are safely wed, I shall not force my attentions on you and you may take your time at settling down at Black Top Farm, I promise you. But Mr Armstrong will not be placated by anything but marriage and your son does need a home.'

He didn't tell her that Nathaniel Armstrong had written him a letter urging him to wait before wedding a woman with such a fiery temper, begging him to consider more fully what he was doing. That letter had annoyed Caleb and made him more determined than ever to see the thing done quickly. Rachel was his. He had waited so long for her and would not wait any longer. Even if he could not fully claim her yet, no one else would know. But she would be his wife. At last.

CHAPTER TWENTY-SEVEN

Since the wedding was taking place in Setherby, Bill Withers took a fancy to stroll down the hill to catch a glimpse of the bride. He was annoyed that so many other folk had come to watch and stood glowering in a corner of the church yard as *that woman* was brought to the ceremony in a carriage like a fine lady. He had hoped to jeer at her, even throw a clart of mud at her skirts, but she was surrounded by gentry so he did not dare. How did a woman like her worm her way into their good books like that?

He waited for Caleb to arrive, scowling to see how strong and happy the fellow looked. What had *he* to look happy about? And he was even taller than *her*. Well, it was being clever as mattered most, and making money, as Bill had shown. He smiled, a mere baring of the teeth that would have warned his wife to tread carefully for a while. Hesketh would be looking a lot less happy soon, Bill intended to make very sure of that. The rest of those fancy sheep would simply vanish one day, as the others had. Tam was only waiting for a bit of bad weather to make folk grow careless, then he'd do the job. He was a good planner, Tam was. And working with him, Bill knew, would make him a nice bit of money, as well as helping him get his own back. See how you find a living for yourself and your new wife then, Caleb Hesketh, he thought spitefully.

And he would find a way to hurt *her*, whether she had a husband or not! It was only then that Bill admitted to himself what he really intended to do, what he had tried to do last time and would have done if Walter hadn't stopped him. It wasn't enough to have her living out at Hepstone. He didn't want her living at all.

A minute later, as he crossed the market square, Bill had an idea that was so right, he stopped dead in his tracks to grin and nod at his own cleverness, then set off running to find his friend Tam Barker and share it with him.

Inside the church, Maggie Kellett sat in her usual pew and scowled down at her prayer book. She had tried to avoid coming to this ceremony because she didn't want to see poor Caleb throwing himself away. And she was feeling really bad today, worse than ever before, but Justin had commanded her attendance. She rubbed her lower belly surreptitiously, for it felt as if someone was sticking a red-hot needle into it. She winced as the pain jabbed again.

She saw Adam enter the church with his stepsister and tried to catch his eye, sure he would come running over to speak to her, but he did not even seem to notice she was there. She had seen him outside, too, speaking animatedly to Peg. The two of them were as close as the brother and sister they were meant to be. Why could Justin not see that? She would have gone over to join them then, but Justin had held her arm and prevented her. He had *forced* her into the church and after escorting her to their pew had told her to stay there.

In Maggie's opinion, things had been better in the old days when people didn't have to get married in church. It was a poor Act of Parliament that changed all that and look what it had led to – a parading of themselves by common persons who should have had the decency to get married quietly. Public weddings like this should be reserved for the gentry, not for those who were bastard born like Caleb and Rachel.

Ruth Thorpe was there too, having travelled over from Todmorden to stay with Mrs Bretherton the night before. She was looking quite grown up now, and was very smartly dressed for one who served customers in a shop. Dressing above her station.

The pain stabbed again and Maggie nearly groaned aloud. She tried to distract herself by watching Mrs Hannah Armstrong in her special chair being wheeled into the church by the new maid and a brawny footman. When the chair had been placed carefully at the end of the Armstrong pew, Mrs Hannah looked round and nodded briefly to the parson's wife. Maggie nodded back, thinking how the old lady had sadly fallen away of late. As for Mrs Catherine Armstrong, sitting in the front pew, she was getting very stout now. Well, she'd soon learn that being rich was no help when it came to bearing children.

Mr Armstrong was nowhere to be seen, but that was not to be wondered at. A man like him wouldn't be attending the wedding of a former maid, would he? And why he'd allowed his wife and aunt to come today, Maggie could not think. She scowled as she watched Caleb and Rachel move into place in front of the altar. The woman had no attendants, of course – well, who would act as bridesmaid to someone like her? Caleb had done very ill for himself with this wife and Maggie didn't intend to receive them in her house. Whatever Justin said.

Since the couple were to travel to Hepstone afterwards for their wedding night, there would be no bedding ceremonies, such as Maggie had had at her own wedding. She smiled at the memory of how her bridesmaids had put her into bed and taken all the pins from her clothing, so that no ill luck should attend the marriage. And then they had taken off her stockings, so that when Justin got into bed, they could stand at the foot of the bed, turn their backs and toss the stockings over their heads to land on her and Justin and bring them luck. How everyone had cheered when the stockings landed just so.

Another pain speared through her and she began rocking to and fro as it continued to niggle at her. She wished desperately that Justin would get through the service quickly.

'You are now man and wife,' he said at last, smiling at the couple standing before him.

Maggie put her hand over her mouth to hold in a groan

and did not even see the bride and groom kiss one another, let alone walk out of the church. It was Justin tapping her shoulder that made her realise she must now leave the church, only she couldn't even stand up. She let out a stifled mew of pain and begged him to get her home, but he would not. Only pride got her upright and she had to lean on his arm to move.

As the ceremony ended Rachel stared up at her new husband, and found him smiling down at her with what in anyone else would have been taken for fondness. Her heart lifted a little. That was not the expression of a man who had come reluctantly and only out of duty into marriage; it was surely the expression of a man who really wanted to marry the woman beside him. Hesitantly she smiled back at him and was pleased to see his happy expression deepen.

A voice beside them said, 'You may kiss the bride!' and as he bent his head towards her, she lifted her face, expecting a quick, impersonal buss on the cheek. But he did not merely press his lips against hers, he took her in his arms and gave her a long, hard kiss. And when he drew his head back, she had to clutch him for a moment, because that kiss had unsettled her, it really had. Why, even Thomas had never kissed her like that.

'I shall try to make you happy, Rachel lass,' he said softly, still smiling.

Her voice was a whisper echoing his. 'And I you.' Suddenly she really did feel married to him and was glad he and Mrs Bretherton had insisted on such a public ceremony, because she was proud to be his wife.

He offered her his arm, for the law now said they must sign the parish register. She was glad to let him guide her to the side of the church, where it was kept, for she was feeling disoriented, her thoughts in a turmoil. He really did seem happy to have wed her. Perhaps – perhaps they would do better than she had expected together. Oh, she did pray so!

After the church business was concluded, the guests all walked together to the inn, with the footman carrying Mrs Hannah across the cobbled square in his arms and the maid pushing the chair behind them, though it rattled and squeaked a protest at the rough surface.

Caleb had gone to the expense of bespeaking refreshments and wine so that everyone could drink the health of the newlyweds. For a moment, Rachel remembered how Thomas had done a similar thing, though it had been a much more humble inn, with only the six of them to sit and eat together. And now three of those six were dead, only her and the two girls left alive.

Caleb stopped walking to ask, 'Are you all right, Rachel? You look sad.'

She shook away the memories and smiled at him. 'I'm fine. Really.'

During the meal and the speeches, Rachel saw Maggie Kellett sitting in a corner on her own. How pale she looked! And how bad-tempered, too. Her glances towards the two ladies from Cleving were resentful, but every now and then she stared at Adam with a naked hunger on her face which upset Rachel, disturbing her warm glow for a minute or two. It was wrong to covet another woman's son like this. And surely that was a wince. Yes, Maggie was pressing one hand to her belly. Had she got the gripes?

The children were all sitting together at the far end of the long table: Adam, Peg, Lizbet, Ruth and Kitty. Kitty was chattering in a lively way, clearly enjoying this holiday from her duties. Catching Rachel's eye, she gave a quick wave and a nod of approval towards Caleb. And Ruth smiled at her stepmother too. Thank goodness they were not upset about this marriage.

Mrs Hannah leaned across the corner of the table towards the bride to say, 'He's a fine lad, your Adam is!'

Rachel turned to beam at her old mistress. 'Yes. And – and thank you so much for coming here today.' Living at Cleving had made her more aware of the ways of the world and she fully understood how important it was that the landowner's family had signified their approval of the match publicly.

Catherine, who was sitting on the far side of her aunt, joined in. 'Mr Armstrong had to go over to Halifax today but he sends his best wishes for your future happiness.' Nathaniel had indeed gone over to Halifax, and very early, too, but he had not sent any good wishes. Still, he would never know she had taken his name in vain.

'Pray give him our thanks,' Rachel said. After a moment, as the conversation grew more general, she turned to Caleb's mother, sitting nearby. 'I shall try to be a good wife to your son, Mistress Hesketh.'

Joanna nodded. 'Good. I think a lot of my Caleb. And – and he's looking for a cottage for me to move to,' her voice faltered for a moment, 'so I shan't be in your way at the farm for long.'

Rachel frowned. Caleb had said nothing of this to her. 'Why do you need to move away, Mrs Hesketh? Is not the farm big enough for us all?'

Joanna stared at her. 'But – you won't want another woman there, surely.'

And then Rachel understood why Joanna had been so stiff with her. 'I lived with my first husband's aunt for several years in perfect amity. No reason on my side I can't do the same with you. And many hands make light work. My weaving brings in good money and I'd rather do that than tend the house, I must admit.'

'But Caleb said—' Joanna broke off and shook her head in bewilderment.

'We can discuss all that tomorrow,' Rachel said in her decisive way. 'But I'd not want to turn anyone out of their home, believe me.'

Which brought tears to Joanna's eyes and a flicker of hope creeping into her heart.

Nathaniel set off for Halifax before daylight, since the road was in reasonable order and his horse very sure-footed. He took his groom with him and a loaded pistol, too. Just let anyone try to rob him! He had not intended to make this trip but the previous day had received important news from the man looking into the question of sheep stealing for him. He was so furious about what he had heard that he hardly noticed the cold, or a light shower which fell just as they were riding into the town. The effrontery of those thieving rascals! That they should sell their booty so openly! Did they think the owner of Cleving Park too stupid to notice anything amiss? Well, they would soon find out their mistake, they would indeed!

He left Timothy to take the horses to the stables of the inn he always patronised and spent the morning with his informant. At one point, he even donned a shabby borrowed cloak and hat to hide his gentleman's clothing and followed Harry Grebbling to a field on the outskirts of the town. He examined the lug marks on the sheep's ears and was betrayed into an exclamation of anger.

'This ear bears my own clip mark,' he said in a low voice, holding the animal between his legs. 'And this, unless I am mistaken, is the mark of Caleb Hesketh, the man of whom I told you, who has lost a great many sheep lately. They take mine in twos and threes, but they take his in larger numbers.' He tapped the ear and although the animal continued to struggle, he did not let it go until he had made his point. 'They may have added a new notch to this animal's ear, but you can see the difference between the two marks. One has clearly been made quite recently, while the other is long healed.'

The man nodded – a quiet man, Harry Gebbling, but becoming known in the district for scenting out trouble. He had done a few jobs now for the lawyer whose services Nathaniel was using in Halifax.

'I came to that conclusion myself.' He waved one hand towards the sheep. 'Besides, these are rather different from Owen Blair's usual sheep – fatter, and with thicker fleeces. When I saw them, I felt sure I was on the right track. But they'll be sent to market tomorrow, so I had to get you over here before that.'

'You have well and truly earned your money,' Nathaniel assured him as they made their way quietly back to the inn. It was the greatest compliment he could pay anyone working for him.

Harry just nodded acceptance of it. He knew he'd done well.

After that Nathaniel went and laid a complaint before the local magistrate, a gentleman he knew slightly, asking that some excuse be made to prevent the sheep being sold until he could catch the culprits red-handed. Perhaps a claim that they were diseased? He confided his suspicions as to who the thieves were, which shocked the magistrate greatly, since these men were respected members of the community.

Ignoring his rumbling stomach, Nathaniel then went to sit with his lawyer, going over the discrepancies in his account books, and explaining about the sheep Harry Gebbling had found. In these matters, with villains as well placed as these, he and his lawyer needed to be abreast of every single detail of the case before he made his move.

And as it turned out, it was a good thing he had not hurried home, even though it meant he would now be returning after dark, because Harry came pounding on the lawyer's door with further news that necessitated a change of plan.

Adam and Joanna were to spend the night at High Fell House with Mrs Bretherton to allow the newlyweds some privacy on their wedding night. Rachel and Caleb were driven out of Setherby sitting together in the small carriage the inn hired out. It smelled musty and was very old-fashioned, since there was not enough custom in Whin Vale to justify the expense of a new vehicle, but it was better than going on foot.

The snow had cleared up now and the roads dried out somewhat, so they made reasonable progress, though Rachel felt as if every bone in her body had been jarred by the time they approached Hepstone.

'I think I should learn to ride,' she said. 'It looks an easier way of travelling than this.'

He smiled. 'I'll buy you a mare and teach you.' A little later, he said quietly, 'My farm is on the other side of the village.'

Her spirits rose suddenly. 'I hadn't realised you were right on the edge of the moors. I shall enjoy that, for I love to walk across the tops in fine weather.'

'Why, so do I. When I can steal a day from my work, that is.'

She saw his eyes crinkle at the corners and guessed that it was a sign of pleasure, a smile in the making. I begin to know him a little, she thought, and was pleased by that.

'I had hoped to show you the farm before we got wed, but I didn't think you should risk going out to it in the snow till you were fully recovered.'

She made a soft but scornful noise in her throat. 'I'm well again now and you won't find me a weakly sort, afraid of a bit of weather.'

His face grew stubborn. 'I would not allow you to be exposed to the icy conditions until you were fully recovered. You're my wife now and I look after my own.'

She smiled at him. ''Tis nice to be part of a family again. I missed it.'

He looked down at their hands, so close, but not linked, and wondered if he dared take hold of hers.

She followed his gaze and realised another thing about him. He was afraid of being rejected, this big silent fellow she had married. So, being Rachel, she reached out and took his hand in her own, joking that, 'We can look out for one another from now on.'

But the amusement faded as something else took its place, an awareness of one another that seemed to fill the whole carriage with tension. She had never felt quite like this with Thomas, never felt that each part of her was totally aware of a man's body. At that moment, the carriage lurched into a deep rut and threw her against him. She cried out in shock, but the cry died to a whimper in her throat as she felt him catch hold of her and brace her body against the strength of his. She had never in her life felt small and feminine before, but she did now. She had never trembled in Thomas's arms like this either. And she wanted Caleb to kiss her, so that when he bent towards her, she raised her face gladly.

Soft they were, his lips, and so warmly alive against her own that she murmured in satisfaction and gave herself to the kiss with all that was in her.

Neither was aware that the carriage had stopped until an icy draught swirled around them and the groom who had come along to help the driver if there were troubles with the muddy roads cleared his throat.

They jerked apart and Rachel felt a hot blush scalding her face.

'Are we here already?' Caleb asked in a slow, befuddled voice, then straightened up and said more clearly, 'Of course we are. Come, Rachel, let me show you our home.'

He swung down from the carriage, helped her to get out and put one arm round her shoulders as they walked across towards the front door, which was sheltered by a small porch with a little pointed gable roof. The ground was slippery, with a thin layer of ice over the mud, and so aware was she of his arm that she didn't watch her footing properly. She cried out involuntarily as she found herself slipping but he laughed and picked her up in his arms as if she weighed nothing at all. He nudged open the door and, still carrying her, stepped inside.

She clung to him, gasping, afraid he would drop her, for no one had picked her up like this since her early childhood, but although Caleb bumped into the door frame, he righted himself with a breathless laugh and did not set her down until he had walked the length of the hall into a huge kitchen.

There, his eyes on her face, he slowly lowered her to the ground, but kept hold of her for a moment to say, flushing, 'My mother said I ought to carry you into the house. 'Tis good luck, she says. And – and I do want things to go well for us, Rachel.' Then he stepped back. 'I'd better go and say goodbye to Sam. He wants to get away before nightfall.'

Rachel's trunk and other possessions were already standing in the kitchen, having been sent across from High Fell House once she, Mrs Bretherton and Adam had left for the church.

She went to glance out of the window at what some might have considered a bleak scene, with the rolling expanse of greyish moors and the remnants of snow piled in corners near the house and spread in dirty-looking smears across the undulating landscape. The farm seemed trim and prosperous from here, set in a little hollow of its own, a place not big enough to be called a valley but large enough to shelter the house from the worst of the gales that swept across the tops. It was surrounded by fields rising in an irregular pattern, separated from one another by neat, drystone walls. Sheep were huddled in the enclosures nearest the house and a few fields away was a cottage with smoke trailing from its chimney. An outcrop of dark, weathered stone just above the small valley showed how the place had got the name Black Top Farm.

'It looks a fine farm,' she said as Caleb came back in.

'I hope you'll continue to think so. Let me show you round. I built the new part of the house myself and have plans to build more rooms on that side of the house.'

'This is a good, big kitchen,' she offered. Someone had been up to the house not too long before and had stoked the fire for them. A big, blackened kettle was steaming gently on its crane to one side of the flames and some food stood on the table covered by a cloth.

'My mother will show you how everything works before she leaves,' he offered as she strolled round the room, fingering the carving on the big oak dresser and admiring the oblong table, strong enough to support the most sumptuous feast.

'I can see no reason for her to leave.'

'It's better that way.' He looked at her in slight puzzlement as she shook her head decisively. 'Better for us, I mean.'

'No. I don't think so. And – and I would never want to be the cause of another woman losing her home.'

'But—'

'I can live with another woman without quarrelling, believe me. And did so happily with my husband's aunt. Is your mother quarrelsome?'

'No. A bit sharp at times, but not quarrelsome.' He hesitated, then added, 'I think the world of her. She's been the best of mothers.'

'Then she should stay.'

He looked at her earnestly. 'Are you sure of that?'

'Aye. I'm very sure.'

'We'll see what she thinks, then.'

Rachel flushed. Joanna Hesketh might not want to live with her. She had not thought of that.

'Come and see the bedrooms.'

He led her upstairs, where the air was considerably colder, and showed her the largest room, which was also the newest, and the two smaller bedrooms, one of which was his mother's.

'There is no bed for you to sleep in if you don't sleep with me,' she said quietly.

'No.'

She looked sideways at him.

'You need not be afraid. I shall not touch you unless you want me to.' He turned on his heel and stamped off down the stairs again.

She stayed where she was for a moment or two, wishing now she had not made that a condition of marrying, and wondering how to set it right, what to say to him when the time came for them to go to bed.

Adam sat in the carriage next to Mrs Hesketh and opposite Mrs Bretherton, wishing his mother was here with them. Kitty had gone back to Cleving and Ruth to Todmorden, so there was just him now.

'Did you enjoy the wedding, child?' Georgiana asked, seeing that Joanna was somewhat overawed by her company.

He nodded. 'Oh, yes. My mother looks happier now. She's been sad for a long time.' Then he frowned. 'Mrs Kellett looked funny today, though, all yellow and twisted. Peg says her mother isn't well.'

The two women exchanged glances. Out of the mouths of babes, thought Georgiana. 'Perhaps she has a fever.'

He pulled a face. 'She tried to catch hold of me when we were going into the inn, but Mr Kellett pulled her back. I was glad. But,' he cocked his head on one side to consider it, 'I don't want her to be ill.' Then he forgot that topic and asked something much more important. 'Do you think Dusty will have missed me?'

'I'm sure he will,' Georgiana assured him. 'You can go and play with him in the stables when we get back.'

At the house, Joanna hesitated. 'Where shall I go, Mrs Bretherton?'

'Come and sit with me in my parlour.'

A flush stained Joanna's cheeks. 'It isn't proper.'

'Fiddle-de-dee! I'm the one who says what is proper in my own home. If I did only what other people tell me is proper, I'd be sitting on my own in that parlour all day long. It was your son who taught me to do things and meet people of all sorts. I shall always be grateful to him for that.'

'Caleb's a fine man.' Joanna paused and said in tones of surprise, 'And now that I think of it, Adam's a lot like he was at that age.'

'Then you have been blessed in your son.'

Joanna nodded, catching the hint of sadness in the other woman's tone, which made her lose a little more of her diffidence.

'This way!' Georgiana led her guest into the parlour willy-nilly and settled down for a discussion of every stage of the wedding, finding her companion as intelligent as her son and thoroughly enjoying another woman's company.

Nathaniel's wrong, Georgiana thought, as she got ready for bed. People do not just come 'in their stations'. There are interesting people everywhere.

It was dark before Nathaniel got home to Cleving, accompanied by a group of militia riding behind his carriage, and he sent commands flying in every direction before he went into the house.

There he had a quiet word with an astonished Catherine before he changed into warmer clothing. After a hasty snack, he kissed her farewell and prepared to ride out again.

★　★　★

When Justin escorted his wife back to the parsonage, he took her into the parlour and saw how gingerly she sat down in her chair. He had noticed her stiffen and gasp a few times during the wedding service, and after it ended it had been a minute or two before she professed herself able to leave the church. But he had refused to let her go home because he wanted to show support for Rachel.

He was now regretting that and was worried about Maggie, for her face was the colour of old bleached bones and her eyes were huge with pain and suffering. 'You look – ill, my dear. Perhaps you should go to bed. Is there anything I can do for you?'

She glared at him, still holding a hand pressed against her belly. 'I told you I wasn't well and should not have been dragged out to that farce of a wedding. There's nothing you can do for me. Nothing! Why, you're *glad* I've lost my son. You're a cruel man, Justin Kellett, and I rue the day I ever married you.' Then she bent her head and began rocking to and fro.

'You're in pain.'

'Did I not tell you so? But what do you care about me these days? The meanest of your parishioners is more important than I am.'

He closed his eyes for a minute, wondering if she would ever accept the truth about Adam, or if he was going to face such recriminations for the rest of his life.

'Tell Mrs Charnley to send me a tea tray. I'm parched.' Maggie saw him still staring at her and added pointedly, 'And I'm tired. I need a rest. So leave me alone.'

He went along to the kitchen, genuinely worried about her now. How bad was her pain? He never knew with her whether she was telling the truth or not. Perhaps another woman would be able to find out more. As he passed on the order for a tea tray, he asked Mrs Charnley to do that. 'If you think we should send for the doctor, come and tell me straightaway.'

But Jane Charnley had no more luck with Maggie than he had had. As she came out of the small parlour, she saw her master standing waiting in the doorway of his study. Closing the door behind her, she walked across to him and whispered, 'Mrs Kellett says she wants only to be left in peace.'

It was over an hour later that Justin heard a scream from the parlour and ran out of his study to find his wife doubled up on the floor, whimpering, and then jerking into rigidity as pain slashed through her again.

After that the evening passed in a blur. He carried her upstairs to bed, sent for the doctor and told the girls to stay in the kitchen. And all the time, screams punctuated the air, on and on.

He had never quite realised before how helpless a man could feel in the face of such trouble. It was different from when he was with his parishioners. This was his wife and he was suddenly beginning to remember how much he had loved her when she was eighteen and foolish, but pretty enough to haunt a young man's dreams.

The doctor came but did not seem able to help, though he administered a draught which would, he said, help Mrs Kellett to get some healing sleep.

Justin accompanied him to the door. 'Have you seen this before?'

The doctor hesitated, then nodded.

'What – what is it?'

'An inflammation of the vital organs.'

'And—'

'We can only pray. Sometimes they recover – but not often, I'm afraid.'

Justin didn't hear the front door close. He just stood in the hall with the words 'We can only pray' echoing round his head. Only he couldn't pray. Not this time.

The draught didn't help Maggie to sleep. All it did was dull the edges of the pain. And by now, her belly was red and distended and her voice was growing ragged with screaming. Justin would have given his soul for his sister Bella's presence, and if Maggie did not improve by morning, he decided he'd send a message across to her, begging for her help.

Later, when word came from Cleving asking for Justin's

ANNA JACOBS

presence there, he left his wife's bedside only long enough to
tell the groom who'd brought the note that Mrs Kellett was
seriously ill and he could not leave her.

As Maggie's screams were still punctuating the night at
regular intervals, he did not have to labour the point.

He went to the kitchen to find Peg weeping and Lizbet
asleep on a blanket in a corner. He did not urge them to go
up to bed. This room was the furthest away from the sound
of screaming. He could think of no words of comfort to offer
his elder daughter, only the shelter of his arms. And that only
for a little time, for he felt his place was beside Maggie –
just in case.

CHAPTER TWENTY-EIGHT

Rachel and Caleb ate some food, then sat and made careful conversation.

We're both frightened to say something that will upset the other, she decided after a while. Eh, it wasn't like that with Thomas. And yet, she had never had the same tingling awareness of Thomas that she did of this man. She was beginning to feel more and more nervous, so in the end she said abruptly, 'I'd be glad to go to bed early. It seems to have been a long day and I'm tired.'

He nodded. 'Yes. You go up first. I'll join you in a few minutes when I've banked up the fire.'

In the bedroom, she undressed slowly, getting between good linen sheets still icy cold because she had been too agitated to remember a warming pan. When Caleb came up, she was lying shivering but trying not to show it.

He blew out the candle and got undressed, filling the silence with small intimate sounds, each of which seemed to echo round the room. She wanted to tell him to hurry up, to come and share the warmth of his body with her as Thomas always had, but she could not force the words out, for she still felt him to be a near stranger. Maybe he wouldn't want to take her in his arms anyway.

He got into bed and lay on the very edge without touching her.

She tried to think of something to say and could not, could only shiver.

'You're cold,' he said abruptly.

'Mmm.'

'Shall I – hold you? I won't if you prefer not to, but it'd get you warm.'

'Yes. Please do.'

She could feel his hesitancy as he took her in his arms, and indeed she felt strangely shy herself. They had seemed in the coach to be getting a bit closer, but any warmth between them had faded in the long silences that had punctuated the evening. She sighed involuntarily and murmured, 'I'd forgotten how comforting it was to have someone in bed with you.'

'Comforting? That's a strange word to use on your wedding night.'

'I'm not good with words. You should not pick me up on them like that, Caleb.'

Silence, then, 'I'm not good with words either.'

She chuckled, for she had found that out for herself already. 'Then we're well matched, my lad.'

They lay together and warmth crept through her.

'I've never shared a bed with a woman,' he confided suddenly.

'But you have – you've lain with a woman, haven't you?'

'Aye. A few times when I was young. But I got so worried afterwards I stopped seeking congress.'

'What were you worried about?' she asked before she could stop herself.

His voice became bitter. 'That I'd bring another bastard like me into the world. That I'd make a child of mine go through what I've had to go through. That I'd have to marry a woman like that for the sake of a child – and I didn't want to marry any of them.'

Her heart ached for him, for the lad he had been and for the solitary man he had grown up into. 'I've only lain with Thomas,' she admitted as the silence grew heavy again. 'And he – he couldn't kiss like you can. Towards the end, he was too tired even to want—' She broke off and was glad when he didn't ask her to finish the sentence.

Caleb shifted to get more comfortable and she ventured to put one arm round his neck and snuggle closer. 'We used to talk in bed, me and Thomas,' she remembered. 'All sorts of things we talked about. We were busy in the daytime, but in bed – well, we talked.'

'They tell me I'm a man of few words.'

She chuckled. 'They're right, too.' She could sense the smile on his face and that heartened her.

They must both have been tired, for they drifted off to sleep in one another's arms, but not before she had felt a hardness pressed against her belly. But by that time, the long day and the strain of everything was taking its toll and she fell asleep suddenly, before she could do anything about it.

Caleb lay there, listening to her slow, even breaths. She was not, he decided, averse to him, but they were such strangers that it was all very difficult. If only she hadn't said she didn't want him making love to her, he might have tried it tonight, for he wanted her quite desperately. He smiled and dared to drop a kiss on her hair. Mind you, the talking was nice, too. It was easier to say things in the darkness, somehow.

As the parsonage clock struck one, Maggie Kellett died suddenly. One minute she was screaming hoarsely, the next the bedroom was silent.

Justin had seen death too often not to recognise it on her face. He bent his head and tried to pray for her soul, but could not, could only sit there, numb and bewildered. It had happened so quickly, without any warning, it seemed. And he had been harsh to her, forcing her to church. He would have to live with guilt for that now, and it wouldn't be easy.

A little later, Jane Charnley came into the room. 'It's very quiet. Is she—' She saw the still face on the pillow and her shoulders sagged.

'She was only six and thirty,' he said, his voice coming out harshly. 'And she's not been happy for a long time now, but – but it seems unfair that she should be taken so young.' He reached forward to close the staring eyes, but as he sat back, tears came welling from his eyes and suddenly he was sobbing.

When he felt arms go round him, he gave in to the need to lean against someone. So many times he had been the one to hold a bereaved person. Now, he needed holding.

He wept for a very long time, wept for the death of their love as well as for Maggie's death, wept for his children, too, who would not even be able to remember her as a loving mother. That seemed the saddest thing of all.

In the middle of the night a dog began to bark in the fields near Black Top Farm.

Caleb woke and stiffened.

Rachel stirred beside him. 'What's—'

'Shh!' He listened and the dog went on barking, so he pushed her away from him abruptly. 'We've had sheep stolen recently. There's supposed to be a lad on watch, but that dog of Joseph's doesn't bark for no reason. I'd better go out and see what's happening.'

She sat up. 'I'll come with you.'

'No. It's probably nothing. You stay here in the warmth.'

But as he rolled out of bed, she did too, and although he slipped into his clothes more quickly, she was not far behind him in leaving the house.

In the nearest field, a voice cried out, a man's voice, angry. It started to shout again, then cut off abruptly.

Rachel stopped, fearful now. She saw Caleb start running forward, heard him call out, and then as the dog started barking furiously, the moon slipped behind a cloud. She strained her ears, shivering in the biting cold. It seemed – it really did seem that men were fighting, grunting with the effort and landing dull thumps on one another.

Since she could not fight like a man, she looked round and in the moonlight spied some shapes leaning against a wall of the barn. She went to grab one of them and found herself with a hoe in her hand. The moon came from behind the clouds as she moved towards the noise, keeping to the shadows as much as possible. She held the hoe across her body, ready to strike out with it. If these intruders were trying to hurt her husband, she would attack them herself, fight by Caleb's side if necessary.

Beyond one of the walls she spied a knot of men wrestling desperately, three against one it seemed, with the dog darting in and out of the fray, nipping at arms or legs. Sheep were milling round at the far side of the field, pressing together and making distressed bleating noises. She tripped and when she looked down she saw the body of another man sprawled half on a pile of dirty snow, half on some muddy ground near the gateway. She bent over it. Not Caleb. But the man was breathing, at least. Was her husband the one under the heaving pile of men, then? He must be.

At that thought, she forgot her caution and hurried forward, desperately afraid for him. There were no neighbours to hear calls for help, no one to come running, so she would have to rely on herself. As she was about to pass through the open gate, a man rose from the shadows behind the wall to bar the path and the moon came out to show his face.

She stopped dead. 'Bill Withers. I might have known you'd be involved in this.'

He smiled, the moon above shadowing his face to turn him into an evil gargoyle like the ones on the church roof. 'I'm glad you recognise me, Rachel Thorpe. I want you to know who it is – before you die.' He brandished a knife at her.

She gave no ground, just hefted the hoe and prepared to die fighting if necessary. But as she watched him carefully, something hit her on the back of the head and the world turned black around her.

Just before midnight, the grooms Nathaniel had sent out came back and reported that Bill Withers was not at his house and his wife said he had gone into Setherby in the morning and hadn't been home since. Walter Smedling was at home, though, but had been behaving very strangely. They hadn't been able to get a word of sense out of him.

'The problem is, where has Withers gone?' Nathaniel was

ANNA JACOBS

not anxious to make a fool of himself. It had seemed so obvious
when he was in Halifax, with Harry Grebbling, who had found
out about the thieves' plans, but now that he was back in his
own comfortable home, it seemed very far-fetched, that men
could openly take so many animals.

'You said he was suspected of stealing, of being involved
in the taking of other men's sheep,' the captain of the militia
prompted. 'And of a violent crime here in Whin Vale. Which
is why we've come. Surely someone will know where he is.'

'Yes, I suppose so, but I don't know who to ask except
Smedling, any more than we know whose sheep he's after
tonight.' He pursed his lips, then said, 'I don't want to leave my
own flocks unprotected either. We'd better leave half your men
to guard my home farm, and let the others sleep in the stables
until we need them. If nothing happens, we'll make our way
to Hesketh's place tomorrow and check that he's all right.'

The captain sighed. It was a freezing night. He was already
half convinced that this was a wild goose chase. Or that this
landowner was only concerned with his own property and not
with the welfare of his tenants. They'd been rushed away from
Halifax so quickly they had not had time to put on their proper
uniforms. A fine showing they'd make tomorrow! And a fine
waste of time this was!

Up at North Beck Cottage, once the groom from Cleving had
left, Hetty sat and fretted, while Walter paced up and down
talking first to his dead wife, then from time to time turning to
his present wife and making perfect sense. Each time she thought
the fit of madness had passed, he would suddenly ramble off into
nonsense again.

'Bill Withers is up to no good,' Hetty said in one of Walter's
more sensible moments.

'He's a murderer, that one.'

'Eh, what do you mean?'

Walter heaved a sigh and looked into a distance only he
could see. 'He killed Thomas Thorpe. Threw a rock at him
and hit his head. I saw him. I was there. But I would never

406

have killed a man. Alice, you have to believe me!' He stared into the fire for so long that Hetty wondered if he'd fallen asleep on the settle, as he sometimes did.

'Walter?' she ventured, longing for her bed but afraid to leave him on his own in this state.

He twitched upright and stared round the room wildly, then turned to her, grasping her arm so tightly she cried out. 'Bill Withers tried to kill Rachel too. If I hadn't been there to drag him off her, she'd be dead now.' He let go of her and crossed his arms over his chest, rubbing his hands up and down his forearms, and groaning in his throat.

Hetty gasped and clutched her breast. 'He never did! That time she was beaten, you mean? It was him?'

'Aye.'

She thought about it for a minute, then said angrily, 'And you took part in it? Beating your own daughter near to death?'

He groaned more loudly and buried his face in his hands. 'She's *not* my daughter.'

'You were the only father she knew, so she's as good as your daughter.'

He looked to the side and began to sob, tears rolling down his face. 'That's what Alice keeps saying too.'

'It's a downright shame, that is. He's a wicked man, that Bill Withers, and you should never have got mixed up with him. What does your Alice say about them going off to steal Caleb Hesketh's sheep tonight?'

'She says we should go and tell Mr Armstrong about it. To make up for what I did. She says she'll forgive me if I do that. But I daren't, I daren't!'

A minute later, he was ranting and raving again and Hetty could get no sense from him.

Out at Black Top Farm, the shepherd's wife paced up and down the kitchen. Her Joseph had been gone for too long and there was a dog barking somewhere across the fields, on and on. She took a sudden decision to go and see if her husband was all right, threw an extra shawl round her shoulders and then flung her old cloak on top of that.

Feeling foolish but still determined, Dinah left the house quietly and crept towards the fields, keeping to the shadows. No need to say anything to Joseph about her fears if he was all right. He'd only laugh at her. But when she heard the sound of footsteps, she shrank back into the shadows and remained motionless, suddenly overwhelmed with terror. Those weren't her Joseph's footsteps. He didn't walk heavily like that. And – and there were several men.

When one of them passed close by, holding a cudgel as if he was ready to use it at any moment, she pressed one hand to her mouth to hold in a scream. She was sure then that her Joseph was in trouble. What had they done to him? He'd never have let strangers make free with Caleb's flock. He'd have stood his ground and fought. And where was Caleb? Surely he'd have heard the noise.

She waited till the stranger had moved away, waited long enough to see him burst into her house and breathe a prayer that he would not come out and find her. Then, with her heart thudding fit to burst out of her chest, she left the path she was on and began to make her way out of their small valley, keeping behind walls as much as possible and scuttling from one piece of black shadow to another. They'd come looking for her, she was sure.

Once she was over the highest part of the land, just under the jutting black rocks, she began to move more quickly downhill, breath rasping in her throat and fear swirling round her like a mist. In the next sheltered space, she found the first of the shepherd lads fast asleep in the little three-sided shelter and shook him awake roughly.

'What's—'

She clamped one hand across his mouth. 'Shh! Them thieving rascals have come back again and they've captured my Joseph. And Mr Hesketh too, I should think, for he wouldn't just stand back and let 'em take his animals.'

The lad goggled at her for a moment, his mouth opening and shutting.

LIKE NO OTHER

'Pull yoursen together, Jack, do. You need to go and get help!' She whispered her instructions, looking over her shoulder every now and then, fearful that she might have been pursued. 'Go into Hepstone and waken everyone you can. Tell 'em to come here quick, else who knows what mischief will happen next.' She only hoped they'd be in time to prevent murder – hoped murder hadn't taken place already.

Joseph, she prayed as she crept back towards the sheepfold again, *Lord save my Joseph!* She had to know what had happened to her man. She just had to go back and find out, even though she trembled every step of the way.

For all Caleb's struggles, he was overpowered and even his dog was driven away with rocks tossed at it. When one hit the animal on the side, it limped off to hide behind a wall, growling in its throat but not attacking again.

Bill made sure Caleb was securely bound, then had him dragged towards the barn, chuckling to see his semi-conscious body bumping over the rough ground. In the barn, the prisoner began to buck and struggle anew at the sight of his wife's unconscious body on the floor, also tightly bound.

'Drag him over beside her,' Bill mocked. 'Let the lovebirds lie together.'

'Ah, leave them be an' get on with it,' said Tam Barker, staying in the shadows and tugging at his fellow thief's arm as their helpers pulled him across the floor. 'Them two won't hinder us while they're lying here trussed like fowls for market. An' by the time anyone does find 'em, we'll be long gone. Or at least I will. You're stupid to have let them see your face. They'll be able to tell the magistrate who did it.'

Bill smiled. He had wanted them to see his face, but they wouldn't be able to tell anyone anything by the time he'd finished with them.

Tam looked at him and realised what he was planning. 'Ach, you're a fool. And I'm telling you straight, I'm having nothing to do with any killing.'

Bill turned to him. 'Who asked you to? I pay back my

409

grudges mysen. I don't need your help. I don't want it, neither. This is for me to do.'

Caleb stopped struggling and pretended to lapse into semi-consciousness again. He did not look in Tam Barker's direction, just lay beside Rachel, trying to seem muddle-headed. But all the time he was testing his bonds, hoping to find some purchase, some way to twist out of them or break them. But however he tried, he couldn't do anything. Bill had made sure of that, tying them with a weaver's thorough understanding of yarn and thread and knots.

The men went outside again, taking their lanterns with them and only then did Caleb whisper to his wife, 'Rachel! Wake up, lass!'

He nudged her with his shoulder, but she didn't stir. He looked round to see what he could use to cut his bonds, but there was nothing within reach. Despair filled him, but he didn't give in to it. He continued to roll around the floor, searching for something, anything that might help.

Outside, the sheep were rounded up and sent off down the lane in the charge of men who had done this before several times, men who had tied up their own dogs at a distance while they made the theft and now unleashed them to help drive the sheep. One man walked along at the front, and the others at the end of the procession, trailing bundles of branches along the ground behind them to wipe out any clear indications of who exactly had passed that way. Once they got on to a certain stony moorland track, they knew they'd leave very little by way of a trail. No one had found them the last few times they'd come this way, and they wouldn't this time, either.

When they had all left, Tam turned to Bill, uneasy at what he proposed, for murder would make folk hunt even harder to find those who'd done it. 'You're mad to think of killing them two.'

'Only way to make sure they say nowt.'

'You needn't have let them see who you were.'

Bill stuck his face close to Tam's. 'I *wanted* 'em to see me!

I *wanted* 'em to know who it was. She's been mockin' me all her life, that one has, but I s'll have the last word, I shall that. An' she'll know it afore she dies.'

The gloating in his voice sickened Tam, but he had no time to lose, so he fumbled in his pocket. 'Here's what I owe you. You won't see me again.'

'Where are you going, then?'

'Best you don't know, then you can't tell anyone. But I shan't be back in these parts again.'

Bill watched him stride away, then turned round to stare at the barn. 'It'll burn nicely, I reckon,' he muttered. 'Plenty of wood in the building and plenty of hay inside. But I'll have a look in that house of theirs first. Might be something worth picking up there.' He looked up at the sky. 'Still be dark for a good while yet. I'll be home in my bed long afore anyone discovers this.'

Walter jerked suddenly into sense again. 'We mun set off!' he said. 'Hetty, lass, we mun go an' tell Mester Armstrong what they're doin'. It's the only thing I can do to make it right for Alice.'

And suddenly Hetty, too, wanted to do that, wanted to shed the burden of guilt about what her husband was doing, a burden she had carried all too long. 'Aye, then, come on, lad. Here!' She grabbed hold of him as he moved towards the door. 'Get your cloak on first, you fool. It's freezing out there.'

He hardly seemed to notice as she flung the cloak round him. As they walked down the valley, he kept up a monologue with Alice, telling her what he was doing, thanking her for showing him how to make amends. It made Hetty's skin prickle with gooseflesh to listen to him.

It seemed a long time till they reached Cleving Park. The gates were locked and Walter was still talking earnestly to Alice's ghost, so Hetty hammered on them, and kept on hammering until the gatekeeper came out.

At first he didn't want to let them through, but when she

explained, he not only opened the small side gate but went with them to the big house.

Cleving was not shrouded in its usual darkness but had faint lights flickering here and there behind windows upstairs, as if people had only just gone to bed.

Hetty went and hammered on the big front door. 'Mr Armstrong!' she called. 'Mr Armstrong, come quick! They're stealing sheep up Hepstone way.'

'And Bill Withers is going to murder Rachel Thorpe,' Walter added. 'Like he murdered her husband.'

By the time Nathaniel flung the door open, Walter had relapsed into madness. They shut him in the cellar, put his wife in the charge of the housekeeper and got ready to go out into the cold night again. Because the things Hetty had told them made sense, knowing what they already did.

The shepherd's lad ran all the way to Hepstone, slipping and slithering and more than once measuring his length on the icy ground. He pounded on the first door he came to, then went on to pound on others. At first he had trouble convincing people he was telling the truth, then, when he couldn't say how many men were attacking Black Top Farm, only that several were involved, some were hesitant about coming with him.

'Maybe we should send for a magistrate,' one suggested.

'Or send for help,' another said. 'If there are a lot of them, we could be in trouble too.'

In the end, they decided to send a man off on ponyback to High Fell House, because Mrs Bretherton had plenty of good horses and could send someone riding to tell Mr Armstrong in Whin Vale, for he was the nearest magistrate. The rest of the men decided to go and scout the land carefully before they leaped into the fray.

When Rachel muttered something and stirred, Caleb rolled back across the barn floor to her. 'Are you all right, Rachel? Answer me if you can.'

Her eyes opened and she blinked in bewilderment. She tried to move and couldn't.

'Are you all right?'

She took a deep shuddering breath. 'My head hurts.'

'Oh, my love, I thought they'd killed you.' He stared towards the door. 'And they *will* kill us if we don't manage to escape.'

'Bill Withers. It was him again!'

'Aye. And Tam Barker. Eh, I nearly died when I thought they'd killed you.'

She stared at him. 'You sound as if you – you care about me.'

'Of course I care about you. Why else did you think I married you?'

'For – for convenience. Like Thomas did.'

And even in those wretched circumstances, his face softened into a smile as he said what he'd been longing to say ever since they got married. 'Nay, Rachel lass, I've loved you for years. Only you'd wed someone else before I had time to tell you.' Then he realised they were wasting time and clicked his tongue in annoyance. 'We've got to get shut of these ropes. Them buggers have trussed me up so tightly I cannot free my hands. And they've locked us in here, too. All I can do is roll around and I can't find anything to rub these ropes against.'

Bill searched the farmhouse but to his disappointment did not find any money. 'Eh, you'd think someone like him would live richer nor this,' he muttered, staring around sourly.

In a fit of pique he swept the ornaments off the dresser, hurled the pewter plates that lined the backs of its shelves across the room and then overturned the dresser itself for good measure. 'Serve 'em right!' he said, as he'd been saying all night.

Then he left the house and started walking towards the barn. 'I'll just finish my business here, then I'll be off. And after this, I'll be free of her. But I'll make her suffer first. Before she dies, she'll regret the day she ever treated me so ill an' she'll say she's sorry for it, too.'

CHAPTER TWENTY-NINE

Bill paused outside the big double door of the barn, wondering why he didn't want to enter it. He took a deep breath and muttered, 'She deserves it!' then he lifted the big wooden latch from its socket and marched inside, lantern held high.

He stopped dead when he saw no bodies lying on the floor. Where were they? They couldn't have escaped! He'd checked their bonds himself.

Flattening himself against the wall, he swung the lantern from side to side, trying to see beyond the wavering circle of light cast by it. They *couldn't* have got free of those bonds. No one could. Suddenly he remembered how big Caleb was and fear crept along his spine. He took out his knife and fingered it. If they came at him, he'd just stab them and be done with it. The main thing was to see them dead.

Hearing a rustling sound, he swung in that direction and his eyes narrowed. Holding the lantern higher, he moved forward one step at a time, ready to run if threatened. Then he kicked some straw away and laughed as he found Rachel lying there, still bound, glaring up at him. 'You'll not hide from me,' he said thickly, anticipation replacing some of the fear in his belly and making his loins tingle.

Suddenly something slammed into his legs and he yelled as he fell over, the lantern crashing from his hand, its light winking out even before it hit the ground.

Then a desperate struggle began, with two bound people

trying to hold down one unbound man with the sheer weight of their bodies, and almost succeeding, too.

But in the end Bill got free of them, dragged Rachel away and tied her quickly to a post supporting the wooden upper level, where most of the straw and grain was stored. It was a lot harder to capture Caleb and tie the sod up, but he managed that, too, in the end. When he had pinned him into place, he kicked him several times, then went over and kicked her, too.

'I'll kill you for that!' Caleb yelled.

He turned then and smiled. 'No, you won't. You'll be dead yourself afore it's light.'

He was rewarded by silence, but the way they were both glaring at him made him glad they were bound, very glad.

Feeling better, he searched for his lantern and took it back to the house to light it again from the kitchen fire. He wanted to see Caleb Hesketh's face as she died – slowly. He wanted to make sure she saw his own face as he killed her. He'd laugh as he did it. Laugh, he would.

The folk from Hepstone took so long to get organised that the lad left them and set off back to the farm on his own. He knew every inch of the fields, so he soon found Dinah crouching over her husband's unconscious body, sobbing.

'Is Joseph dead, missus?'

She gasped and whirled round, reaching for a rock as a weapon, then saw who it was. 'No. But he will be if we don't get him inside out of the cold.' She looked beyond him. 'Didn't you fetch anyone?'

'They're still talking about how to do it, so I came back to see what was happening.' He glanced over his shoulder, afraid of someone coming up behind him and hitting him.

'They've took the sheep,' she whispered, 'but there's some of the murdering rascals still around. I seen a light in the house and then in the barn.'

'Oh.'

She gave him a poke. 'You creep over an' see if they've gone yet, then come back and tell me. We have to get my

Joseph home where I can tend him. See how they've hurt him.' She began to weep, but silently, afraid of calling attention to herself.

The lad gulped. He didn't want to get too close to such men. But then he looked down at Joseph's face, the blood that had dried on it looking like black tar in the darkness, and he remembered the many kindnesses he'd had from the old shepherd. 'All right.'

He set off creeping through the darkness, narrowly missing Bill Withers who came stumbling from the barn with his unlit lantern.

Heart thumping, he watched the man enter the house, then turned and made his way towards the barn, terrified of what he'd find there. It took him a moment to pluck up the courage to go inside and just as he was doing that, he saw someone come out of the farmhouse, so hid himself behind a pile of straw and waited, heart pounding, to see what happened.

The group of people from Hepstone were halfway towards Black Top Farm when they heard hoofbeats behind them. They scattered to each side of the road, not knowing what to expect. Several men were coming, from the sounds of it.

At the sight of them, the mounted men slowed down and the first one hailed the nearest man. 'What's happening?'

'Trouble over at Black Top Farm. Hesketh's shepherd lad came seeking help. There's a lot of men there, it seems, taking the sheep and killing folk.'

Nathaniel shouted, 'Follow us there as quickly as you can!' and urged his horse into movement.

The captain spurred his horse forward and rode shoulder to shoulder with him.

In the kitchen, Bill lit the lantern, paused to take a swig of small ale from the barrel, laughed and then left the tap running on to the scrubbed flagstones of the floor.

Holding his lantern high, he stumbled back across the icy ground towards the barn. For some reason, he was not looking forward to killing a woman who stared back at him as she did. And as Caleb Hesketh did. It was one thing to beat a person senseless, quite another to stab them while they stared at you. Then he looked at the lantern and made up his mind. No need to stab them at all. He could let fire do the job for him. He needn't even go near them again.

Outside the barn was a pile of dirty straw. He gathered some together, pleased to see that the eaves had kept it dry, then opened the little door of the lantern. Very carefully, he set fire to a small bundle of it, murmuring approval as the flames caught. He waited till the straw was burning fiercely, then opened the barn door and tossed the flaming bundle inside. He waited only long enough to see the piled straw inside catch fire, knowing his victims were tied to posts and helpless to put it out, then he slammed the door shut and dropped the wooden latch into place.

'That'll fettle 'em,' he said, relieved. Eh, it wasn't easy to kill someone in cold blood, even her. He turned and set off towards the moors, not even waiting to see the barn burn down. There was no one out here to rescue them and he had a long walk back to Lower Clough. He had to get there before his children woke and folk started their day's work. He had to make out he'd been sleeping in his bed all night.

At the rim of the small valley, he turned to see the barn flaming like a torch and watched it for a few moments, then threw back his head to laugh. They'd be well roasted, those two would. 'Serve her bloody right!' he told the night sky and walked on.

Just as he was starting across the moors he heard hoofbeats and hid behind a wall. He goggled at the sight of several horsemen pounding along the lane to the farm but didn't wait to see what they did, just turned and ran for his life. He'd take a short cut across the tops because he had to get back home as quickly as he could now. And he had to hope those two had perished before anyone opened the barn door. Surely they would have! Smoke could kill you as well as flames, everyone knew that.

★ ★ ★

Nathaniel and his men rode into the farmyard. Sliding from his horse, the captain was the first to reach the flaming barn. Someone was beating against the door, thumping at it as if trying to get out. He lifted the latch from its slot just as the person inside slammed against the door again. It burst open, knocking him aside.

Three figures stumbled out of the barn, smoke-blackened, coughing and standing defensively, as if they expected to be attacked.

Then one of them, a woman with singed skirts and blackened face, said in a husky voice, 'It's Mr Armstrong, Caleb! It's Mr Armstrong! Oh, thank heavens, thank heavens!'

The tall man peered through the wildly flickering light cast by the roaring flames, then he also sighed in relief. 'Thank God you're here, sir!' He turned to the lad who had released them and added, 'You saved our lives there, Jack. I'll not forget that.'

He didn't wait for an answer, but turned to his wife, pulled her into his arms and cradled her there for a minute, needing desperately to hold her close. 'Oh, my love, my love,' he muttered into her hair. 'If I'd lost you now!'

And Rachel dragged his head down to hers to kiss him on the lips, tasting smoke and soot and joy, and murmuring between kisses, 'Caleb! Caleb!'

An angry voice interrupted them. 'This is no time for fondling and caressing, Hesketh!'

They turned, still closely embraced, to give Mr Armstrong their attention.

'You're right, sir,' said Caleb, grinning, 'but you must excuse a man who's barely escaped dying on his wedding night. I needed to hold this wife of mine, needed to feel her safe in my arms.'

The captain chuckled. 'Wedding night, eh?' He gestured towards the burning barn. 'Well, you've certainly lit a big enough bonfire to celebrate.'

Then Caleb realised what was happening. 'My barn! Are you just going to stand there and watch it burn?'

Feet came pounding along the lane and a line of people soon formed to swing buckets of water from the duck pond and try to put out the blaze. The members of the militia joined them and no one had time to ask exactly what had happened until the fire was out.

As they were standing looking at the sodden mess of the barn, saved by its stout stone walls, the captain felt something touch his cheek and looked up. 'Oh, hell, 'tis starting to snow again. We'll never find those sheep now. This'll cover the tracks.'

It was fully light before Caleb and Rachel managed any real privacy. He said farewell to Mr Armstrong and the militia, thanked his neighbours for their timely help and came into the kitchen to find her still clearing up the mess left by Bill Withers.

She turned and smiled shyly at him.

For a moment they stood there, then moved together. In his arms, she said softly, 'I have grown to love you too, Caleb. I realised that when I thought we were to die.'

'I've loved you for years.' He smoothed one tumbled lock from her brow. 'Some of your beautiful hair is singed.'

She touched his hair. 'So is yours. I've washed my face but I must look a mess.'

'You look wonderful to me,' he said simply. 'You always have done, a fine strong woman, one to fight beside her man, to lie beside him warm in bed and mother a brood of children.'

'Oh, Caleb!' And she lost herself in his embrace.

A boy's voice brought them from their closeness. 'Mam! Mam, where are you?'

'It's Adam!' She turned towards the door, allowing Caleb to walk with her, his arm still round her waist. This man was of exactly the right size for a woman like her, she thought inconsequentially, then the door was flung open and Adam rushed inside.

'Mam! Are you hurt?'

She and Caleb both held out an arm to him and he ran towards them without hesitation.

'We're a little singed round the edges,' she said, 'but we're not hurt. Well, not much, any road.'

Adam looked up at them and made a discovery. 'You look happy.'

'Aye,' said Caleb, 'happy we're wed, happy we're still alive and happy to see you, lad.'

For a moment, all three stood there, nestling closely together, then Nathaniel Armstrong came into the room, pausing to look disapproving.

Caleb exchanged smiles with Rachel then moved forward to greet the landowner. 'I thought you'd gone back to Setherby, sir.'

'I met Mrs Bretherton who was quite determined to come and see you, so I decided to escort her here. My men are still out hunting the moors for that villain now that it's light.'

'Any sign of him?'

'Some tracks above the farm, but they peter out on the higher ground, and the snow is coming down thick and fast. Do you wish me to leave some men here in case he comes back?'

Caleb shook his head. 'Nay, we're forewarned now. I'll take Joseph and Dinah into my house for a night or two, and we'll keep watch together. You get off towards Halifax, sir, and see if you can catch the scoundrels that end. I want my sheep back.'

Nathaniel nodded to Rachel and turned to leave. He had thought her more sensible than this, but she was acting like a lovesick girl, smiling and cuddling Hesketh as if she had not just escaped being murdered. He shook his head in disapproval, then mounted his horse, feeling stiff and tired, but determined not to let the villains get away with this. And after that, he'd go back to his own wife and hope never to spend such a night again.

On the moors a man with a broken back lay in the snow at the foot of a steep drop and cursed. As daylight came and the snow continued to fall, Bill tried to drag himself along towards a track. But he grew colder and colder, and soon gave up the attempt to move, lying huddled on the ground, letting the snow cover him as it would.

After a while, he made the discovery that snow kept you warm and closed his eyes in relief. He'd just lie here till they found him. They'd be out looking.

He did not open his eyes again.

It was nightfall before Nathaniel Armstrong and his groom got back to Cleving and both men were exhausted.

'Find someone else to tend the horses,' Nathaniel ordered. 'Get yourself some food from the kitchens and then go to bed. And my thanks for your help, Timothy.'

Inside the house, he let his wife and servants take over and fuss about him. His aunt smiled at him from her wheeled chair, maids beamed at him and his manservant came to throw a warm shawl round his shoulders and talk of hot baths.

The idea of that pleased Nathaniel so much, he sent them scurrying to the outhouse for the big wooden bathtub and, after he had eaten, led the way eagerly up to his bedroom. When Catherine would have left him to undress, he shook his head. 'Stay with me, my dear.' He stood by the fire until the bath was ready, let his man help him remove his damp garments, then sank gratefully into the hot water, leaning his head against the rim.

When he was well settled, he sent the manservant away. 'I'll ring when I need you.'

Catherine, pleased to be asked to stay, waited until her husband had lost that pinched white look before asking, 'Did you catch all the thieves, then?' For he had only had time to tell her about the doings out at Hepstone, not what had happened in Halifax.

He smiled and nodded, wriggling in pleasure at the wonderful warmth of the water. 'Aye. It'll cause a scandal of no mean order, though, for there were men of property involved, but we caught them red-handed. The snow slowed the thieves down nicely. And we've found quite a few of Hesketh's other lost sheep – though the scoundrels seem to have sent most of mine to the butcher's.' He scowled at that thought. 'But they shall make restitution for it, believe me.'

'I'm just glad that you're back safely, Nathaniel,' she said, kneeling beside him to trickle hot water over his back with a washcloth.

'You shouldn't be doing this in your condition.' But he lay back against the towel folded over the high end of the wooden tub and made soft noises of pleasure.

'I keep telling you I'm feeling well,' she teased. 'And since I intend to gift you with a large family, you must get used to seeing me like this and stop fussing.' She gestured to her belly.

He stared at her and surprised himself as much as her by saying, 'You are the best gift of all, Catherine. I could not be more pleased with my wife.'

She stared at him, tears in her eyes. 'Oh, Nathaniel!' For he was not a demonstrative man and she had never expected to hear such words from him.

He flushed, then made a puffing noise and added recklessly, 'But I should like to get out of this water now and hold you in my arms, my love.' For if a mere sheep farmer like Caleb Hesketh could show his love so plainly, then a gentleman could certainly do the same.

A few days later, Rachel and Caleb stood in their doorway staring out across fields once again full of sheep.

'They seem fine, fat beasts,' she said. 'But I have a lot to learn if I am to be a sheep farmer's wife. Especially since your mother is to stay at High Fell and keep Mrs Bretherton company.'

'I shall be more than a sheep farmer,' he said with quiet confidence. 'I have ambitions which may make you smile, but—'

'I should never smile at a man for having ambitions,' she said. 'Indeed, I hope those ambitions will include me. I am,' she paused, afraid of him scorning her, 'good with figures and – and I should like to help you.'

He beamed at her. 'That would be wonderful, for I do not enjoy casting accounts.'

'Do you mean that?'

ANNA JACOBS

He hugged her to him. 'Rachel, Rachel, how many times must I tell you that I want you working beside me and am proud of your intelligence and skills?'

'Oh, Caleb—'

A voice interrupted them and they turned to see Adam standing there, arms akimbo. 'Why do you two keep cuddling all the time?'

'Because we are newly wed.'

'Well, it seems very strange to me. I shan't ever get married if you have to keep cuddling a girl. And you said you'd show me the boundaries of the farm today, Caleb.' He had decided he did not want to call any other man 'father'.

'Indeed I shall.' He hugged Rachel once more, then let her go. 'Shall you come with us, my little love?' For it was a joke between them now that she was smaller than he was.

'I shall be happy to.'

So they walked arm in arm round the borders of his farm, with Adam rushing here and there, Dusty padding behind them in an uneasy truce with the sheep dogs, and Caleb explaining just how he had acquired each piece and where the original holding had been.

And none of them noticed the cold or the icy wind. Indeed, if you had asked them, they would have said it was a very fine day indeed.